JAN - - 2012

D0041986

Also available from
GENA SHOWALTER
and Harlequin TEEN

Intertwined
Unraveled

GENA SHOWALTER

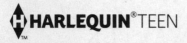 HARLEQUIN®TEEN

ISBN-13: 978-0-373-21038-1

TWISTED

Recycling programs
for this product may
not exist in your area.

Copyright © 2011 by Gena Showalter

All rights reserved. Except for use in any review, the reproduction or utilization of
this work in whole or in part in any form by any electronic, mechanical or other means,
now known or hereafter invented, including xerography, photocopying and recording, or
in any information storage or retrieval system, is forbidden without the written permission
of the publisher, Harlequin Enterprises Limited, 225 Duncan Mill Road, Don Mills, Ontario
M3B 3K9, Canada.

This is a work of fiction. Names, characters, places and incidents are either the product of
the author's imagination or are used fictitiously, and any resemblance to actual persons,
living or dead, business establishments, events or locales is entirely coincidental.

This edition published by arrangement with Harlequin Books S.A.

For questions and comments about the quality of this book please contact us at
Customer_eCare@Harlequin.ca.

® and TM are trademarks of the publisher. Trademarks indicated with ® are registered in
the United States Patent and Trademark Office, the Canadian Trade Marks Office and in
other countries.

www.HarlequinTEEN.com

Printed in U.S.A.

To the usual suspects: Haden, Seth, Chloe, Riley, Victoria, Nathan, Meg, Parks, Lauren, Stephanie, Brittany, and Brianna. What can I say, guys? In a world where I am Queen Decision Maker, fangs sprout. Claws grow. Dark descends. You're welcome.

Once again to The Awesome, editor Natashya Wilson, for her brilliant insight and dedicated beyond-the-call-of-dutying. Yes, I just made that entire phrase a verb. Not once did she freak out when I said, "I don't know. I'll figure it out later." (Which pretty much sums up my writing process.)

To the wonderful folks at Harlequin, who took me in and made me one of their own!

To P.C. Cast, Rachel Caine, Marley Gibson, Rosemary Clement-Moore, Linda Gerber and Tina Ferraro for helping me run the *Unraveled* puzzle contest last year. *Such* a blast. I owe you, ladies!

To Pennye Edwards, the best mother-in-law a girl could have. Honest to God, she kept me sane while I was writing this book. Well, as sane as a girl like me can be.

To my Love Bunny. When I locked myself in my writing cave, he made sure the beast was fed. Even if he had to slide the food under the door and run for his life.

To Jill Monroe and Kresley Cole. If I wasn't already married, and they weren't already married, I'd marry them. For reals.

And this time, I'm not going to dedicate the book to myself, but to Loreal hair color (medium to dark brown). After writing this book, I needed this miracle worker more than ever.

ONE

ADEN STONE STARED DOWN at the girl sleeping on the rocky dais. Long hair the color of a wintry midnight, dark yet glimmering like the moonlight on snow, spilled over slender shoulders. Spiky black lashes cast shadows over high, model-sharp cheekbones. Lush pink lips glistened with a sheen of moisture.

He'd watched her lick those lips several times, and he knew. Even lost to slumber as she was, she scented something delicious and craved a taste.

Taste… Yes…

Her skin was snow-white yet constantly flushed a deep rose in all the right places. Not one flaw did she possess. Not a single line or wrinkle—even though she was over eighty years old.

Young, for her kind.

She wore a tattered black robe that draped from just

under her arms to the tips of her toes. Or would have, if she hadn't rucked the material up one of her legs. The slender limb was bent and angled outward. A feast for his gaze, perhaps even an I-want-you-to-drink-from-the-vein-in-my-thigh invitation.

He should resist.

He couldn't resist.

She was the most beautiful female he'd ever seen. Fragile-looking, dainty. Like a priceless piece of art in the one and only museum he'd ever toured. The curator had slapped his hand for trying to touch something he shouldn't.

No need to guard this one, he thought with a small smile. She could protect herself, snapping a man's neck with a single twist of her wrist.

She was a vampire. *His* vampire. His sickness and his cure.

Aden placed one of his knees on the makeshift bed. The T-shirt that stretched underneath the girl, cushioning her ever so slightly, snagged underneath his weight and pulled tight, rolling her in his direction. She didn't moan or utter a breathy sigh as a human might have done. She was quiet, eerily so. Her expression remained the same: serene, innocent…trusting.

You shouldn't do this.

He was going to do this.

He wore a pair of ripped, bloodstained jeans. The same jeans he'd worn the night of their first date. The night his entire world changed. She wore the robe and nothing else. Sometimes their clothing was the only thing that kept them from doing more than drinking from each other.

Drinking from each other. Or "feeding." So mild a word for what happened. He would never purposely hurt her, but when the madness came upon him—hell, when the madness came upon *her*—affection was forgotten. They became animals.

You shouldn't do this, what was left of his conscience repeated.

One more drink, and I'll leave her alone.

That's what you said last time. And the time before that. And the time before that.

Yeah, but I mean it this time. He hoped.

Once, he would have been talking to the three souls trapped inside his head. But they weren't inside his head anymore, they were inside hers, and he'd reverted to talking to himself. At least until the monster awoke. An honest to God monster, prowling through his conscious, roaring, desperate for blood. The monster the sleeping girl had inadvertently given him, the monster responsible for his new favorite sport—jugular tapping. Then he didn't talk to anyone at all.

Down…down Aden leaned until his chest flattened against the vampire's. He placed his hands at her temples and balanced his weight. The tips of their noses were a mere whisper apart, yet he wanted to be closer to her. Always closer.

He applied more pressure to his left hand, the soft strands of her hair pulling as tight as the T-shirt had done, causing her head to loll in that direction and exposing the elegant length of her neck. At the base, her pulse thumped steadily.

Unlike the bloodsuckers of myth, she was not dead. She was a living, breathing being, born rather than created, and more alive than anyone he'd ever met. Unless he accidently killed her, of course.

I won't.

You might. Don't do this.

Just a sip…

His mouth watered. He inhaled…and felt as if he were breathing for the very first time. Everything was so new, wondrous…he held the breath…held…could almost taste the sweetness of her blood already…slowly released. No relief was forthcoming, just an increased awareness of that ever-present hunger. He ran his tongue over his teeth, his aching gums. He didn't have fangs, but, oh, he wanted to bite her. Wanted to drink her down. Savor, drink again. Drink, drink, drink.

Even without fangs, he could bite her. And, if she were human, he could drain her dry. But because she was vampire, her skin was as hard and smooth as polished ivory. Reaching a vein with his teeth was impossible. He needed *je la nune,* the only substance capable of burning through that ivory. Problem was, they'd run out. Now, there was only one way to get what he wanted.

"Victoria," he rasped.

She must not have recovered from their last interlude, because she gave no indication that she heard him. A flicker of guilt pierced his hunger. He should get up, move away from her. Let her rest, recover. She'd fed him so much blood over the past few days—weeks? years?— she couldn't have much left.

"Victoria." He couldn't stop her name from rolling off his tongue. The hunger…truly, it never left him. Only grew, slithering around him, clamping down on his soul. Still. He'd take just a drop, the taste he'd promised himself, and then he would at last leave her alone. She could go back to sleep.

Until he needed more.

You won't take any more, remember? This is the last time.

"Wake up for me, sweetheart." He pressed their lips together, harder than he'd intended. A kiss for his Sleeping Beauty.

Like the girl in the fairy tale, Victoria blinked open her lids, the length of her lashes separating, connecting, separating for good. Then he was peering into eyes of the purest crystal. Deep, fathomless. Glazed with a hunger of their own.

"Aden?" She stretched like a kitten, her arms rising above her head, her back arching. A purr rumbled from her throat. "Is it bad again?"

The robe gaped over her chest, just a little, but enough, and he caught a glimpse of the tattoo etched above her heart. A faded black—soon to disappear altogether, just as her others had done—with multiple circles swirling into each other and connecting in the middle. Not just a pretty decoration, but a ward, a spell inked into her skin to protect her against death, and the only thing that had saved her life as she'd poured most of her blood down his throat that first time.

He wished he knew how long ago that was, but time had ceased to exist for him. There was only here and now and her. Always her. Always this, the hunger and the thirst blending into a feral, consuming urge.

Her knee came up to rest against his hip bone, and he

settled more firmly against her. Such an intimate position. No time to enjoy. They had a minute, maybe two,
before the voices would destroy her concentration and
the roar of the beast would claim his.

A minute before they both became as dark as their
natures demanded.

"Please," was all he said. Black spiderwebs were forming in his line of vision, thickening, closing in, until her
neck was all that he could see. The ache in his gums was
unbearable, and he was afraid he was drooling.

"Yes." She didn't hesitate. She wound her arms around
him, her nails sinking into his scalp, and drew him down
for a kiss.

Their tongues met, thrust together, and for a moment,
he lost himself in her sweetness. She was rich chocolate
smoothly mixed with chili peppers, creamy yet spicy.

If only he were simply a boy and she were simply a
girl, they would kiss, and he would try for more. She
might deny him. She might beg him to continue. Either
way, they would care only about each other. Now, as
they were, nothing mattered more than the blood.

"Ready?" she breathed. She was his dealer, his sup-
plier and his drug, all wrapped in the same irresistible
package. He wanted to hate her for that. Part of him—

the new, sinister part—did hate her. The rest of him loved her immeasurably.

Sadly, he feared the two parts would one day war.

Someone always died in a war.

"Ready?" she asked again.

"Do it." A growl so hoarse he sounded more animal than human.

Was he human anymore? He'd been a magnet for the paranormal his entire life. Maybe he'd never been human. Not that he cared about the answer right now. Blood…

The ferocity of their kiss increased. Without pulling away, Victoria flicked her tongue across her fangs, cutting the tissue straight down the center. Nectar of the gods welled, the taste of chocolate and spice instantly replaced by champagne and honey, intoxicating him. His head swam with dizziness as his body temperature rose.

He sucked the blood quickly, before her wound had time to close, taking every drop he could, every swallow ringing a groan of rapture from him. His temperature rose another degree, another still, until fire poured through him, burning him up, scorching him to ash.

He recognized the sensation. Not too long ago, his mind had merged with that of a male vampire. A vampire roasting inside a death pyre. Aden had felt as if *he* were the one drenched in flames.

Soon after that, his mind had merged with a fairy's. A fairy with a knife in his chest, the beat of his heart no longer saving him but destroying him, the blade sinking deeper and deeper.

Both instances had been a lesson in pain, but neither compared to Aden's own stabbing, when *his* body had been the one violated. And if not for the girl beneath him, he would have died.

He and Victoria had thought to celebrate their victory against a coven of witches and a contingent of fairies... alone, together. From the shadows had jumped a demon in human skin, his knife embedded in Aden's chest— yes, everyone always went for the heart—before he could blink.

Victoria should have let him go. *His* stabbing had been predicted by one of the souls. Aden had expected it. He might not have been prepared for it, but he had known he wasn't meant to have a future beyond that point.

And really, he and Victoria would have been better off if she'd let him go. Fact: you didn't mess with fate without paying a price. He should be dead, and Victoria should be free of his baggage. But panic had bloomed inside her. He knew, because he remembered the high-pitched tenor of her screams. Could still feel the way her hands had clutched at him, shaking him as life flowed out of him. Worse, he could still feel the white-hot tears slipping from her face onto his.

Now, she was paying for her actions. She might continue to pay until Aden accidentally killed her—or until *she* killed *him*. A life for a life. Wasn't that how the universe worked?

This time, he expected to die from the inferno Victoria's blood was creating inside him. Instead, he found himself…calming. Not just calming, but thriving, his limbs growing stronger, his bones vibrating with energy, his muscles flexing with purpose.

This had never happened during a feeding. Wasn't supposed to happen now. They drank, they fought and they passed out. He didn't recharge like a battery.

When the blood on her tongue dried up—far too soon—he was reminded of his need, need, need *now,* and he stopped worrying about the repercussions, stopped caring about his reactions.

"Victoria," he croaked.

"More?" she asked, breath emerging shallowly. Her nails were leaving track marks down his nape and along his shoulders. The hunger must be coming upon her, too.

Even without her monster, the beating heart of her vampire nature and the driving force of Aden's new menu selection, she craved blood. Maybe because it was all she'd ever known. Maybe because she was as addicted as he was.

"More," he confirmed.

Once again she razed her tongue against her fangs. A new wound opened up. Blood welled, though not as much and not as quickly. Still he sucked and sucked and sucked.

Not enough, not enough, never enough.

Within seconds the blood stopped leaking. He didn't want to hurt her, couldn't let himself hurt her, but he found himself biting her tongue; unlike her skin, this flesh was soft and malleable. She moaned, but not in pain. He'd accidentally cut his tongue, too, and *his* blood was trickling into *her* mouth.

"More," she said, a demand now.

His hands tangled in the silky length of her hair, fisted. He angled her head, allowing deeper access for them both. *So good.*

She'd once told him humans died when vampires attempted to turn them. She'd also mentioned that the vampires attempting the turning died as well. At the time, he hadn't understood why.

Now, he understood—but the knowledge cost him.

When she'd taken what remained of his blood and poured her own straight into his mouth, they'd done more than swap DNA, more than trade his souls for her monster. They'd swapped and traded *everything*. Memories, likes, dislikes, abilities and desires, back and forth, back and forth, until he sometimes couldn't tell what was his and what was hers.

Had he once been whipped with a cat-o'-nine-tails? Had he once drained a human to death? Had he once stumbled upon a sick shape-shifting bear clan and doctored them to health?

A muted rumble—a yawn?—in the back of his mind claimed his attention. The monster. Actually, *demon* was a better description for Chompers. Aden felt utterly possessed by him. A feeling he should have been used to. Only, Chompers was nothing like the souls—he wasn't affable like Julian, perverted like Caleb, or caring like Elijah. Chompers thought only of blood and pain. The taking of blood—and the giving of pain.

When he took over, Aden became more predator than man. He hated himself as much as he hated Victoria. Which was surreal. Chompers adored Aden. He truly did. He enjoyed being inside Aden's mind and didn't fight to leave him as he'd always fought Victoria. But even still, Chompers had a violent temperament, and that violent temperament demanded its due.

Sometimes Aden and Victoria switched back, the souls returning to him, Chompers returning to her. They would quickly switch again, however. And again and again and again. And each time edged them closer and closer to insanity. Too many memories swirling together, too many conflicting needs. One day soon, they would tumble off that edge completely.

"Aden," Victoria said, panting, his name broken. "I must...have to..."

He knew what came next.

She angled his head, just as he'd done to her, and a moment later, her mouth left his. He didn't like that. Her fangs sank into his jugular. He didn't like that, either, and hissed out a breath. Once upon a time, her bite had felt *good*. In her mindless state of hunger, she'd lost her finesse, and those fangs sliced into a tendon. He didn't try to stop her, though. She needed to drink just as much as he did.

Footsteps echoed through their cave, resonating like a buzzer.

Aden didn't panic. Victoria could teleport anywhere she'd been before, had even whisked them here the night of his stabbing. He didn't know where "here" was, or when she'd visited, he knew only that hikers occasionally wandered inside. None had ever traveled this far and this deep, and he doubted that would change.

He and Victoria could have gone somewhere else, he supposed, somewhere even more remote. Might have been safer, being as far away from civilization as possible. There was a target on Aden's back, after all, Victoria's father having come back from the dead to reclaim his throne. Or rather, Vlad the Impaler was *trying* to reclaim the throne.

Aden might be human—emphasis on *might*—but *he* was now the vampire king. He'd killed for the right to rule. So, *he* would be reclaiming the throne. Just as soon as he could wean himself from Victoria's blood.

His thoughts, he wondered, or the monster's?

His, he decided next. Had to be his. He wanted to be king as intently as he wanted to feed.

You didn't before. In fact, he'd been on the hunt for a replacement.

That was before. Besides, there at the end, I had started to make plans for my people.

His people?

That was the adrenaline talking.

Yeah? And this is me talking—shut up.

The footsteps reverberated, closer…closer…

Victoria ripped her fangs from his neck and hissed at the only entrance to the cavern. Normally, if she were lucid, she would simply compel visitors away before they could step inside. Her voice was powerful, and no one human could resist doing what she commanded. Except Aden. He must have built up an immunity to that voice, because she could no longer work her magic on him. She'd tried, here in the cave, every time the madness had come upon her. *Tilt your head, offer your neck…* Yet he'd done only what *he* wanted.

"If the human comes any closer, I will eat his liver and rip out his heart," she snarled.

A threat she wouldn't see through, Aden didn't think. These past few days—years?—she craved only Aden's blood, as he craved only hers. He could always smell the hikers the moment they entered the winding maze of the caves, just as he knew Victoria could, but the thought of drinking from one of them, even to save his life, caused acid and bile to churn in his stomach. And yet, they were the reason he stayed in this location. If he or Victoria ever needed someone else's blood, whether they wanted it or not, they could get it.

Footsteps, closer and closer still, hurried now, determined. "Is someone back there?" The man's voice was slightly accented. Spanish, perhaps. "I mean you no harm. I heard voices and thought you might need some help."

Victoria was off the dais, and a second later Aden was smashing face-first into the thin T-shirt she'd used as a cushion. A tall, lanky man with dark hair and skin, perhaps forty years old, stepped into their private sanctuary. Victoria latched onto the human's shirt, moving so swiftly Aden saw only a blur. The guy's backpack rattled against his canteen of water. With a flick of her wrist— see?—she flung him deeper inside.

He landed with a hard thud, skidding backward until he hit the wall. Instinctively he rolled and sat up. Confusion and fear battled for supremacy in his expression.

"What—" He held out his hands in a protective gesture.

Another blur of motion, and Victoria was crouched in front of him, gripping his chin. Aden's blood dripped from the corners of her mouth. That jet-black hair was a wild tangle around her head, and her fangs extended past her upper lip, cutting into the bottom one. She was a hauntingly lovely sight, as nightmarish as she was angelic.

Little beads of sweat broke out over the man's brow. His eyes widened, fear finally winning and glazing his irises. His chest rose and fell quickly, shallowly, his breath wheezing from his nostrils.

"I—I'm so sorry. Didn't mean to…will leave…never tell…swear…just let me go…please, *please*."

Victoria continued to study him as if he were a rat in a wheel.

"Tell him to go away," Aden said. "Tell him to forget." She would despise herself if she hurt an innocent human. One day. Not today, probably not tomorrow, but one day, when their wits returned.

If they returned.

Silence. Her fingers tightened on the man. So much so, he grimaced in pain, bruises already branching along his jaw.

Aden opened his mouth to issue another command, but in the back of his mind, he heard another rumble. Stronger this time, more than a yawn. Every muscle in his body tensed.

Chompers had awakened.

A sense of urgency filled Aden. "Victoria. Now! Or I swear I'll never feed you again."

Another beat of silence, then, "You will go away," she said, thrums of subdued power wafting from her voice. Why subdued? "You saw no one, spoke to no one."

Unlike before, several seconds passed before the

human responded to her command. In the end, his brown eyes dulled, and his pupils contracted. "No trouble," he said in a monotone. "Leave. No one."

"Good," she said, anger pulsing from her now. Her arm fell to her side. "Go. Before it's too late."

He stood. Walked to the entrance. Exited without looking back. He would never know how close he'd come to dying.

The rumble in Aden's head intensified yet again. Any moment now, and the rumble would become—

A roar.

So loud, consuming, rocking him to his soul. Aden covered his ears, hoping to block the sound, even though he knew how ineffective the action was. Louder and louder, the roar became a scream, high-pitched, slashing through his mind like a razor until his thoughts broke apart and two words hacked their way to center stage.

Feed.

Destroy.

No, no, no. *I did feed,* he said to Chompers. *Let's not—*

FEED. DESTROY.

The spiderwebs returned to his vision, interspaced with red. Both zeroed in on Victoria. Still she crouched, her gaze leveled on him, wary. She knew what would happen next.

FEEDDESTROY.

Yes. Aden rolled from the rocky dais and settled his weight on unsteady legs. Victoria unfolded to her full height, reed slender and lovely. Wild. Her hands curled into fists. He'd just eaten, true, but he needed more. Had to have more.

"Feed," he heard himself say, two voices layered together, one familiar, the other smoky and harsh. Fight this, he had to fight this. Couldn't let Chompers tug his puppet strings.

A whimper escaped Victoria as she scratched at her ears. The souls must be waking up. He knew how loud their voices could be. As loud as Chompers' roar.

"Protect," she said, her eyes suddenly sparkling with brown, green and blue. Oh, yes. The souls were in there, chattering.

Protect her, as she'd said. He must protect her. But he ground out, "Destroy." And even though he tried to root his feet into the floor, he found himself stalking toward her, his mouth watering.

D e s t r o y d e s t r o y d e s t r o y .
DESTROYDESTROYDESTROY.

Chompers had always been insistent. But this…this was savagery at its most basic.

Somehow, some way, Aden's time with Victoria was about to come to an end—the knowledge was suddenly as much a part of him as his healed heart—and he had a feeling only one of them would be walking away.

+WO

VICTORIA TEPES, DAUGHTER of Vlad the Impaler and one of the three princesses of Wallachia, braced herself for impact. Good thing. A split second later, Aden slammed into her, knocking her into the same cave wall against which she'd thrown the human. Goodbye, beloved oxygen.

There was no time to refill her lungs, either. One of Aden's hands closed around her neck and squeezed. Not enough to damage her but enough to trap her. He was fighting the monster's urges with every bit of his strength, she knew. Otherwise he would have already crushed her.

Soon, he would lose the battle.

Anger would have helped her push him away, but she couldn't summon a single spark of it. *She* had done this to him, and the guilt ate at her, a malignant cancer without a cure. He'd told her not to try and save him. He'd told her bad things would happen if she did. But as she'd peered down at the boy she'd come to love, the one person who had ever accepted her for who and what she was without any strings or expectations, she hadn't been able to let him go. She'd thought, *He's mine, I need him.*

So, before death could claim him, she'd acted. She still didn't regret what she'd done—how could she? He was here!—and *that* was why the guilt had chewed such a big hole in her. Her Aden had to abhor what he was becoming. Aggressive, domineering...a warrior without a soul.

Normally he was gentle with her, treating her like a precious treasure, a need to safeguard her somehow hardwired into his brain. Even though she could rip him apart in seconds. Or rather, *could have* ripped him apart. More than changing mentally, he was changing physically. Already he was taller, stronger, quicker—and he'd been tall, strong and quick to begin with.

His eyes, usually a collage of glittering colors as the souls he (once) possessed peered through them, were now the startling shade of a violet. "Thirsty," he rasped, and she would have sworn she felt the singe of smoke wafting from him.

Isn't this just a peach, a male voice piped up inside her

head. *We're with the vamp again.* And there was Julian, the corpse whisperer. He could raise the dead. So far, however, all he'd raised was her blood pressure.

Sweet! Hey Vicki. Another voice immediately joined the conversation. *You should take a shower. You know, get that blood cleaned off you. And remember to scrub really hard. Everywhere. Cleanliness is next to godliness.* This one belonged to Caleb, the body possessor and naked-curves aficionado.

"Let me take over Aden's body," she said. She'd seen him step into and disappear inside other people, snapping up the reins of command. Just *boom,* one second he was there, and the next he was a part of them, forcing them to do whatever he wanted.

He no longer needed Caleb's help to perform the task. He could control the ability, turning it on and off at will. Not her, though. She'd tried multiple times and failed miserably. Maybe because the souls were not a natural extension of her being. Maybe because they were new to her, there was a certain way to deal with them, and she hadn't yet found that way. Maybe because they constantly fought her. Whatever the reason, she needed their...gag...permission to use them.

A chorus of *No, no, no,* rang out. As always.

"I'll be careful with him," she added. "I'll force him

to sit still until the madness passes." If she could. Sometimes the madness overtook *her,* and she forgot her purpose.

Nope, sorry. The guys and I—wait, the guys and me— wait, how do you say that properly?

"Does it matter?" she snapped.

Anyway, Caleb went on smoothly, *we talked, and we're not gonna help you use us. That might create a permanent connection, you know? Like a bond. You're hot, and I'd love to bond with you, and in fact, I voted in your favor, but majority rules and we're not staying any longer than necessary. Now about that shower...*

"Congratulations on your little talk. If he's hurt, you have only yourselves to blame."

No, we'll know who to blame. Because you're right. This will not end well, Elijah, the death predictor, suddenly chimed in. He never had anything good to say. At least, not to her.

Caleb snorted. *Bite your tongue, E. Showers always end well if you know what you're doing.*

Aden shook her, his grip tightening in a demand for her attention. "Thirsty," he repeated, clearly expecting her to do something about it.

"I know." So. She was on her own. Foolish souls. Not only did they refuse to help her, they stole her concentration, preventing her from helping herself. "But you can't drink from me. I haven't yet fully recovered from the last time." Especially considering *last time* had happened roughly five minutes ago. He shouldn't have been this desperate.

"Thirsty."

"Listen to me, Aden. This isn't you, but Chompers." Such a silly name for such a ferocious beast. "Fight him. You have to keep fighting him."

You won't get through to him, Elijah told her. The soul's new nickname, she decided—The Good News Bear. *I've seen this encounter play out. Aden's lost in there.*

"Oh, just shut up!" she snapped. "I don't need your commentary. And you know what else? You've been wrong before! Aden didn't die after he was stabbed. Either time!"

Yes, and look where that got you both.

Stating the obvious. Such a low blow. "Shut. Up."

A flicker of sympathy in those petal-toned eyes before the cold, frothing hunger returned. "Thirsty. Drink. Now." Aden flashed his teeth at her just before diving for her neck. On some level, he knew he couldn't reach her vein, but at this stage, that never stopped him from trying.

Victoria gripped him by the hair and flung him. *Gentle, gentle.* He flew across the cave into the far wall, and she winced. Oops. Dust and debris exploded around him, drifting to her as he slid to the ground. She sucked in a much-needed breath, then had to cough to clear her throat of the rubble.

Hey! Be careful with our boy, Julian commanded. *I plan to move back inside him, you know.*

"I'm trying to be careful," she wanted to scream. How had Aden dealt with these beings all his life? They chattered constantly, commenting on *everything.* Julian found fault with her every action, Caleb took nothing seriously and Elijah was the biggest downer of all time.

To be honest, she would have more fun overdosing on sedatives than speaking to him.

Where were human junkies when you needed to top yourself off?

Aden stood, his gaze locked on her.

How can I stop him without harming him? She'd wondered this a thousand times before, but the solution had never come to her. Surely there was a way to facilitate—

Hey, I kinda feel funny, Caleb announced, his voice booming as if there had never been anyone or anything more important than him and his feelings in the history of the world.

Will you give it a rest? You've got a funny feeling in your invisible pants and the only way to fix you is for Victoria to undress. We know! Julian snapped. *Why don't you do our boy Aden a solid and stop trying to play Naughty Shower Time with his girlfriend?*

Victoria clawed at her ears, trying to reach the souls and finally kill them. They were so loud. So *there,* like shadows slinking through her skull, untouchable, darting just out of reach every time she closed in.

No, I'm not horny. A laborious pause. *Well, I am, but that's not what I'm talking about right now. I…I think I'm… dizzy.*

Caleb was telling the truth. That dizziness was now spilling into her, and she wavered on her feet.

Hey, Julian said a second later. *Me, too. What did you do to us, princess?*

Of course he blamed her, even though it wasn't her fault. The dizziness always hit them a few minutes before they returned to Aden, and they were always surprised.

Here comes Aden, Elijah warned her. *I hope you're prepared for the changes about to unfold. I know I'm not.*

Hey, don't help the enemy! Julian growled.

"I'm not the—" The scent of Aden's blood hit her first, potent and tantalizing, making her mouth water, reminding her of *her* body's needs. Then, suddenly, she was falling, hard hands pushing her down. Cold rock scraped against her back, and she gasped out the rest of her sentence "—enemy."

"Feed." Aden's weight pinned her, his teeth chewing at her neck a moment later. She latched onto his hair again, but this time, when she tugged, he bit down harder—*into* her vein. Her skin actually split open.

Never before had something like this happened, and a scream of pain tore from her. A scream that died as quickly as it had begun. Her throat clogged as the dizziness returned, accompanied by a tidal wave of unexpected fatigue. Her muscles quivered, and she thought she heard Caleb moan.

Caleb. Reminded of his presence, she gasped out his name, willing to beg the soul to help her now. "Let me possess—"

His second moan cut her off. *What's happening to me?*

"Concentrate. Please. Let me—"

Am I dying? I don't want to die. I'm too young to die.

He and his babbling would be no help. Nor would the others. Julian and Elijah were moaning, too. But they weren't leaving her, weren't returning to Aden. And then their moans became shouts, fogging her mind, derailing her good sense.

Flashes in her mind, like a camera switching views. Her bodyguard, Riley—tall and dark-haired, smiling with wicked humor. Her sisters, Lauren and Stephanie, both blonde and beautiful, teasing her mercilessly.

Her mother, Edina, with black-as-a-midnight-sky hair swinging as she twirled. Her long-lost brother, Sorin, a warrior she'd been commanded to forget, she'd *tried* to forget as he'd walked away and never looked back.

More flashes, the camera revealing only black and white now. Shannon, her roommate, kind, caring, concerned. No, not her roommate, but Aden's. Ryder, the boy Shannon had wanted to date, even though he'd rejected him. Dan, beloved owner of the D and M ranch, her home for the last few months. No, not *her* home. Aden's.

Her own thoughts and memories were blending with Aden's, forming a hazy cloud around her. Then the flashes disappeared all together. She was weakening... fighting the need to sleep...

Come on, Tepes! You're royalty. You can do this!

A pep talk courtesy of herself, one that worked. She *could* do this.

Determination driving her, she managed to tug on Aden's hair, lifting his head. Unfortunately, she wasn't strong enough to throw him. Not this time. And for a moment, their gazes clashed. His eyes were red now, glowing. Demonic. Blood dripped from his mouth—her blood—and splashed onto her chin. Blood she desperately needed to keep.

She should have been frightened. Because, as she looked up at the fiend she had created, she saw her death. A death that made sense. Elijah had claimed Aden was now lost to the beast, and Elijah was never wrong. And yet...

Blood...her own hunger rose again, filling her up, becoming all that she knew, strengthening her. She would not be taken down without feasting on *him,* she decided.

Her fangs sharpened as she surged up to bite. Only, she could not pierce his skin. Something blocked her. What blocked her? She looked, determined to remove the obstacle, but she saw only the bronze of Aden's skin. Nothing covered that hammering pulse.

Taste, taste, must taste. A mantra she couldn't blame on the souls.

Snarling, she released his hair and clawed at him. A tiny cut, that's all she needed to make. So easy, but her nails failed her as thoroughly as her teeth.

"Feed." Aden dove back down. Clearly, her jugular was his favorite chew toy.

TASTE. She surged back up, trying to bite him again.

"Taste," the beast said, as if he'd heard her thought and mirrored it.

They rolled on the floor in a bid for dominance. Whenever she managed to toss him away, he always flew back in less than a blink. They crashed into the walls, slammed into the dais and splashed in the shallow puddles of water.

Whoever won would feed. Whoever lost would die, drained, the circle of life proven once again. For only the strongest could survive; everyone else became a snack. Until Aden, her every action had been motivated by that principle. After him, she had fought to protect those weaker than herself. Fought her instinct to take, to have. Now, she couldn't fight. She wanted. She would have.

All too soon, however, Aden pinned her, and this time, he held her down so firmly, she was unable to wrestle her way free. Their bodies rubbed together as she still continued to struggle, their limbs tangling. Finally, he managed to grab her wrists and brace them over her head.

Game over. She had lost.

She took stock. She was panting, sweating, her neck throbbing, her mind locked on one thought: *TASTETASTETASTE.*

Yes.

"Let go," she snarled.

Above her, Aden stilled. He, too, was panting and sweating. His eyes were still glowing that bright crimson, but now there were flecks of amber mixed with the red. Amber, his natural color. That meant, for once, Elijah had been wrong. Aden *was* in there, still battling the beast for control.

She could do no less.

The thought was a lifeline, and she clung. Victoria concentrated on her breathing, in and out, slow and measured. Voices other than her own began to penetrate her awareness.

—*feeling worse,* Caleb was saying.

The dizziness had never been this bad before. And once the switch-switch-switch had begun, the souls should not have been able to stay put. Why hadn't they left her?

We all have to stay calm, Elijah said. *Okay? We'll be fine. I know we'll be fine.*

You're lying. Julian's words were slurred. *Hurts too badly for us to be fine.*

Yes, lying. Panic drenched Caleb's voice. *This is terrible, I'm dying, and you're dying, too. We're all dying. I know we're dying.*

Stop saying the word dying *and calm down,* Elijah commanded. *Now. Your little anxiety attacks are placing Aden and Victoria in more danger.*

At last, concern. But it was too little, too late. They were already in danger.

I just…I need…

Caleb! You're placing all of us in danger, too. Please, calm down.

"Thirsty," Aden said, his gravelly voice drawing her back to the hated present.

The amber was fading in his eyes, the red expanding. He was losing the battle…would soon attack her, his gaze already zeroing in on the still-seeping wound in her neck. He licked his lips, his eyes closing as he savored the lingering flavor of her.

This was the perfect time for her to strike, she thought, reverting to her baser urges. Her opponent was distracted. "Taste," she said, the word garbled.

Victoria. You love him. You fought to save him. Don't undermine your own efforts by succumbing to a hunger you can control. A voice of reason in the chaos of her mind. But of course, Elijah, the psychic, would know exactly what to say to reach her. *All right? Okay? I can't deal with both you and Caleb right now, on top of the dizziness. One of you has to act like a grown-up. And since you're eighty-something years old, I pick you.*

Aden's eyelids popped open. Bright red, no longer any hint of his humanity.

Control herself, yes. She could. She would. "Aden, please." Save him, yes. She would try that, too. He meant everything to her. "I know you can hear me. I know you don't really want to hurt me."

A pause, heavy and laden with tension. Then, miraculously, another flicker of amber, deep in those beloved eyes. "Can't hurt..." he said. "Don't want to hurt."

Tears of relief pooled in her lashes, leaked onto her cheeks. "Let go of my hands, Aden. Please."

Another pause, this one lasting an eternity. Slowly, so slowly, he uncurled his fingers from her wrists and lifted his arms away from her. He straightened until he was straddling her, his knees pressing into her hips.

"Victoria...sorry, so sorry. Your poor, beautiful neck." The dual voice, one his, one the beast's, tendrils of sympathy and smoke, blending together, wafting over her.

She offered him a soft smile. "Nothing to apologize for." *I did this to you.*

I...need...you must... Caleb couldn't quite catch his breath—and suddenly, Victoria couldn't quite catch her breath, either. *Something's happening...I can't...*

Listen to me carefully, Caleb, Elijah lashed out. *We can't go back to Aden yet. We'll be killed.*

Killed? Caleb gasped. *Figures. I knew we were going to die.*

What do you mean, killed? Julian snarled.

I mean, we'll be fine unless you two keep this up! Your panic is going to drive us out of Victoria, and we can't leave Victoria. Not yet. So you have to calm down like I told you. Do you hear me? We can return to Aden later. After the…just after. So, Caleb, Julian, are you listening to—

His speech ended abruptly. Caleb screamed, then Julian screamed, the sounds blending with Elijah's sudden groan of distress. No, they hadn't listened.

Neither had she, apparently. Victoria was the next to scream, and the sound of *that* busted her eardrums. Loud, loud, so loud. Hurt, hurt, *so* hurt. Then, she didn't care. The pain left, and her scream softened into a purr.

Somehow, some way, absolute power was birthed inside her, blasting through her, fusing with her. Now, a part of her. Good, good, so good.

Throughout the decades of her life, she had drained several witches. A bad thing for vampires. Witches were their drug of no-choice, and once sampled, it was difficult to think about anything else. She knew that very well. Though years had passed since her last bender, some days the cravings hit her, and she'd find herself running through the woods, searching, searching, desperate to find a witch. Any witch. And that was reason number one why witches and vampires usually avoided each other.

But, oh, this sudden burst of power…it was witchlike, intoxicating, warmth and sunlight, yet cold like a snowstorm. Dizzying, overwhelming, everything and nothing. She floated on clouds, swept away from the cave. She dozed on a beach, water lapping at her feet. She danced in the rain, as carefree as the child she'd never been allowed to be.

Such a beautiful eternity awaited her here. She never wanted to leave.

She thought she heard the souls crying, soft, almost childlike. Where they not experiencing this, too?

A roar cut through her euphoria. That roar stretched out wispy tentacles, and those tentacles wrapped around her, surprisingly strong, tugging her away. Frowning, she dug her heels into the ground. *I'm staying!*

A second roar inside her head, louder now, threatening, causing a chilled, clammy sheen of perspiration to coat her….

In a snap, she was jerked back to the present. And just like that, her sense of tranquility vanished. No. No, no, *no.*

Oh, yes. The souls were no longer chattering, screaming, crying, *anything,* and the sense of power had evaporated with the tranquility. More than that, Chompers had returned, and he didn't want her to hurt Aden.

Before, each time her beast had returned to her, she had experienced a sharp lance of acknowledgment. Nothing more. Then he'd left her again. Then returned. An endless cycle as she and Aden endlessly drank. But this...this was something different. Something stronger. A passing of energy, perhaps. Or had that been a final break of the ever-changing cycle of possession?

Chompers' hunger blended with her own, familiar, yet utterly unwelcome because he would not allow her to do anything about it. He never did, not with Aden.

Victoria blinked open her eyes, gasped. She had never left the cave, but she'd been *busy*. She was on her feet, her arms outstretched. A golden glow radiated from between her fingers, dimming...gone. Aden lay in a crumpled heap against the far wall. He was unconscious, unmoving, maybe even—no. No!

Her bare feet dug into the rocks as she raced to him. The moment she reached him, she was crouching and feeling for a pulse. *No, no, no. Please, please.* There! Fast, too fast and too weak, but there. He was alive.

Relief flooded her, followed quickly by remorse. What had she done to him? Beaten him? Drained him?

No, she couldn't have. Chompers wouldn't have allowed that, either. Right?

"Oh, Aden." She smoothed the hair from his brow. There were no bruises on his face, no punctures in his neck. "What's wrong with you?"

A sound wafted to her ears. Frowning, she leaned down. Was he…humming? She blinked, listened more intently. Yes, yes, he was. And if he was humming, he wasn't hurting. Right? He must be experiencing some sort of euphoria. Perhaps even the same euphoria she'd basked in. *Right?*

Please, be right.

She studied him more intently. His expression was serene, his lips edged upward. He looked boyish, innocent, almost angelic. He *was* experiencing the euphoria, then.

Relaxing, she traced her fingertip along his hairline. He was so striking, with his hair dyed black and those two-inch blond roots. Perfectly arched eyebrows rose above perfectly uptilted eyes. His nose was perfectly sloped. His lips were soft, his chin stubborn. Again, perfectly. His was a face a girl would never tire of looking at. Maybe because every new glance revealed a previously undiscovered nuance. This time, she saw the thick, feathering fan of his lashes, a golden chocolate in the haze of the cave.

"Wake up for me, Aden. Please."

Nothing, no response.

Perhaps, like her, he didn't want to leave. Well, too bad. They had some chatting to do.

"Aden. Aden, wake up."

Again nothing. No, not nothing. He scowled, and the scowl soon became a grimace.

Her heart galloped against her ribs. All right. What if he wasn't floating and carefree? What if he was stuck? Or worse, agonized? That grimace...

He panted out a breath once, twice, shallow and rasping. Crackling. She'd heard that crackle before—each time she'd taken too much blood from a human.

He won't die. He can't. They'd been here a week. Seven days, three hours and eighteen minutes. They'd fought and kissed and drank from each other the entire time. Aden had survived all of that; surely he would survive this. Whatever *this* was.

Shame suddenly outweighed her ever-present guilt. And maybe that shame was what corralled her beast, stopping him from screaming for release the way he had every time before.

Wait. Chompers wasn't screaming. The realization caused her to blink with confusion. A quick glance at her chest, and she saw that *all* of her wards had faded.

Even still, the beast was silent. That had never happened before.

What else was different? Her gaze fell to Aden's neck, where his pulse drummed sporadically. Her mouth watered, but the urge, the electrifying *need* to bite him, wasn't there.

No, not true. It was there, it simply wasn't as strong. It was controllable. Even still, she was thirsty, desperate to drink from *someone*. And if *she* could now take from someone else, perhaps Aden could, as well. If so...

He could be saved. Completely. She hoped. There was only one way to find out. Though she was still weak, she twined her fingers with Aden's and closed her eyes, imagining her bedroom at the vampire stronghold near Crossroads, Oklahoma. White carpet, white walls, white bed covers.

Please work, she thought. *Please.*

A cold breeze kicked up, blowing her hair up and down, the strands winding together and knotting. It was working! Her grip tightened on Aden, and her lips curved into a grin. The floor fell away, leaving them suspended in the air. Any moment now and they would be—

Her feet settled on a soft, plush foundation. Carpet.

Home. They were home.

†HREE

Three days later

THE BEDROOM DOOR CRASHED against the wall as a harsh male voice snarled, "I hear you've threatened to disembowel anyone who steps foot in your room. Well, here I am. But before you disembowel me, you better tell me what the *hell* is going on."

Victoria stopped pacing and whipped around to face the intruder. Riley. Her bodyguard. Her best friend. Tall, as muscled as Aden now was, with a face roughened by life and fist fights.

Her chest constricted. He wasn't handsome in a Prince of Your Dreams way like Aden, but in a sexy I'll Kick Your Ass No Matter What It Takes and Laugh way, and that was exactly what she needed at the moment. A willingness to do whatever was necessary.

He might be the one person able to help her.

And though he was obviously fuming, his eyes glittering with angry heat, he was the best thing she'd seen in days. He had dark, shaggy hair, bright green eyes fringed by long lashes of the darkest jet, and a nose broken too many times to count, with a slight bump in the center. Certain injuries, when received repeatedly, simply couldn't heal properly.

He wore a green Lucky Charms T-shirt and jeans— or what looked to be jeans, since she knew they weren't really denim. He was the only slash of color in her white-as-the-clouds bedroom.

"Nice shirt," she said. One, to distract him from his anger before she spilled her secrets, and two, to showcase the sense of humor she was desperately trying to develop. Once, his human girlfriend, Mary Ann Gray, had accused Victoria of being too somber.

"Only thing I could find. Victoria. Talk. Now. Before I assume the worst and just start offing everyone in the house."

The pretend sense of humor vanished, and tears filled her eyes, those stupid human tears she'd never shed before coming to the States. She raced to Riley, throwing herself into his strong, capable arms.

"I'm so glad you're here."

"You might not be so glad if I have to force you to start talking." Despite the threat, he hugged her tight, exactly as he'd done when they were younger and other vampires refused to play with her.

Because she was a daughter of Vlad the Impaler, everyone had feared punishment if she were hurt—or worse—on their watch. But not Riley. Never Riley. He was like the brother she had always wanted, her comforter and her shield.

Oh, she had a blood brother. Sorin. Except, Vlad had forbidden her from looking at, talking to or even acknowledging him. Father Dearest hadn't wanted his only son tainted by his "too soft" daughters. In fact, when Aden had asked Victoria about her siblings back when they'd first met, she'd named only her sisters. Last she'd inadvertently heard, Sorin was leading half of the vampire army through Europe, keeping Bloody Mary, the leader of the Scottish faction, in line. Combine all of that, and Sorin didn't count.

Besides, Vlad had long ago given Riley charge of Victoria's care, and the wolf shifter had taken the job seriously. Not just out of a sense of duty, or fear of torture and death if he failed, but also because he liked her. They were friends first and everything else second.

"*Why* are you here, though?" she asked, ignoring his demand. Again.

"My brothers hunted me down and scared two centuries off my life when they told me you'd ventured into Crazy Town. Now, enough about me." Riley pulled back and cupped her cheeks, forcing her to peer up at him. "Have you fed properly? You look like crap."

His concern—and insult—offered more comfort than anything else could have and was so wonderfully Riley she responded in a way she knew he would approve. "Yes, Daddy. I've fed properly." Truth. Five minutes after arriving home and settling Aden in her bed, she'd had her fangs buried deep inside one of the blood-slaves who lived here at the stronghold.

So thirsty had she been, she'd nearly drained the human dry. Her sister Lauren had managed to jerk her away just in time. Her other sister, Stephanie, had found her a second human, and a third and a fourth, and she'd drunk until her stomach could hold no more.

"Smart-ass." Riley's lips twitched with his amusement. "When did you learn to wield sarcasm?"

"I can't remember exactly." All she knew was that she'd had a choice. Find the humor in what happened to her or drown in her misery. "Two weeks ago, maybe."

The mention of time wiped away his delighted expression, leaving him with a cold frown.

Only one person affected him that way. Mary Ann Gray. The girl had struck out on her own the same night Aden had been stabbed, and Riley the Besotted Wolf had charged after her, determined to protect her despite the hazard to himself.

"Where's your human?" Wait. Mary Ann wasn't quite human anymore. The girl had become a drainer—something Victoria had not seen coming—able to suck the magic from witches, the beasts from vampires, the power from fairies and the ability to shift forms from the wolves.

Victoria had begun to wonder if Mary Ann had *ever* been human. After all, fairies were drainers. The difference was, the fairies could control their hunger and feedings. Mary Ann could not. Still. That raised a startling question. Could Mary Ann be a human/fairy hybrid?

Victoria had never heard of such a pairing, but as she was learning, anything was possible. If Mary Ann *was* somehow a hybrid, every vampire and shifter in this stronghold—besides Riley, of course—would want the girl dead. More than they already did. Fae were Enemy One. Dangerous in the extreme. A threat to otherworld existence.

"Well?" Victoria insisted when Riley offered no reply.

"I lost her." A muscle underneath his eye jerked, a sure sign of his upset.

"Wait. You, an expert tracker, lost a teenager who wouldn't know how to hide if she were invisible?" Another sign that Mary Ann was more than she seemed.

The ticking migrated to Riley's jaw. "Yes."

"You should be ashamed."

"I don't want to talk about it," he said. "I'm here to talk about you. How are you? Seriously?"

"I'm fine."

"All right. I'll pretend I believe that. Any word from your father?"

"No." Vlad had ordered Aden's execution while remaining in the shadows. Shadows he had yet to vacate.

She'd never been so grateful for her father's vanity. He wanted to be seen as invincible, always. So, no one here knew Vlad was still alive, and if she had her way, they never would. The vampires might rebel against Aden before he was officially crowned king, and if they rebelled while he was in this condition, he would lose. Everything he'd already endured would have been for nothing.

Even healthy and whole, he needed every edge he

could get. Not just to remain in charge, but to stay alive.

Right now, he had time. Victoria knew her father. Vlad would not return until he was at top strength. Then...well, then there would be a war. Vlad would punish those who'd submitted to Aden's rule. Herself and Riley included. He would make an example of Aden. And his preferred method of "exampling," as she'd come to call it, was placing a severed head on a pike and displaying that pike at his front door.

Would Aden fight him? If so, could Aden hope to win?

"How's Aden?" Riley asked. The wolf could read auras and had probably sensed the direction of her thoughts. "Did he...survive?"

Yes and no. Her stomach twisted into thousands of little knots. She tugged from Riley's hold, turned and motioned to the bed with a wave of her hand. "Behold. Our king."

Green eyes narrowed as they lanced to the lump atop the mattress. Five sure steps, and the shifter was at the side of the bed, peering down. Victoria joined him, trying to see Aden as Riley must.

He lay on his back, as motionless as a corpse. His normally bronzed skin was pallid, the blue tracery of his veins evident. His cheeks were hollowed out, his lips chapped and cracked. His hair was soaked with sweat and plastered to his scalp.

"What's wrong with him?" Riley demanded in a quiet, yet all the harsher for it, tone.

"I don't know."

"You know something."

She gulped. "Well, I think I told you that Tucker stabbed him."

"Yes, and Tucker will die for that." A flat, cold statement of fact. "Soon."

The homicidal confession didn't surprise her. Retaliation was Riley's way. Tit for tat, and never anything in between. That way, an enemy never tried to harm you twice. "I wanted to save him—save Aden I mean—so I…I tried to…" *Just say it.* "Tried to turn him. I told you that, too."

"And I thought you'd change your mind, see reason."

"Well, I didn't. I know I shouldn't have done it, but I couldn't… I didn't want… I did what I had to do to keep him alive!"

"Aden told you the consequences of messing with one of Elijah's predictions, Vic. The few times he did it, people suffered more than they would have if he'd left them alone."

Her back went ramrod straight, her nose lifting in the air. "Yes, he did, and no, that didn't stop me or change my mind. I fed him my blood, every drop I could, drank from him, and then he drank from me. We repeated the process, over and over again."

"And?"

Of course he knew there was more to the story. Her shoulders sagged. "And…somehow I absorbed his souls inside my head, and he absorbed my beast."

Riley's mouth dropped open. "*You* have the souls?"

"Not anymore. We kept switching back and forth, and we kept drinking from each other, even though we barely had anything left. I thought we would kill each other. We…almost…did." Her chin trembled, breaking the words apart.

"There's more. Tell me." Riley was merciless when he wanted something, and right now he wanted information. He'd warned her she wouldn't like him if he had to force her to talk, and she took the threat seriously.

"Our last day in the cave, I did something to him. I don't know what, and it's killing me! I blacked out, and when I came to, he was like this."

"You just blacked out? For how long?"

"Yes, and I don't know."

"Was he bleeding?"

"No." Truth. But that didn't mean she hadn't injured him internally.

Why couldn't she remember what happened?

"Why did you bring him here? In this condition, he's weak and vulnerable. There's no better time to strike at him. Your people could rise up and finally rid themselves of the human king they never wanted."

Her nose went back into the air. "I've been guarding him, and no one has even tried to enter my room. I think they remember how much their beasts love him." Every vampire possessed one, and without the wards they etched into their skin, those beasts could emerge, take solid form and attack. And when they attacked, no one, especially not their vampire "master," was safe.

And yet, those same beasts acted like trained, slobbery house dogs in Aden's presence, doing everything he commanded, protecting him against any and all threats.

"Or maybe the people haven't yet realized Aden's here," she finished.

"Oh, they realize. Everyone I ran into was on edge. Their beasts want out of them and in here with Aden."

That she could believe. The precious silence she'd experienced those last minutes in the cave had ended the moment she arrived home. Chompers wanted to move inside Aden's mind permanently and wasn't afraid to roar his displeasure about being stuck with Victoria.

After feeding him, she'd had to double up on her wards to quiet him.

"Is Aden now a vampire?" Riley asked.

"No. Yes. I don't know. Before passing out, he craved blood. My blood." *All of my blood.* She kept that little gem to herself. No telling how Riley would react.

He reached out and lifted Aden's lips from his teeth. "No fangs."

"No, but his skin…"

"Is like yours?" Frown deepening, Riley unleashed his claws, his nails lengthening and sharpening. Before Victoria could protest, he raked those claws over Aden's cheek.

"Don't—"

Not a single wound formed.

"Interesting." A clear liquid—*je la nune*—beaded on the end of those claws, and Riley once more sliced at Aden's cheek. This time, the skin sizzled as it split apart.

"Stop it!" With a screech, Victoria threw herself over Aden's body, preventing Riley from making another pass at him. Not that he tried.

"You're right. He has a vampire's skin," Riley said.

"Which is what I was trying to tell you!" What she wouldn't admit, not yet, because she still couldn't believe it herself, was that she now had *human* skin. Vulnerable, so easily harmed. Feeding hadn't reversed the damage, either. She wasn't sure anything would. "You didn't need to hurt him like that. The *je la nune* would burn through a human, too."

Riley ignored her. "How long has he been like this?"

"Three days." She sat up, remaining beside Aden, and glared at her bodyguard, daring him to blame her.

"Give me a minute to mentally calculate." With barely a pause, he added, "Yep, that's three days too long. Has he fed recently?"

"Yes." She'd tested every blood-slave she'd allowed him to drink from, then, when she knew they were safe, she'd given him a little at a time to gauge how he would respond. There'd been no reaction, good or bad, so she'd given him more and more, until the blood had practically seeped from his pores. Still there'd been no reaction.

For hours she had debated the wisdom of giving him more of *her* blood. What if he became addicted again? Then she'd thought, what if he was *still* addicted, and only her blood could help him?

So, she'd done it. She'd sliced her wrist—and oh, how that had hurt—pouring her blood straight down his throat. The wound had healed slowly for her, swiftly for a human, but Aden had gotten several mouthfuls in the interim. His cheeks had suddenly bloomed with color, and she'd been so hopeful—for both of them. But a few minutes later, the color had withered, then disappeared altogether, and his sleep had become fitful. Too fitful. He'd moaned in pain, writhed and finally vomited.

She explained all of that to Riley.

"Maybe that's the problem, then," he said. "Maybe he doesn't need the blood."

"I let him go twenty-four hours without it, and he got even worse. He only improved to this comalike state when I started feeding him again."

A heavy sigh. "All right, here's what we're gonna do," Riley said, taking charge. As always. "I'm gonna post guards at your door. No one but you and I are to enter this room. Understand?"

"No. Because I'm foolish. News flash, Riley. That's why I threatened to disembowel anyone who entered." Well, well. Stress and lack of rest were making her snappy.

He continued, unperturbed, "You're going to feed him your blood, exactly as you've been doing, and you will alert me if there's a change. Any change. I will go to the D and M ranch and grab his medication."

The D and M ranch. Aden's home. Well, perhaps former home now. Troubled teenagers lived there, and it was a last stop on the road to redemption—or damnation. One broken rule, and those teens were kicked out. Leaving without contacting Dan, the owner of that ranch, was probably the biggest no-no of all.

"Victoria, are you listening to me?"

"What? Oh, yes. Sorry." She was still so easily distracted. "But Aden hates his medication." And if he wanted back inside that ranch, Victoria would make it happen. A few spoken commands, and the humans there would do and think whatever she wanted them to do and think.

If she still possessed the Voice, she thought with a swirl of dread. She'd lost her ultratough skin and could have lost her ultrapowerful voice, too. Since returning, she had tried to compel a few of the human slaves to do her bidding. They had smiled at her and gone on their way, *without* doing what she'd told them.

You're out of practice, that's all, and still haven't completely regained your strength.

The pep talk failed to comfort her.

"You're worse than Aden," Riley muttered. "And I

don't care if he hates his meds or not. We've seen him like this before, minus the need for blood, and the medication was the only thing that helped him. If the souls are responsible, like they were before, we have to knock them out for a little while."

"But what if the medication hurts him, now that he's a blood drinker?"

"Doubtful, since human meds don't really hurt you. But there's only one way to find out, isn't there?"

Good point. One that bothered her. Most everyone in Aden's life considered him a schizophrenic. Not only had his parents given him up when he was little, but he'd been shuffled from one mental institution to another. Different "cures" had been shoved down his throat for years, and he'd hated them all.

And, really, he liked the souls, loud and obnoxious as they were, and his newest medicinal regimen shut them down entirely. But Riley was right. Aden wouldn't last much longer in his current state. They had to try something, anything. Everything.

"All right." She hated that she hadn't thought of this. If it worked, she could have saved Aden three days of... distress? Pain? Mental torment? Probably a mix of all three. "We'll try."

"Good. I'll be back." Riley turned on his booted heels and headed for the door.

"Riley."

He stopped, but didn't face her.

"Be careful. Thomas's ghost is still there." Thomas, the fairy prince Riley and Aden had killed to save her. Now his very nasty ghost haunted the ranch, and he craved vengeance.

"I will."

"And thank you." Being here was probably difficult for him. Mary Ann was his love, and knowing him, he was frothing over her disappearance. Was probably frantic to be out there, searching for her. Yet, he stayed because Victoria needed him.

When Aden improved, she would help Riley hunt for Mary Ann, she decided. A danger to her loved ones or not.

A stiff nod, and then Riley was gone, the door closing behind him. Sighing, Victoria turned back to Aden. Her beautiful Aden. What was going on in that head of his? Was he aware of his surroundings? Hurting, as she suspected?

Did he know what she had done to him, those last few minutes in their cave?

She ran her fingers through his hair, lifting the strands

and revealing the blond roots. There was a slight curl at the ends, the locks winding around her knuckles. He didn't lean into her touch as she was used to, and that saddened her.

How much turmoil could one boy endure before he crumbled? Since the moment she'd entered his life, he'd known only war and pain. Because of her, goblin poison had ravaged him. Because of her, the witches had cursed his friends to die. Because of her, the fairies had tried to take over the D and M ranch.

Fine. Maybe all those things weren't exactly because of her, but she still felt responsible. A humorless laugh escaped her. How human of her. To carry the weight of blame, despite everything. Aden would be so proud.

"You woke up from this kind of thing before," she whispered. "You will wake up this time, too." *Please.*

Unable to bear the thought of separation, she remained where she was until Riley returned a half hour later. He was without his shirt and wearing new pants that weren't yet fastened. He'd dressed hastily, his other clothes ruined during his shift to wolf, she was sure.

Wolves tended to wear clothing that ripped easily. Because, when they shifted, they were stuck wearing whatever didn't fall off. And wearing human underwear while in wolf form was something they preferred to avoid.

He carried a small wicker basket filled with medicine, the pill bottles rattling together. Victoria hopped to her feet, and he placed the basket where she'd sat.

"Sorry I took so long."

"Thomas give you any trouble?"

"Nope. I didn't even catch a glimpse of him. But then, unlike Aden, I've never been able to see or hear the dead. The delay had to do with the pills. I didn't know which ones to give our boy and didn't want him to have a reaction to the wrong combination, so I just grabbed the bottles with his name on them, stopped in my room, and Googled."

What he didn't say: Mary Ann was the Google queen, and she was the one who'd taught him how to use the search engine. Although, calling it an engine always confused Victoria. There were no workable parts that she could see.

"So, what happened at the ranch?" she asked.

"Here. See for yourself." He extended his free hand, and she twined their fingers. They'd been together so long, they'd developed a very strong mental connection and were able to "share" their experiences.

As if a television screen were switched on inside her

mind with a view straight from Riley's eyes, she saw Dan, an ex-football star, tall, blond and rugged, standing in the kitchen of the ranch. His wife, petite, pretty Meg, bustled around him, tossing ingredients into a pot.

"—really worried," Meg was saying.

"Me, too. But Aden's not the first to run away. He won't be the last." While the words were accepting, the tone was not.

"He's the first to surprise you with his actions, though."

"Yeah. He's just such a great kid. All heart."

Meg's smile was soft. "And not knowing why he left kills you. I know, baby."

"I hope he's okay. Maybe if I'd given him more one-on-one time, he wouldn't have—"

"No. Don't you dare do that to yourself. We can't control the actions of others. All we can do is support them, and pray we make a difference."

The conversation faded as Riley stealthily maneuvered from the main house and into the bunkhouse behind it. Aden's friends were there. Seth, Ryder and Shannon lounged on the couch, watching TV. Terry, RJ and Brian were in front of the computer, playing games. Relaxing activities, but there was an undeniable tension radiating from each boy.

They must feel the loss of Aden, too.

I have to fix this, Victoria thought.

Shannon stood, a chalky cast to his mocha skin, his gaze sweeping the room—and clashing with Riley's.

In the present, Riley released her hand, the images flickering, disappearing, and she was once again inside her bedroom.

"Shannon saw you," she said.

"Yeah, but he didn't do anything and I was able to get what we needed without incident." Riley dug inside the basket, setting aside what he wanted and discarding what he didn't. "There wasn't a whole lot of information, just enough to tell me he needs the antipsychotics. This, this, and this." As he spoke, he placed the desired pills in her palm.

She studied them. One was yellow and round, one blue and oblong, and one white and scored in the center. These tiny things were supposed to help him when she could not?

"Fetch a glass of water from my bathroom," she said.

Commands were not something Riley usually responded to, but he didn't hesitate to obey, soon thrusting the desired glass in her hand. His concern for Aden was as great as hers.

"Lift his head and tilt it back," she said, and again, Riley jumped to obey.

She pried Aden's mouth open and set the pills on his tongue. Then she placed the rim of the glass at his mouth and poured. Just a little, but enough. Without looking away, she reached out and set the remaining water on her nightstand. Or tried to. Her aim was off, and the glass thudded and splashed to the floor. She didn't care. She closed Aden's mouth with one hand and worked his throat with the other, until all the pills made their way into his stomach.

That done, she straightened and peered down at her patient. "Now what?" she whispered, watching for any kind of response…and not seeing one.

"Now," Riley said, grim, "we wait."

FOUR

MARY ANN GRAY SAT AT THE corner desk in the back
of the library, reading countless microfiches—the same
thing she'd done every night for a week. Days were beginning to blend together, her temples were throbbing,
the muscles in her back were knotted, and there were
(probably permanent) marks along her butt and thighs
that were a perfect match to the scuffs in the freakishly
uncomfortable chair she'd commandeered.

According to all the "How To" info she'd read for
people on the run, she knew developing a routine was
bad. Like flashing a neon arrow just above your head.
Problem was, this routine was necessary.

"They close in thirty, you know."

She flicked an irritated glance at her companion. AKA
the boy she couldn't ditch no matter what she tried. And
she'd tried a lot. Dine and dash. The old "wait here, I'll

be right back." The classic "what's that over there?" And even brutal honesty—"just leave me alone, I hate you."

"So I'll finish in thirty," she said. "Now get lost."

"Let's not start that argument again." Tucker Harbor perched at the edge of her desk, pushing books and newspapers on top of each other and crinkling their precious pages. Just to irritate her, she was sure. "I'm not going anywhere."

"Do you mind? This stuff is important."

"Yes, I do mind, thanks for asking," he said, staying put.

She glared up at him. A mix of blond and brown hair shagged around the boyish face of an angel. Which was one hundred percent false advertising, considering he'd been spawned from a demon. Or would that be spawned from *the devil?*

"When are you going to tell me what you're looking for?" he asked.

"When I stop wanting to rip out your trachea. In other words, never."

He shook his head in mock despondency. A hard thing to pull off while he was freaking grinning. "Harsh, Mary Ann. Harsh."

He was *so* annoying. She'd dated him for months, then dropped him like the used condom he was when she found out he'd cheated on her with her best friend Penny. Penny, who was now pregnant with his kid.

Penny, whom she'd forgiven and still called. As of this morning, her friend was suffering from all-day sickness. Despite that, she'd managed to crawl her way out of bed to check on Mary Ann's dad.

Her friend's words played through her head.

"Sweet Jesus, Mary Contrary," Penny had crackled over the line. *"He's, like, the walking dead. He doesn't even go to work anymore. He just stays in the house. I peeked in the window last night, and he was just staring at your picture. You know I'm as hard core as a girl can be, but that almost broke me."*

Me, too, she thought now. *Nothing I can do about that, however. I'm saving his life.* She'd had him freed from a vengeful fairy's compulsion to never leave his room and to ignore everything around him. That would have to be enough. Better he was despondent than murdered to get to her.

And, now it was time to change the subject inside her head. What had she been thinking about before? Oh, yeah. Tucker.

Why, why, why had she convinced Aden, Riley and Victoria to save Tucker's life after a group of vampires used his body as an appetizer? If she hadn't, he wouldn't have been alive to stab Aden in the heart.

Weirdly enough, Tucker had confessed to the crime without any prompting from her. He'd even cried while telling her. Not that she had forgiven him. Maybe when the shock wore off. Then again, maybe not.

"What you did to Aden was harsh," she said softly.

He blanched, but still he didn't move away. "I told you. Vlad made me do it."

"And how do I know you're not here under Vlad's orders, watching me and reporting what I do?"

"Because I told you I wasn't."

"And you're known for your honesty and integrity?"

"Sarcasm is an ugly thing, Mary Ann. Look, I did what he wanted and then I ran. I haven't seen him or heard from him since."

The "heard from him" part gave her pause. She knew Vlad had spoken to Tucker inside his head, as if standing next to him and whispering when he hadn't actually been standing next to him and whispering. Maybe Tucker was telling the truth right now, but again, maybe he wasn't.

Bottom line: at any moment Vlad could whisper, command him to drag her home, hurt her, bury her, and Tucker would obey without hesitation. She wasn't willing to risk it.

So she said, "I don't care about your reasons or that you're desperate to escape the head vamp. The facts are, you hurt Penny, hurt Aden, and you're a liability. I'd be stupid to trust you."

"You don't have to trust me. You just have to use me. And in my defense, *again,* Aden is still alive. I can feel the pull of him."

So could she, and that was the only reason she hadn't followed through with her threat to get up close and personal with his windpipe. Okay, that wasn't the only reason. She wasn't violent by nature. Usually.

Neither was Aden, but life had shaped him differently than it had shaped her. While she'd grown up in the comfort of her parents' love, he'd grown up in the cold, uncaring walls of mental institutions, his doctors constantly shoving pills at him. Pills he hadn't wanted and hadn't liked.

The docs had assumed he was crazy, never digging deeper to get to the truth. And the truth was, Aden was a paranormal magnet. Anyone or anything with supernatural abilities was drawn to him, and their powers—whatever they were—were magnified.

Mary Ann, on the other hand, was the exact

opposite. She tended to repel the supernatural and suppress powers.

The suppression thing was the reason Tucker had glued himself to her side. Around her, the darkest urges of his demonic nature were eased, even forgotten. He liked that. In fact, *that* was the reason he'd dated her. Not because he'd been attracted to her, but because he liked feeling normal.

So not flattering.

"Look," he said. "I've helped you, haven't I?"

She refused to admit that, yes, in the past few days he'd helped her. She still wanted him to suck it.

"Riley was closing in on you, and I cast an illusion, hiding you inside it. He passed you."

Don't take the bait. And don't you dare think about Riley! Riley, who was probably—*argh!* She pressed her lips together, once again remaining silent.

Tucker sighed. "*Such* a stubborn girl."

Though she tried to stop them, thoughts of Riley continued to flood her. Riley, chasing after her the night she discovered the truth about her mother. Riley, catching her, carrying her to his car. Riley, kissing her. Comforting her. He would comfort her now, if she let him. But as much as she wanted to see him, she couldn't. She would definitely hurt him and quite possibly kill him.

And really, seeing him that last time, when he'd bypassed her, unaware she was right there hidden in Tucker's illusion, had nearly killed *her*. She loved that boy. So much so she'd come close to giving him her virginity. Twice. Both times he had been the one to stop them, wanting to make sure she was ready. That she wouldn't regret what happened. That she was with him because she wanted him, and for no other reason.

Now she regretted that they hadn't.

Walking away from him—fine, running as fast as her feet would carry her—had been hard. Was still hard. Harder by the second. How easy would it be to call him and ask him to pick her up? Beyond easy. He'd do it, too. Meet her wherever she asked, sweep her up and cart her to safety. That's just how he was.

So, she had to be the same way for him. Anything to keep him safe. Even if that meant being apart. Forever.

"I had to stand far away from you," Tucker went on, either oblivious to her inner turmoil or simply not caring, "so you wouldn't mess with my mojo. You know, stifle it."

"No. I don't know what mojo is because I'm a moron."

"Sarcasm again. Seriously, rethink it. *Anyway.* I had to

be close enough to you to still be able to force Riley to see only what I wanted him to see. That wasn't easy."

She made a big production of leaning forward and "studying" the screen. When, in actuality, the words were kinda blurred together and had been for a while. Fatigue rode her hard. Nowadays, fatigue always rode her hard. She felt like she hadn't slept in years.

Every night, when she laid her head on whatever motel pillow she could afford—or when she couldn't, whatever building she stumbled upon—she tossed and turned, her mind lost to the things she'd witnessed and done what seemed an eternity ago.

Wow. An eternity that was really only about two craptastic weeks ago. Bodies had been writhing in pain all around her. *Because* of her. People had begged for mercy. Because of her. Because she had placed her hands on their chests and absorbed their powers, warmth and energy, leaving them with nothing, turning them into empty husks.

"Did you *want* to see the wolf?" Tucker asked, head tilting to the side as he measured her expression.

"Yes." The truth left her before she could stop it. How big and strong and capable Riley had looked. How frustrated and angry. How…frightened. For her.

Exasperated, Tucker threw up his arms. "Then why are you running from him?"

Because she was dangerous. She wouldn't mean to, but one day she would drain the energy out of him, too. *Without* touching him. Truly, she didn't need to touch people to kill them. Touching helped, yes, but she could simply stand in front of them and inadvertently start tugging their life force into her own body.

Those life forces had become her food, after all.

Though she'd tried, she hadn't drained Tucker yet. For some reason, she couldn't. He possessed some kind of block. Either that, or her previous overindulgence prevented her from feeding. Yet.

She should feel guilty that she'd tried, because, if she had succeeded, he would never have recovered. The witches hadn't. The fairies hadn't. Only the ones who'd left the fray before she'd reached them had survived the carnage.

She sighed. Despite her failure with Tucker, she thought it was just a matter of time before her hunger returned in full. Every few hours, she experienced slight pangs. She feared those pangs would only grow. That they would develop invisible arms and reach out, grabbing onto whatever creature happened to be in her vicinity.

Fingers crossed, Tucker was victim one.

She found herself wondering what demons tasted like and had to shake away the thought. See? She couldn't control this newest aspect of her nature. Bile burned a path up her throat. She needed a distraction. Big-time.

Mary Ann swiveled in her chair, leaned back and rested her hands on her middle. Peering up at her ex through the thick shield of her lashes, she said, "Tucker, I'm no good for you. You should leave while you can." He'd get one warning. Only one.

He frowned. "What does that mean?"

"You saw what I did that night." A statement not a question. And she didn't have to specify what night she meant.

"Yeah." His frown disappeared, a high-wattage grin taking its place. "And it was impressive as hell."

Impressive? Hardly. Her cheeks suffused with heat. "If you stay, I'll do that to you. I won't mean to—at least, that's what I'll tell anyone who questions me—but I will."

The person next to her, a college-aged girl, shushed her. "Trying to work here."

"Trying to converse here," Tucker said, flashing a scowl at her. "You don't like it, you can move."

She moved, her ponytail angrily swishing back and forth.

Mary Ann fought a small wave of jealousy. She'd always wanted to be strong and assertive, and while she was working on it, she wasn't there yet. For Tucker, it came so effortlessly.

Tucker studied her, one brow arched. "Liked that, did you?"

Took a Herculean effort, but she maintained a neutral expression. "No."

"Liar." He rolled his eyes, then rested his elbows on his knees. "Back to what we were *discussing*." He threw the last word at the girl, now four desks away, before refocusing on Mary Ann. "Let's say I like to live on the edge, and the fact that you could one day hurt me revs my engine. But guess what, baby doll? You need me. Riley wasn't the only one chasing you, you know."

"What?" That was news to her.

"Yep. Two girls. Both blondes. You kinda fought them before." He gave a low, raspy wolf-whistle. "And BTW, they're hot."

The bile gave her throat another good singeing. "Were they wearing robes? Red robes?" If so…

"Yes. You saw them this go-round?"

"No." But hot blondes she'd "fought" before were

rare. So, she knew exactly whom he spoke of and suddenly wanted to vomit.

"Too bad. You could have put in a good word for me. Because, yeah, I'd do 'em."

"A good word?" she scoffed, though inside she trembled. "When you'd do anyone? Please." The blondes were witches, no question. Witches who had escaped her wrath. Witches who now hated her for destroying their brethren. Witches with power beyond imagining.

Mmm, power...

The fear momentarily left her, and her mouth watered. Witches tasted so good...

When she realized what thoughts were pouring through her mind, she slapped herself on the cheek. *Bad Mary Ann! Bad!*

"Okay, what was *that* about?"

She ignored Tucker to concentrate on her new top priority. More wards. If witches were on her tail, she needed to be ready for their attack. And they would attack. New wards would protect her from specific spells they might cast. Spells of death, destruction and even mind control.

Yeah, the Red Robed Wretches could go there.

"Hey, you're getting paler by the second. There's no reason for you to worry. I sent them away just like I sent the wolf away. Oh, and I sent the other group chasing you away, too. A mix of males and females with sparkly skin."

Please, no. Not—

"Fairies," Tucker said. "They were definitely fairies."

Confirmation. Wonderful. As many as she had drained, they had to want revenge just as badly as the witches. Tucker might have sent them away, but they'd be back. All of them.

"So what do you come here every day to read about, huh?" Tucker asked, changing the subject. To give her time to calm down? To distract her? "Tell me, and maybe I can help. More, that is. Help *more*."

Subtle. "It involves Aden, and secrets he's shared with me. And I am *not* sharing those secrets with you."

A moment passed in silence. Then, "Secrets, secrets, let's see. There are so many to choose from, I don't know where to start."

"What do you mean?"

"Vlad had me research Aden before I stabbed him, and guess what? You're not the only one who's good at researching."

Heart thundering with a storm of dread, she whipped upright. "What did you learn?" Aden did not like any-one knowing about him. He was embarrassed, but also cautious. If the wrong person found out about him—and actually believed the truth—he could be used, tested, locked away, killed. Take your pick.

Tucker held up one hand and began ticking off items like he was reading from a list. "He has three souls trapped inside his head. He used to have four, and one of them was your mother—your real mother, not the aunt who raised you as if you were hers—but Eve's gone now. What else? Oh, yeah. He's now king of the vampires. Until Vlad decides to step in and take the crown back."

Right on all counts. Her mouth went dry, and she croaked out, "How did you learn all that?"

"Honey, I can listen to any conversation, anytime, and no one ever knows I'm there. And I listened to a *lot* of yours."

"You spied on me."

"Isn't that what I just said?"

How many times? What all had he seen? She popped her jaw. Perhaps, if she was never able to drain him, she'd just stab him the same way he'd stabbed Aden. "What makes you think Vlad will succeed?"

Gray eyes went flat. "Please. As if there can be any other outcome. I researched Vlad, too, and he is a warrior who has won countless battles and survived for thousands of years. He's flat-out mean, underhanded and has no concept of honor. What is Aden? Nothing but a bag of meat to a guy like Vlad. Why? Because Aden will want to fight fair and will actually care about collateral damage, both of which will handicap him."

Phrased like that, there was no denying the truth. She needed all the help she could get for her original mission. Even from someone like Tucker.

Mary Ann fell back into her chair, closed her eyes for a moment and breathed. Just breathed. In and out, trying to relax, to come to grips with what she was about to do. If Tucker betrayed her, she would have done more harm than good to her friend. If he didn't, well, he could actually help keep Aden alive.

So. No contest. She had to do this.

"Okay," she said, meeting his gaze dead-on. "Here it is, the whole story, the unvarnished truth."

He rubbed his hands together with glee.

That didn't comfort her and, in fact, intensified her tension. But she said, "A few weeks ago, Riley and Victoria gave Aden and me a list. Because, on December twelfth, seventeen years ago—"

"Wait. December twelfth, your birthday?"

She blinked in surprise. He remembered. How had he remembered? "Yes. Anyway, fifty-three people died in the same hospital where Aden and I were born. St. Mary's." At his look of confusion, she added, "Did I forget to mention Aden and I share a birthday?"

"Yes, but I already knew."

"*Anyway.* A lot of those people died because of a bus accident. My mom died giving birth to me." Her mom had been like Aden, a force of nature, able to do things "normal" people couldn't, and infant Mary Ann had drained her dry. *Don't think about that, either, or you'll, what? Cry.* "Somewhere on that list are the three other souls that Aden inadvertently sucked inside his head." Maybe, they thought, hoped.

"You're sure? Maybe they died nearby, and their names aren't there."

"A possibility, I guess." One she wouldn't entertain at the moment. "Through my research, I've managed to cross off more than half the names already."

"That seems excessive."

Not really. "The remaining souls are male, so that automatically eliminated the females."

Tucker arched a brow. "Unless they're transgender souls. I mean, really. Aden seems like the type to host a pink panty party inside his—"

"Tucker."

"What? He *does*. And his friend Shannon is as gay as—"

"*Shut. Up.* The *males* possess the same special abilities now that they possessed when they were alive. I know this because my mother did, too. So I've been going through the names, looking for stories about raising the dead, body possession and predicting death. Even the minutest hint."

He thought for a moment. "Backtrack a little. Why exactly do you want to identify the souls?"

"Because they need to remember what their last wish was, and do it. Then, they'll leave Aden and he'll be stronger, able to concentrate and defend himself from Vlad."

"You really think that will help?"

"What is this? Twenty questions? Hell, yes, I do." She had to. Otherwise her friend's chances were nil.

Once again Tucker was blinking down at her. "Mary Ann, you just cussed."

"*Hell* isn't a cuss word."

"To me it is."

"Why? Because you're afraid of spending eternity there?"

Good humor, gone. "Something like that."

He looked so sad, she actually felt bad for her waspishness. "Maybe, by the time this is over, I'll have earned myself a spot right next to you. We can keep each other company while roasting."

He barked out a laugh, as she'd hoped, but that earned them another glare from Hush Girl. He flipped HG off and said to Mary Ann, "You *wish* I'd spend eternity with you. So, you got any leads?"

"Before you interrupted me—" she paused, waiting for an apology, but of course he didn't offer one "—I was reading a story about a mortician at the hospital. Dr. Daniel Smart. Apparently he was murdered there. Defense wounds on his arms and legs, as if he'd rolled into a ball to protect himself while someone—" or something "—bit and punched him."

"Great story. But what does that have to do with Aden's souls?"

"One of them can raise the dead. What if Dr. Smart raised a dead body in the morgue, and it killed him?"

"But wouldn't he have raised a dead body before? And if he had, why would he have continued to work there? He would have been in constant danger, and his secret would have gotten out. But it didn't, which means he didn't."

"Maybe he could control the ability."

"Maybe he couldn't."

"I don't care what you say," she grumbled, hating that he was right. Again. "This is the best lead I've got."

"Our definition for the word *best* differs. Still," Tucker went on blithely, "it's worth checking out."

"I know." How irritating! As if she needed his permission. "That's next on my To Do list."

"What about his parents?"

"Who, Smart's?"

Tucker rolled his eyes. "No, moron. Aden's."

"What about them?" Their current address was burning a hole in her pocket. Finding them had been first on that To Do list she'd mentioned, in fact, and she'd already crossed it off with shocking ease. A search engine, a (stolen) credit card Tucker had given her, and *boom*. Results.

They were still local; the shame of abandoning their son, when they might have been the only people in the world who could truly help him, hadn't driven them away. Were they happy with their decision? Regretful?

She'd debated: call Aden and tell him, or not call Aden? In the end, she'd opted for *not*. For the moment. He had a lot to deal with right now and if she met with the couple first—fine, spied on them—she could make a more informed decision.

"Close up for today," Tucker said, drawing her back into the conversation, "and let's find a place to sleep. We'll head out for..." He paused, waiting.

"Smart's wife is still here in Tulsa, close to St. Mary's, the hospital where her husband used to work." Tulsa, Oklahoma. Which was two hours away from Crossroads, Oklahoma. Two hours away from Riley.

Not that she'd imagined him driving that stretch of highway a thousand times.

"Good." Tucker nodded. "Did you read the man's obituary?"

"Yes."

"Checked out his family?"

"As best as I could." He'd left the wife behind, but no one else had been mentioned.

"And you have an exact address?"

"No. I thought I'd drive around until a golden ray of sunlight shined down from the heavens and spotlighted the house."

"Sarcasm again. Not your best look."

"Then stop asking dumb questions."

He sighed, the last sane guy in existence. "We'll drive there in the morning. Does that work for your timetable?" He didn't give her a chance to respond. He stretched out his hand and waved at her. "Come on."

With a sigh of her own, she placed her hand in his. As he stood, he pulled her to her feet. He helped her into her jacket and tugged her out of the microfiche area. Just before they walked into the main library, someone screamed. A girl. Hush Girl, maybe. Fearing the worst, Mary Ann tried to turn around and see what was going on. Tucker threw his arm around her shoulders and forced her attention straight ahead.

"Believe me. You don't want to see."

No attacking witches or fairies, then. "What did you do?" she whispered fiercely. And she knew he'd done something, the turd.

"Let's just say the snake under her desk is trying to converse with her," he replied with another wicked grin.

Of course.

They stepped outside, into the moonlight and cold. She tugged the lapels of her jacket closer and glared up at him. "I thought you couldn't cast illusions when you were so close to me."

His grin widened, and all she could see was straight white teeth flashing down at her in the darkness. She looked away before she gave into the urge to slap him. Repeatedly. Cars whizzed along the street in a *zoom, zoom* rhythm. No one stood on the sidewalk, and there were no insidious shadows lurking nearby. Searching had become a habit.

"Well?" she insisted.

He leaned down, as if sharing a naughty secret. "Let's just say my skills are going nuclear."

Or her ability to mute was fading, she thought suddenly, and her eyes widened. Oh, please, please, please, let her ability be fading. If she stopped muting powers, she might stop draining energy, too. And if she stopped, she could see Riley again. Could kiss him again. Could finally—please, finally—do more. Without worry.

"Okay, why did that make you so happy?" Tucker asked, suspicious.

What did he have to be suspicious about? "Nothing."

"Liar."

"Demon."

He cleared his throat as if fighting a laugh. "That's not really an insult for me, you know."

"I know." She practically skipped along the concrete. Even the *thought* of safely seeing Riley lightened her mood. "Let's just enjoy the moment, okay?"

Tucker had to quicken his step to remain beside her. "What moment?"

"*This* moment."

"Why? There's nothing special about it."

"There could be if you shut your mouth."

This time, he laughed outright. "Remind me why I dated you."

"No. I'd only throw up in my mouth."

"Nice, Mary Ann," he said, but he was still grinning.

"I try."

FIVE

THE SCREAMS THAT HAD RAZED Aden's mind for such a torturous eternity ceased abruptly, and he knew only silence. Yet, the silence was worse because, without the distraction, he became aware of a thick, gloomy fog surrounding him, writhing with malicious glee.

Escape, he needed to escape. He would die if he stayed here. Surely the fog would suffocate him. Was even now trying to do so. Determined, he clawed his way through, climbing…climbing…his body broken, throbbing… climbing…climbing…higher and higher until—

His eyelids sprang apart.

First thing he noticed, the fog had dissipated. Still, the world around him was hazy, as though smeared with Vaseline. He sucked in a deep breath to center himself, then growled. There was something sweet in the air, and his mouth watered. His blood heated.

Taste…

Someone called his name. A girl, her voice layered with concern and relief. He blinked, gradually clearing away the film, and sat up, ignoring the aches and pains shooting through him. His gaze panned the…bedroom. Yes, he was inside a bedroom. Or a snowstorm. All that white—white walls, white carpet, white furnishings— was as overwhelming as it was familiar.

A girl approached him, her hands wringing together and twisting the fabric of her black robe. Finally, a shade other than white. Long dark hair cascaded over one delicate shoulder. She had pale skin, smooth and flawless, and the loveliest blue eyes he'd ever seen.

She reached out, slowly, so slow, to feel his brow. The sweetness in the air thickened, and the urge to taste increased. Though he wanted to bite her, he leaned away from her touch.

Hurt consumed her features.

Within seconds, she masked the emotion and squared her shoulders. "I'm glad you're awake," she said, voice devoid of any emotion as well.

Fangs peeked from between her lips, he noted. Vampire. She was a vampire. A vampire princess. Her name was Victoria, and she was his girlfriend. The details came at him like they were baseballs being shot from a pitching machine. Yet no reaction accompanied them.

"How do you feel?" she asked.

He just looked at her. Feel? His nerve endings had calmed, and he didn't feel anything.

She gulped. "You were asleep for nearly four days. We gave you medication to quiet the souls, just in case they were the ones keeping you under." Chewing on her bottom lip, she glanced over her shoulder. "We didn't feel we had any other choice."

We, she kept saying. Implying someone had helped her.

"Can we get you anything?"

We again. Aden panned the room a second time and noticed a guy standing in the far corner. Tall, strong, dark hair, green eyes. Riley. A wolf shape-shifter and an all-around pain in the ass, but he was a good guy nonetheless.

A human girl stood beside him. How Aden knew she was human, he wasn't sure. He'd never met her before. She was nervous, moving her weight from one sandaled foot to the other, her short crop of blond hair dancing over her shoulders, her brown eyes looking anywhere but at him, and her freckled skin chalk white.

Again the sweetness in the air intensified. Except now

it was layered with something spicy, and his entire body vibrated with anticipation.

Anticipation. His first emotion since waking up, and it consumed him.

"Thirsty," he croaked.

Victoria reached out, not to touch him but to offer her wrist. Distantly he recalled drinking from that wrist. His gaze lifted. And from that elegant neck. And that gorgeous mouth. He'd been besieged with need, utterly intoxicated. And he'd hated himself. He recalled that, too.

Also, he'd hated *her*. Or at least, a part of him had.

That part of him must have grown, taken over. Because, looking at her now, so lovely and serene, he wanted to grab her arms and shake her. To hurt her as she'd hurt him. To punish her for what she'd done to him.

The urges surprised him. What *had* she done to him? Besides try to turn him into a vampire. Besides feed him and feed from him. Besides fight him to survive. All of which he understood and accepted.

"Aden?" She wiggled her wrist.

The moisture in his mouth heated and burned, demanding relief, demanding…blood. He recognized the sensation and was leaning toward her before he registered the fact that he was moving at all. Just before he sank his teeth into her skin, he stopped. What was he doing? He needed blood, yes, but not hers. Hers was dangerous. Addictive.

Shaking, he pushed her arm away—the part of him that still craved her screamed in protest. Her skin was warm, and though not as hot as before, he tingled where they'd touched all the same. He wanted to be touched again and again and again.

Focus on the human. "You," he said, nodding to her. He refused to fall under another girl's spell. If he did, he might not recover. There was no way anyone would affect him the way Victoria did. Surely. "Do you want to feed me?"

That dark gaze at last zoomed in on him. "Y-yes."

Truth or lie? "Are you nervous?"

"Of you?" She shook her head with conviction, but her subsequent stuttering contradicted the motion. "N-no."

She wasn't scared of him, but she *was* scared of something. That wouldn't stop him. "Good. Come here."

Riley and Victoria shared a long, dark look. More than a look, actually. He knew Riley was pushing his thoughts into Victoria's head, and shrugged. Let them say—or not say—what they wanted. Nothing would change his decided course of action.

Finally Victoria nodded, moved backward, and the wolf shifter gave the human a little push in Aden's direction. She scooted around the princess, remaining out of striking distance, and Aden suddenly comprehended the reason for her upset. She feared *Victoria*.

Smart of her. Victoria watched her through narrowed eyes, poised to launch into an attack at any second. Were they enemies? No, they couldn't be. No one was more protective of Victoria than Riley, and the wolf never would have let the human through the door if that had been the case. So...what was the problem?

Only when the girl was at Aden's side did she relax. She curtsied, grinned. "What can I do for you, my king?"

He didn't allow himself to study his vampire and her reaction to the girl's query. "Let me have your arm."

Instantly she reached out. He wrapped his fingers around her wrist. It was thicker than Victoria's, with a little more meat under her skin. As hot as Aden's body temperature now was, the human felt chilled.

He absorbed her scent, testing it. Sharper than what he craved, he mused, with more spice than sweetness, but he could deal. Already his stomach was twisting, knotting. He urged her closer...opened his mouth...

"Wait. You're going to hurt her," Victoria snapped, beside the girl in the blink of an eye and jerking her from Aden's hold.

The human gasped and trembled.

Aden growled, even as the scent of the vampire stirred up some kind of animal inside him. A wild thing, co-habitating in a place where there was no room for emotion, only instinct honed on a battlefield.

Mine, that wild thing said.

Never yours, the other part of him hissed.

"You don't have fangs." Victoria raised her chin. "So, like I said, you'll hurt her. I'll bite her and—"

"*I'll* bite her." Fangs or not, he knew how to feed. Hadn't he proven that to Victoria, over and over again?

The memory had his gaze falling to her neck, where her pulse hammered swiftly. The ache in his gums returned. *Mine,* he thought again. *Mine to bite and to drink from and to kiss.*

You don't even like her. Not anymore.

"I'll bite her," she continued through gritted teeth, "and you can drink from her." She didn't give him a chance to respond. She simply lifted and bit.

The human closed her eyes, moaning as the pleasure

hit her. Pleasure Aden knew very well and still craved, despite his determination to remain aloof.

Vampire fangs produced some kind of drug that numbed your skin and flowed straight into your veins, warming you up, making you feel good, *too good*. Which was exactly why so many humans became addicted, willing to do anything for another nibbling.

Not him. Never him. Not again.

A second passed, then another. Victoria lifted her head. Blood wetted her lips a deep scarlet, and Aden wanted to lick them. Instead, he forced his gaze on the two punctures in the human's wrist. Blood wetted there, too, and he groaned. What he didn't do was chastise Victoria for disobeying him. *What right do I have to chastise her?* He simply claimed the arm offered to him and brought the wound to his mouth.

He licked once, twice, tasting ambrosia, groaning again, before sucking, letting the nectar fill his mouth, swallowing, his eyes closing in the same surrender the human had experienced. And yet, in the back of his mind, he thought that as wonderful as this blood tasted, it should have tasted *better*. Should have been sweeter, with only a little hint of that spice.

"—has no fangs, yet he *still* craves blood," Riley was

saying as Aden became aware of his surroundings again. "It's unheard of."

"Apparently not," Victoria snapped. "Look at him. He's enjoying every moment of this."

"Enjoying? His eyes look dead, and have ever since he woke up. Something's wrong with him."

Aden knew they were talking about him, but just as before, he didn't care.

"Well, she's enjoying it, then," Victoria added, words sharp as a whip. "If I wasn't holding her back she'd be grinding on him."

"Do you want me to deny that?" the wolf muttered. "Because we both know I'd be lying."

"You're a terrible friend."

"Whatever. Just don't kill her afterward. To borrow her, I had to promise Lauren you'd do her laundry for a week. And I had to promise you'd do it forever if any harm came to her slave."

"Thanks a lot. You couldn't have asked Lauren for a male?"

A tremor rocked the human. Of fear? Or was she still too lost to the pleasure to care, either?

"I'm only guessing here, but I don't think humans— even former humans—are like us. They can't separate feeding from sex. I figured Aden would appreciate a female."

"Well, he's appreciating her too much!"

Riley arched a brow at Victoria. "Are you jealous, princess?"

"No. Yes. He's mine." A pause. "Well, he *was*. Now... he pushed me away. Twice. Did you see him push me away?"

"Yeah, I did, but he loves you, Vic. You know that."

"Do I?" she asked softly.

Did he? Aden wondered. Even though he didn't like her at the moment? Because, as he knew, you didn't have to like someone to love them. A lesson he'd learned as a child, when his parents had him committed, then walked away and never looked back.

He hadn't liked them, might even have hated them, but even still, he'd loved them. At least at first. But as the days had passed in a medicated haze, as other patients beat him up and called him names, that love had withered, leaving only the hate. Then, the hate, too, had left him, and he simply hadn't cared. He'd had the souls.

His souls. Where were his souls? They weren't chattering, and he couldn't feel them in the back of his mind. Did Victoria have them?

No longer was she watching him. Her gaze had moved just over his shoulder, perhaps even outside the room. Her eyes were as blue as before, no longer mixed with green, brown and gray. No, the souls were not inside her head.

They must be in his, and the medication must have put them to sleep. Another reason to dislike Victoria. The souls were his best friends, and a few times over the years, they'd been his only reason to live. They despised his medication and would not be happy when they woke up. She'd known that, yet she'd forced the pills down his throat anyway.

"Yes," Victoria finally said. "He loves me. I know it."

She did? She was a step ahead of him, then. Once, he *had* loved her; he knew that much. And why wouldn't he have? She was flawless, a walking fantasy. But what did he really know about her?

Bad—to her, humans were nothing more than food. Bad—she could enslave with a single bite. Good—she cared about her family. Bad—her father wanted to kill him. Good—she knew he was different than other humans and vampires, and she liked him anyway. Bad—she was insensitive to humans and their needs. Good—she was *trying* to be sensitive to humans and their needs.

During their one and only date, she had danced around him, telling jokes. Lame ones, but she'd been trying. For him. Trying to be what she thought he wanted and needed. So, yes, he had loved her. But now? He couldn't summon a single spark or hint of softness.

Oh, the attraction was still there. He wanted to push the human away and fall on the vampire. He wanted his teeth in her neck and his body pinning hers. He wanted her hands on him, and her mouth on him, and he wanted her gasping his name.

Even as the thoughts drifted through his head, images formed. Of her, of him, of the two of them together, doing exactly what he wanted. What he wanted so badly he was actually growling, the guttural sound rising in his throat and spilling into the bedroom, echoing menacingly between them.

Victoria must have assumed the growl was for the human. Suddenly she vibrated with anger and concern. He could actually taste the emotions in the air, and they had him sucking at the human with renewed fervor.

The human moaned her approval.

Strength was infusing his cells. His muscles were expanding, his bones humming. And, wow. If this human female affected him so powerfully, how would the vampire affect him?

"Okay, enough." Riley strode to the bed, grabbed the human, and jerked her away from him. "Leave," the wolf told the girl.

"I...I..." She swayed. "Yes, of course." Then footsteps sounded, the slam of a door.

"Victoria." When the wolf stretched a hand out to the vampire, Aden jumped to his feet and moved between them, preventing contact. An instinctive urge to protect what was his.

"Are you thinking to fight me or her?" Riley asked, seemingly unconcerned by either choice.

"Neither." Both. He might not like Victoria, but he still wanted her. He didn't want anyone else to have her. The impulse...the two needs...warring...what the hell was wrong with him? He was like two different people.

"O-kay. Why are your claws out?"

Claws? Aden looked down, and sure enough, his nails had lengthened and sharpened, little daggers tipping his fingers. He should be freaked out but could only lift his hands to the light, studying this newest development. "How is this possible?"

Riley blew out a breath and said, "Either you're changing into a vampire slowly, one modification at a time, or you're the first human–vamp hybrid. To my knowledge. Now, are you going to back off or do I have to make you?"

A little bark of amusement escaped him. Little, yes, but amusement all the same. "You could try."

Clearly not the response the wolf had expected. He blinked, shook his head. "Look, we'll come back to the male pissing contest in a second. There's something wrong with you, and I don't know how deep the problem goes. So we're gonna have a little chat and find out."

Behind him, Aden heard Victoria shift from one foot to the other. The fine hairs on the back of his neck lifted, his skin doing that tingling thing. He scowled. He was *that* aware of her? "There's nothing wrong with me. There, we talked. Now, gather my people in the great hall."

The words echoed with threat, surprising Aden as much as they did Riley. Only recently had he accepted his right to rule, but never once had he thought of the vampires as "my people." But they were, and now he had plenty to say to them.

"There *is* something wrong with you, Aden," Riley insisted. "You haven't even asked about Mary Ann. She's out there somewhere, on her own, perhaps in danger. Do you not care about her anymore?"

A flicker of emotion sparked in his chest, extinguished before he could figure out what it was. Or what it meant. "She'll be fine," he said.

"Are you sure about that? Has Elijah told you?"

"Yes, I'm sure. And no, he hasn't."

Hope bloomed and died in Riley's eyes. "Then how are you sure?"

Because he wanted to be, and in that moment Aden was certain he got what he wanted. Always. And if he didn't, he did whatever was necessary to change the circumstances.

Wait. Was that true? He couldn't think of a specific example, buuut...he simply *knew*. He shrugged. That was good enough for him.

Maybe there *was* something wrong with him. Not that he cared about that, either, he realized. He would talk to his people, as planned.

"Perhaps you didn't hear me," Aden said. "You've got some gathering to do."

"Gather them yourself, *majesty*." Riley huffed and puffed, his shoulders straightening, squaring. Aden's lips twitched in renewed humor, but he wasn't sure why that would be funny to him. "I'm going after Mary Ann. Victoria?"

"She stays," Aden said, the words leaving him before

he could stop them. Despite everything, or maybe because of it, he wanted her with him.

"Victoria?" the wolf snapped.

"I did this to him," she said softly. "I have to stay with him and make sure…you know."

Aden didn't know what "you know" was, and he still didn't care. He was getting what he wanted: her presence. That was enough. For now.

Riley popped his jaw. "Very well. Keep your cell with you at all times, and call if you need anything. Anything at all. And I'll call you if I learn anything. Be careful."

"Always."

A stiff nod in Aden's direction, and then Riley was turning on his heel, marching away.

Aden didn't spare Victoria a glance and certainly didn't thank her. He wasn't one to say thanks, ever. Right? Even though the desire to do so sparked and died in the same place as that unnameable emotion for Mary Ann. He simply strode to the room's only window, a bay that opened on to a balcony, determined to call his people together on his own.

SIX

VICTORIA REMAINED IN PLACE AS Aden stood on her balcony, doing nothing…waiting for…she wasn't sure. He wasn't "chatting with his people," though. He was alone, barefoot and unconcerned by everything around him. Oh, and someone else's blood flowed in his veins. The knowledge irritated her when it should have delighted her. He was alive. He was awake.

She was still irritated. Despite everything, she wanted *her* blood in his veins. *Her* blood making him stronger.

Get over yourself already. The open balcony doors let the chilled morning air inside the room, and she shivered. For the first time in her life, she would have welcomed a coat. Something, anything, to melt the frost practically glossing her exposed skin.

How was Aden not shivering? He was bare-chested, deliciously so. Rope after rope of muscle lined his stomach and neatly patterned his back. Tragically, he wore jeans. Clean jeans, at least. She'd washed and changed him while he'd slept. And she hadn't looked at anything improper. Except for those two—*four*—times. Riley had been too distracted to ask about those sponge baths, for which she was grateful.

Looking where she shouldn't, how very human of her. Once, Aden would have been proud about that. Now... she had no idea what was going on inside his head or how he'd react to, well, anything. She knew only that Riley was right. Something was wrong with Aden. He wasn't himself. He was colder, harsher.

Challenging.

Vampires were all about tossing challenges at the weak and vulnerable. And the weak and vulnerable accepted those challenges or they endured an eternity of slavery by declining. Then, when they lost, they endured an eternity of slavery anyway. Difference was, by accepting and losing, they weren't teased and tormented, too.

Vlad had set the rules, of course. He despised weakness and cowardice, he'd claimed, and the challenges were a way to weed out the "unworthy."

Did Aden plan to challenge everyone?

A movement in the sky captured her attention, and she watched a black bird soar past. The sun was hidden behind gray clouds, and perhaps even a thick layer of glassy rime. The angels were ice-skating up there, her mother would have said.

Her mother. How Victoria missed her. For the past seven years, her mother had been locked away in Romania, a prisoner charged with sharing information about vampires with humans. Vlad had even forbidden his people from speaking her name. Edina the Swan.

Even thinking it gave Victoria a thrill. Rebellion was new to her.

Then, when Aden was dubbed the man in charge, he'd freed the woman at Victoria's behest. She had expected her mother to teleport to Crossroads so they could be together again. Only, Edina had decided to remain in her homeland.

As if Victoria wasn't important enough to bother with.

She wanted to be important to someone. And had been. To Aden. Since the first moment he'd spotted her, he'd made her feel special. Now...

Her stomach jumbled as she stepped beside him. His attention never strayed from the surrounding forest. Large oaks knifed toward that icy sky, a smattering of blood-red leaves hanging on for dear life. Mostly gnarled limbs stretched out and interlocked, as if the trees were holding hands, bracing themselves for the coming winter.

She wanted to take *Aden*'s hand but wasn't sure how he would react.

"I think you should travel back in time," she said, breaking the silence. She'd given this some thought. If he traveled back to the night Tucker stabbed him, he could prevent all of this. Not just the stabbing, but her attempt to turn him. Their week of feeding, of nearly draining each other, their fighting, this…none of this would happen.

"No."

That's it? That's all her intense pondering got? "No? Just like that?"

"Just like that."

"But Aden, you can stop Tucker, once and for all."

"Too many things could go wrong, and we don't know what would happen in the new reality. Could be far worse than this one."

She doubted that. "There's only one way to know for sure." Her new favorite phrase.

"No."

So adamant. He couldn't *like* this reality. Could he?

"This is mine," he said matter-of-factly, reminding her of her father.

All right, maybe he could. "Yes," she said with a shudder.

His gaze moved to the ground below them, and hers followed, seeing the hidden stretch of land as he must. Bleak, yet fighting to survive. Not a single bloom colored the garden, but the bushes were yellow and orange. Ivy still clung to each trellis, though the leaves were light and brittle.

In the center of the yard was a large metal circle, a ward welded into the dirt, seemingly innocuous whirls intersecting through every inch. The metal could move and open, creating a platform that lowered into the crypt where her father had been buried.

Without a word, Aden climbed the balcony railing and straightened, his balance precarious at best.

"What are you doing? We're too many stories up. Come down! You—"

He stepped off.

A yelp escaped her as she bent over the rail, her heart stopping as she watched him fall…fall…land. He didn't splat or crumple as expected. He simply uncoiled from a crouch and walked out of the backyard, all liquid grace and lethal determination.

Victoria had done the same a thousand times before. Perhaps that was why she didn't hesitate to follow him over. "Aden, wait!" Cold, biting air lifted her hair and robe.

As she tumbled toward the flat, hard surface, she remembered her new, human skin. She flailed, trying to claw her way back up. Then it was too late. She—

Hit.

Her knees vibrated from impact, and she collapsed, slamming into one of the ward's metal bars. During *that* impact, oxygen heaved from her lungs. Worse, her shoulder popped out of place and the agony nearly undid her. For hours—maybe just a few minutes—she lay panting, shivering from cold and shock, tears scalding her eyes and catching in her lashes.

"Stupid, stupid, *stupid,*" she said through chattering teeth. Though the sun was hidden behind those clouds, though the air seemed layered with frost, her skin began to prickle as if she were close to reaching vampire maturity and burning.

What was wrong with her? Besides the thousand other things she'd been dealing with lately?

Footsteps reverberated, and suddenly she could scent Aden in the air. That amazing fragrance of—she sniffed, frowned. He smelled different. Still amazing, but different. Familiar. Like sandalwood and evergreen. A mystic from long ago, yet coldly alive, and now as spicy as the human girl had been.

I will not let jealousy overtake me.

Victoria opened her eyes, unsure when she'd closed them. Aden was leaning down, spotlighted by rogue rays of light that had escaped their cloudy prison. His expression was as impassive as before. Dark hair fell over his eyes—eyes of startling violet.

Since she'd known him, she'd seen him with eyes of gold, green, brown, blue and black, but the violet had not appeared until their time in the cave.

When he reached out, she thought he meant to help her up. She offered him a small, waxen smile. "Thank you."

"I would not thank me, if I were you." He latched onto her shoulder, and sharp pain lashed through her.

"What do you—"

He forced the bone to pop back into place, and she discovered what true pain really was. A scream ripped from deep inside her. Birds took flight, probably desperate to escape the horrendous, ear-piercing sound.

"You're welcome," he said, straightening.

She would take that to mean *I'm really truly very sorry I hurt you, my love.* "Next time—"

"There won't be a next time. You won't be jumping from the railing again. Promise me."

"No, I—"

"Promise me," he insisted.

"Stop cutting me off."

"All right."

When he offered nothing else, exasperating her, she rasped, "Why did you jump? You could have walked through the house to reach the bottom." And saved her a panic attack and dislocated shoulder.

"This way was faster." He pivoted on his heel and marched away. Again.

"Wait."

He didn't wait.

Cursing under her breath, Victoria gathered enough strength to stand. Her knees trembled and nearly buckled, but she somehow found the will to remain upright. She trailed after Aden, feeling like a puppy on a leash. A bad puppy who didn't want to go on a walk and had to be dragged.

Aden never once glanced back to make sure she was okay or even to ascertain that she was there. He just didn't care, and that hurt worse than her shoulder, cutting at her insides, making her cringe. To him, she either followed or she didn't, and neither choice evoked emotion.

"Why do you want to talk to everyone?" she asked.

"A few things need to be straightened out." He strode to the front of the house, up the porch steps and stopped at the towering, arched front doors. Few vampires were out and about at this time of day, even with the hazy milieu, but those who traipsed the grounds blinked in shock when they spotted him, then quickly bowed to show their respect.

A minute ticked by.

More minutes ticked by.

"Um, Aden. You have to walk through a door to enter a house. Standing here won't do anything."

"I will. First, I'm surveying what's mine."

Once again, he sounded like her father—or Dmitri, her former betrothed—and she chewed at the inside of her cheek in disgust. She hadn't been fond of either man. *Please, please let Aden return to his normal self when the pills wear off.*

What would she do if he didn't?

She wouldn't think about that right now. She would just get through the day, help Aden conduct his meeting, for whatever reason, guarding him all the while, and then, later, if necessary, she would worry.

"Do you like what you see?" she asked, recalling the first time she'd brought him here. He'd taken one look at the Queen Anne–style mansion—the asymmetrical towers, the gothic stones and glasswork, the narrow windows with their prominent eave brackets sharpened to deadly points and the steeply pitched roofs, all painted a grim black—and grimaced.

"Yes."

One-word answers were annoying, she decided.

Finally he pushed the double doors open and entered. His gaze swept the spacious foyer, taking in the black walls, the crimson carpet, the antique furniture polished to a perfect shine, and he frowned.

"I know the layout of this place. There are thirty bedrooms, most of them upstairs. There are twenty ornate fireplaces, several rooms with parquet floors, several with red sandstone, a great hall, a throne room and two dining rooms. But I've never seen more than this room, your bedroom and the backyard. How is that possible?"

Excellent question. "Maybe…maybe when we exchanged memories all those times, some of mine stuck."

"Maybe." He flicked her a blank glance. "Do you recall anything about me?"

Oh, yes. Mostly she remembered the beatings he'd

received in a few of the mental institutions he'd lived in—she wished to punish those responsible. She also remembered the isolation he'd endured in several of the foster homes he'd stayed in, the parents afraid of him but willing to take on his "care" for the paycheck that came with him. Not to mention the rejection he'd suffered time after time from peers who considered him too different to deal with. Too weird.

That was why she couldn't walk away from him now. No matter how distant or unlike himself he was, she wouldn't reject him.

"Well?" he prompted.

"Yes, I do." She didn't tell him what, though. "Do you recall anything specific about me? Besides this home?"

"No."

"Oh." A memory could have sparked compassion. Compassion could have sparked a thousand other emotions, one of them reminding him of just how much he freaking *loved her.* Or maybe this was for the best. There were some things a girl didn't want her boyfriend to know about her.

"Wait," he said, blinking. "I do remember something."

Hope and dread battled for supremacy. "Yes?"

"When you first came to Crossroads, summoned here because of the supernatural blast Mary Ann and I inadvertently created, you spotted me from a distance and thought, *I should kill him*."

Ouch. See? *That* was one of those things. "First, I told you about that. Second, taken out of context, the thought seems worse than it was."

"You mean a desire to kill me is a good thing when in context?"

Her teeth gnashed. "No, but you're forgetting how strange your pull was to us. We didn't know why you'd summoned us here, what you had planned for us, or if you were helping our enemy. We—"

"Enem*ies*."

"What?"

"You don't have one, you have many. In fact, the only race you aren't at war with is the wolves, and they'd be fighting you, too, if they weren't so loyal by nature."

Well, well. An emotion from him. Only, it wasn't one she'd wanted. He was disappointed. She didn't understand why. "You have no idea the things that have taken place between the races throughout the centuries. How could you? You've been living in your little humanity bubble, unaware of the creatures that stalk the night."

"And yet I know alliances *can* be formed."

"With who? The witches? They know we crave their blood and can't control our hunger in their presence. They would laugh in your face if you offered a truce. So who does that leave? The fairies? We feed off the humans they consider their children. They would wipe us out if they could. Don't forget the fairy prince you helped kill, and the fairy princess who then tried to kill you. What about the goblins? They are mindless beings, caring only about their next meal, which just so happens to be living flesh. *Our* flesh. Shall I go on?"

"Yes." Glitter in his eyes, a twitch of his lips. "Explain to me why you war with other vampire factions."

"Explain to me why humans war with other humans."

He ran his tongue over his teeth. "Most humans desire peace."

"And yet they still have not found a way to facilitate it."

"Nor have the vampires."

They stood there, simply staring at each other in the silence. She was panting again, her aching shoulder rousing her fervor for the subject and perhaps making her snappier than she should have been when Aden had so calmly stated his case.

"Aden," she said, gentling her tone. "Peace is a wonderful thing. But that's all it is. A thing—and sometimes the wrong thing. Will you roll over in the name of peace, allowing my father to reclaim his throne, or will you fight him?"

"Fight," he said without hesitation. "Then I will wage war until the other vampire factions are brought to heel. And if they can't be brought to heel, they will be annihilated. Examples will be made, and peace will finally reign."

War at any cost was classic Vlad the Impaler ideology, and not something Aden Stone had ever before supported. Yet, this was the second time in the last five minutes that Aden had sounded exactly like her father. The third time that day.

An idea rolled through her mind, frightening her.

Were bits of her father somehow trapped inside him, driving him? If so, how? Aden had tangled with *Victoria's* memories, not her father's. Unless…were these *her* beliefs? Had they remained with him along with a few of her memories?

Vlad had always viewed humans as food and nothing more, even though he'd once been human himself, and he had taught his children to view them the same way. Power had gone to his head, she supposed. To all their heads. But more than thinking himself superior to humans, he'd thought himself superior to *all* races. King of Kings, Lord of Lords. Peace had been an afterthought, the road to that peace violent and gruesome.

Better others were wiped out than living and opposing every directive he gave them, Vlad had often said.

After meeting Aden and seeing what he was willing to endure for those he loved, her entire perspective had changed. Vlad shattered. Aden restored. Vlad enjoyed the downfall of others, Aden mourned it. Vlad was never satisfied. Aden found joy where he could.

She envied him for all of that. Not that she was now completely opposed to war. One day, she would have to face off with her father. One day, she would have to destroy him, for he would never allow Aden to rule. Vlad would fight until the end, and he would fight without mercy. Therefore, someone had to deliver that end, and she would rather that someone be her.

Having been inside Aden's head, she knew just how deeply his past hacked at his joy. He'd hurt people. He'd possessed other bodies, forcing people to do what he wanted, rather than what they believed. All to protect himself or someone he cared about, true, yet the guilt had never left him.

I know the feeling. She still had no idea what she'd done to him, those last few minutes inside their cave, but the guilt was slicing at her, leaving raw, open wounds inside her.

"Distracted?"

Victoria focused on Aden. Were his lips curling into a grin? Surely not. That would mean she had amused him. "Yes. Sorry."

"You should—" He stiffened, his ears twitching. "Someone's coming."

She looked up, and sure enough, two females were pounding down the stairs, black robes dancing at their ankles. Victoria wanted to ask how he'd heard them when she had not but didn't want to admit her observational skills were inferior.

"My king," one of the girls said when she spotted him, stopping at the second to last step. She executed a perfect curtsy, pale hair falling over one shoulder.

"My...Aden." The other girl stopped, as well. Her curtsy was less graceful, but maybe that was because she was eyeing Aden as if he were a slice of candy and she had a sweet fang.

She wasn't attracted to him, Victoria knew. No, the dark-haired beauty was attracted to power. Which was why she'd challenged Victoria for rights to him.

According to their laws, any vampire could challenge any other vampire for rights to a human blood-slave.

Though Aden was acting king, he was still human—or had been, at the time the challenge was issued—and Draven had used the loophole to her advantage, hoping she would take over his "care" and become queen.

They had yet to fight. Soon, though. Soon. Aden had only to announce when and where.

Victoria seethed with the need to put Draven in her place—the crypt outside. There was protecting your loved ones out of duty, and then there was protecting your loved ones for fun. Draven would be given a taste of the latter.

Perhaps Victoria was still like her father, after all.

"Is today my birthday? Look who decided to stop hiding in her room," Draven said with a pointed look at Victoria. "How courageous of you."

"You were welcome to knock on that door at any time. And yet you didn't. I wonder why."

Draven flashed her fangs.

Bring it.

"Maddie. Draven." Aden nodded to them both, inserting himself into the "conversation" and taking it over. With no other preamble, he added, "Go to my throne room and await me. I wish to speak with everyone who lives here."

Victoria's hands fisted at her sides. He knew the sisters'

names, yet she didn't think he'd ever before met Maddie the Lovely. Draven the Cunning, yes. Or as Victoria suddenly wanted to call her, Draven the Soon to Die Painfully.

The vampire council had chosen the bitch—oops, was her anger showing again?—to date Aden, along with four others, one of whom had been Victoria's sister Stephanie, hoping he would choose a wife, while at the same time pacifying mothers and fathers who wanted their daughters aligned with the royal house. Back then, Aden had claimed to desire only Victoria.

Had that changed like everything else?

"What is this meeting about?" Draven asked, batting her lashes at him.

"You will find out when everyone else does."

While Victoria rejoiced over his abrupt answer, Draven struggled to hide her flare of anger.

When she succeeded, she propped her hip to one side and twirled a lock of hair around her finger. "May I stand on your dais?"

Simpering cow.

The forcefulness—the *humanness*—of the thought surprised her. At least Aden seemed as unaffected by Draven's seduction attempt as he had about everything else.

"No, you may not," he said, then added flatly, "But you may sit on the steps next to the dais. I want you close to me."

She threw Victoria a smug glance. "Because I'm beautiful and you can't keep your eyes off me?"

Maddie pinched her, clearly trying to shut her up, but Draven waved her hand away. She'd always been her own number one fan.

Aden frowned. "No. The fact is, I don't trust you, don't like you and want to make sure I can see your hands. If you go for a weapon, you will be deemed a traitor and imprisoned."

Every bit of color drained from Draven's cheeks. "Wh-what?"

All right, Victoria loved this new Aden.

"May we change our clothing before we enter the throne room, majesty?" Maddie asked softly, and when Aden nodded she pulled her sister away before the girl could say anything else.

Victoria's mouth opened, snapped closed, opened again, yet no words escaped. Not that she knew what to say. That had been spectacular. Simply spectacular.

Back to business, Aden strode to the far wall and lifted the gold summoning horn hanging there. A thing of beauty, that horn. Solid gold, intricately carved, a

dragon's head curving from the top, scaled claws curving from the bottom and a mouthpiece rounding up into
a tail. He placed that mouthpiece at his lips.

"Wait. What are you doing? Don't—" Victoria raced
toward him, only to stop when he blew. A loud wail
echoed throughout the entire mansion, bouncing off the
walls, vibrating against the floors, rattling the very foundation. "—do that," she finished weakly.

He must have interpreted "don't do that" as "do it
again," an easy mistake to make when you *failed to listen,* because he blew a second time, and another wail
resounded.

Dread worked through her, and she pinched the
bridge of her nose. Finally the wailing ceased, leaving a
strange, deafening silence.

"You shouldn't have done that," she said.

"Why?"

Her hand fell to her side. "Uh, because I said not
to?"

"Why not use the horn," he continued, "when it's out
in the open, *waiting* to be used?"

"It's out in the open for emergencies only."

"This is an emergency."

I will not scream at him. "How so?" Gritted, but not
screamed. Good.

"I didn't want to climb the stairs, call, text, email or wait for the grapevine to inform everyone about my meeting."

I will not slap him. I absolutely will not. "Well, do you know what your laziness just did?"

"Yes. I summoned my vampires. Efficiently. Quickly."

Maybe one little slap wouldn't hurt. "Yes. You also summoned your allies and let your enemies know you are in need of aid. Wait. Let me rephrase. You summoned my *father's* allies, and—" she lowered her voice in case anyone was eavesdropping "—he wants you dead—in case you've forgotten—and now he'll have help. Because when he shows up—and he will—they'll offer their support *to him* rather than to you."

Which meant... Her brother would return, she realized. Her brother would return and assist her father.

What would she do if her brother fought her boyfriend?

She'd always loathed the decree that kept her segregated from Sorin, had hoped he would one day seek her out, but he never had. Neither of them had been willing to risk their father's ire. She'd spied on him a few times, though, watching him flirt with women before coldly maiming the vampires he trained with.

She'd come to think of him as half irreverent brat, half homicidal maniac, and to this day she wondered what he thought of her, or if he would even care to learn. He'd always been Vlad's staunchest supporter.

Aden winning against her father was a long shot, but Aden winning against her father *and* her brother? Impossible. Because the only thing that would be sliced was Aden.

She would talk to Sorin—for the first time ever, and sweet mercy, she wanted to vomit from nerves at just the thought—and ask him not to fight. And when she asked him, he would…she didn't know what he would do.

"If what you say is true," Aden said, "your father would have snuck in here and used the horn himself. But he didn't, which means he didn't want anyone summoned."

"I—" Had no argument, and he had a point. Still!

Aden shrugged. "Let him—and them—come."

What would it take to shake him out of this emotionless stupor? "Some will teleport into the surrounding forest. Some will travel as humans travel, but all will make their way here to hurt you."

"I know. And that's a good thing. I want my opposition disposed of quickly, in one swoop."

Back to spouting Vlad's—*her*—philosophy, was he? "My brother will be among those who travel here."

"I know."

He knew? And he didn't care?

"He'll die like the others."

No, he didn't care. She stared up at him for a long, silent moment. "Who *are* you?" Her Aden never would have planned something so cruel.

"I'm your king." His head tilted as his study of her intensified. "Unless you choose to serve your father now?"

"Why? Would you kill me, too?"

His expression became thoughtful, as if he were actually pondering his answer.

"Never mind," she gritted out. The conversation was only making her angrier. "But my brother—"

"Is not up for discussion. Until Vlad develops the courage to show himself, our little war can't begin. And it needs to begin, out in the open this time, so that it can end. We cannot have one without the other."

He'd just spouted another facet of *her* beliefs. How many times had she said *You cannot have an end without a beginning* to Riley throughout the years? Countless. Of course, she'd been trying to talk the shifter into letting her misbehave, not trying to convince him to ramp up the hostilities. But here was a question to last the ages: had *she* been this annoying?

"You. Are. Frustrating. Me."

Aden shrugged, but underneath the casual, un-concerned action, she saw a glimmer of unease work through his expression. First thoughtful, now uneasy. He must not like frustrating her. She hoped.

Hope that was demolished when he said, "Enough. We have things to do," and strode to the throne room to at last host his precious meeting.

Once again Victoria found herself trailing after him like a puppy. And she didn't need Elijah to tell her bad, bad things were about to happen.

SEVEN

ADEN STEPPED INTO THE throne room, his bare footfalls silent against the plush red carpeting that formed a path directly to his throne. Black wards were woven into that carpet, and for the first time he could feel the full force of the power wafting from them, slithering around his feet. With every step, that power twined higher and higher, around his calves, his thighs, his waist. His stomach, chest and arms.

He breathed deeply, the constant buzzing in his head finally quieting. The power swirled, forming a halo that lifted strands of his hair, as if he'd just stuck his fingers into a light socket.

He experienced a startling moment of clarity. Of... *emotion*. Suddenly he was Aden, not the cold-hearted vampire king he'd somehow become. He *felt*. Guilt, joy, remorse, excitement, sorrow...love.

He reached back, extending his hand, needing to touch Victoria, even in so small a way. He knew she was behind him, each of his cells aware of her every move, her every breath. Every second that passed.

A momentary pause, a gasp of surprise. Her fingers tentatively twined with his, meltingly warm and familiar. "Aden?"

"Yes?"

Her step faltered, and she stumbled into him. He stopped and wrapped his arm around her to hold her up, loving the way she fit against his side. Like a puzzle piece he'd been missing.

"Your eyes…they're normal." Hope bubbled in the undertone of her voice.

Normal? "I take it that's a good thing."

"Very good."

He glanced around. Black candelabras lined the front of the concrete bleachers stretching at his sides. Between them were thick marble columns. "I can't believe this," he said, shocked that he was really here. "Forget the danger I caused by using the horn. I summoned everyone in here to prove a point, and that point could kill them."

"What point?"

"I'm too embarrassed to say. I…need to sit down." He kicked back into motion. When he reached the throne, he eased down, more candles flickering around him, smoke swirling from the tips.

The buzzing in his head started up again. A split second later a grumble sounded, subdued, yet all the more savage and brutal because of that. And just like that, the veil of emotion lifted, leaving him feeling both a biting cold and a sizzling heat, neither of which could surpass his determination to lead his vampires to victory against Vlad.

"I'm so happy, I could cry. How human of me, right? But then, I'm becoming more human by the second, I think. And that's okay. Yes? That's good?" A grinning Victoria crouched in front of him, resting her palms on his thighs. "Let's go back to my bedroom and talk. We'll..." Slowly her grin faded. "Your eyes." Her voice was now flat.

"What about them?"

"They're violet again. Dead."

He shrugged, unconcerned. "Do I have Chompers inside my head?" The grumbling had tapered off as suddenly as it had begun, but he knew there was something—someone—at the edge of his conscious, waiting, listening...controlling?

If not Chompers, who? Or...what?

A frown as she straightened. "No. He's with me."

Aden looked her over. She wore a long black robe, thin straps tying the material on her shoulders. Two tugs, and that robe would drop to the floor, and he could drink from her neck, her chest, even her thighs. Any place he wanted, really.

He gripped the solid gold arms of the throne to ensure his hands behaved. Where were these thoughts coming from? Earlier, he hadn't been able to decide if he even liked this girl. Now he was imagining undressing her and feasting on her?

"You're sure about Chompers?" he croaked.

"Completely. I'm warded from neck to ankle just to keep him under control, but I can still hear him."

A miracle he didn't ask for proof.

"Let's talk about this tomorrow, after your medication has worn off," she said on a sigh. "All right?"

He watched her lips as she spoke. They were red and lush, and he wanted to bite them, too.

Maybe he hadn't taken enough blood from the human. Wait. Scratch maybe. He hadn't. Otherwise, his mouth would not be watering. His gums would not be aching, his muscles clenching.

"Aden?"

He almost leaped from the throne and threw himself

at her. If he didn't look away, he *would* throw himself at her. "Stand behind me." *Please.*

The demand was harsher than he'd intended, but he didn't apologize.

Shock rather then affront claimed her delicate features. Then her eyes narrowed, and she pivoted, standing beside him rather than behind him as ordered.

He could still feel the heat of her body, the warmth of her breath trekking over him. Close vicinity of any kind was also a problem, then. But before he could send her away, a female moan echoed, followed by the grunt of a male. Instinctively Aden reached for the daggers strapped to his ankles.

There were no daggers strapped to his ankles.

Didn't matter. He stood, surveying his throne room. His subjects had yet to enter—he could hear them gathering outside the room, speculating about what he desired. How long would they—

A couple locked in a heated kiss entered through the far left door. The male had his back to Aden, was walking the female toward a column, pressing her against it. Aden saw dark hair in disarray and a T-shirt ripped along the ribs. Saw jeans worn loose and bagging around lean hips. In fact, the only things holding up those jeans were the girl's legs.

They must not have heard about the meeting.

The female was a blonde Aden hadn't seen before but somehow recognized. Her eyes were closed, but he knew her irises were hazel. Her fangs chewed at her bottom lip as blood dripped down her chin. Clearly, she had fed before they'd started this.

This. In his throne room. Without his permission.

Aden's ire rose. And yet, deep, deep inside, he was also amused. Maybe even a bit envious.

Victoria must have only just realized what was happening, because she gasped. Aden didn't need to turn around to know her cheeks were flushed a pretty pink. The heat blasting off her had intensified, wrapping around him like an invisible chain.

He waited until the pair finished and the boy was zipping up his pants, the girl straightening her robe. A robe very much like Victoria's. Long, dark and easily removable. *Don't go there.* The couple was lucky the others hadn't ceased their debate outside the doors.

Aden cleared his throat as he sat back down.

The boy wheeled around, and the first thing Aden noticed were the perfect punctures in his neck, set in the eyes of the snake tattooed there, both still seeping with bright crimson nectar.

His mouth watered again. Was he drooling?

Seeing him, the girl gasped in horror and dropped to her knees, her head bowed. "Your majesty. I'm so sorry. I should not have entered without your express permission. I will shear my hair, rip my skin to ribbons and throw myself over a cliff. Just say the word. I would never have intentionally offended you."

"Be quiet." Blood...taste...

He must have stiffened or made ready to rise, because Victoria settled her hand on his shoulder and held him down. He could have brushed her aside but didn't. He liked the weight there, slight though it was. Liked knowing he had only to grab her wrist and tug and she would be in his lap. Her neck, close. Her blood, in his mouth.

Deep breath in, deep breath out. Again. Again. The bloodlust faded, but only slightly. Slightly, but enough.

"Yo, Ad," the boy said.

Aden studied a face he'd seen every day for months. Rough, scarred in a few places. "Seth. What are you doing here?"

Seth flashed an unrepentant smile. "Came looking for you. Dan's worried. Everyone's worried."

Emotions came back in a flood, guilt the front-runner, but each evaporated in the blink of an eye. "How did you find me?"

"Shannon. He followed your friend Riley, who snuck into your room to grab some of your crap."

Shannon lived at the D and M, had been his roommate, and was one of the good guys. He also had tracking skills Aden hadn't known about.

"Gotta admit, though, I didn't expect *this*." Seth waved his hand across the gothicly designed room. "I mean *vampires?* Can you say incredible?"

Aden's attention returned to the girl, who was still kneeling, her body quaking as she silently cried. "Enough. You had permission to be here. I summoned everyone for a meeting. Now rise and take a seat."

"Thank you. Thank you so much, majesty." She straightened, her gaze never finding the courage to meet his, and backtracked to obey.

Part of him took great satisfaction in that. The other part of him was distressed. "Have you been claimed as a blood-slave?" he asked Seth.

"No, way! I'm no one's slave." Seth flicked an invisible piece of lint off his shoulder. "Did someone try to claim me, though? Yeah. Some dude. Until I mentioned how tight you and I are, and he couldn't get away from me fast enough. Had the opposite affect on the girls. It's been open season on my body, baby."

Tight? Once upon a time, Seth had wanted to hack him to pieces and nail those pieces to the ranch walls.

"No wonder you kept this place a secret. You got all the tail you could want—and more."

"How long have you been here?" Victoria asked, her voice as sharp as one of the daggers Aden had wanted. "How many times have you been bitten?"

Dark eyes swung to her. And stayed. And fell over her, taking all of her in. Aden stiffened and forced himself to hold on to the armrests before he did something he'd regret. Namely, rip out his friend's eyeballs.

Hinges creaked as a door was opened. Footsteps sounded. Multiple pairs. No conversation, however. That had ended. Vampires and blood-slaves came into view, each finally taking their places on the tiers, as ordered.

Seth looked back at them, waved with enthusiasm, then returned his attention to Aden. "I haven't been here long," he answered. "And I've been bitten a lot."

"No symptoms of losing too much blood?" Aden asked at the same time Victoria said, "Are you craving the bites?"

"What is this? National Interrogate Seth Day? No symptoms. And yes, I'm craving. Who could have guessed how fun those fangs could be?"

Aden heard her swallow a mouthful of crackling air,

knew she was concerned and confused. "But your eyes are not glazed."

"I know," Seth replied. "They're straight up awesome."

"But..." Victoria twirled the ends of her hair around her finger. "How have you not become a blood-slave, addicted to the bite?"

Seth wiggled his brows. "Maybe I haven't been bitten by the right girl. Hey, so, you want to give me a go?"

Victoria rolled her eyes, and Aden gnashed his teeth. Flirting with the princess was not allowed. Ever. "Does Dan know where you are?"

Seth shifted from one foot to the other, at last uncomfortable. "Not really."

"So you *disappeared,* like me? Worried him?"

"Well, it's not like I can tell him what I found, now, is it?"

More and more vampires were filing into the room. He could feel their eyes on him, their curiosity blistering him. More than that, he could feel the desires of their beasts. Those beasts wanted to be with him, to touch him. They'd missed him.

"What about the other boys?" he asked, continuing his conversation with Seth. He was king. He could do whatever he wished. "How are they?"

"Well, Terry and RJ are moving out as planned. Next week, in fact. Oh, and Dan caught Shannon and Ryder together."

"What?" He'd known Shannon was gay. Known Shannon had thought—hoped—Ryder was gay. But Ryder had treated Shannon as if he had the plague ever since Shannon had made a pass at him. "And?"

"And, Dan was pretty cool about it. He told them the rest of us aren't allowed to date while we're on the ranch, so they aren't allowed to, either. They can't be alone together or anything like that."

Dan was a better guy than Aden had given him credit for—and he'd given the guy a lot of credit. "You have to go back."

"No. No way. This setup is too sweet. The chicks come on to me like they're flies and I'm honey." Seth pursed his lips. "I mean, like they're bears and I'm honey."

Aden didn't want to know how many bears the boy had entertained. "Have there been fights over you?"

Seth's chest puffed up. "Don't mean to brag, but... hell, it's not bragging if it's true, right? Yeah, there's been a fight. Just a few hours ago, in fact."

And the loser was now enslaved. "You're going back, and that's final," he said, something inside him—some kind of heat—wrapping around the words as they left his mouth.

Seth straightened abruptly, and his eyes glazed over. "Yes. Going back." He spun on his heels and strode down the red carpet without another word.

Shocking.

"Wait," Victoria called, a bit of panic in her voice.

He kept walking.

"I said wait!" she shouted.

Again, he kept walking.

"Aden, stop him," she pleaded.

Her desperation reached the core of him, and he found himself reacting, obeying. "Seth, stop," he called, the heat still pulsing around the words.

Seth halted but didn't turn around.

"Tell him to forget his time here." Her hand, which had never left his shoulder, tightened its grip, her fingertips digging into his muscle. "Tell him there's no such thing as a vampire."

"And he'll believe me? Just like that?"

"Yes."

Doubtful. Still. Aden thought about it, wanting to please her in this, but unsure *why* he wanted to please her in this. In the end, he said, "Seth, return to Dan. Tell him you found me, that I'm alive and well and living somewhere else, but do not mention the vampires."

"Return. Dan. Found. Well. No vampires."

That's when realization struck. His heart beat a ragged tattoo in his chest. Voice Voodoo, Mary Ann called the vampire ability to speak and manipulate. Right now, Aden was using Voice Voodoo. He didn't know how, wasn't sure it would last, but damned if he wouldn't enjoy it.

You hated when Victoria used Voice Voodoo on others.

Well, that was before.

Before you became an asshole? Power is going to your head, and if you don't fight this, you'll stay like this forever.

Great. He was still talking to himself. And wasn't *that* a wonderful development. One half of him loathed the other half of him. At this rate, he'd soon be fist fighting himself.

"Tell him to forget us," Victoria begged. "Please."

"No."

"Why?"

Because Aden could use a human ally. Because having eyes and ears on the outside was a good thing. Because he'd said so. "Seth. Go."

Seth went, leaving Aden alone with his vampires. The tiers were now overflowing with bodies. A sea of pale faces, both male and female. There was Draven at the front, a fake smile aimed up at him.

Lauren and Stephanie, Victoria's sisters, were up front, as well. They were scowling at him. Scowls that did nothing to diminish their beauty. Both were blonde, but one had blue eyes and the other green. One was a warrior, the other a wannabe human.

And there were the silver-haired councilmen, paler than all the rest because they'd been alive so much longer and could no longer tolerate the sunlight.

Every vampire wore some type of black robe, and every slave wore some type of white robe. White and black, white and black, interspersed, hypnotizing.

Shifters in full wolf form lined the bottom of the rows, guarding their beloved vamps and watching him warily. While the vamps might follow him blindly, the wolves never would. Oh, they would serve whoever was crowned king, but he would have to work for their affection.

Affection was important to cultivate, for the wolves produced the substance that could slaughter Aden's people.

"I brought you here for two reasons," he said, not deigning to rise. Silence greeted the announcement. "The first, to remind you that I am alive and well."

Now, murmurs arose. Whether they were of approval or disappointment, he wasn't sure and didn't care.

"The second reason is to remind you of what I can do. Beasts," he called, ready to make his point. "Come to me."

Expressions morphed to differing degrees of horror. Someone whimpered. Someone else groaned. Behind him, he heard a scream. Then, shadows began to rise over a few of the vampires. A few more. More. All. Dark wings expanded, flapping, filling empty air.

Slowly those shadows solidified, becoming monsters straight out of nightmares. Snouts formed and scarlet eyes glowed. Thick, dragonlike torsos rose…rose…and those solidified as well. Hoofed feet appeared next and stomped down the steps.

Vampires screeched and scrambled away. These monsters had been inside them, but when freed, even they couldn't control them. And usually, a beast went for its host first, chomping and chewing until vampire organs were mush inside the supposedly indestructible skin. This time, the beasts raced for Aden.

He stood, cast a quick glance over his shoulder to ensure that Victoria was safe—she'd pressed herself against the far wall, her eyes wide with fear. Chompers stood beside her, clawed feet scraping at the dais as he tried to hold himself back, his nostrils flared, his fangs exposed, his saliva blowing at Victoria with every exhalation he made.

"To me," Aden reminded him.

That beastly head swung around, and their gazes met. Like a favored pet who knew he'd get a treat, Chompers lost his air of aggression and clomped his way over. His tongue rolled out and his tail wagged. Then Aden was surrounded, being licked and nudged by others.

Chompers shoved his way to the front, snorting once, twice. He seemed to…frown?

"What's wrong?" Aden asked him.

The beast sniffed, sniffed, and yes, he was indeed frowning.

"Do I smell different, boy?" Like a vampire?

A nod.

"And you don't like it?"

Another nod.

The cold part of Aden took offence. The other part of him, still buried so deeply, wanted to fix it. "Come on," he said, scratching behind Chompers' ear. "Let's all go outside and play. Maybe that'll help."

None of the vampires protested as he led the beasts outside the throne room and through the hallway and foyer. The floor shook, and the furniture rattled.

Knickknacks—probably priceless vases and things collected throughout the ages—fell and shattered.

Aden didn't pause, didn't ask them to be careful, and finally stepped into the gloomy morning, his army behind him, practically ripping the front door from its hinges as they hurried to once again surround him.

He picked up a few sticks and tossed them. Those sticks were chased and grabbed between strong jaws in seconds, then brought back to him. How surreal they must look out here, playing fetch. A true stranger-than-fiction moment.

For a while, he was able to forget his troubles. But deep down, he suspected that the moment he left this clearing, his life would change—again—and still not for the better.

EIGHT

RILEY OF THE MANY NAMES raced through forests, along paved, graveled and dirt roads, through neighborhoods, congested shop ways and back alleys, his stride never slowing. Not when the sun fought free of the patchwork sky and burned him despite the chill in the air, not when that same chill agonized his lungs, and not when the moon at last appeared, a half crescent of gold he *so* wanted to howl at. Hour after hour disappeared, the miles eaten up.

To distract himself, he let his mind roll with everything he'd been called throughout the years. His brothers called him Riley the Randy. Or Riley the Shut the Hell Up. Victoria had recently begun to call him Riley the Pain Who Never Lets Me Get Away With *Anything*. And it was usually said with a stomp of her royal foot.

To enroll in Aden's school, he'd taken Connall as a

last name. Connall meant "great, mighty hound" in the ancient language. Victoria had suggested Ulrich, which meant "female warrior." One of the first jokes she'd ever cracked. He'd been so proud of her, he'd almost done it. But Riley Ulrich was a little too foreign-sounding when he'd wanted only to blend in.

Maybe he should have gone with Riley Smith. Or Riley Jones.

Some of his past girlfriends had called him Riley the Asshat. Or, his personal favorite, Riley the I Hope You Contract VD, You Rotten Piece of Shit.

His relationships never tended to work out, for whatever reason. "Whatever" was always his fault, he knew. And not just because the girls told him so. He purposefully kept himself at a distance, for their good as well as his own. He had a possessive streak that went bone deep, and if he ever decided a girl was his, well, he'd keep her. Forever.

Sure, the girls might have wanted him in the moment, or even for a few weeks or months into the relationship, but that could change. She could change.

He wouldn't change.

You couldn't teach old dogs new tricks because the old dogs just freaking didn't care to learn. Riley had lived over a hundred years. Among humans, he was old. Therefore, he wasn't learning anything new.

Among his own people, he was still a babe, but that didn't help his argument, so he wasn't going to toss that into the equation.

Also, the girlfriend, when she truly got to know him, might not understand his lifestyle, might not like it and might decide to leave him. But if he'd taken things to the next level, it would be too late. Anyone you brought to Vlad's home stayed in Vlad's home.

Vlad wasn't calling the shots anymore, but Riley understood the reasoning behind the edict. Protection of the species. Still. By bringing someone into the fold, you opened yourself up to challenges.

Look at Vic and Draven.

Riley hated challenges. What was his was his, and he didn't share. And maybe he felt that way because he'd grown up in a pack, and every scrap of food, every piece of clothing, every room, bed and unmated female—and yes, every unmated male—had been considered community property. That had gotten old fast. So, like he'd said, he kept a part of himself distanced from his girlfriends and never allowed himself to consider one exclusively "his."

Until Mary Ann.

Somehow she'd snuck past his defenses. Hell, maybe she'd muted them like she muted everything else. He'd wondered, finding it strange that he'd been intrigued by her since the beginning. And yeah, he'd also been panting for a little action. All that dark hair he'd wanted to fist, those so-deep-you-could-be-lost-forever eyes of fall-brown he'd wanted to search. That olive skin, pale with the slightest hint of color, he'd wanted to lick. (Hey, he was a dog.)

She was tall and slender, pretty in a quiet way, graceful in an even quieter way. Like, she might trip while she was walking, her mind lost in thought, but when she reached up to brush her hair out of her face, her fingers tracing over her cheeks and temples, she was all fluid motion, a study of sensuality.

She didn't know her own appeal, and that had been obvious in the beginning, too. She sometimes looked down at her feet, shyly kicking stones. She never purposely sought attention; she sometimes blushed. She was reserved and nervous, yet determined to overcome every test tossed her way.

At first, he hadn't known how smart she was. He'd just thought, *wow, she's pretty…and sweet…and more concerned with others than she is with herself.* But he'd learned fast. Real fast. Her mind worked at an amazing speed.

She took nothing at face value, researched everything and, though reserved and nervous, had no problem voicing her opinions with people she was comfortable with, believing what she said one hundred percent.

What's more, she told the truth, always. No matter how harsh. He admired that trait because he was the same way.

She was emotional, too. Something he was not and had not realized he liked. Until her. She wasn't afraid to cry all over him or hug him. Or to laugh and twirl around a room with happiness. Quite simply, she held nothing back. The complete opposite of him and everyone he'd ever dated, really.

She was vulnerable, and she didn't care. She just... lived.

Leaving him hadn't been about protecting herself. He knew that. Leaving him had been about protecting *him*. She didn't want to hurt him, and he got that. He did. He didn't want to hurt her, either. But separation? That wasn't the answer.

So she was a drainer. So what? They'd deal. Every couple had their problems. And okay, okay. Her problem could kill him. They'd find a solution before that happened. Guaranteed.

A rock sliced into his paw, but he didn't stumble. He

kept running, sweat dripping in his eyes. Unlike non-shifter dogs, he could sweat (among other things) as human and animal collided inside him. And sweat he did. A lot. His fur was plastered to his pelt by the time he reached the big, bad city.

Panting, he whizzed past people—all of whom yelped in shock at the large (*really* large) animal streaking by—bypassed cars and barreled past other animals. Pets on leashes, wild things foraging for food.

So many auras, each boasting colorful layer after colorful layer. One for the physical body, one for self-directed emotions, one for emotions directed at others, for the logical mind, the creative mind, the practical mind, for truth and lie, for love and hate, for passion and finally, for peace and chaos.

People wore those layers like coats. Glowing coats that broadcast their thoughts and emotions—their *everything.* Wouldn't be so bad, if each layer was a simple color from an organized chart. Red, blue, green or yellow, something easy like that. But, no. He saw varying shades of the same colors, different colors on top of different colors, colors blending together, colors, colors and more colors.

That was another thing he liked about Mary Ann. Her aura. He didn't have to waste time interpreting the colors pulsing around her. They were too pure, too strong, each one stacked on top of the other, nothing murky or open for interpretation.

Where are you, sweetheart?

Last time he'd seen her, too many days ago, she'd been in Tulsa, Oklahoma. How she'd escaped him, he didn't yet know. One moment he'd seen her, the next, when she turned a corner, he hadn't. He'd smelled her, though. That sweet fragrance of wildflowers and honey. But just like her, the scent had faded, leading nowhere, and he'd lost her trail completely.

He would have stayed and continued searching, but when he'd called his brother Nate for an update on Vic, Aden and life at the mansion, he'd flipped. Hearing his personal charge was "crying a lot" and "shut in her room," as well as "worked into a blood craze and threatening to damage people" had sent him into a tailspin of panic. He'd stolen a car and broken every speed law known to man to reach her.

He could have driven back here, that would have taken him only three hours, but he preferred to run in his animal form. To scent Mary Ann. To know who had interacted with her.

When he reached the street where he'd last seen her walking—smack in the middle of a busy shopping center—he at last slowed. Horns honked, cars swerved to avoid him. He moved into the shadows, staying close to building walls. Would be a major pain in the ass to deal with Animal Control and their tranq guns.

Adrenaline surged through him, thick and potent, making his blood like fire in his veins. The sweat kept dripping from him, leaving a noticeable trail along the sidewalk. He probably smelled. Good. Everyone would stay the hell away from him.

He sniffed…sniffed…so many odors, blending together. He sorted through them, continuing to sniff… caught a hint of magic, and the hair on his spine lifted, even wet and weighted as it was. Magic equaled witches, and the witches hated Mary Ann with a murderous passion.

A coven could live here, unaware of the drainer now in their midst. Or a coven could be following her.

He sniffed, sniffed…there. The *drum, drum* of his heart increased in speed and ferocity. Mary Ann. The scent of her hadn't just lingered; it had grown stronger. She must have taken this path several times—and recently. Why? Had she run into the witches? If so, had she sucked the magic out of them or had they captured her? Or worse?

He studied the area. Clothing boutiques, a deli, cafés, a coffee shop. A short distance ahead was a hill, highlighted by a multitude of lamps, a yellowing lawn and a tall, sprawling building. It was older, comprised of brownstone, with steepled roofs and concrete steps. A library.

Bingo. Mary Ann's mother ship.

Riley closed the distance and clomped up the steps. Closing time had already passed, which meant the building was empty for the night. He turned, sniffing. Oh, yes. The sweet scent of Mary Ann saturated the air. She'd been here many times. Researching, as her nature dictated.

What was she researching? Drainers? Even the thought caused his stomach to churn with a bucket of acid. Paper trails were a bitch, and yeah, witches tracked that kind of thing. Who didn't? They'd be on her—if they weren't already—before she could click her heels together and pray for home.

Sniff, sniff. He frowned. He also caught the scent of something, someone, familiar. Dark, a little citrusy. Familiar, yes, but not enough to immediately register a name.

Then, Riley lost the scent altogether. Cigarette smoke wafted through the air, masking everything else as it wound around him. He growled, low and throaty. He hated that crap, and as soon as he found the source he was going to—

A dirty guy with a whiskey bottle sat behind one of the columns, the smoke snaking around him. "Here doggie, doggie," he slurred.

Seriously? Riley threw another growl the guy's way.

That earned him a drunken chortle. "Mean little thing, ain't ya?"

Little? Hardly. *Dude, you're lucky I don't piss all over you.* Riley flashed his sharp canines and turned. He could see the shopping area he'd just left and a good expanse beyond that, rundown apartments, most likely crack houses, and what looked to be several crime scenes, police lights flashing red and blue. Beyond even that was downtown Tulsa. Lots of lights and towering buildings, both glass and chrome.

Mary Ann wouldn't have traveled so far from the library, even to lose herself in the crowd. One, she couldn't afford it, and two, information was her crack, and she'd want to be close to the source, just in case a new idea struck her and she needed a snort.

So. *Cheap motel, here I come.* Riley trotted from the building, always sniffing, until he found the correct trail. There! Anticipation flooded him, and he picked up speed.

First thing he'd do when he found her was shake her. Second thing, kiss her. Third, shake her again. Fourth, kiss her again.

He was sensing a pattern.

She'd probably taken a hundred years off his life. And he wasn't grateful! Shifters didn't live forever, but they did have a long, long life, and he wanted every moment of his.

His parents had died before their time, with too many regrets. He didn't want that for himself. 'Course, they'd died in a fairy raid and not because of one little human girl who drove them crazy.

Fairies, man. They had such a God complex, always slaughtering other supernatural races in the name of protecting humans, when the truth was, they just wanted to be the most powerful beings on the block.

Kinda like Vlad, who had raised Riley. Whom Riley had always served. Until Aden had taken the crown. Then Riley's loyalty had switched, and even when he'd discovered Vlad still lived, Riley hadn't betrayed Aden. The bond had already formed.

This new Aden, though... There was something different about him, something Riley didn't like. What, he wasn't sure. Still, he wouldn't betray his new king. Once he had Mary Ann safely tucked away and guarded, he would help Aden rediscover his old personality. Somehow.

The scent of magic increased, and Riley slowed. His gaze sharpened, darting past colors, slicing past shadows. Across the street, he spotted two telling glows. One a metallic gold, the other a brownish gold. Magic.

Hello, mentor and apprentice.

His ears twitched as he listened to all the conversations around him—and even those miles away, and inside buildings—discarding idle chatter, focusing, focusing...

"—have to strike now, while she's without protection."

He knew the voice. Marie. A witch. The leader of the coven that had come to Crossroads.

"I know. But her wards are a problem." He knew that voice, as well. Jennifer. Also witch. The student. "We'll have to plan our strike precisely. We can't allow those wards to save her."

Mary Ann was currently protected against death by physical injury and mind control. To bypass those, the witches would have to...what? Cause mental injury through some kind of trickery? He wasn't sure how they'd pull something like that off.

How many others were nearby? Had they seen Mary Ann already? They obviously hadn't attacked her. Determined to discover the truth, he drew closer to them.

"The boy will have to be taken care of, as well," Marie said on a sigh.

What boy? Him? Or someone else? Jealousy sparked.

"He's done nothing wrong," Jennifer said.

"Doesn't matter. He's powerful. He'll be trouble," Marie replied.

Powerful could mean Aden but could also mean Riley. However, the "done nothing wrong" part eliminated them both. Riley's jealousy sprouted wings with razored tips and flew through his entire body.

Marie continued, "We can't risk his coming after us. He could do serious damage. Especially if he decides to aid the other one, the new king. And since Aden has Tyson stuck inside him…"

"I know." Fear coated Jennifer's voice.

Tyson? One of the souls BD? Before Death.

Riley made a mental note to tell Aden, see if the name sparked a memory in a soul. He stopped when he reached the front doors of an apartment building. One of the crumbling, rundown ones. The witches were inside, their auras practically crackling beyond the bricks. So badly he wanted to charge through the building, biting and chewing the magic wielders to pieces. Threaten

Mary Ann and hurt. That was the lesson they needed to learn. But he was without wards. His wolf skin couldn't hold them. The witches could cast a thousand different spells—death, destruction, pain—and he would be helpless.

That was why wolves never challenged witches without a vampire by their side.

A low growl slipped from him. He hated walking away from a fight, but he did it. He clomped back into the shadows and saw the motel across the street—and the four telling auras inside it. Those auras crackled, glitter swirling in a rainbow of colors.

Fairies.

They were here, too. Dread slithered through him. His ears twitched as he honed in, listened.

"—reach her before the witches," someone was saying. Female. Possibly Brendal, the fairy who'd tried to mind-control Aden into doing as she wanted. A princess, and the dead and ghostly Thomas's determined sister. "She's mine."

"Yes, princess."

Oh, yes. That was Brendal.

Riley sped into action, Mary Ann's scent strengthening the moment he reached the Charleston Motel. The sign underneath read Weekly Rapes Available. *Nice.* Someone had screwed with the letters.

Would Mary Ann have gone inside such a dilapidated facility? Doing so was completely out of character for someone known as a Goody Two-shoes. (And what the hell did that mean, anyway? Why were shoes considered good?) She might have, though, simply to throw off whoever was following her.

And the witches and fairies *had* seen her. No question of that now. Why else would they be here, talking about her?

As his anticipation and concern returned, strengthened, he raced across the street. Headlights washed over him, a car horn blared, tires squealed. Shoulda looked both ways, he supposed, jumping out of the way. The motel doors opened from the outside, rather than from an inner hallway. His favorite. He sniffed each one until he caught another whiff of Mary Ann.

The instant he did, his blood heated with all kinds of gooey emotions only girls were supposed to feel. She was here.

He shifted to his human form, naked and suddenly cold, picked the lock, shifted back to his wolf form, settled his mouth around the knob and gave a little twist. Or tried to. No movement, which meant she'd done more than lock it. Good. Not that any kind of rigging would stop the witches, the fae or him.

Rather than shift back to his human form and undo her handiwork—perhaps waking Mary Ann and giving her time to run, hide or call "the boy" the witches had mentioned—Riley slammed into the door with all his considerable wolf weight. Hinges snapped, and wood shards rained.

He remained there in the entrance, taking stock. First thing he noticed: there was someone on the floor, sitting up, glaring. Tucker Harbor. Second thing: someone on the bed, sitting up, gasping. Mary Ann. That fall of dark hair, her aura the dark red of fear, the blue of hope.

In an instant he knew. Tucker was "the boy." The powerful, supposedly done-nothing-wrong boy.

In a blink, the scene changed. No longer was anyone on the floor. No longer was the person on the bed gasping at him with a combination of fear and hope.

Now, there were two people on the bed—and they were having sex.

Another growl left him, this one as savage and lethal as a dagger. Probably cutting much deeper. He'd already decided to kill Tucker, but now he was going to make it hurt.

Riley shifted—uncaring that he was naked—and

closed the door as best he could. With the damage to the hinges, he could only prop the fake wood against the opening. Then he turned and crossed his arms over his chest.

"I know what you're doing, you bastard, and you can stop." Illusions. This was an illusion, and he knew it soul deep. Neither person on the bed, so lost to pleasure, cast any kind of aura.

"Riley," Mary Ann said on a raspy breath.

The sound of his name on those lips affected him. His blood heated another degree and not with fury.

"Tucker," she said next, pleasure giving way to irritation. "Stop, or I'll stab you."

A funny threat, coming from her, but effective. Tucker dropped the illusion, and once again Riley saw that Tucker was on the floor and Mary Ann was on the bed.

She looked away from Riley, even as she tossed him a sheet, a hot blush staining her cheeks. "For frick's sake, Riley, cover yourself. Tucker's here."

Had she just said *for frick's sake?* And, if he didn't obey? He wanted to ask but didn't. He caught the sheet and wound the material around his waist, tucking in the end to ensure it stayed put. He recrossed his arms over his chest. "I'm sure Tucker's already come to grips with the fact that everyone he encounters is bigger than he is, so don't worry that he'll slip into a shame spiral and kill himself. Just start talking." *Before I start maiming.* "What's going on?"

"Can't you tell?" Tucker asked, smug enough to boil Riley's good intentions. "We're dating again, and she's playing hard to get."

Riley ran his tongue over his teeth. "Not another word out of you, demon. Mary Ann?" She'd ditched him to go on the run with her cheating, evil ex. Riley had never been more stunned—or more pissed. "You've got witches across the street, fairies here in this building, and both are planning your execution. You can either tell me what's going on now, or tell me after I kill Tucker."

She gulped. "Now is fine."

"Good choice." Man, she was beautiful. Not just quietly pretty, he realized, but drop-dead beautiful. And, yeah, maybe the fact that he'd missed her so much was responsible for the change, but just then she was perfect in every way. Except for the ex. Tucker was an accessory that would not go with any of Mary Ann's outfits.

Tucker stood. He wore a T-shirt and a pair of boxers. Both would look so much nicer torn to ribbons. Along with his skin. "You want a piece of me, wolf? Then come and get it. 'Cause your girlfriend sure did earlier."

Another gasp left Mary Ann. "You are such a liar! I've changed my mind, Riley. We can talk after you kill him," she added primly.

He flashed a grin. Until he heard "—wolf is back! What should we do?" The speaker was Jennifer. Through magic, they could watch anyone at any time. Why the hell hadn't he thought of that?

"The slaughter will have to wait," he said. "Grab your stuff. We need to leave. The witches are watching you." And he needed to do something to stop them.

"Okay. Yes." She was pale and trembling as she unfolded from the bed, but her bag was already packed, the same backpack she'd left home with, so the moment she slid her feet into her tennis shoes, she was ready.

They were racing into the night a second later.

Tucker, the bastard, followed them. "You'll need me," he said, smug again. "*If* you want to succeed."

"Like you did such a good job before," Riley snapped.

"She's alive, isn't she?"

No arguing with that.

"Zip it, both of you," Mary Ann said, exasperated. "We can yell and threaten each other when we're safe."

He heard her unspoken question: Would they ever be safe? Truly safe? He wanted to reply but zipped his lips as ordered and shifted back to wolf form, the sheet falling away.

He'd make sure she was safe. Whatever he had to do, he'd make sure.

NINE

WHEN ADEN FINISHED PLAYING fetch with the beasts, he asked them to return to their hosts. They snorted and groused, but ultimately they obeyed, wanting so badly to please him. After that, he ordered his people to go about their business and no one—*no one*—was to disturb him.

After *that,* he spent a few hours walking the grounds (pristine), the house (immaculate), listening to gossip (boring) and ignoring the councilmen, who obeyed his edict to leave him alone but who purposely cast their voices his way as they argued about his future marriage plans (not gonna happen).

They also discussed his coronation ceremony having been canceled because he'd been missing, and then picked a new date, agreeing they could have everything ready in a week. Which, miracle of miracles, was nearly the same date as the ceremony they'd canceled, but whatever.

He was king, and he didn't need a coronation to feel the part. Nor did the people need a coronation to follow him. Not after they'd seen what he could do with their beasts.

And now...now he was weary. He found a shirt, pulled it on and spent the rest of the night in the throne room, the power wafting from the wards woven into the carpet quieting the buzzing in his head, comforting him but not reassuring him. At least no one tried to enter, leaving him alone with his thoughts.

He wondered where Victoria was and what she was doing. Fine. He didn't care about either. He just wanted to know who she was doing *whatever it was* with and kill the guy.

Victoria was his girlfriend. Right? So, warning other males away with violence was his prerogative. *Right?*

He massaged the back of his neck. *Something is wrong with you,* Riley had said. Victoria had agreed, and now Aden did as well. He was uncaring, cold and murderous, his emotions dying before they had a chance to grow, his thoughts traveling dark, dangerous paths he didn't understand.

More than that, he knew things he shouldn't. Like the

names, faults and strengths of vampires he'd never met. Like how blowing the golden horn would summon his allies. Or Vlad's. He knew his way around this home. Every secret passage, every forgotten hidey-hole. And his desire to start a war with anyone and everyone who opposed his rule? That topped the list of weird.

He had become someone else.

How was he supposed to fight this when part of him actually *liked* the changes?

By the time the sun rose, he hadn't yet come up with a decent answer. He was tired, but still too restless to try and sleep. Good thing, too. Being vulnerable in a nest of vipers wasn't wise. On top of that, his meds were wearing off, and the souls were murmuring inside his head. Nothing distinguishable yet but enough to assure him they were with him still.

He was relieved—he supposed.

Mostly, he was hungry. Not for pancakes or cereal or even a bagel, but for blood from a living host. Something else he should care about but didn't. All he wanted was to feed. And he wanted to do it before the souls woke completely and decided to comment about his new eating habits. Although they might understand and accept, considering what they'd witnessed inside the cave.

He stood, his bones creaking from the hours of disuse,

and finally strode out of the throne room. He waited, expectant, but the buzzing never started up again.

Two wolves stood sentry at the double doors, one the pure white of a snowflake, the other a rainbow of golds. They followed him as he walked, not even trying to hide their purpose.

Nathan and Maxwell, Riley's brothers. Undoubtedly his new guards. He'd met them before, so it wasn't strange that he knew them. They were good guys, if a bit irreverent.

One of his feet knocked into the other. See? Those weren't his thoughts. Nathan and Maxwell were good guys, yeah, but Aden had never considered them irreverent before.

Younger vampires wandered in every direction, blood-slaves trailing behind them, worship glazing their eyes. *That could have been me.* In the cave, he'd craved Victoria's bite more than anything in the world. Had wanted to bite her even more than that.

The way his gums throbbed and his teeth ached in a sudden chorus of *oh, please, now,* he still wanted to bite her. Her, and no one else. And he could do so. He was her king. He *would* bite her. He had only to find her.

Or not, he realized next. That's what minions were for.

Minions? Really?

Maybe…maybe the only way to fight this strange new part of himself was to do the opposite of what it wanted. He nodded. That made sense. The first hurdle, of course, was Victoria. He yearned to feed from her, therefore he couldn't feed from her. The second hurdle would be telling her they couldn't spend any more time together.

Telling her would require seeing her. A tingle of anticipation swept through him. Deep down, in the part of himself that he *did* know and *did* understand, he would cut off an arm to see her.

"Take me to Victoria," he commanded the wolves. There would be no sending minions. Not for this.

Nathan's ears perked up. Maxwell chomped his teeth at him. Then the pair of them bounded in front of him, a silent demand for him to follow. He did and soon found himself in the backyard. The sun was brighter than usual, and despite the chill in the air, he experienced a rush of burning bristles against his skin. Not enough to send him back inside but just enough to annoy him.

Aden? Is that you? an unsure male voice asked. Julian, alert at last.

Aden should have been happy—the soul sounded like himself and hadn't changed like Aden. Yes, he should have been. "It's me," he said, and the wolves stopped to look back at him. He waved them forward.

Comprehension dawned in their gazes, and they obeyed. Aden wished he could think his replies to the souls, but his inner voice was always lost in the chaos.

Dude! The uncertainty fell away. *We're back with Aden,* Julian whooped happily. *Are we here to stay, E? Come on, Great Oracle of Doom, and help a guy out. Tell me what I want to hear.*

Silence.

Elijah must still be sleeping. Caleb, too. Lazy bums.

The wolves stopped, their spines stiffening, their hair standing on end. They looked around, growling at—Aden followed their line of vision through the surrounding forest—nothing but air. Did they sense a threat he couldn't see? He waited, but no one stepped from the trees, and not a single leaf swayed from nearby motion. Had some of his—or Vlad's—allies arrived yet? Would they even come?

The horn was bespelled and had been for over a thousand years, ever since several vampire factions had agreed to aid each other whenever necessary. And yet, not one of those factions had ever used their horn. Would they remember what the summons meant? Would they care?

The growling intensified a split second before a

woman danced her way into the metal circle that desig-
nated the crypt. Aden was hypnotized by her. She wore
a black robe like all the vampires here, but a hood draped
her head, concealing her features. Still, he could see the
long length of hair, black as night and cascading like a
waterfall over her shoulder.

The wolves didn't stop growling, but they didn't attack her. They must have been as transfixed as he was.

Twirling, twirling, mesmerizing.

There was something familiar about her, something that lit Aden up inside, even as it dragged him
down. Whoever she was, she raised the same emotions
Mary Ann did. An urge to hug, followed by a need to
run.

"Maxwell, Nathan," he said.

They quieted as they looked over their furry shoulders.

Using minions wasn't a bad idea, really. "Bring Victoria to me," he said absently.

We should stay with you. Nathan's voice echoed inside
his head. *There's danger here, my king.*

Wolves could speak into the minds of those around
them. Something Riley had done to him before, so he
wasn't startled. And neither was Julian, who probably

couldn't hear the new voice. "From this woman? No. Now go get Victoria and bring her to me."

They shared a confused look before nodding and clomping off.

He sat down, right there, in front of the circle, watching the woman. She didn't seem to notice him. Her graceful, twirling steps never faltered. Twirling, twirling, a ballerina on ice, her arms outstretched, one leg lifted behind her and bent. Twirling and twirling.

Who was she?

A cough inside his head. *Hello, Aden,* Elijah finally said, then yawned. *How are you feeling?*

"Fine." Kind of.

So are we here to stay or what? Julian demanded, practically jumping up and down.

I…don't know, the psychic replied.

O-kay. That was a first.

Explain yourself, please, Julian huffed.

Elijah sighed. *I just woke up. Do we have to do the heavy stuff—*

Explain, explain, explain!

You are such *a child. But fine. Aden's path has been altered so much lately, I can no longer see a clear future for him. He was supposed to die, and that was supposed to be the end of us all. But he didn't, we didn't, and now I can't see what lies ahead.*

Perhaps that was a good thing.

That better not mean we're going to die soon. Really die, I mean, Julian replied, and if he'd had a body he would have been pacing. *Or that we're gonna wake up back inside the vamp. I like her and everything, when she's not going for our jugular, but come on. A guy needs to be a guy.*

Nothing wrong with the vamp, Caleb said, piping up for the first time. Like Elijah, he yawned. *No offense, Aden, but she's hotter than you.*

A milk jug is hotter than our Ad, Julian said with a snicker.

Caleb snorted. *Buuurn.*

"Good. The gang's all here."

Why don't you sound happy? Julian asked, pouting now. *More important question—why didn't you laugh at my amazing joke?*

And why are you so...cold inside? Caleb asked. *Seriously, it's like a meat locker in here.*

Meat locker? When his skin felt molten? "I'm fine. And I don't know."

I might. What do you remember about your last hour inside that cave with Victoria? Elijah asked. *Think for a minute, okay, then you can go back to doing whatever it is you're doing.*

"Why do you want to know?"

Please. Just do what I told you.

Not an answer, but fine. Whatever. "All right." Arguing required too much energy. So he thought about it, replaying the events through his head. He'd just bitten Victoria. Just drank from her. She'd just bitten and drunk from him. That hadn't been enough for either of them. They'd fought, tossing each other around like rag dolls, both lost to a hunger that never seemed to be satisfied.

The dancing woman laughed, and Aden wanted to look at her, to see her face softened by humor, but forced himself to concentrate, thinking back...back. The cave. Victoria. The fighting had stopped, and they'd faced off. She'd...glowed. Yes, he remembered now. A glorious golden glow had seeped from her pores, so bright he hadn't been able to look at her. Seeing it, Chompers had gone crazy inside his head, wanting out, desperate to protect him, sensing a predator far stronger than himself was about to be unleashed.

Then, Chompers had gotten his wish. He'd emerged from Aden's body, solidified into dragon form and attacked. Aden had shouted, racing forward, afraid for his girl, willing to throw himself in front of Victoria to save her from being clamped between those too-strong jaws. Only, Victoria had stretched out her hands. The glow had lanced away from her body and into Chompers, knocking him backward, pinning him to the cave wall.

Victoria had turned her attention to Aden. Again the glow had lanced from her, then slammed into him. He, too, had been thrown backward, pinned on the opposite side, as far away from Chompers as possible. She had closed the distance between them.

Her eyes, usually blue, had then been filled with lavender ice chips and devoid of any emotion. She'd looked him over from head to toe, taking his measure.

A pause. Aden had tried to breathe, couldn't breathe. The energy, or whatever she'd thrown at him, had been tightening its hold on him, shoving his ribs into his lungs, piercing the membrane. Pain had shot through him.

"Victoria," Aden had gasped out.

She'd blinked at him, as if she'd heard him but hadn't quite understood him.

"Victoria."

She'd opened her mouth to speak. Had spoken. He'd heard the words. Or should have. The sounds she'd made, they'd been—

Enough! Elijah shouted inside Aden's head, drowning out everything else.

Aden sucked in a breath, suddenly back in the present, the past fading, gone.

That's enough, Elijah said again, calm this time.

"You wanted me to think back," Aden said, confused.

"I did. You should have let the scene play until the end." He wanted to know what Victoria had said—and who had been speaking through her. Because that had not been her voice. Too raw, too guttural. Too animalistic.

What are you talking about? What scene? I didn't see anything, Julian groused.

Me, either, Caleb said. *What happened?*

Nothing, Elijah lied. *Leave it alone, Aden. You saw all that you needed to see. Frankly, I didn't expect you to remember that much.*

Another lie? Elijah never lied. What was going on? "Then why did you have me think back?"

I just wanted you to know that Victoria didn't hurt you on purpose.

Was that why he'd been wondering if he even liked her? Because of something she'd done in the cave? Something he couldn't remember? Or hadn't *yet* remembered.

He pursed his lips. His past was there, all of it, every memory accessible, but those memories weren't the main focus of his mind. He had to actively consider something—like what had happened in the cave—before the event crystallized.

After all the blood exchanges, Victoria left pieces of herself inside you. Her past, her thoughts and desires. Or rather, former thoughts and desires. They seem like yours now.

"That can't be right. Earlier I wondered if I even liked her."

And once upon a time, she didn't like herself.

"I want to kill her father. She loved her father."

She's wanted to harm him many times over the past few decades. He wasn't always nice to her, you know. But Aden? You're still here, too. The desire to harm him could very well spring from deep inside you.

Pieces of Victoria's psyche. Inside him. Driving him, changing him. Right or wrong? True or false? "How do you know this?"

I'm all-knowing, remember? The self-deprecating tone held a layer of truth and dread.

"Not anymore. *Remember?*"

The dancing woman stopped, laughed, such a tinkling sound—he loved that sound, hated that sound—and pushed back her hood to look directly at him. Her face was lovely, delicate and hauntingly sweet.

"There you are, my darling. What are you doing, sitting so far away? Come and dance with me."

Darling? Oh, yes, he knew her. *Should* know her, but still couldn't quite place her. His brain kept getting caught up on the words *mother* and *exasperating*. She wasn't his mother—was she?—and he wasn't sure why she exasperated him.

"I don't know how to dance," he told her.

"I'll take the blame, I swear."

He blinked in confusion. She wanted to take the blame for his lack of skill?

If you get up and dance right now, I'll never forgive you, Caleb said. *You'll look like an idiot, and in turn make us look like idiots.*

You're unwillingness to groove surprises me, C-man. Julian chuckled. *Flailing around would probably look like some kind of mating ritual, luring the ladies. Or something.*

Aden. Dude. If you're thinking about dancing, you should just get up and dance. Caleb's abrupt switch was almost comical. *It's all about the bump and grind.*

Another tinkling laugh, and the woman pulled her hood back up. "Very well, my darling, be that way. I'll dance on my own." The twirling started up again. "But you're missing out, I promise you."

"Aden." The pureness of Victoria's voice captured his attention. "You summoned me?"

He forced himself to look up. She stood just off to

the side, the wolves flanking her. The sun framed her, creating an angelic halo around her. She'd pulled her dark hair into a ponytail and wore a black robe, as usual, only this one boasted long sleeves and a coarser, thicker material. She looked…human, so beautifully human, her cheeks and nose a bright pink, her eyes watering from the cold.

"Do you know that woman?" He motioned to where—she was gone. The dancing female had spun her way out of the backyard.

"Who?" Victoria asked.

"Never mind." The scent of her hit him, as sweet as she looked. Gums, throbbing. Teeth, aching. Mouth, watering.

And wouldn't you know it? The buzzing returned to his head, followed by a muted cry. The same muted cry he'd heard last night. Small, almost whining. Grumbling for attention. Like a newborn baby.

What was that? Julian demanded.

"Probably just echoes from before, in the cave," he said, the words slurred. God. His tongue felt as big as a golf ball. His gaze latched onto Victoria's thumping pulse. Mmm.

"What?" Victoria asked, brow furrowing in confusion.

This is dangerous, Elijah said. *Look away from her. You can't drink from her. What if you become addicted to her again?*

Or worse, what if there's another switch and we end up back inside her? Julian's fear was palpable.

Am I the only one with a sense of adventure? Caleb asked. *Do it! Drink her!*

Ignore him. Drink from someone else, Elijah commanded.

But…Aden didn't want to drink from anyone else, even though his stomach was twisting painfully, even though he'd decided to send Victoria away.

His hunger must have overridden his good sense because he now wanted to keep her with him. And what he wanted, he got. Always. Sighing, he stood and held out his hand, another plaintive cry resounding in his head before he could speak.

Seriously, what is that? Julian's fear gave way to irritation. *Caleb, are you acting like a brat again, pretending to be a baby?*

You know I hold my breath to get what I want. I don't whine.

Uh, hate to break it to you, but you don't have any breath, Elijah said.

And yet it works for me. Why would I change my methods?

Aden tuned them out as best he could. "Walk with

me," he said to Victoria. She hadn't taken his hand, was merely peering down at it, unsure.

Hope flickered in her blue, blue eyes as she glanced up. "Really?"

As I was saying earlier, you do like her, Elijah said, voice pushing through his mental blocks. *Don't forget that. Any negative feelings toward her are not your own. Okay? Yes?*

Why the insistence?

Victoria placed her hand in his, and ignoring the souls was no longer an issue. The princess became his sole focus.

Her scent did more than envelop him, it invaded him, consumed him, and his mouth watered a little more. Just then, he *really* liked her. Her softness, her warmth— not hot, not anymore, but warm and sweet. Her... everything.

"Scout ahead and make sure we'll be alone," he commanded the wolves before leading Victoria out of the backyard and into the forest. They bounded in front of him and soon disappeared. No howls of warning were forthcoming, so he continued on.

What he would do with Victoria, well, he wasn't sure about that, either. But they would find out together. For better or worse.

ten

Was this walk for business or pleasure?

Victoria strolled hand in hand with Aden for a long while, just as they'd done before The Incident, as she was now calling their last minutes in the cave, silent—if she didn't count the now-constant, though gradually quieting, roaring in the back of her head—moving farther and farther away from the mansion. And protection.

She'd never feared Aden before, and really, she didn't fear him now. It was just, he was so different, she didn't know what to expect from him. At least she'd been smart enough to choose a winter robe to somewhat fight the early morning chill. Something she'd never had to do before. In fact, she'd had to borrow the stupid, constrictive thing from a human blood-slave.

Weather had never before mattered to her. *Temperature* had never before mattered. Now, she was freakishly cold.

All. The. Time. She'd tossed and turned all night, shivering, her teeth chattering.

"I like it out here," Aden said.

Casual conversation. Fabulous. "I'm surprised." The trees were sparse, their limbs gnarled, offering very little shade overhead. Not that Victoria needed much shade. Her now vulnerable skin loved the sun, soaking in every ray, though still not warming her.

"Yeah. No prying eyes, nowhere for anyone to hide."

Anyone—like her? "Should I be scared?"

"I don't know."

His honesty relaxed her enough to leave her smiling. "Just warn me if you decide to attack."

"All right." A moment passed. "Here's your warning. I'm hungry."

Goodbye relaxation. Tensing, she waited for him to pounce. When he didn't, she cleared her throat and asked, "Hungry for human food or for blood?"

"Blood." The word was as slurred as before, when he'd been staring at her pulse.

If that was the only reason he'd asked her to walk with him, she'd…she didn't know what she'd do. What she did know—the thought hurt with the same jolting force as a car slamming into her and angered with a flash of fire usually found only in hearths. To calm herself, she breathed in and out, distantly heard the rattle of locusts and the call of the birds.

"Before you drink from anyone else, I need to teach you how to eat." Good. No hurt, no anger.

"I think I know how to drink," he said dryly.

"Properly?" Because what they'd done in the cave didn't count.

"Meaning?"

"Veins and arteries taste different. Arteries are sweeter, but they're deeper and harder for humans to heal, so you go for them only if you want to kill. And each vein tastes different, too. The ones in the neck are deoxygenated, so they have a little bit of a—'delicious'—fizz to them, but if you don't know what you're doing you'll, what? Kill."

"I knew that," he said, then thought for a moment. He nodded. "Yes, I knew that."

She didn't ask whether he'd learned from her memories, as she had learned a few things from his, or if he'd learned on his own, like, say, sometime during the night, while they'd been apart and she'd had no idea what he was doing. Some things you were better off not knowing.

"Well, either way, you can't drink from me." So there!

The frown Aden leveled on her was all about intimidation. "*I* know I shouldn't drink from you, but why are *you* so against it?"

Because he would find out how vulnerable she was. Because his still-human teeth would cut through her skin without any problem and probably damage her. Because she might like it more than he did.

Because *she* might now become addicted to *his* bite.

The way that blood-slave had reacted to him, all pleasure and delight and eagerness, meant that even without fangs, he now produced the chemical needed to intoxicate.

"Victoria?"

Oh, yeah. She hadn't yet answered. What should she say? "I just don't want you to," she finally lied. Time to change the subject. "So...did you drink from anyone last night or this morning?"

The moment she asked, and so snappily, too, she wished she hadn't. Finally she understood what he had gone through every time he'd thought of her mouth pressed into someone else, their blood filling her up. How he'd hated it but had had to accept it, because she'd needed to drink from others to survive.

She despised the thought of him drinking from some-one else. Despised the thought of his teeth inside some other girl's vein. And yes, she wanted to kill the stupid girl!

Stupid—because anyone who messed with Victoria's boyfriend deserved what she got.

Who are you?

And was he still her boyfriend?

"I haven't drunk from anyone. Yet. I'll find someone," he replied, completely unaware—or unconcerned—with her rising anger. "When I'm ready." He flicked her a glance, his gaze dropping straight to her neck, tracking her pulse like the predator he'd become.

Perhaps she was the stupid one, because she tossed her hair over one shoulder, offering him an irresistible view. *Trying to tempt him, Vic?*

No. Never.

Really?

Fine. Yes. I am trying to tempt him. He's mine!

And now she was talking to herself. The day improved by the minute.

"Have *you* fed today?" he asked in that casual tone.

Disappointment crashed through her. So much for tempting him. "Yes. Of course, I have."

His eyes narrowed, creating tiny slits where each

individual lash was visible and his violet eyes were able to laser down at her. Violet eyes? Again? "On who?" he demanded.

On what was a more fitting question. For the first time in *ever,* she'd eaten food. Real food, with weird textures and flavors she'd before tasted only in liquid nutrient form. As of last night, her need for blood had begun to dwindle. Oh, she still craved it (kind of), still needed it (sort of), but she also needed something else. Something solid.

She'd had to sneak down to the slave quarters and raid their fridge. She could have gone to the wolf quarters, but they would have scented her out and known she'd been there, and she'd rather avoid a conversation about her new eating habits.

She hadn't known what to pick, so she'd hidden two balls of cheese in her robe—her breasts had looked so perky and large!—snuck back to her room, and nibbled on them, surprised by how much she enjoyed the rich, smoky flavor.

Maybe her declining interest in blood was the reason Chompers wouldn't shut up. *He* was the reason she still needed to drink, after all, and since she hadn't fed him breakfast, he was probably starving. Poor guy.

Poor guy?

Her wards were in place, so that wasn't the issue. Before, with her vampire skin, those wards had lasted a few weeks, no longer, and she'd had to re-ink them. She'd had these new ones for four days and they hadn't even begun to fade.

"Victoria. I asked you a question."

Right. She had to stop retreating into her own head. "Uh, you don't know him." Truth. Cheese came from cows, and there was no way Aden had met this particular cow.

"Tell me his name anyway."

"So you can kill him?" she asked hopefully. Soliciting a massacre wasn't her objective, but a jealous Aden was a caring Aden.

"Never mind." He waved away her reply. "It doesn't matter."

Hopes dashed again.

Something vibrated against her side, and she yelped. Aden glanced down at her, confused and maybe just a little concerned. Hopes reignited.

A yo-yo, that's what she was.

"Are you okay?" he asked.

"I think—" Another vibration, another yelp. What the—her phone, she realized with relief. Only her phone. "Yes, I'm fine."

She stuffed her free hand into the robe's only pocket and withdrew the small, plastic devise. She'd started to carry one after meeting Aden, so that he could call if he needed her. So far, he hadn't called, but Riley was certainly taking advantage. His number was different every time, the little thief, but his message was always the same. How many *This is bullshit!* texts could she get from him?

"A message from Riley," she said. "Give me a sec. I have to reply."

This is bullshit! she read. Got MA 2 safety & T is about 2 ruin it.

T. Tucker. Victoria hated Tucker. After releasing Aden's hand—which she hated to do—she typed, Kill him. Make it hurt. In her haste, she typed "hart" but didn't realize until too late.

"How is he?" Aden asked. He wound his arm around her waist, guiding her out of the way of trees as her attention wavered between her phone and what was ahead of her. Well, well. While the hand-holding had been as delightful as finding a rainbow, this was like finding the pot of gold at the end of it. She absorbed his heat, felt her cells waking up, responding to him.

"Good." Another vibration and she read, Hart? Ha!

CID. Soon. SOB's helping 2. Another vibration, a new text. How's BK doing?

BK. Boy King. Riley had started calling Aden by the stupid nickname in earlier texts and hadn't stopped. On mend.

Ask him if the name Tyson means anything.

"Does the name Tyson mean anything to you?"

"Tyson?" Aden asked.

"Mmm-hmm."

A moment passed. "No. Should it?"

"Don't know." She asked Riley.

We'll talk about it later. Call if u need me.

K.

I'll call when Tuck has bled out.

Her lips twitched as she returned the phone to her pocket.

Aden didn't ask what they'd discussed. He just changed the subject, saying, "Elijah says I'm now like you. My personality, I mean."

"Of course Elijah is blaming me for the change. He doesn't like me. None of them do," she said, then his words sank in, and she gasped. "Wait, what?" Her step faltered, tripping her, dislodging Aden's hold. When she straightened, she glared at his still moving form. Never mind that she'd had the same thought yesterday. She'd been more inclined to blame her father. "Aden!"

He turned back to face her, frowned at the distance between them and approached. Again she absorbed his heat. Now that her cells were fully awake, they practically quivered in rapture, being this close to him.

How she would have loved it if he'd deigned to return her glare, but no. His expression remained blank. "He says you left pieces of your character inside me. Like when I gave you the souls, and you gave me Chompers." His head tilted to the side, his gaze moving past her, past the forest, as if he were listening to someone else. He probably was. Then he nodded and said, "And when we drank from each other."

She ran her tongue over her teeth. Her sharp, useless teeth. "You're saying this uncaring, very nearly unlikable act is because of *me?*" *You thought the same thing,* she reminded herself. *How can you be mad at him?*

She didn't know, but she was. *Very* mad.

"Yes. That's what I'm saying." Offered with no hesitation.

That was how people saw her? Cold, distant? Oh, she'd known they considered her too serious, but this... Ugh, ugh, *ugh.* "Why aren't I acting like you, then?"

"Maybe you are."

"What does that mean?"

"I don't know. You tell me."

Her chin lifted. "You mean I'm acting confused, tuning in and out of our conversations, distracted all the time, and throwing jealous fits?" Wait. She *was*. Her eyes widened as realization struck. She really was.

"Was that how you saw me?" he asked, parroting her thoughts. He took a menacing step toward her, then another.

She backed away slowly, trying not to be obvious in her cowardice—and her desire. Her quivering became outright shaking, her need to be touched by him overshadowing everything else, making her ache.

He didn't stop coming, and she didn't stop retreating until her back pressed into a thick tree trunk. She might crave him, but she didn't know this Aden, didn't know how he'd react to the things she did and said.

Although, if Elijah was correct, she could guess. If Aden was acting like her, he would try and resist her, but he would fail. Just as she'd always failed to resist him. He would try and dislike her, try to detach himself from her, but again, he would fail.

Finally, a blessing amidst a curse.

When she'd first met him, she had been following orders from her father. Find him, interrogate him, and kill him. She'd found him all right. She'd interrogated him—kind of. While her father had expected screams of pain to spring from the question-and-answer session, she'd ended up swimming with Aden, playing with him. Kissing him.

She'd told herself she didn't—couldn't—like him. He was food, nothing more. She'd told herself to remain disconnected from the situation, to do what needed to be done. Aden had summoned her kind to Oklahoma, he hummed with a kind of power none of them understood but were drawn to, a power the beasts inside them yearned for and basically worshipped, and he could do serious damage to their race. Killing him would have been a mercy to her people.

Killing him, though, had never been an option for Victoria. She had been intrigued by him, had identified with him. He was an outsider to his own kind; he was misunderstood, unwanted. She wasn't an outsider, but as a princess she *was* set apart. And it hadn't helped that she'd always been a disappointment to her father. She wasn't a warrior like her sister Lauren, and she wasn't a volatile force of nature like Stephanie.

She was just…herself.

Aden flattened his hands at her temples, his lower body brushing against hers and pulling a delighted gasp right out of her. He'd caged her in, surrounded her, becoming all that she saw. All she wanted to see.

"You *are* tuning in and out of our conversations," he said. There was no heat to his tone, but maybe…maybe there were threads of amusement?

"That doesn't prove anything," she said, just to provoke him. What would he do? How far would he take this?

"Let's test the theory, then."

"How?"

His nose brushed against hers, his breath fanning over her cheeks, warm and minty. "How would you like to test it?"

Was he going to kiss her? Her heart sped into hyperdrive, her veins expanding to accommodate the increase of blood flow. She ran her tongue over her lips, her gaze melting into his. "I—I don't know."

"I do," he said darkly, huskily. "First, do I have *all* your attention?"

"Yes."

"Good. That's step one. Now for step two."

Without any more explanation, he settled his mouth over hers, soft, exploring. Her breath hitched as she tasted him. Then, he pressed harder, opened up, and licked at her. She opened up, too, welcoming him inside, and their tongues rolled together. Her hands slid up his chest, around his neck and tangled in his hair.

"I like step two," she rasped, so happy this was happening, she could have burst. "But it doesn't prove anything."

Kiss. "Well, we'll worry about that later." Kiss.

She chuckled, loving this teasing side of him. A side she'd missed terribly.

They stayed like that, kissing and touching, for countless minutes, hours maybe, and finally, blessedly, her body began to warm. As delighted as she was about that, she wished Aden would pet her as he'd used to do. She wanted his hands on her, all over her.

Soon she got her wish. Not skin-to-skin contact, but his hands began to roam, exploring her, molding her, shaping, driving her to kiss him harder, until little moans were escaping the back of her throat, until she was panting, biting at him.

To his credit, he didn't bite her back. His touch did strengthen, though, becoming rougher. And she liked it.

"Aden," she said, not sure why she was saying his name.

A moment later, she felt as if she were falling... falling...brittle leaves and cold dirt suddenly supporting her, Aden's weight pinning her down. The kiss never slowed. They clutched at each other, rubbed at each other. Her body was sensitized, racing toward…something with every move she made.

He did finally pull away to cup her jaw. He, too, was panting. Little beads of sweat popped up on his brow.

"Have you been with anybody?" he asked. There was a gruff quality to his voice. A quality she loved.

"You mean sex?"

He nodded, his gaze straying to her neck. A second later, he was kissing her there, licking, sucking but still not biting. And, oh, the sensations he evoked. She was being devoured by them, every inch of her ablaze.

Rather than answer, she said shakily, "Have you?"

"No."

But…but…he was so beautiful. Even if human girls considered him crazy, they should have been all over him. Actually, they should have been all over him *because* they considered him crazy. Weren't bad boys attractive to one and all? Someone to be tamed or something?

Her betrothed, Dmitri, had been a bad boy among the vampires, and the females had flocked to him.

"Why not?" Her hands began an exploration of their own, sliding down the strength of his chest, tugging at the softness of his shirt, then slipping under it. Finally. Hot-as-a-furnace skin.

"Never trusted anyone enough."

Did he trust her enough? Or at all? She hoped so, because she would never betray him. Ever.

"What about you?" he asked, planting kisses along her jaw.

Her nails curled into him. She didn't want to answer. Not after hearing his reply. "Well…"

He lifted his head, and she moaned in frustration. His eyes glowed a brilliant amber-brown now, tiny flecks of violet and green swirling in the background. Such gorgeous, mesmerizing eyes.

"Yes," she admitted softly. "I have."

His hold tightened on her. "With who?"

Would he think badly of her now? She didn't want to tell him, so she said, "I was curious. I was betrothed to Dmitri, as you know, and as you also know, I hated him and, well—"

"Dmitri? You slept with *Dmitri?* Whom you hated?" There was a faint trace of outrage in his tone.

Even that minute amount angered her, cooling the hottest of the flames licking over her. "No. Not Dmitri. But what if it *was* him? What would you do? What would you say?"

"I don't know," he answered honestly.

A few more flames crackled and hissed their way to extinction. "*Anyway*. I didn't want him to be my first because, as you said, I hated him." She'd debated keeping herself pure for him, even though that wasn't a vampire tradition or requirement. She'd debated simply because Dmitri had been a jealous, possessive sort, and he would have hurt whoever she'd picked.

Finally, a few months before traveling to Oklahoma, she'd decided to go for it, just get it over with and pick someone who could hold his own against her fiancé. A mistake that she regretted, but one she couldn't change.

"And for your information," she went on, "we don't have as staunch a view about sex as you humans do. My father had about a thousand wives, you know."

Frost glazed his eyes. "So who were you with?"

Like she'd go there with him. "It doesn't matter."

"He's still alive and here, then. And that means I can—" Suddenly silent, Aden stiffened against her, his gaze jolting up and narrowing. "Someone's coming." He sniffed. "Female. Familiar."

Her ears perked, but she didn't hear anything.

He lifted from her and stood, and though she'd been on a downward spiral and had despised the direction of their conversation, she already mourned the separation, resented the interruption.

Without a word, he reached down and helped her do the same. Her knees almost buckled as she brushed the debris from her robe, her attention never leaving him. His skin was flushed, tension vibrating from him. While he didn't have fangs, his teeth were bared in a fearsome scowl. His lips were swollen—perhaps she'd bitten too hard—and his hair nearly stood on end.

Crunching leaves, snapping twigs.

Someone *was* coming. How had Aden heard before she had? *Again?* She swung around and saw Maddie the Lovely rushing toward them, long blond hair flying behind her.

"Your majesty," the girl called, grinding to a halt when she spotted him.

Aden stepped in front of Victoria. To shield her from a possible threat? *Please, please, please.* That would mean her Aden was returning, the parts of Victoria fading. Right?

"Yes?" Aden prompted.

"You have visitors." Maddie focused on Victoria, worry in her eyes, before returning her attention to Aden. "The councilmen suggested you hurry."

Dread slithered through Victoria, a snake determined

to squeeze the life out of her. Visitors. Allies? Or enemies? Either way, Aden was hungry and hadn't yet fed. Until he did, everyone in the mansion would be in danger. Because the longer he went without blood, the more he would weaken, the more the hunger would strengthen, until he just sort of snapped, attacking everyone around him.

"You need to feed first," she said to him. Though it pained her, she added, "On Maddie." The sooner the better.

Vampires *could* satisfactorily feed on other vampires. It wasn't ideal, not only because of the skin issue, but also because, when you drank from another vampire, you saw the world through their eyes. At least for a little while.

A distraction like that could cost Aden his life. But, he would have a few hours before his focus merged with Maddie's. That should give him plenty of time to deal with the visitors. And later, Victoria could guard him in her bedroom.

"No. No vampires," Aden said with a shake of his head. "Victoria, teleport to the stronghold and bring me a blood-slave."

He wasn't fighting her on the issue, and she wasn't sure if that made her happy or sad. Or angry. "I...can't," she admitted quietly. She'd tried to teleport to him this morning, when Riley's brothers had informed her of his summons, and she'd failed miserably.

Depression had nearly overwhelmed her. She wasn't normal anymore. She was a freak among her own kind. And honest to God, walking from one place to the other, without the option of simply appearing, sucked.

Sucked. Another human word. When would the madness end?

"Why?" Aden asked.

"I just can't."

He remained quiet for a moment, absorbing her claim. Whether he deduced what it meant or not, when even she wasn't one hundred percent certain herself, he didn't say. He just nodded. "All right, then. We'll walk back to the stronghold together."

"But you need to—"

"Maddie," he said, cutting Victoria off. "Lead the way."

The girl nodded and obeyed, and Aden followed after her. Victoria remained in place for several heartbeats of time. Neither Aden nor Maddie looked back at her. Or around for her. She wanted to do something to keep Aden from the house and whoever had come for him. She wanted to protect him. But how?

The farther away Aden got, the more the roaring in

her head increased in volume, until she couldn't concentrate. "Shut up, Chompers!"

Another roar.

"Fine." And wouldn't you know it? Now she was talking to the thing in her head like Aden often had. Gritting her teeth, she trudged after him.

ELEVEN

MARY ANN WANTED TO SCREAM. In the end, she allowed herself only to snap, "That's enough. Both of you."

Ignoring her, Tucker and Riley faced off. Again. After running all night, stealing a car, stealing bleach for her hair—she was still rebelling about that and hadn't used it—stealing tattoo equipment, breaking into a motel room, commandeering it, she needed a freaking moment of peace before the three of them had to leave and steal another car.

"I can't believe you want this piece of crap to live," Riley said.

"Apparently she likes pieces of crap. Look who she's dating." Tucker snickered at him.

"I do not like crap." Geez! They were like children. Feral, rabies-infected children who needed to be put down. "And I was dating him. *Was*. Not anymore." Sadly.

Riley growled low in his throat, a definite war cry, looking from Tucker to her, her to Tucker, as if he didn't know who to be angrier at. Great. That was just great. If he turned that snarl on her, she'd be the one to do a little murdering!

"Just shut up, Tucker, before Riley stops listening to me and finally snacks on your bone marrow. Riley, I believe we have a few things to do before we head out."

He considered her, the menace draining from him.

"Take off your shirt," he said, clearly deciding to play nice, "and lie on the bed. And if you sneak a peek, T-man, I will break every bone in your body."

"Oh, I'll sneak a peek. I'll sneak several." Tucker rubbed his hands together with glee. "And guess what, *R-man*. There will be one more bone in my body for you to break."

Gross. Just gross.

Another growl erupted from Riley. He stepped closer to Tucker, only a whisper of air separating them.

Mary Ann jumped between them and shoved, keeping both of her arms extended. A puny effort, but they were kind enough to pretend she could do some damage of her own and remained apart.

Of course, that didn't stop the verbal sparring.

"Jackass."

"Pansy."

"Pervert."

"Asshole."

Silence—except for the harshness of Riley's breathing.

"Very mature," she said on a sigh.

"What are wards, anyway?" Tucker asked, as if he hadn't just acted like a baby and Riley wasn't once again planning his murder.

"Do you not care about the rabid dog about to chew off your face?" she muttered. Before he could answer with something snide, she replied, "Wards are protective spells. That way, the witches have less power over us. Now back off. Both of you."

"No one can overpower *me,*" Tucker said, ignoring her demand.

"Underestimating them is a mistake," she said. "They once cast a death curse over me, Riley and Victoria, and we barely survived."

"Let's not forget the witches are viewing you through magic," Riley said. "We need to get on with this."

Mary Ann watched Tucker raze a hand through his hair. "I always knew there were other...things out there," he said. "Different, like me. I just didn't know it'd be something lame like witches and wolves."

She arched a brow. Her arms were shaking—*note to self: start working out*—but she kept them extended. "And demons are cool?"

"Hell, yeah." Just then, his tone was *too* cocky. And she knew.

He was lying. For sure. He hated himself. And having heard tidbits of gossip about his abusive father, she knew Tucker hated him, too. "Anyway," she went on, "once a spell is cast, not even the witches can stop it from being fulfilled. Whatever conditions they set have to be met. Like with the death curse, we had a week to make a meeting. If we failed to appear, or rather, if Aden did, we all died."

"If Vlad had known you guys were cursed, he would have simply locked Aden away, allowing that week to tick by, rather than siccing me on him. The whole stabbing thing could have been avoided. So really, you guys carry the blame for the past. Had you told people—"

"Riley, Victoria and me would have died."

Tucker shrugged. "That wouldn't have been my problem."

"And now?" Riley demanded. "Are you helping Vlad now?"

"He stopped summoning me after I stabbed Aden, so I took off. I didn't like helping him, you know. And for the record, I apologized to Aden. Before *and* after I sliced his heart in two. Cut me some slack."

Anger had Riley's eyes snapping with green fire. "You apologized. Oh, well, then. That smoothes everything over."

"Finally." Tucker raised his arms, the last sane man in the world. "Someone understands."

Riley stepped around Mary Ann and shoved the guy. Hard. "I'm sorry." Shoved again. "Oops. Sorry. My bad. All smoothed? Forgive me?" Another shove.

Tucker took the abuse without striking back. *Shocking.*

Mary Ann maneuvered them back on track. "I'm not taking off my shirt. Okay? So just stand down, boys. And you can ward my arms, Riley. That'll work just as well as my back and chest."

"Fine." At least he stopped pushing.

Already she had tattoos on her back to protect her against mind manipulation and mortal wounds. Now he wanted to ensure she was protected against another death curse, as well as magical illusions—he'd learned his lesson with Tucker—and pain and panic and spying spells.

"Wait, wait, wait. Back up." Riley shook his head, the tension draining from him as he faced her. "Your dad will see your arms."

Yes, she knew that. And that would absolutely matter if she ever planned to see her dad again.

A wave of homesickness hit her, tears suddenly welling in her eyes. She'd been gone only two weeks, but she already missed her dad like crazy. But she had to stay away from him, too. She would not bring a supernatural war to his doorstep.

Rather than offering a reply, however, she sat at the edge of the bed and rolled up her shirtsleeves. "Stop wasting time. Get to work."

"You really don't plan on going back, do you?" Tucker asked. For once, his tone was without sarcasm, flippancy or pure meanness.

"No," she said flatly. "I don't. Riley." She stretched out on the creaking mattress, praying she didn't leave with bedbugs. Or worse. "Begin." Or she might chicken out.

He looked her over before closing the distance, kneeling at her side and settling her arm in his lap. Contact. Sizzling, earth-shattering, necessary. Somehow, she maintained a blank expression.

"You've changed," he said.

"In two weeks?" She wanted to snort. She couldn't. He was right.

"Yeah." He'd already placed the equipment on the nightstand, the ink ready to go. He lifted the tiny gun and pressed the needle deep. There was a sharp sting, a persistent burn and the buzz of the little motor. Maybe her homesickness had toughened her up—she didn't even flinch.

"Do you think I've changed for the better?" *Stop. Don't pursue this. You might not like what you learn.*

"I liked you how you were."

He sounded bitter. She *had* to pursue. "Which was weak? Reliant on you?"

"You weren't weak."

"Well, I wasn't strong, either."

"And you're strong now?"

Ouch. "I'm *stronger.* So you don't like me now?" *Why are you pursuing this?*

"I like you. What I don't like is the company you keep," he added loudly.

"This is boring," Tucker said, pacing at the edge of the bed. "Someone entertain me."

They ignored him.

"How did you and Tucker hook up?" Riley asked. His touch became more aggressive. "And I don't mean that in the romantic sense. Unless there's something you need to tell me. And if that's the case—"

"It's not, there's not," she rushed to assure him. Things might be over between them, but she didn't want him to think she'd jumped into something with Tucker. "After stabbing Aden—which I still haven't forgiven him for—" she said just as loudly as Riley had "—Tucker came looking for me. He saw me leave my house with a bag and followed me."

"*I* followed you. You did everything in your power to lose me. Him, you kept around." Yep. That was bitterness, pure and fervent. More than that, "him" had been said with so much disgust, Riley could have been discussing a case of raging diarrhea.

In his mind, he probably was.

"Yeah," she said, tone softening, "but I *care* about hurting you."

"Nice, Mary Ann," Tucker said dryly. "Real nice."

They ignored him.

Riley paused. Set the ink gun aside, and reached for her. His fingers traced over her jaw, caressing. Mary Ann didn't mean to, but she leaned into the familiar, calloused touch, her eyes closing. Just then, they were the only two people in the world.

She breathed him in, pretending she was normal, he

was normal, everything was normal. That wild, earthy scent of his reminded her of the outdoors, and she wished for more, was desperate for more—until she remembered what had happened to the last creatures of the night she'd encountered and couldn't pretend anymore.

They'd convulsed, their skin paling…paling…until they'd become chalk white, resembling painted Halloween decorations. Bruises had formed under their eyes, their lips had chapped, and they'd screamed. And screamed and screamed and screamed, the pain too much to bear.

"Mary Ann."

She must have stiffened. Her eyelids sprang apart, and she saw that Riley was frowning with concern. Concern. No, no, no. "Did I hurt you?" she asked in a rush. Had she drained him, even a little?

"I'm fine. You didn't hurt me."

The concern had been for her, then. She relaxed, but only slightly. Why did he have to be so wonderful? "You'd tell me if I did?"

"Of course. I'm not the suffer-in-silence type."

No, he wasn't. Something she'd always loved about him.

"How are *you?*" he asked. "Are you…feeding properly?"

"Not yet. I've been living off my immense overindulgence, but the full feeling is fading," she admitted. "I'll be hungry very soon."

"Very soon isn't now. We have time."

Time together, he was saying. Time before she had to start worrying.

When would he learn? She *always* worried. "Just finish the wards," she said on a sigh.

"All right. But this conversation isn't over."

Yeah, it was, but she didn't comment, and a few hours later, she was the proud owner of six new wards.

"Sexy," Tucker said, wiggling his brows at her.

"Do you want me to pluck out your eyes?" Riley snapped as he dismantled the equipment and stuffed it into a bag.

"Fine." Tucker held up his hands, all innocence. "She looks disgusting."

Disgusting? "Thanks a lot, you traitor."

Tucker shrugged, unapologetic. "We tried dating, we failed. Therefore I know not to put my eggs in your basket. If I do, they'll be met with a hammer."

Okay. Were eggs a metaphor for his balls? Because *that* was disgusting. Still, it had Riley nodding, genuinely happy for the first time all day.

"You're not putting your eggs in my basket, either," she informed him.

He, too, shrugged. "You'll change your mind."

"Just...keep your lips away from me!" If he kissed her, she'd cave, she always did. His mouth weakened her, and that was that.

He gave her a secret smile, one that promised he'd be all over her when they were alone. And she'd like it. She shivered. *No being alone with the wolf!*

"I didn't say anything about kissing you. Did I?"

"Sick, just sick." Tucker pretended to gag. "Stop flirting in front of the innocent bystander."

"I doubt you've ever been innocent," she said dryly.

"And don't you have somewhere to be?" Riley demanded. "Like with your pregnant girlfriend?"

Penny. Mary Ann hadn't yet called her today and wondered if the girl was still hunched over a toilet, vomiting out her guts.

For the first time since Tucker had stepped in front of Mary Ann, begging her to let him help her so that he could make up for what he'd done to Aden, claiming he only felt "right" when he was with her, that he could fight his darker urges as long as he kept her close, he appeared utterly defeated.

"Penny will find happiness without me," he said without emotion.

"Well, her—your—baby won't. He'll be part demon, and Pen needs help raising him."

His defeated pallor washed away with the flush of longing.

Did he…could he really…love Penny and want the baby? Maybe some part of him did. But maybe he also knew being with them would destroy them in ways leaving them alone wouldn't. His dark nature might cause him to do things he would regret for the rest of his life.

Mary Ann knew the feeling. Being without Riley was *killing* her. She missed him a little more every day—even missed him while he was beside her—but she would do anything, *anything,* to keep him safe.

"So, are you done with Mary Ann? Tell me you're done. Because I'm ready for my turn," Tucker said, rubbing his hands together a second time.

Riley snorted. "Yeah. Right."

"Hey, I don't want to be cursed, either. And as I'm a valued member of this team."

"Our definition of *valued* must differ."

Tucker popped his jaw. "Just like our definition for *shifter* must differ. To you it probably means *one who can change shapes.* To me it just means *asshole.*"

"How about I ward you with permanent impotence?" Riley withdrew the gun and shook it at him. "How about that?"

"Unnecessarily cruel, wolf. I'm hurt. Really." Tucker wiped pretend tears from his eyes. "Those witches and fairies are hot, and if I'm captured by one of them, I need to be in working order. You remember how I like to *work,* don't you, Mary Ann?"

Oh, no. He wasn't dragging her into this. "We never had sex, and you know it."

"You were too busy nailing everyone else," Riley snarled at him.

"Yeah, like your mom," Tucker said.

"My mother is dead."

There was a beat of silence. "Yeah, like your dad," Tucker said without an ounce of remorse.

Actually, Riley's dad was dead, too. No reason to mention that aloud, allowing Tucker to come up with someone else he could have nailed. "You two are such… guys," she said, standing.

"He's a guy." Riley shrugged. "For the most part."

Tucker's eyes narrowed. "What are you saying? The rest of me is a girl?"

"Hey." Riley held up his hands, palms out, in a mimic

of Tucker's earlier profession of innocence. "I'm not the one who admitted to nailing a dude."

"That was a lie, Fido. An insult to your parents that you're clearly too dumb to get."

"Can we go now?" Mary Ann asked before they could fight. Again.

"Yes," Riley said at the same time Tucker said, "Whatever."

Thankfully they traveled the fifteen miles to Dr. Daniel Smart's former residence without incident. She would have preferred to go alone, but hey. At five, she'd wanted a pony. She'd learned to live with disappointment.

No one answered the door after a bout of hard knocking from Riley, followed by an equally hard bout of knocking from Tucker, as if even that was a competition, but their little group of dysfunction didn't leave. They sat on the porch swing, Mary Ann the meat in a testosterone sandwich, and waited.

She'd checked the county records, and Dr. Smart's wife still owned this place. So, Tonya Smart hadn't changed the name on the deed, which most likely meant she hadn't remarried.

Maybe she'd rented it out, though. Maybe she wasn't here because she worked weekends. Maybe she would take one look at Mary Ann and tell her to get lost. She definitely wouldn't want to answer questions akin to, "Was your husband a weirdo who could raise the dead?" But Mary Ann was going to try.

The sun shone brightly, clouds floating by and obscuring the golden rays every few minutes. Mist formed in front of her face every time she breathed. As she unrolled her shirtsleeves for added warmth, she asked, "How's Aden?" ashamed for not asking sooner. In her defense, he was the reason she was here.

"Recovering," was all Riley said. "No thanks to Tuck."

"Can you just let it go?" Tucker snapped. "I said I was sorry."

"Absolutely I can let it go. The day you're dead."

Mary Ann pinched the bridge of her nose, certain her head would explode by the end of the day. She had never wanted to become a referee, but that's what they had reduced her to. Next go-round, she was going to demand a paycheck!

After two hours of the back-and-forth insults, her headache was more of an enemy than the witches and the fairies, and she was very close to convincing herself Tonya Smart *couldn't* help her. Of course, that's when she heard the purr of a car motor, the crunch of tires coming up the drive.

Mary Ann hopped to her feet. Her butt had fallen asleep, and the abrupt movement awakened it with a vengeance.

"Let me do the talking," she told the boys.

"What are you going to say?" Tucker asked.

"Just watch and learn, demon," Riley said. "She'll say the right thing, that's what."

Tucker pouted. "You told him your plan, but didn't tell me?"

"No. He just trusts me. Now zip it." She hadn't told either one of them because she hadn't yet figured out what angle to pursue. But this was crunch time. She had to figure it out *now*.

Ms. Smart emerged from the vehicle. She was in her mid-fifties, with light brown hair, a trim form, her clothes neat and tidy. She was pretty in a motherly way, and at one time, she'd probably been beautiful.

She carried a sack of groceries and smiled warmly as she approached. Mary Ann wished she could see her eyes, but they were hidden behind sunglasses.

"Can I help you?"

She was human, Mary Ann thought, surprised her

mind now worked that way. Nowadays, the first time she met someone new, she immediately sized them up.

"Her aura is black," Riley muttered, and he sounded confused.

What exactly did that mean? No time to ask. "Yes, you can help me. My name is Mary Ann. You're Tonya Smart, right?"

"Right," she replied, just a bit hesitant now.

Finally. A break. "I'm just...well, my mother died the same day as your husband." Was she really going there, right from the beginning? "In the same hospital." Yep. She was. "She gave birth to me, and...that was it. The end." How stupid did she sound?

Some of the warmth faded, wariness taking its place. "I'm sorry for your loss."

"Thank you. I'm sorry for yours, as well."

Ms. Smart nodded in acknowledgment, shifting the grocery sack to her other arm. Her gaze must have skidded over the boys, because the wariness became laced with fear. "Why are you telling me this? Why are you here?"

"We won't hurt you," Mary Ann assured her. "The boys can leave if they bother you. In fact," she said, glancing at them, "go. Now."

Though Riley looked like he wanted to protest, he

reached out, grabbed Tucker by the shirt collar and dragged him away. They didn't go far, stopping under a large oak in the front yard.

"So which one are you dating?" Ms. Smart asked.

"Neither. The dark-haired one. Neither," she added.

Smart laughed, relaxing once more. "Oh, to be young again."

Mary Ann found herself studying the boys. Riley, with his dark hair and rough, fighter face, resembled a devil. Tucker, with his pale hair and innocent features, resembled an angel. Yet, personality-wise, the opposite was true. *Doesn't matter right now.*

She returned her focus to the woman and cleared her throat. "One of my friends was born that same day in the same hospital. St. Mary's," she added, in case Ms. Smart thought she was lying. Proof was in the details, after all. "He's looking for his parents."

Confusion flittered across that aging face. "And you think my Daniel could be his father?"

"No, nothing like that. It's just, my friend…and me… we…can do…things. Weird things." From the corner of her eye, she could see Riley fighting the urge to close the distance and sweep her away. She shouldn't be admitting this. To anyone. Especially not to a virtual stranger who might mention what she'd said to the wrong people. People who could come after Mary Ann and Aden. There was no other way, however.

Besides, she'd done her homework. Daniel Smart had to be Julian. The pieces just fit. "I wondered if…"

"What?" Smart insisted.

"I wondered if Mr. Smart could do…weird things, too."

A heavy pause, then, "Weird things. Like what?"

She couldn't say it. She just couldn't.

"Never mind," Smart said a split second later, her voice cold. "I want you to leave. Don't come here again."

"Please, Mrs. Smart. This is a matter of life and death."

The older woman pounded up the stairs and skidded around Mary Ann. At the mention of *death*, however, she paused at the door. Without facing Mary Ann, she whispered, "Are you trying to…raise someone?"

Raise someone—from the dead. She knew. She really knew! Someone ignorant of what Julian could do would not have known to ask that kind of question. Mary Ann wanted to whoop. "No, no, I promise you. Nothing like that." By sheer will alone, she managed to remain sedate. "I'm just trying to find the person who could… raise something. A person who died the same day I was born. Someone who might have…passed that ability to someone else."

If Daniel Smart *was* Julian, his last wish might have been to talk with this woman. Tossing out these half truths as she was, Mary Ann risked alienating her, but she couldn't just spill the entire truth, either. Not yet.

Silence. More of that dreadful silence.

Then, "My Daniel couldn't do what you're asking."

"Oh." She'd been so certain. Maybe…maybe Smart was lying. There simply wasn't another explanation for what Mary Ann had read.

"But his brother could," the woman finished.

Okay. There *was* another explanation.

"He disappeared that night, too, and hasn't been heard from since. Now please. Leave. And remember what I told you. Don't come back here. You're not welcome."

✝WELVE

An hour later, Mary Ann found herself nestled inside The Wire Bean. The ridiculous name aside, she liked the place. The internet café was cozy, with plush couches and small round tables, as well as booths with multiple plug-ins right there on the side.

She pretended to sip a mocha latte—because actually drinking it would have made her sick. Human food was no longer hers to enjoy, only the magic and powers of others. Not that she was bitter. Except that she was freaking bitter!

Anyway. The drink had been "paid for" by Tucker.

His version of "let me get this" was casting an illusion so that the girl at the register—who'd smiled and flirted with him and Riley to an annoying degree—thought she'd been handed a twenty when in reality, Tucker had handed her a nice helping of air.

Riley had voiced a complaint. Tucker had looked at him and said, "Really, Rover? You stole Mary Ann a laptop, and you question *my* methods? Really?"

"Yes, really."

"At least my victim isn't going to cry all night about losing the first ten pages of his book report."

"Well, aren't you just the do-gooder," the shifter sneered.

At one time—like, an hour ago—all of this bickering would have bothered her. Right now? Hardly a blip on her radar. She was busy.

Of course, then they'd argued about who got to sit next to her. Flattering, as well as insulting, since it was merely a pissing contest and not a true desire to be near her. Riley won. Barely. And only because he tripped Tucker and the boy fell face-first into the coffee-stained tile.

Now her shifter was leaning back, his arm stretched out behind her, and Tucker sat across from her, scowling at them. Mary Ann continued to pretend to sip and type, breathing in the delightful fumes while searching for answers about Daniel Smart's brother, Robert.

"You know," Tucker said. "I'm actually a pretty good guy when it's just me and Mary Ann. You kind of harsh my mellow, Fido."

"I'll pretend *that's* true."

"It's true," Mary Ann said without looking up from the screen. "Just like I negate Aden's abilities when I'm around him, I negate Tucker's evil."

"I'd argue the word *evil*," Tucker said.

"And you," she went on, ignoring the demon, "negate my negating ability."

"Poor Tucker," Riley sneered. "Having to deal with being a bad boy."

"And don't you care that I'm calling you by different dog names, *Max?*" Tucker said with an obvious sulk.

"No. And by the way, Max is my brother's name."

"Wait." Tucker leaned forward, lips twitching into a grin. "Your brother is a wolf-shifter and his name is Max?"

"Yeah. So?"

"So you do know that's, like, the most popular dog name of the year?"

"What are you, a statistical handbook?"

Frowning, Tucker ran a hand through his hair. "If you're not gonna react to insults the right way, I'm not sticking around. First I called you Fido. No reaction. Then I called you Max, and you corrected me. You're lame." He slid from the booth. "I'll be outside. Smoking. Maybe drinking."

"Don't stab anyone," Riley said with a wave of his fingers.

His expression darkened. "Do you have anything to add to this conversation, Mary Ann?"

"That's great," she said distractedly, having already tuned them out.

He pushed out a sigh. "Find me when you're done."

"Sure, sure," Riley assured him. Then flipped him off.

Tucker stomped out of the café, the bell chiming over the door.

"What a douche," Riley muttered. "I'm going to kill him before this is over, you know that, right?"

"That's great."

"And you'll be okay with that?"

"That's great."

"You're not listening to a word I'm saying, either, are you?"

"That's great." Seventeen years ago, people had not Facebooked or tweeted their every thought, so finding Robert Smart was a little more than difficult. But she was finally getting somewhere.

She found a news story about him, and that led to another, and another and still another. Each one had to do with Robert Smart's ability to locate dead bodies and communicate with the dead. But none of them mentioned *raising* the dead. More than that, there was no mention of his death. So, she might be getting somewhere, but it wasn't doing her any good. Until—

Bingo! A story about his disappearance. Excitement rushed through her as she read the first few lines. He'd disappeared the same night his brother was killed. And… oh. Disappointment replaced her excitement. "His body was never found, and he never married," she said. "He had no children, no relatives other than Daniel and Tonya." Which meant talking to his family was out. Tonya was likely to call the police if she caught sight of Mary Ann again.

"That's great," Riley said, mimicking her. Then, without taking a breath, he added, "But he could be out there talking to the witches or the fairies, you know."

And if he had no family, what kind of last wish would he have had? Not to say goodbye to them, of course, as Mary Ann's mother had wanted to do with her. So, what had he wanted?

She needed to know. In order to leave Aden, Julian had to do what his human self regretted not doing. But the souls didn't remember their human lives until someone reminded them. Right now, she was the only one who could remind Julian.

"Mary Ann," Riley prompted.

Maybe if she printed out his (previous) life story and read it to him? Maybe then he'd remember. Or, maybe it was time to switch gears and spy on Aden's parents. Yeah, maybe. The deed to their house belonged to Joe Stone. Paula, the mom, hadn't been mentioned. Were they still together? Separated?

"Mary Ann?"

"What?" Oh, yeah. Riley had said something. Robert, witches, fairies. "Of course he's not talking to the witches or the fairies. He's dead."

A long, drawn-out sigh had warm, minty breath washing over her. "I meant Tucker."

"Oh. Then go follow him. Kill him. Whatever. *Please.* I just need a few minutes of peace."

A beat of stunned silence. "Are you trying to get rid of me?"

"Yes. But for some reason, it's not working."

Wonderfully calloused fingers settled on her chin and turned her face. "Mary Ann?" His eyes glittered with amusement.

"What?"

"You're sexy when you're focused." With that, he leaned over and kissed her. Right there in front of everyone, he slipped his tongue into her mouth. He was warm and wet and as delicious as she remembered. She'd never been one for public displays of affection, but she found herself leaning closer, wrapping her arms around him, sinking her hands in his hair.

He knew just how to move his tongue against hers. Just how to apply pressure, how to ease off, how to take her breath and give her his. And the warmth, she couldn't get enough. She pressed closer to him, so close she could feel tendrils of energy flowing into her mouth, down her throat and swirling inside her stomach.

She knew that sensation.

Panic infused her, and she wrenched away. They were both panting, but Riley was glazed with a sheen of perspiration. Her heart raced as she gasped out, "I was about to feed off you."

"I know." There was no upset in his tone, which surprised her.

"And you didn't pull away from me? You idiot!"

His lips quirked up at the corners. "I liked what we were doing."

He was *amused? Idiot* was too kind a word for him. But, see? This was exactly why she'd run away from him. He didn't take his safety seriously.

Scowling at him, Mary Ann dragged her legs between them and pushed him. Right out of the booth.

He landed on his butt with a shocked *humph*. "Get out of here before I...before I...knee you in the balls!"

More quirking. He took his time standing up. "I'll find a witch. If you're hungry, you can—"

Her anger deflated. He was trying to take care of her. How could she stay mad at him? "I'm not." And she wasn't. Not fully. Not yet.

"You know what happens when you let yourself go without...eating. Just let me—"

"No." Yes, she knew what happened. She hurt. Worse than she'd ever hurt in her life. "I'm fine." She didn't want him messing with the witches, possibly getting bespelled—although the impotency thing he'd mentioned to Tucker might do them both some good—and she certainly didn't want to be responsible for another death.

"The witches were going to hurt you. Now you can hurt them first."

Technically that was true. She could hurt them. When her hunger reached the point of pain, she fed without thought or intent. Witches first, fairies second, but one day neither race would be enough. She'd crave the others. The vampires, the shifters. Even humans. But as she was now, only partially hungry, she would have to touch the witch to feed, and she just didn't want to get that up close and personal if she didn't have to. For all the reasons she'd previously mentioned, but also because, well, she *liked* a few of them.

Two—Marie and Jennifer—could have killed her a dozen times. They hadn't. They'd talked to her, instead, and walked away. She kinda felt like she owed them.

"Go find Tucker before I decide *you'll* make a tasty snack," she said. "Wait. First tell me what you meant about Tonya's aura being black."

He frowned as he slid back into the booth. "Usually that means the person is going to die. But hers was an old black, kind of faded to a gray. I've seen that kind of aura a few times before, but usually on people who had somehow cheated death through magic or been cursed for a long, long time."

Was that what would happen to Aden's aura, then? Slowly fade, maybe rot? "So her life was saved through magic? Or she was cursed? Which one?"

"I don't know. I didn't get a magical vibe off her." He shrugged. "But that could just mean the curse is so much a part of her, like her lungs or her heart, that no one can sense it. Or it could mean that magic wasn't used."

"So what you're telling me is that you have no freaking clue?"

"Correct. So what *you're* telling *me* is that you don't

want me to stay with you? Because after that tasty snack comment, I *want* you to—"

"Go, you nympho!"

Laughing, he stood and blew her a kiss, then stalked from the shop. Mary Ann forced her attention to return to her laptop. Her hands were shaking as she typed. And what do you know? She typed without thinking and ended up with a search on Aden's parents. Again. Maybe her subconscious was trying to tell her something.

Fine. She'd go with it. And another thing. Her next ward, she decided, was going to prevent boys from muddying up her thoughts and ruining her concentration. But somehow, she doubted even that could protect her from Riley's appeal.

ADEN SURPRISED VICTORIA. Rather than walking into the throne room, where his "guests" awaited him, and demanding answers, rather than feeding himself, he first prepared himself for the possibility of battle. A task that caused several tension-filled hours to tick by, morning giving way to afternoon.

She listened to a one-sided conversation he had with Elijah and knew Aden was upset because the soul hadn't predicted this, and he hadn't prepared. She listened as he spoke with the councilmen, then Maddie, learning what he could about the nine warriors awaiting him. She breathed a sigh of relief when he placed guards and look-outs in every room in the house as well as outside. She watched as he armed himself, looked away as he changed into a new T-shirt and jeans, and waited with him for the wolves, already tired from patrolling, to come in from the forest.

There was no time to think about their kiss and his anger over her lack of virginity, which was out of char-acter for both past and present Aden. Did he suspect the boy's identity? Would he hate her when the suspicion was confirmed?

Okay, there was time to think about all of that, but she couldn't allow herself the luxury. She needed to focus, to be at her best. Just in case Aden wasn't. He still hadn't eaten, and she didn't know why.

Something else she didn't know—why he had stopped what he was doing, twice, to announce that he wasn't going to dance.

Now he marched along the scarlet rug, Victoria just behind him, wolves flanking him, and a handful of his strongest vampire warriors behind them. Vampire citi-zens lined the walls, watching him, forming a hallway that led straight to the throne room.

Victoria caught whispers like "just appeared,"

"trouble" and "war," and each caused dread to work through her.

Whoever the warriors were, they could obviously teleport, since they had not stormed through the house but had "just appeared" in the throne room. And to appear somewhere, a teleporter had to have been there before. Which meant Vlad had once entertained the warriors.

As Aden approached the throne room, two of his sentries threw open the tall, arched doorways. Without a pause in his stride, the new and as-yet-uncrowned vampire king entered the room. Victoria expected more whispers, something, but the only thing to be heard was the thump of multiple pairs of boots and the scrape of wolf claws. Then Aden stopped, as did everyone behind him, and there wasn't even that. Just silence.

The newcomers—taller and stronger than Victoria had imagined, and she'd imagined *very* tall and *very* strong—formed a backward V. A war formation. Too many times to count, she'd seen her father act as the center of just such a V. It was a pose meant to intimidate, to show unity. A kind of "you mess with one, you mess with all" thing.

The man in front tilted his head to the side. There was no deference to the action, of course, just an I-am-the-scientist-and-you-are-the-lab-rat surety. "At last.

You arrive." He didn't sneer, but the insult was there, an implication that Aden was a coward for having made him wait.

The old Aden might have ignored the implication. The new Aden raised his chin and said, "At last, I honor you with my presence."

A fierce scowl. "We are not your subjects, and we are not honored by you."

"Of course you are."

"No."

"Yes."

"Why, you little—"

The warrior to the speaker's right placed a firm hand on his shoulder, and he pressed his lips together in an obvious bid for calm. The second man said, "We are not the ones who wish to speak with you, Aden the Beast Tamer."

At least they acknowledged his power. Names were important to her kind, identifiers of personality, skill and conquest. Vlad the Impaler. Lauren the Bloodthirsty— which was saying something among a horde of vampires. Stephanie the Exuberant. Victoria the Mediator.

"Who, then?" Aden demanded.

A pause, the eye of the storm, before another male teleported to the head of the V, and every person in the room, save for the newcomers and Aden, gasped in astonishment.

"Me."

"Sorin," she breathed. She'd known he would come, yet seeing him live and in person still managed to astonish and amaze her. Her brother was here. *Her brother was actually here!*

The little girl she used to be wanted to run to him, to throw herself in his arms. They'd never before touched, never spoken, and they'd only met gazes a total of six times. Yet still, the forgotten part of her wanted to do those things and more.

"You know him?" Aden asked her, but didn't wait for her answer. "I think I know him, too." His eyes darkened, then lit back up, going from violet to black, black to violet, as he looked through her. "Is there a way to stop him?"

"Stop…Sorin?"

He frowned, shook his head. "I don't believe you, Elijah."

Of course. The souls were bothering him, but sadly, they were not helping him.

Victoria reached out and twined their fingers, offering what comfort she could while trying to bring him back to the here and now. He blinked, the black gobbling up his eyes and remaining. He gave her a reassuring squeeze, comforting *her*.

Sorin snorted. "I heard you were insane, human. I am glad to see the gossips can get things right every now and then."

Aden's grip tightened, but he did not reply.

"Has Elijah…has he predicted something terrible?" she whispered.

A muscle ticked under his eye. Again he remained silent.

Was he lost to a prediction even now? Trembling, she returned her attention to her brother. "He is not insane," she said. Maybe she could convince these boys to get along. "Underestimating him will get you killed."

Sorin met her gaze. Seven, she thought, keeping score in her head, just as before. His hard expression did not change or soften. Did he even remember her? He'd been gone so very long.

Vampires aged much more slowly than humans. While Victoria was eighty-one years old, she was the equivalent of an eighteen-year-old human. Sorin was just over four hundred years old, yet he looked to be in his mid-twenties, with pale hair and eyes as blue as hers. He was taller than Aden by almost a foot and packed with more muscle than any football star.

"Sister," he said, bowing his head in tribute. "I also heard you were dating the insane human king, but I did not believe it until this moment. And do you really think he could harm me?"

Her first thought: *He remembers.* Her second: *Have I ever been so happy?* Her third: *There is going to be trouble.* Her last: *He remembers!*

"Do not anger him," she said, pleased by the evenness of her voice. No matter what happened, no matter what was said, she had to remain emotionally distanced. If there was one thing Riley had taught her during their many self-defense training sessions, it was that emotions ruined perspective and rationality. "Your beast will not like it and will punish you for it."

A muscle began to tick under *Sorin's* eye. Interesting. He must have experienced his beast's displeasure already.

Sorin's gaze left her to rake Aden up and down. "You do not look like a vampire king."

"Thank you," Aden replied with a nod of his head. Good. He was back in the throne room and out of his head.

"That wasn't a compliment."

A pause. A sigh from Aden. "I'm to tell you that what you're planning will not end well."

Victoria's stomach rolled.

"And exactly what am I planning?" Sorin asked, unconcerned.

"Why spoil the surprise for everyone?"

"Very well. Let's not. Let's just get started." With that, Sorin advanced, reaching up and clutching the hilts of the blades peeking above his shoulders. Metal whistled against leather, then the silver tips were gleaming in the light of the chandelier.

Aden stood as still as a statue until the wolves erupted in a chorus of growls and snarls. He held up his hand for silence. They obeyed, but their bodies remained taut, the hair on their backs standing on end. And though he didn't order any of the vampires to fight, though he shouted for them to return to their formation, several of them rushed forward, closing in on her brother.

She knew why they did so. Their beasts. Chompers was going crazy inside her head, banging against her temples with enough force to hurt, wanting out, wanting to stand guard over Aden. Every bit of her strength was required to keep him inside, to keep her own feet in place as his failure to escape drove him to try and control her body.

She watched, shaking, as Sorin spun—and there went someone's internal organs. He spun again—and there went a head. He went low, and a leg separated at the knee, each piece falling in a different direction. Gruesome, but all Victoria could think was how good the spurting blood looked. Not just to Chompers, who finally stopped fighting her as he focused on the substance he so craved, but to her. And if it looked good to her...

She glanced over at Aden. He was licking his lips, and his eyes were electric, crackling with lightning. Was he entranced? If so, there would be no saving him.

Sorin stopped just in front of Aden, who continued to watch the blood. He was. He was entranced.

I should have forced him to eat before coming here. Now he might dive for one of those puddles. Might lie there and lap up every drop, leaving his body vulnerable to attack.

"Get the bodies out of here," she shouted, fearing Aden's ability to raise the dead would kick in, and the walking corpses would attack.

Vampire soldiers rushed to obey her.

"Aren't you frightened?" her brother demanded. The tips of his swords were pointed toward the floor, blood dripping down, down, down, sliding so perfectly. She had only to crouch and stick out her tongue, and the flavor would explode through her mouth.

What are you doing? Trembling, she directed her

attention to the boys. They were still nose to nose. She must have squeezed Aden's hand with every bit of her strength because she'd cut off circulation in her own fingers. They were tingling. *Relax, just relax.*

Aden cleared his throat, somehow pulled himself out of the entrancement as only an older, practiced vampire could, and straightened. "Frightened? Of you?"

Sorin grinned slowly. "Of death."

"Why would I be? I'm already dead."

That gave her brother pause, wiping away his amusement. "You were told wrong, were you not? So far, this has been very good for me."

"I never said this wouldn't end well *for you.*"

A confused shake of that pale head. "You, then?"

"No."

"Then why—never mind." Sorin met Victoria's gaze. Eight. "Is he always this cryptic?"

The fact that her brother was speaking directly to her again thrilled her, and she couldn't deny it. In fact, she was so thrilled she couldn't think up an intelligent reply. She could only stand there, staring at him, openmouthed and sputtering like a fool.

"Just say what you have to say," Aden commanded, "so that we can get started."

Get started? With what? Fear replaced her pleasure.

Sorin sucked in a breath. "Very well, then. I came to tell you that your allies are dead. I killed them."

"Killed them? When Aden only just took the throne?" she gasped out. Finally. Words.

An impish shrug. "I've been knocking them off for the past decade, striking at Vlad every chance I could."

Father had never told her Sorin had turned on their clan. *You're shocked by that?* He'd never told her anything. "I don't understand," Victoria said. "Why would you do such a thing?"

She was ignored.

"I know your secret," her brother said to Aden.

"I know you do," he replied evenly.

So frustrating. What secret?

"His strength grows daily, you know. He will return one day soon. He will attack."

His. Sorin knew Vlad still lived. No one else knew, but if they found out... They won't connect the dots, she assured herself before she could work up a good panic. For all they knew, Aden and Sorin were discussing Dmitri. Or someone else, someone they didn't know. Yes, that worked. *Please, yes.*

"I know that, too," Aden said. "I also know you want to be king. You want to be the one to destroy him when he reappears. You're willing to challenge me to get what you want. Even to the detriment of the clan."

"Insane yet clever. You are correct, Aden the Beast Tamer."

"No." Victoria shook her head violently. "Maybe we can talk this out. Maybe we can compromise." Vampire battles of this magnitude were bloody and sadistic, and she couldn't bear the thought of either of them hurt...or worse. And after witnessing Sorin's skill, she wasn't sure even Aden's ability could save him.

Aden knew it, too. Hadn't he predicted this wouldn't end well? And yet still he said, "I accept your challenge, Sorin the Vicious. We fight for the crown at sunset tomorrow."

THIRTEEN

"Why did you give him so long to prepare?"

Aden sat on the lid of the toilet in Victoria's private bathroom, hungry, *so* hungry, tired and unsure. Had he done the right thing?

He'd soon find out.

He held clippers in one hand and a small trash bin in the other. He passed the first to Victoria and set the second on the floor between his feet before he replied. "I gave *myself* so long to prepare."

"Oh."

She was paler than usual and shaky rather than sturdy. Agitated, even. He understood. He did. Aden had threatened her brother. Was going to *fight* her brother. She was probably confused, upset and unsure.

An hour ago, that might not have bothered him. But as they'd stood in the throne room, danger torpedoing toward him, she'd taken his hand and offered comfort. Somehow, some way, that contact had tugged him out of the cold, emotionless wasteland he'd been living in. He was feeling. Hope, admiration, affection, each like the warm rays from the sun.

Now he rested his elbows on his knees. "I'm going to ask you a question, Victoria, and I don't mean anything by it, okay? So don't get the wrong idea. I'm just curious."

She stiffened, and he could feel the worry pouring off her already. "All right."

"You're helping me, but you obviously love your brother." He'd felt her desire to run to the homicidal maniac. Only, instead of attacking him, she would have hugged him. Would Sorin have murdered her, too? "So, *why* are you here, helping me?"

Some of the worry faded. "Fishing for compliments? Or an *I love you* confession?" Before he could respond, not that he knew what to say, she added, "I don't want the two of you to fight, that's all."

Did she expect him to walk away from this? "We will fight. That, I can promise you." Blunt of him, perhaps, but he didn't want any misunderstandings.

Her shoulders slumped a little. "I know you will.

Believe me, if I thought I could talk sense into either one of you..."

He watched her, trying to gauge her reaction to his next words without looking like he was trying to gauge her reaction. "Do you *want* me to walk away?"

A moment passed. She sighed. "No. You can't. He would come after you. Others would come after you. The challenge has been issued and accepted, and if it's not followed through, everyone will think you are weak, that they can have what's yours. You'll never have peace. I just..."

Wanted them both to be okay. Understandable.

"And before you ask, I want you to win."

That, he hadn't anticipated. "Why?"

"Because there's a possibility you will spare him. He will not extend you the same courtesy. Do—do you know what's going to happen?"

"I don't know about the outcome of the fight, no." Truth. Through Elijah, he'd seen it, but he'd seen several different versions of it. "I do know your brother won't cause any trouble while he waits for the challenge. Meaning, no one else will try and attack him. Or me. If that helps. Elijah told me."

She shuddered. "It doesn't help. And I...I don't think we should talk about this anymore. My body is reacting negatively to your every word. Any more, and I might throw up on your feet."

Great. He'd meant to reassure her, not sicken her. "Is an upset stomach your only symptom?"

"My blood is chilled and thick, and my heart is drumming too forcefully against my ribs."

Not as terrible as he'd feared. She'd just described a mild panic attack. "And you've never experienced this type of reaction before?"

"Not to this degree." She frowned down at the clippers. "So what do you want me to do with these?"

If she wanted to topic switch, they'd topic switch. He wasn't sure how else to calm her. "I'd like you to shave my head."

"Shave your—*what?*"

"Shave my head."

Horror blanketed her beautiful face. "But you'll be bald."

He felt a small wave of amusement rush through him. "There are worse things."

No, there are not! That will seriously affect our lady action, Caleb said. He'd been fuming since Aden had made the decision to say goodbye to his dye job.

"Anyway, I won't be bald. I'll be blond. There's a

guard on the clippers that'll leave a couple inches of hair."

"Oh," she repeated, then fumbled around for a moment as she tried to turn them on. Finally the little motor revved to life. "And you're sure about this? There's no going back if you don't like the results."

"I'm sure."

"Then tell me why you want a cut."

Yeah, Julian said. *This is dumb. We'll look like an idiot.* Elijah had no comment.

After everything that had happened, Aden felt like a new person. He *was* a new person. Yet every time he passed a mirror—and as a lot of the walls here were, in fact, mirrors, he saw more of himself than he wanted—he looked the same. That had to change, too.

"I just do," was all he said.

"Very well, then." Resigned, tentative, Victoria got to work, and he watched black lock after black lock fall to the floor.

Stop her, Caleb practically cried. *Grab her hand and stop her.*

For a moment, Aden felt something—a rope, maybe—pulling at his arm, lifting it, his fingers twitching, ready to close around Victoria's wrist, and he frowned. A conscious effort was required to keep his arm at his side.

What the hell?

Come on, man, Caleb continued. *All you have to do is lift your arm and grab her wrist.*

Lift his arm. Grab her wrist. The answer popped into place. "You trying to take over the body, Caleb?"

Maybe, was the grumbled reply.

None of the souls had tried anything like that in years. Probably because they couldn't take over without his permission. Or hadn't been able to. But that tug…it was stronger than anything they'd done before. He wasn't exactly sure what that meant.

"Don't do that again," he snapped.

Fine!

Victoria had moved between his spread knees, and at his words, she stiffened. "I didn't…I'm just…you told me to do this!"

Immediately repentant, he said, "Sorry. I wasn't talking to you."

"Oh. Good. You had me worried." She returned her attention to the trim job.

Her scent hit him with the force of a swinging baseball bat. Aden forgot the souls as his mouth watered, and his stomach curled into itself. He'd been on the verge of starvation ever since her brother had maimed and killed those vampires, and he'd barely made it out of the throne room without falling to his face and licking the oh, so delicious-looking blood off the floor.

Only two things had stopped him. The desire for Victoria's blood, and only Victoria's blood, which fortified itself by the minute, and the knowledge that showing weakness of any kind would be used against him during the big battle. And the battle *would* happen, just as he'd promised Victoria.

Elijah might have seen several different outcomes, but circumventing the battle altogether hadn't been one of them.

A few times, Aden had seen himself die, his head removed by a sword covered in *je la nune*. Victoria wouldn't be able to save him from that. But then he'd thought, *I won't go low, I'll dart to the side.* And the visions had instantly changed. So, when the new outcome played through his mind, he'd seen Sorin swing, encountering air as Aden ducked and went in for his own attack.

He'd realized then that his future was uncertain. Completely changeable. And he could win—maybe— but at a price. His victory would mark the beginning of a downward spiral for Victoria. Maybe because she would see him standing over her brother's body, vampires cheering his success while she cried.

He didn't want that for her. Didn't want her depressed

or angry, or worse, hating him with every fiber of her being. Therefore, he had to figure out a solution.

"Did you know you have small black dots on your scalp?" she asked.

"Freckles?"

"Most likely. They're cute."

Cute kicked the butt of *hideous,* but just barely. "Thanks."

"Welcome." A soft hum drifted from her as she finished up. "There," she finally announced. "Done." She cupped his cheeks in her less than warm hands and looked him over. "You are——" She gasped.

"What?" Was it *that* bad?

I don't like to say I told you so, Caleb announced. *But I freaking TOLD YOU SO.*

While Victoria's mouth opened and closed, Aden unfolded to a stand. His reflection in the mirror above the sink slowly came into view. He'd expected a real ugh-o to stare back at him, but that wasn't the case. He had two inches of hair left, the strands spiked. They were a dirty blond, his natural color, and they made his skin appear a deeper bronze. And his eyes, which had once been black and had recently converted to violet, were now a golden brown.

Oh, Caleb breathed. *Well, okay then. Will wonders never cease?*

"You don't like it?" he asked Victoria.

"Like it?" With a trembling hand, she reached up to run her fingers along his newly shorn scalp. "I love it. And I finally see the appeal of the bad boy."

He looked like a bad boy, he wondered, leaning into her touch, hoping it would deepen.

Kiss her, Caleb prompted. *Now, now, now! Before the mood is tainted.*

For once, I gotta agree with the pervert, Julian said. *French that girl within an inch of her life.*

Yes.

Before Aden realized he'd moved, his hands were on her waist, drawing her closer to him. Automatically his gaze dropped to her neck, to her hammering pulse. A high-pitched roar, similar to what he'd heard outside, only a bit louder now, suddenly echoed inside his head.

Victoria noticed the direction of his gaze. "You need to feed or you'll be too weak to survive tomorrow."

I'll do more than survive. He hoped. "You offering?"

"N-no." She gulped, sending a shiver down the rest of her body. "Aden, you have to stop this."

"Stop what? Holding you?"

Nooo! Caleb cried, and Aden's fingers clenched on Victoria, making her wince. *I've missed her.*

"That's enough," Aden snapped at him. "Loosen your hold, and give me a minute."

"The souls?" she asked sympathetically.

His nod was clipped, scattering Caleb's mutterings. Then the pressure eased and Aden was able to gentle his grip on his own. Caleb kept that up, and something would have to be done. What, though, Aden didn't know. Other than finding the soul's way out.

"And no," Victoria said, picking their conversation up where it had ended, "I didn't mean I wanted you to stop holding me. Or maybe I did. You want me one minute, you don't the next, then you want me again, like now, and I can't keep up. I just—*sweet heavens above!*"

The innocent curse didn't surprise him, but the panicked shock bubbling from it did. "What's wrong?" No one had stepped into the bathroom. No threat had jumped out at them.

She pulled from his hold and withdrew her phone, her hand trembling, her breathing ragged. "Riley just texted, and the vibration freaks me out every time."

He wanted her back in his arms. "Easy fix. Turn it off vibrate."

"Sure thing. As soon as I figure out how to do that."

She read the screen, her pale skin tinting with gray. "Will you, uh, excuse me?" She didn't wait for his reply but raced from the bathroom, throwing over her shoulder, "I'll send a blood-slave to see to your hunger, maybe the same one from before," before slamming the door shut behind her.

"Don't do that," he called. If she heard him, he didn't know. Even then, he wanted only Victoria. He strode into the bedroom, but she was already gone.

I can't believe you let her get away without a goodbye kiss, Caleb whined.

Elijah made a noise that sounded like a cross between a wheeze and a cough. *First the hair, and now the kiss. Will you stop already? You're driving* me *crazy.*

No! This is important.

I shut you down once, Caleb. Don't make me do it again.

Shut me down? What do you mean? How and when did this alleged shutdown happen? Because Aden can tell you that, of the three of us, I'm the most powerful, and if any shutting down needs to occur, I'll be the one doing it.

Elijah's annoyance bled into unease. *Never mind. Just—*

Wait! Hold on a sec. I'm not gonna let this drop. You're talking about the cave, right? Because the end of our stay is like the same black hole Mary Ann sends us to whenever Aden nears her. Did you do that to us, E? Huh, huh, did you?

A, uh, black hole, you say?

What did you do, E? Julian demanded.

For the love of God! "I need Elijah to help me during the battle with Sorin, but if you guys don't shut up, I'll find the meds Victoria gave us and send you to a black hole right here and now."

Sorry, Ad, Julian said.

Fine, be that way, Caleb said.

Thank you, Elijah said.

"Good." They understood each other.

From the corner of his eye, Aden spotted the dancing woman from this morning gliding toward Victoria's bed, leaning over. A little girl with long black hair lay there, sleeping. He frowned in confusion. Neither female had been there a moment ago.

"You," he said, approaching.

She ignored him, saying to the little girl, somehow equally as familiar to him, "Come on now, precious." She threw a panicked glance over her shoulder. Not at Aden, but at somewhere far, far past him. "We have to leave now. Before he returns."

The little girl stretched and yawned. "But I don't want

to go," she said in the sweetest angel voice he'd ever heard.

"You must. Now."

"If she doesn't want to go, you're not taking her." Aden reached the woman, tried to latch onto her shoulder—but his hand ghosted through her.

FOURTEEN

AFTER ARRANGING FOR A blood-slave to be sent to Aden, as promised, Victoria locked herself in Riley's bedroom, knowing no one would enter without permission, and she could have as much privacy as she wanted for as long as she needed.

She hadn't lied to Aden. Riley *had* sent her a text. Think we found J's ID. Being tracked by WBs & FS. Except 4 raging fungus, all good. BK?

J for Julian. WB for witch-bitches. FS for fairy spawn. Raging fungus had to be Tucker. Shocking that Riley hadn't killed him already. Or maybe not. Mary Ann must have put her dainty foot down, and, lovestruck idiot that he was, Riley caved.

Like Aden used to cave for Victoria. And might again, one day soon, if the looks he'd given her in the bathroom meant anything.

BK good, she typed. U B careful.

And the Boy King *was* good. He was finally returning to his normal self. Only, things were about to change for him yet again, and in a way that would hurt him deeply. Because, if Riley and Mary Ann had discovered Julian's true identity, it was only a matter of time before Aden had to say goodbye to the soul.

She wouldn't tell him. Not yet. He had too much to worry about already. And that brought her to the other text she'd received, one she hadn't mentioned.

I'm in the forest. Find me. Sorin.

Her brother wanted to speak with her. *Her brother.* About building a relationship with her, or about Aden? Or both? Either way, she would be taking a huge risk simply to see him.

Although, on one hand, she might be able to change his mind about the fight. *Big* might. On the other, he might try to use her to force *Aden* to back out. Having witnessed his merciless skill with a sword, that seemed more likely. But…

The desire to see him was overwhelming.

She would go see him, she decided, but she would be smart about it. She wouldn't go alone, and she wouldn't stay long. *Neither of those concessions makes you smart*. Didn't matter. Hope was a silly but completely undeniable thing.

She gathered her sisters as backup and headed outside, careful not to shiver at the sudden drop in temperature.

"I don't want to meet him," Lauren said firmly. "I'm only going so I can murder him if he threatens you." Tall, slender and as blond as Sorin, she wore a skintight black leather halter top and pants. Barbed wire circled both of her wrists. She'd been training to be a warrior her entire life, and she'd killed more witches and fae than the leader of Vlad's army had. The fact that she was female had kept her from advancing up the ranks. "He had decades to convince Vlad to let us talk to him, years to visit, and he didn't."

"You should probably shut up now," Stephanie said after popping a bubble. Shorter than either Lauren or Victoria, she had long blond hair and moss-green eyes. Rather than traditional vampire garb, she wore a blue tank top and a black micro-mini. The length of her hair was braided and twisted into tiny buns all over her head. "You're only showing your dumb side."

"Dumb side! I don't have a dumb side, and you know it."

"Ha! I've met pet rocks who were smarter than you."

"Do you want me to murder you, too? Because I will!"

They loved each other, but they also loved to snipe at each other.

Victoria was envious. These two had always possessed the courage to be who and what they wanted to be. But then again, Lauren had been favored by Vlad, and Stephanie's mother had been the favorite of all his wives. He'd gone easy on both of them. Victoria had not been favored, and her mother had been the most despised, so she'd always borne the brunt of his rage.

She'd tried to please him, as well as her mother, but they'd admired such different traits that, in the end, she hadn't pleased either of them. Vlad had wanted a fearless soldier who threw herself into every battle; her mother had wanted a sweet-tempered, fun-loving brat. She was neither.

As she made her way through the trees, she endured the bitter cold, savored the scent of the coming storm. The sky was darkening, the clouds growing thick and black. Hadn't taken long to learn Oklahoma weather could change in the blink of an eye.

Footsteps just ahead, branches slapping together. She and her sisters halted just as her brother's men stepped forward, forming a circle around them. They were camouflaged so well, she had to stare and stare hard to see them.

Sorin moved from the center of them. "Sisters," he said with a nod.

With a whoop, Stephanie ran to him. She threw herself in his arms. He caught her, twirling her around. Envy returned, nearly swallowing Victoria whole. The pair had spent time together, that much was obvious. They knew each other, were comfortable with each other, perhaps even loved each other.

Why hadn't Sorin wanted to spend time with Victoria?

"What are you doing, you cow?" Lauren snarled at the youngest princess. "Get back here before he double-crosses you and you're watching your head roll away from your body."

Stephanie smirked. *Still* snuggling in Sorin's arms, she said, "I'm not the one who failed to visit our brother in secret. And who are you calling a cow, you whale? Have you seen your ass in those pants?" A mocking shudder raked her. "Actually, forget the question. *Everyone's* seen your ass in those pants."

"Everyone's about to see your blood sprayed all over the trees."

Perhaps Victoria should have come out here on her

own. "Lauren, you're gorgeous," she said, holding out her arms to keep the two sniping females apart, just in case they decided to leap at each other and slap fight. Yes, they'd done it before, and it was humiliating for everyone. "Stephanie, you're beautiful, too. Now, can I speak with my brother? Please?"

Sorin kissed Stephanie's temple before setting her down. He motioned behind the group with a wave of his hand. "Sit. All of you." So formal now. So polite.

"Sit wh-ere. Oh." Victoria spun around, expecting to see only the brittle leaves and twigs she'd passed. Instead, she found four perfect tree stumps, two facing the other two. Exactly how distracted had she been?

Victoria eased onto the one closest to her. Sorin claimed the one across from her, and Stephanie claimed the one at his side, forcing Lauren to take the one facing her.

All but one of Sorin's men had disappeared, but she knew they were nearby, watching, listening, protecting. Then one of them stepped from the shadows, proving her suspicions, holding a tray of blood-filled goblets.

Victoria accepted one and sipped. The blood was warm, rich and sweet. Not as sweet as Aden's, but Chompers practically whimpered with relief.

"I'm surprised you came," Sorin said, looking right at her.

She had so much to say to him, so much to ask. "Why did you never visit us?" was the first thing to escape her mouth. The question echoed, and she blushed, gulping down the rest of the blood to hide her face for a few precious seconds. She should have chosen to kick things off another way. Not accusing him of neglect right from the beginning and putting him on the defensive.

Amused rather than offended, he said, "I didn't think you wished to risk Father's wrath." Getting comfortable, he removed the swords from his back and propped them against the side of his seat. "Was I wrong?"

Shoulders slumping, she set her empty goblet on the ground. "I could have risked his wrath to see you, so I suppose I must share the blame."

Lauren rolled her eyes. "You're always so quick to take the blame or forgive when you can't. Well, I would have risked it, you backline reject, but still you didn't try to meet with me. And let me tell you something else. If you despised Vlad half as much as you claimed, you would have. So guess what? You're all talk and I'll hate you forever for that. In fact, I might even decide to rip your throat out before I— No way! Is that blade *curved?*" She dropped her still-full goblet, blood spilling in the dirt, and pushed from her stump.

In the next blink, she was crouching in front of his weapons, studying them, running her fingers along the blades, oohing and aahing. "Can I have one? Or both? Please!"

He handled her jump from hatred to gimme-now-now-*now* with ease. "You may have both when I'm done with the human king."

The sickness Victoria had experienced in her bathroom, just before shaving Aden's head, returned full force.

"Awesome. Thanks." Lauren dragged one of the blades back to her seat to continue her study.

Sorin peered at Victoria with eyes so similar to her own that she could have been drowning in her reflection. "And you? What would you have of me? My surrender to the human?"

He's not so human anymore.

Stephanie raised her free hand high in the air. "Me, me. I know. Pick me!"

"You asked me to come, and I did," Victoria said. "Why did you ask me? To *offer* your surrender to the human?"

She expected the comment to enrage him. Had he

been Vlad, it would have. Instead, he surprised her once again by grinning. "I see Father did not beat the fire out of you as I'd assumed."

Vlad had certainly tried. "Well?" she prompted.

Sorin shrugged one of those wide shoulders. "I heard your Aden's summons, and I came to remove him from the throne. I can tell you have great affection for him. I have also heard the reports. But we have become a joke among the races. Soon those races will swarm and attack us, hoping to destroy the vampires at long last."

"How have we become a joke? He defeated the witches and the fae—in one night! Tell me the last time you did that. Or Father. You can't," she added before he could reply. "You're simply making excuses because you desire the crown for yourself."

He gave another shrug, unashamed and unabashed. "Very well. I do. That crown is my right. My birthright. The human seems nice enough—for food—but that's all he is, Victoria. Food."

No, Aden was far more than that. He was courageous, honorable, and had (almost) always made her feel better about herself. He'd never purposely hurt her, and he never would, even when he was at his worst. She could not say the same about Sorin.

So, this was one battle she would not back down from.

"You should have taken the crown from Vlad yourself, but you didn't. You struck at him from behind, waiting, biding your time."

Finally, the reaction she'd expected since the first. Anger. "Your human did *not* strike at Vlad," Sorin said with a glare. "Dmitri did. Aden merely finished off your betrothed."

True. *But.* "If Dmitri defeated Father, Dmitri was stronger than Father. And if Aden defeated Dmitri, that means Aden was stronger than both of them."

"Logical, but wrong. He'll not defeat Vlad. He's too nice. More than that, Father was at his weakest when Dmitri attacked him. That will not happen again. He'll be prepared now. And he'll do anything, fair or foul, but mostly foul, to get what he wants. You know this. *I* can defeat him, however. I *will* defeat him. I've been preparing for this war for years."

"Wait. What is all of this about defeating Vlad?" Lauren said. "He's dead."

The sickness churned more forcefully. "Actually, he's alive."

Lauren looked like she wanted to protest, but a nod of confirmation from Sorin, then Stephanie, had her sputtering. "How did you guys know? Why did no one tell me? What does this mean for us? Our people?"

"Sorin told me," Stephanie said. "And it means nothing. No matter what, Father cannot be allowed to rule again. He's a tyrant."

"But...but..."

"You know I'm right. You hate him, you just don't want a human in charge of us." Stephanie twined her fingers with Sorin's. "And you need to listen to me. Aden isn't as nice as you think. I mean, he is, but he's lived at a ranch for human baddies for months. He's done stuff. He'll not be easy to walk on."

Sorin scoffed. "A baddie human isn't the same as a baddie vampire warrior, now is it?"

"I'm with Steph," Lauren said, abandoning her upset over Vlad's defeat of the grave. Or, really, her upset over not being told. "You're underestimating Aden, and it'll cost you." Metal vibrated and whistled as she ran her fingertip along the center of one of the swords. "You weren't here when he had our beasts slobbering all over him."

"Stop!" Victoria banged her fist against her thigh. "Giving Sorin information about Aden is akin to aiding him. Aiding him is a betrayal to your king."

Sorin waved away her protest. "They've told me nothing I didn't already know. And you can tell your human that I will be leaving my beast behind. He'll not use mine against me."

She absorbed his words, her eyes widening. "You can do that? Leave your beast behind? On purpose? And survive?"

He nodded proudly. "Unlike Father, I have never feared mine. I accept that part of myself—and use it to my advantage. My beast leaves me and returns to me at my discretion."

"He doesn't try to kill you?" Lauren asked, as shocked as Victoria was.

"He did. At first. Now, he accepts." Sorin rested his elbows on his knees, his expression thoughtful. "Perhaps I'll teach you how to release yours. He can fight along-side you. And believe me, you'll never have a stronger, more vigilant partner."

"I would love that!"

Victoria had never heard such excitement from her all-fighting-all-the-time sister. And, she thought with mounting dread, there went Aden's best advantage. Con-trolling Sorin through his beast.

"Things will be much improved under my reign," Sorin said, his gaze pinning her in place. "You'll see."

FIFTEEN

RAIN POURED ALL NIGHT LONG. Rain *still* poured at dawn and throughout the rest of the day. The sky was as black as an abyss, the clouds so thick Aden wasn't sure they'd ever dissipate.

At the appropriate time, he made his way to the backyard of his new home. A home he would not give up easily. He stopped at the edge of the warded circle, quivering with energy. He was shirtless, wearing only jeans and boots, already soaked to the bone.

On his finger perched Vlad's ring, filled with *je la nune*. At his ankles, his daggers were at the ready. Every vampire living in the home stood outside with him, some holding torches under the awning. Victoria stood with her sisters, wringing her hands together, bathed in flickering firelight.

They hadn't spoken since she'd left him yesterday.

She'd tried, she'd wanted to, but still he'd avoided her. His hunger for her would have deepened, and worse, he would have asked her to betray her brother.

He couldn't ask her. Not if he wanted to like himself when this was over.

It would be hard to like himself, though, if he was dead.

"Did you feed?" she mouthed.

He gave one clipped shake of his head. No, he hadn't. He'd tried. A few hours after dismissing the slave she'd sent him, without taking a single drop of blood from the girl, his hunger had overwhelmed him and he'd marched to the slave quarters, an area that was more like a harem than anything, where the humans could roam freely, even though they didn't *want* to roam.

As he'd stood there, watching them, listening to their idle chatter, he'd found his hunger actually dwindling. Even though the scent of their blood, the drum-loud beat of their hearts, had tantalized him. He'd left.

On his way to the throne room, where he'd sat and thought in private, again he'd been more interested in the blood of the *vampires* he'd passed, his hunger returning with a vengeance. Yet he'd opted not to partake, wondering whether he'd spend the next day seeing the world through their eyes rather than his own.

He'd almost hunted Victoria down, almost asked *her* to feed him. But still he'd avoided her. For all his other reasons and one more. Well, many more, but this one was the most important. She didn't want to feed him. The knowledge tore him up inside, even if the fault lay entirely with him. After the way he'd treated her...

An animalistic cry reverberated in the back of his mind. One he'd heard before, one he ignored.

He hadn't gotten to tell Victoria about his encounter with her mother, the dancing woman. He was now certain that was who he'd seen, that he'd watched one of Victoria's memories come to life. A memory of her mother trying to abscond with her, of Vlad catching them. Of Vlad punishing Victoria while her mother watched. A whipping, each of the cat-o'-nine tails laced with the same liquid in his ring.

By the time her father had finished, her back had reminded him of tattered Christmas ribbons. Vlad would pay for that.

And Aden would be the one to kill him, for real this time. Soon. He just had to take care of Sorin first.

Aden, Elijah said nervously.

"Not another word," he muttered. "You guys promised."

I'm sorry, but I only just realized. Only just saw. You need to take your pills. Okay? Please.

What? Caleb and Julian demanded in unison.

"Saw what?"

Just take your pills. As you know, I've seen this fight end with several different outcomes and each one was worse than the last. Well, I just saw another outcome. The images were disjointed and distorted, and I'm not sure I saw things in the proper order, but I think you will walk away from this if you take the pills.

How could that be? "I don't have them with me." If he failed to take them, would he have a vision of Victoria's past, midpunch? Would the souls distract him too much? "Besides, I need your ability." He needed to know what Sorin planned to do to him before the bastard actually did it. Sorin was going for his head, no question.

Just…send Victoria to get them.

"Why?"

I told you. There's a very high chance you won't walk away without them.

A very high chance? "That's not good enough."

Okay, let's look at this from a different angle. You know how cold you've been?

"Yes." Kinda hard to forget.

Well, that's actually been a lifesaver for you. Right now, strong emotion is your enemy. The pills will help you remain unemotional.

"I don't understand."

Yeah, me either, Caleb said.

Just take the pills, Aden, Elijah insisted again. *Trust me, emotion is not your friend.*

Was anything, anymore? "All right." Elijah was never wrong. Or rarely wrong, he guessed he had to say now. If Aden needed the pills, he needed the pills. "I'll—"

Sorin materialized at the edge of the clearing, already marching forward, two of his men holding a banner that stretched over their heads, the rest holding torches of their own. Torches the rain did not affect. They were a collage of shadows and light, menace and redemption.

The wind kicked up, whistling…closer and closer… footsteps…

"It's too late. I can't send her now." He would appear weak. Vulnerable. To vampires, appearance was everything, and if he appeared weak and vulnerable, he would lose this fight even if he won. "We'll have to find another way to bring home the victory."

Elijah groaned. *I was afraid that would happen. Just try to stay calm. No matter what. Okay?*

"Okay." Easily said. Probably impossible to do.

Then Sorin and his men were there, standing just inside the ward, and Aden could see each face clearly—as well as the faces of Seth, Shannon and Ryder, his human friends. They were bound with rope. Prisoners.

To their credit, they didn't appear to be scared. Seth, with his red-and-black hair dripping into his scowl, just looked pissed. Shannon's darker skin blended into the shadows, but his eyes...his eyes were so green they glowed. And they were narrowed on Sorin, throwing daggers of hate. Ryder was the calmest of the three. Maybe because he looked shocked to his marrow.

First things first. "Let them go," Aden demanded. "Now."

The rain slowed to an icy trickle. Sorin nodded, as if happy to oblige. "Of course I'll let them go. Their freedom in exchange for the crown. Simple, easy, and you don't have to die."

He could accept, but as the new king, Sorin could later kill the boys anyway, and there would be nothing Aden could do to stop him. "Only a coward would offer such a bargain."

"Is this the part where I erupt into a rage and attack you? Sorry, no rage from me. Call me whatever you like. It doesn't matter. Very soon everyone here will call me King."

"Cocky."

"Confident. But all right. You don't wish to save your friends. I understand. Callous of you, but let's see if you'll relinquish the crown to save your girlfriend."

During Sorin's speech, one of his men had snuck through the crowd and closed in on Victoria, grabbing her by the back of the neck and forcing her to her knees. She tried to fight, but her strength was clearly no match for his.

"Before you ask, she can't teleport away," Sorin said. "She came to see me last night, and I drugged her drink."

Victoria trembled and gave her brother a look of cutting betrayal. Aden felt a twinge of betrayal himself. She'd left him and gone to see her brother, might have even told him secrets about Aden.

After the way you treated her, could you blame her? Elijah said.

Way to help me remain calm, he thought darkly. Not that the souls could hear him. "How can you treat her that way?" he asked Sorin. "She's your sister."

A negligent shrug. "One thing I've learned over the centuries. *Everyone* is expendable."

Victoria's chin trembled, and Aden knew she was fighting tears. He stiffened. No matter what she'd done, no matter what had gone down, he *hated* the thought of her upset. Strong emotion? Yeah, if anything could cause it, he realized, she could.

Any questions he might have had about his feelings for her were answered in that moment. Aden didn't just like her, he loved her, and he would do anything to protect her. More than that, he trusted her. She might have gone to see her brother, but she wouldn't have done anything to jeopardize Aden's health. Just as, even at his worst, he had not jeopardized hers.

Aden, Elijah began, nervous again.

"No," he said. No more distractions.

"He's without his beast," Victoria called, the last word emerging on a cry of pain. The man must have increased the pressure on her neck.

Elijah cursed as fury sparked to sizzling life inside his chest. In the back of his mind, he heard the plaintive cry of a newborn. Just like before. Only stronger this time, and as angry as he was. The souls began to argue, Caleb and Julian demanding answers, Elijah refusing to give them.

Aden tuned them out as best he could and focused on Sorin. He would pay for Victoria's pain. In blood. "Swords?" he asked, because that was the method the warrior had chosen in every vision Aden had had of this fight.

A moment passed as Sorin unraveled the meaning of his question. There would be no surrender. They would fight. Surprised flickered in those blue eyes before smoothing into eagerness. "Let's make it sort of fair. Hand to hand."

Aden nodded, surprise flooding *him*. Nothing was happening as he'd seen. What did that mean? What had caused things to change? The fact that he hadn't taken the pills?

"If anything happens to Victoria or my humans, I'll kill your men when I'm done with you," Aden said to Sorin. And he meant it.

"Now who's the cocky one, hmm?"

"I want your vow. No harm will come to them. Now, during or after. No question, no matter the outcome."

Sorin nodded. "You have my word."

The ease with which he offered the concession made Aden think he'd never planned to hurt the foursome. That wasn't going to save him, not now, but it did defuse the hottest threads of Aden's fury.

With a shrug, the black robe draping Sorin's shoulders fell to the ground, leaving him as bare-chested as Aden. Difference was, Sorin's torso was covered in fresh wards.

There was not an inch of pale skin visible. Only black ink on top of black ink, circles on top of circles. Aden briefly wondered what the guy was warded against before clearing his mind. He had to concentrate.

Together they approached the center of the metal ring, then stopped, only a whisper away from each other. Aden had been in more fistfights than he could count, but they'd always been spur-of-the-moment, his mind lost to whatever emotion or insult that had brought him to that point. He'd never coldly, calculatingly planned to brawl like this.

"I think I would have liked you in other circumstances," Sorin said. Just before drilling his knuckles into Aden's eye socket.

His arm moved so quickly, Aden registered only a blur before tumbling *backward,* pain exploding through his head. He managed to remain on his feet as the entire world went silent, black. There was no rain, no crowd, no souls. No...anything. Not even time. He was deaf, dumb and blind, his brain completely shut down.

Aden just stood there, lost, barely breathing, until he saw a sudden flash of white. A return to black. Another flash of white, one that lasted a little longer. Black. White. Black, white, as if someone were playing with a light switch inside his head.

Then he heard a little whoosh of noise, the only pre-cursor to the sudden *boom* as the world slammed back into focus. He heard, he knew, he saw, but there was no time to react. Sorin was on him, fists pummeling like a jackhammer, over and over again, raining down, never stopping.

Come on, come on. Get in this thing. Using all of his strength, Aden kneed him in the balls. And if Sorin *had* still possessed his beast, the creature would have come roaring out at exactly that moment in a bid to protect Aden from further damage, because Sorin hunched over and screamed with unholy rage.

The down and dirty action gave Aden a necessary reprieve—and time to jerk his knee up, slamming Sorin under his chin, sending him soaring to his back.

Aden raced to him, intending to pin the guy's shoul-ders with his knees and just start whaling, but Sorin pulled up his legs, rolling with Aden's weight before kicking. This time, Aden was the one to soar to his back. A blink of his swelling eyes, and Sorin was on him.

Punch, punch, punch. "Any time you want to give up, all you have to do is kneel before me and proclaim your loyalty."

"Go screw yourself," he managed between blows.

"Original."

"Appropriate."

Punch, punch. Several of the bones in his face shattered. His nose might have snapped in half; some of the cartilage definitely shifted to one side. Adrenaline shot through his veins as if he'd injected it, warming him up, strengthening him. But was it enough?

Calm. You have to stay calm.

Elijah's voice.

Ignored.

With a roar that matched the one in his head, the one growing, growing, growing in volume, Aden threw a punch of his own. Then another and another and another, until Sorin stopped hitting him to save his own face from a battering. A golden opportunity. Aden reached up, grabbed him under the arms and shoved, flipping the warrior over him. He didn't release his hold, but allowed himself to flip, as well, so that he was finally the one on top.

He spit blood and what looked to be a Chiclet— a tooth! Then he held Sorin's face with one hand and rained down the fury with the other. Boom, boom, boom, so fast he couldn't see even the blur. Or maybe his eyesight was too cloudy, his lids desperate to glue together and (hopefully) heal.

To Elijah's delight, every punch calmed him.

But Sorin didn't stay down for long and gave another kick. They were thrust apart. Aden slammed into the wall of spectators. Some fell with him, others pushed at him, but he felt the desires of their beasts. The desire to emerge and save him.

"No," he yelled. "Don't. Stay."

They obeyed, none slipping from their hosts and solidifying. How much time before they forgot his command and did as they wished? Probably not much. End this, he had to end this.

Sorin must have felt the same, because they leaped at each other, rolling together, throwing elbows and knees, going for soft spots—nose, throat and groin. Every new punch Aden threw would have fortified the calm, if every punch he received hadn't fanned the flames back up.

Soon blood was flowing from a gaping cut across Sorin's hairline. Blood that snared Aden's attention. Maybe because it was a vampire's blood. Maybe because it had the same sweet, dark scent as Victoria's.

Taste…must taste…

As distracted as he was, Sorin managed to knock him sideways. He stumbled into the spectators, and this time he could *hear* their beasts. Roars, so many roars. Still they remained in their cages, but just barely.

Would have served Sorin right to lose that way. To be humbled by the very beasts he'd mocked Aden for taming. But Aden had a point to prove, or Victoria's brother would never take him seriously.

Wait. *You're going to let him live?* He'd decided to end him, hadn't he?

Taste...

Aden shoved from the crowd and dove for Sorin. Again they rolled, again they twisted and fought like animals.

"I didn't want it to end this way, but I'm glad it did." Sorin bared his fangs and swooped down to bite Aden's neck.

Only, he couldn't. His fangs wouldn't pierce the skin. The warrior was shocked, yes, but reacted as if he'd trained for such a thing. Before Aden could extract himself, Sorin raised his hand and removed the covering of a ring very similar to the one Aden wore. He dribbled the contents over Aden's neck. The burn was instantaneous, sweeping through his entire body in seconds and engulfing him with flames. Felt like it, anyway.

His throat clogged up, cutting off his air supply. His fury was joined by fear and pain, all three consuming him.

With a snarl, Sorin pinned him, his fangs drilling

deep into the wound. Suction. So much suction. Taking the flames and replacing them with ice. No matter how much Aden struggled, he couldn't dislodge those teeth.

When his struggles slowed, stopped, he knew. He was going to die.

The roaring inside his head increased so much, became so loud, it was all Aden could hear. Roaring, roaring, roaring—quieting now. No, not quieting, he realized hazily. *Leaving* him. Ripping at his insides. Rising from his head, something sharp shooting from his back. Soon a creature was hovering over him, moving beside him. A black mist, taking shape. A snout, wings, claws. Roaring, roaring, roaring, blending with gasps of terror.

Someone's beast had escaped.

Sorin was torn from him, fangs practically taking Aden's trachea with them. He lay there a moment, panting, sweating but cold. He could still win this, he thought. He hadn't admitted defeat, and he wasn't yet dead. How could he be, when every muscle and bone he possessed ached? First, though, he had to ensure Victoria's safety.

Gingerly he sat up, the wound in his neck pulling, stinging. Blood poured down him, washing away in the steady drizzle of rain. Dizziness was a bitch, and a while passed before he could focus. When he did, he saw Victoria, her face pale, her cheeks wet with rain—and tears? Her chin was still trembling. She was no longer on her knees, but her brother's warrior was still beside her.

Relief speared him. She was okay.

"Aden," she said, both dazed and frightened. "Your beast."

Something whizzed through his line of vision, breaking their connection. He looked—and nearly choked on his own tongue. A baby beast, monster, *whatever* was chasing Sorin around the circle, nipping at him with saber teeth.

Your beast, Victoria had said. That's what the mist had been. And it *had* risen from him. The rending of his insides, the sharp sting at his back...yeah, it had come from him.

The beast was smaller than any of the others Aden had seen, but no less fierce. Those wings stretched into razor sharp points. His scales were a glossy gray, like smoked, polished glass. His arms were short and thin but tipped with ivory claws. His hoofed and clawed feet slammed into the ground, disrupting grass and rattling metal.

He's mine, Aden thought, dazed all over again. *He actually came from me.*

And he's what I didn't want to happen, what I didn't want

any of you to know about, Elijah said on a sigh. *He's been growing inside of you since that last day in the cave. He's who looked through Victoria's eyes before slamming into you and rendering you unconscious.*

"How?" he managed to say despite his wound, having held the torn skin together.

He was birthed to life inside you with the first blood exchange, then entered Victoria's mind when we did, growing all the while, then finally stopping the switching altogether.

"Why keep him secret?" Good. His words were getting stronger, clearer.

I didn't want you or the dynamic duo to panic. Strong emotion was the only thing that could push him out, and yes, I'm purposefully using birthing language because that's basically what happened, and he wasn't ready to be pushed out. He's now, well, a preemie.

Which meant he was...what? Fragile? Vulnerable?

Hungry. He's very hungry, very determined, and will never be easily controlled. I didn't want to tell you, but you've been battling his nature, as well as Victoria's. You were doing an excellent job, too. Until this.

So what does this crap mean for us? Caleb asked.

Elijah sighed. *The little guy's had a taste of freedom now. He will never be happy caged.*

At least Aden survived the fight, Julian pointed out. *You said he'd die without the pills.*

No, I said he could *die. There's a difference. A lot of new mothers die giving birth too soon, and that's what I saw.*

Caleb snickered despite the severity of the circumstances. *Congrats, Ad. You're a mom. Why don't you breastfeed the little guy?*

Julian chortled.

Finally the "little guy" captured Sorin and forced him to the ground, holding him by the stomach. And the funny thing: his own beast could have helped him, but he'd come to this fight without the creature.

Now go finish this fight, Elijah said. *You've been given a golden opportunity. Let's use it and end this the right way.*

Aden stood. Almost fell, but managed to limp over. Grinning, he opened his ring. "Payback." *Je la nune* spilled over Sorin's neck, and *his* skin sizzled open, blood welling. Aden was careful not to splash the baby beast, who was watching him through starving, savage eyes.

While Sorin grunted from pain, Aden reached out and petted the—his—beast. "Good boy," he said, scrambling for a name. Chompers Jr., maybe. Junior for short. Yeah, that worked.

Lips pulled back from sharpened teeth as the creature growled at him. Chompers and the others purred when he petted them. Oh, well. At least Junior didn't release Sorin and snap at Aden.

Aden turned his attention to his opponent and bit hard, sucking back mouthful after mouthful of blood and loving every moment of it. Tasted just like Victoria's, just as he'd suspected it would. He might never stop, might take every drop, *needed* every drop. And wouldn't you know it, his beast purred about that, as if *he* could taste the blood, too.

Maybe he could. Junior released Sorin and joined Aden, drinking at Sorin's neck. Sorin bucked once, twice, before stilling.

We have to stop. If we don't, Sorin will die. He doesn't need to die. You've won.

Elijah again.

Ignored again.

No, he couldn't ignore the soul. Not this time. The outcome. Important. Victoria. Hate him. Love him. The words sliced through the bloodlust and Aden jolted upright, warmth fizzing over him as if he were showering in soda. Already his wounds were knitting back together. He reached out to Junior, but the little guy snarled at him before shaking Sorin's neck like a dog with a bone.

You'll have to wrestle him.

Great. Another fight. Aden dove for him, knocking

him down, away from the body and the blood. Wings flapped frantically, and those saber teeth made a play for his face.

A few of Sorin's warriors rushed forward, clearly intending to help their lord, who lay on his back, as motionless as the dead. "Don't," Aden shouted as he struggled to subdue the creature, and they froze. "Leave, everyone leave." Last thing he needed was for Junior to hurt someone else. Or to be hurt. "And no fighting, or I swear I'll release this one and end you all. You'll wait inside."

Several pounding heartbeats of time passed before footsteps reverberated. Murmurs echoed. Then, only the three of them were left. Sorin, the struggling Junior and Aden. He was surprised at how easily the vampires and wolves had obeyed.

A long while passed like that, so long that the rain stopped. So long that Sorin healed enough to awaken and sit up.

The warrior shook his head, as if clearing cobwebs from his thoughts, then zeroed in on Aden. He could have stood and attacked, but he didn't. He'd lost. He knew it. Everyone knew it. He watched Aden through narrowed eyes.

"You're not human," the warrior accused.

"Not anymore. Hell, maybe not ever." Along with

a beast of his own, he now had the vampire voice and skin. Made him wonder what else had changed—what else he could do.

Miracle of miracles, Junior stilled. He was panting through thick, black nostrils. Aden continued to hold him, cooing soothingly. His eyelids gradually closed, and surprise surprise, Junior had long, curling eyelashes. He appeared almost…cuddly.

Soon his big body went lax, and the panting became snoring. Still Aden held on, not knowing what else to do, knowing only that the beast could awaken any second, start combating him again, and if he wasn't prepared, he'd be blood-buttered toast.

Then Junior's body began to fade, fade, until Aden was utterly saturated by the same sizzling black mist that had left him earlier. He sat up, the mist seeping into his pores, his bones, heating him into a high output furnace.

Weirdest. Thing. Ever. His brain basically scrambled with bewilderment. That was…that had been…he had no words.

Sorin was unfazed. "By the way, my beast is bigger than yours."

"Not for long. Did you see the size of my guy's feet?"

Massive arms crossed over a massive chest. "Forget

the beasts. I've got a few things on my mind, Haden Stone."

Hearing his full name always gave him pause. "Like the fact that you want another go at me? Well, come on. Let's get this over with. Because I am not going to let you come back for seconds at a later date. You either serve me now, or you die now. Those are your only two options."

"I wasn't thinking of attacking," the warrior said, standing carefully. He wobbled on his feet, walked over and held out a hand. "I was thinking I will never live this down. I was thinking we should have fought with swords. I was thinking...I want to help you up. King."

O-kay. *This* was officially the weirdest thing. A turn of events he never could have predicted. A turn of events Elijah *hadn't* predicted. Made him terribly uneasy, but he was too fatigued to argue.

"Thanks." Aden didn't trust the man, but he slapped their palms together anyway.

SIXTEEN

THE VICTORY CELEBRATION was in full swing before Aden and Sorin entered the house. Goblets of blood had been given to each of the vampires, and glasses of wine to each of the wolves and humans. Laughter abounded. The king had proven his strength and cunning, after all, and the people here had followed him wisely.

Whispered theories abounded, too, everyone wondering how a human had finally turned into a vampire, and if other humans could now be turned.

"We haven't tried a turning in so long, the circumstances that prevented our success could have altered."

"But what were those circumstances? We've never known."

"Could have been our blood. Or theirs."

"I'd love to run some tests and find out."

"Yes, but will the new king allow it?"

No one seemed to mind their cold, wet robe or

sopping hair, yet Victoria couldn't stop shivering. Her teeth were chattering so vigorously, she feared everyone in the massive ballroom could hear them over the angelic hum of the harp.

Stupid human skin.

As she claimed a goblet of blood for herself, determined to feed the still-weakening Chompers even if the thought of drinking blood currently upset her stomach anew, she panned her surroundings. The marbled floor, the glass walls, the columns stretching to a web of crystals on the ceiling.

In the center of that web was a glittering chandelier in the shape of a spider, eight legs seeming to move from one corner of the room to another. A lovely space, if you liked a darker, almost gothic atmosphere. She preferred colors and always had. Pink, yellow, blue. Even white. Anything but the black her father had always insisted upon.

Perpetuate the myths, he'd said, and the humans will never take you seriously. They will always underestimate your strength.

She had been half awed and half horrified by her father. But she'd always assumed Sorin adored him utterly. Why hadn't—didn't—he?

Sorin. He was a puzzle to her, the pieces so scattered

she wasn't sure she would ever be able to find them and put them together. And Aden, well, he had won a fight against a seasoned warrior.

Even more shocking, no one here had hindered him or helped Sorin—if she didn't count Lauren and Stephanie, who were watching the doors for Sorin, and after yesterday, she *didn't* count them. More than that, Aden had a beast and the skin of a vampire. *Her* skin.

How much more had they traded?

She'd lost her ability to compel humans with her voice. She'd lost her ability to teleport. Aden could do one, which meant he could probably do the other. And what about her lightning quick speed? He'd moved so swiftly in that ring. Swifter than ever before. What about her strength? Only weeks ago, she had jerked a tree out of the ground with her bare hands, roots and all.

Just then, she wasn't sure she was capable of lifting her hair out of her face.

Would she still have saved Aden if she'd known this would happen?

The answer came in an instant. Yes. Yes, she would have. She would have given up *more*.

You just might have to, she thought.

Her hand shook as she brought her goblet to her lips and sipped. The blood was thick, cooling and had a metallic taste that left her grimacing. Ick. What she wouldn't give for a...sandwich. Yes, that's what those things were called. Thin slices of meat stuffed between bread and slathered with something thick and white. Her mouth watered at the same time her stomach growled.

Soon she would have to sneak back to the slave quarters. Very, very soon.

"V–V–Victoria!" a male called over the noise.

She spun, and there, in the far corner, was Shannon, the speaker, with Seth and Ryder beside him. Two of her brother's soldiers were perched at their sides, expressions foreboding.

How could she have forgotten that the boys had been taken, bound?

She placed her goblet on a passing tray and stalked forward.

"V–Victoria," Shannon said again, his stutter more pronounced than usual. "Do s–something. P–please."

Their gazes met for the briefest of moments, the green of his eyes almost fever bright. His mocha skin had dulled, yet he was no less beautiful. More so than even a lot of the vampires here. He was tall and naturally strong, and when he smiled, his straight white teeth on display, he was a diamond among zirconium. She'd always liked him.

He was in the center of the group, and though he stood straight and proud, his pinky was curled into Ryder's, as if the other boy was his rock, his comfort. Or perhaps he was Ryder's rock, as the usually tanned boy was currently colored a faint shade of green.

Seth was waving and grinning at someone over Victoria's shoulder. He even did the universal sign for *call me*.

Victoria looked the guards over, taking their measure. They lost their air of menace and smiled at her. Well, their version of a smile, anyway. They bared their fangs, their lips peeling back so much that she saw gums.

Both had razored haircuts and thin scars on their cheeks. Scars. How novel. How had they gotten them? The same way Riley had gotten the bump in his nose? Through repeated injury? And would *she* soon be covered in scars? If so, would Aden still think her beautiful?

Don't worry about that right now. She might fall into a spiral of depression. But then again, depression might help her feel normal again.

Concentrate. Right. Despite the "smiles," the one on the right looked like he enjoyed shards of glass and kittens for breakfast. The one on the left looked like he enjoyed just the glass shards, so she'd take her chances with him.

"You're in good spirits, considering your leader just lost his chance to rule," she announced.

One of his brows arched, nearly knitting into his hairline. "Who said he lost?"

An unexpected response. "Me. Aden, I'm sure. Everyone here, definitely. You did notice the party, didn't you?"

He shook his head, a little shell-shocked, as if her literal interpretation of his question threw him for a loop. He shared a glance with his friend before saying, "No, I mean, perhaps he only wished to test your Aden's mettle."

Oh, please. "What a wonderful way to cover the sting of a loss."

A shrug of wide shoulders, reminding her very much of her brother. How long had the warriors been together? "Think whatever you wish. It will not change the facts."

What facts? "So he threw the fight and allowed himself to become the indentured servant of the new king?"

"He would never throw a fight. Your brother is a good man, Princess Victoria. His goal has always been, and will always be, freedom for us all."

People were staring at them, listening unabashedly.

So, all right, then. Pleasantries were over, and a debate was not happening. "Release the boys. Now. Or I'll be forced to—"

"Of course. You'll be happy to note they are in the same condition as when we took them, and no worse for wear."

She folded her arms over her middle. "And the bruises on their wrists? The ones from the rope you used on them?"

"I'm positive they had those already," the other kitten-eating guard said.

Both men actually stepped aside, practically gift wrapping the boys for her. Too easy, she thought, mouth opening and closing as she floundered for a response.

Shannon and Ryder did not falter. They grabbed her hands and tugged her away. Shannon also latched onto Seth to propel him into motion. Midway, when her neurons began firing again, she took the lead. Where to take them, where to take them?

An older female vampire stepped in front of her. Older, but no less beautiful for it. Smooth skin, elegant features. "I wish to speak with you, princess." Gray eyes slid over the boys as a pink tongue ran over sharp white fangs. "How much for the tattooed one?"

"He's not for sale," she said at the same time Seth, the tattooed one, said, "What did you have in mind?"

With an I-mean-business frown, Victoria slapped the back of his head. "Not another word from you."

"Ow!" He glared at her. "What was that for?"

"He's not for sale," she repeated to the vampire. "For any price."

The female pouted. "You're sure?"

"Yes."

That gray gaze switched focus, landing on Shannon. "What about the—"

"*None* of them are for sale." Blood-slaves were traded all the time. For money, for clothes. For fun. Once that hadn't bothered her, but the thought of these boys, so like Aden, being passed around like bags of potato chips did not settle well with her.

"*Such* a pity." The female tossed her rope of blond hair over her shoulder before gliding away.

Victoria was stopped three more times with different offers to buy the humans before she at last ushered her charges through one of the many secret passages at the far end of the room. Secret, even though *everyone* knew about them.

This one opened into a small room that looked into the ballroom with two-way glass. Of course a young vampire couple writhed on the couch, and Victoria had to clear her throat to gain their attention. They sprang apart, both of them blushing as they righted their clothes.

"Uh, hello, princess, what are you—" the male began.

"Out," she said, and the pair scrambled to obey. She shut the door behind them. Squaring her shoulders, she turned to face the humans with the eagerness of a firing squad. "You have questions, I'm sure."

All three spoke at once.

"I was s-sleeping, all right, and a-all of a sudden this g-giant vamp—"

"—minding my own business and then I notice fangs. Fangs! After I pissed my pants, they forced me to—"

"—spare room or something I could stay in? Because I'm sick of going back and forth, and did you happen to notice the hot redhead with the giant—"

"—w-was that thing that came o-out of Aden? A d-dragon? It just r-rose out of h-him—"

"—rope burns. If I scar, I'm suing. I might sue anyway. Dan is going to kill me. If your blood-hungry friends don't snack on my organs first. I'm on my last strike, you know. And this time it's not even my fault. Why the hell—"

"—or even the brunette. You kind of owe me. I don't know if anyone's ever told you this before, but there *is* such a thing as cock-blocking, and you're proof."

Silence.

Okay. Where to begin? Guess she'd start with the basics. "I'm a vampire." And it was odd, talking to humans about her race. It was an offense once punishable by death. Or, at the very least, eternal imprisonment, cutting you off from the rest of the world.

That would have been her mother's fate if Victoria hadn't arranged for her freedom. *And what does she do? Refuse to visit me.* That stung more and more every day. Maybe because Victoria kept thinking of new reasons for her mother's refusal. She wasn't good enough. Wasn't liked anymore. Was a complete disappointment.

Was this how Aden felt when he thought about *his* parents? Abandoned, forgotten, unloved? Probably, and that was yet another thing they had in common.

"This house is full of vampires, as you saw for yourself," she continued. "What you don't know is that Aden is now our king. He fought my brother to defend his crown. He won."

"Yeah, he did," Seth said, raising his hand to high-five someone.

The other two just looked at him.

"What?"

"The monster you saw is..." Very hard to explain. "Something all vampires carry inside themselves."

"Oh, hell, no. *Aden* is a vampire?" Ryder's eyes were as round as saucers.

"Yes."

A smirking Shannon held out his hand to Ryder. "T-told you. Y-you owe me a f-five spot."

"You wagered on his race?" she gasped out.

"Not that. I s-suspected you were s-something different. The way you w-walk, talk, dead giveaways." He flashed her a grin. "The way you sneak into o-our room at the ranch, more so."

Once again she was in danger of falling into that spiral of depression. She'd worked hard to blend in, and yet, she'd failed royally. "How do I walk? Talk?"

"You glide," Seth said, wiggling his brows in approval. "And your accent is...different."

Different. A polite way of saying "creepy"? "How is Dan?" she asked. Still blaming himself?

"He's sad," Seth said.

"Worried," Ryder added.

Shannon shrugged. "G-guilty."

Yes, he still blamed himself. "Maybe, when Aden returns you to the ranch, he'll talk to Dan." She knew

Aden respected Dan, knew just how badly he had wanted to finish high school. And he'd planned to do so. Until she'd saved his life, changing the very fabric of who he was.

Would he look back later and regret the choices he'd made these past few days? She didn't want that. More than anything else, she wanted him happy. Now, always. And if things progressed as she thought they would, he had a long "always" to look forward to—or a long always to dread.

"Hey, what's happening out there?" Seth asked, pressing his face against the glass.

"What do you mean?" Beyond the two-way mirror, Victoria watched as everyone in the ballroom dropped to their knees, heads bowed. Voices tapered to quiet. She knew what that meant. "Aden has arrived," she said, every cell in her body going on alert. And sure enough, a sweep of her gaze, and she could see Aden and Sorin towering in the arched double doors.

Aden's hair no longer fell over his face, so she had a clear view of his swollen eyelids and discolored cheeks and jaw. The damage could have been worse, *much* worse, and should have been, considering the number of times her brother had introduced cartilage and bone to knuckles. At least he was steady on his feet. Not many would be, after receiving a beating like that.

He searched the room, his gaze sliding over vampires, wolves and humans, never pausing, completely determined. Was he...looking for her?

He was so hot and cold with her lately, she dared not hope. Best to think of something else. Something less upsetting. Like her brother. The moron.

Sorin had healed considerably but sported the same cuts and bruises Aden did. Especially in his neck, where the *je la nune* had burned away skin and muscle. Part of her wanted to shove her fingers into that wound and tug. He had used her. He hadn't known her ability to teleport had vanished, and so he had drugged her. Reduced her to a bargaining chip. Yes, he had done so to prevent a fight to the death—Aden's death—but he could have found another way. Aden had.

And there was reason number one Aden was the better choice for king.

"I can't believe I used to give him a hard time about stuff," Ryder muttered. "He could have kicked my ass and then some."

"It's 'cause you're dumb," Seth said.

"I'm not dumb."

"Dude, the only class you've got an A in is lunch. And we both know that A only stands for Appetite."

"He's g-got an A in recess, t-too," Shannon said with a grin.

Ryder shoved him good-naturedly.

Seth gagged. "My eyes! My poor eyes. Dude-on-dude foreplay is just gross."

Ryder lost his tolerant humor, balled his fist, about to take a swing, but Victoria stepped between them. "Enough." But really? What could she do if they decided to go for a knock-down, drag-out? Nothing, that's what. Not anymore.

More than that, if they hit her, they could inflict injuries she might not be able to recover from.

She'd never had to worry about such a thing before.

Suddenly Aden's gaze latched onto the mirror as if glued there—as if he could see through the smoky glass. She hadn't meant to look at him again, but it was habit now and she'd acted automatically.

When she realized they were peering at each other, she froze, helplessly trapped by his scrutiny. Could he see her? Impossible. But...

"You may rise," he said to the crowd.

Clothing rustled as everyone stood, cutting Aden from

her view. Murmurs arose. Giggles and jeers were thrown at Sorin. Right now, he was a laughingstock.

Perhaps that would change in a hundred years or so. Perhaps not.

When the crowd parted like the Red Sea, Victoria was offered another straight shot at Aden. He was striding forward and headed directly toward her.

Had he seen her?

Sorin stalked behind him, ignoring the barbs tossed his way.

A pair of soft, delicate hands reached out, caressing Aden, stopping him. Draven the *So* Going To Die, Victoria realized with a rising tide of anger. Again the crowd quieted, every ear in the room twitching and listening.

"Congratulations on your victory," Draven said silkily. "*My* king."

"Thank you. If you'll excuse me—" He tried to move around her.

She jumped back in front of him. "A moment of your time, if you please."

Indecision played over his features before he nodded. "A moment. Nothing more."

Her eyes glittered with menace, revealing the bitch underneath the beauty. "Very well, I'll jump right in.

I don't know if the wolf-shifter, Riley, or even Victoria herself, told you or not, but two weeks ago I challenged Victoria for rights to you."

Every muscle in his body stiffened, and his narrowed gaze rose to the mirror for one second, two, before returning to Draven. "Go on."

Perhaps the girl was stupid and didn't hear the warning in his tone. Perhaps? Ha! She was, because she actually continued. "You are human, after all, and—"

"*Was* human," he corrected with sharp reproof.

"I realize that," Draven replied. "*Now.*" Stupid was too kind. Obviously she had the IQ of a gutter rat. "But the challenge was issued and accepted weeks ago, as I said, when you were, in fact, human. So the law still applies. Victoria must fight me, as you fought Sorin. That is our way. That has always been our way."

The whispered theories reignited. How had Aden turned? Could someone else be turned?

A grayish tint washed over Aden's skin. "There will be no attempting to turn the humans," he called to one and all.

Even Victoria didn't know how or why Aden—and she herself—had survived when the only successful turnings had happened in the late 1400s. Bloody Mary—the original and not the former queen of England—was now the leader of the Scottish faction, and she had turned in that time frame as well.

Throughout the years, Victoria had heard rumors of a long-ago passionate affair between Vlad and Mary. That Vlad had chosen to turn her rather than his wife. And when Vlad later discarded Mary in favor of another, Mary had gathered her supporters and left, vowing revenge.

There had been battles, lives lost, but neither side had ever backed down. Amid both clans, people had tired of the constant bickering. Willing to abandon the only homes they'd ever known in the name of peace, they had broken all ties with *both* leaders, and more factions were created. So many, all over the world, each with a king or a queen, or both, if the more powerful of the pair was inclined to share.

Victoria thought of Sorin and his claim to have slaughtered Vlad's allies. A claim she was inclined to believe, considering none had arrived after Aden's summons.

A worrisome thought occurred to her. If word of that spread—*hey, everyone, the new vampire king has no backup*—well, he would become an even bigger target.

"As the king's number one adviser," Sorin said to Draven, "I have much to say about this."

Aden tossed him a what-the-hell frown. Victoria hid a smile behind her hand. Number one adviser?

"I am advising him to schedule the fight later today. After the beating I just received, I look forward to seeing someone else receive one. Namely you, little girl. I have watched my sister fight—"

He had?

"—and she is very, very good."

Draven buffed her fingernails. "I am agreeable to the time frame, and need only your approval, majesty."

Victoria's hand fell to her throat. Her oh-so-vulnerable throat. The chill inside her deepened, migrating into bone.

"What are you quaking about? You can take her." Seth tapped her on the butt. "She's straight-up bitch, but you've got a dark side. I can tell."

"Thank you. I think." She *used* to have a dark side. Now she just had a human side. Draven would tear her to pieces. And though she wanted to rush out there and stop the madness, she knew it was already too late. The fight *had* been accepted. To withdraw now was to admit defeat.

As Aden would soon learn, the loser of a challenge gave up everything to the winner. Their possessions... their lives. That's why challenges were so rarely issued.

Sorin was Aden's property now. For the rest of his very long life.

Victoria did not want to be Draven's.

"No, today is unacceptable," Aden said. "I'll set a time after I review my schedule, and an announcement will be made. Until then, stay away from her." He brushed Draven aside and kicked back into motion, Sorin remaining at his side.

The girl watched his back the entire time, her eyes slitted.

When he reached the mirrored wall, he stopped, his gaze roving, searching for the handle. "Victoria," he said. "Let me in."

He did. He knew she was inside. And peering through objects had not been an ability she had ever possessed. Shocked, she opened the door for him.

Their gazes clashed as the boys poured out from behind her and rushed to him, surrounding him, whooping, grinning like loons and shouting. Aden endured everything with flushed cheeks and a frozen expression of disbelief.

She smiled at him, and he smiled back. A moment all their own, despite the chaos. Pleasure bloomed. She cherished every second, knowing the memory was one she'd coddle for a very long time.

"That's the way it's done, bitches," Seth said, extending his arm through the doorway and flipping Sorin off.

Her brother blew him a kiss.

Ryder drilled his knuckles into Seth's arm and chortled. "Now who's the one enjoying guy-on-guy foreplay?"

"Stephanie," Aden called without turning away. "I need you."

Wait. What?

Her sister came rushing from the center of the crowd, chewing gum and twirling the end of her ponytail around her finger. "Present."

"Do me a favor and take the boys back to the ranch."

Frowning, she pointed to her chest. "Me?"

"Yes, you."

"Sweet! Really?" Jumping up and down, clapping her hands, she said, "I can drink them, right? Please, please, *please* tell me I get to drink them."

Aden's horror was instant. "No. Do not drink from them. I want them to arrive home in the same condition they're in now."

The bouncing stopped. She popped a bubble. "That's all you want me to do, then? Escort them? That kind of sucks—without actually sucking."

He glanced at Victoria for guidance. She shrugged.

"Yes, escort them only," he said, massaging the back of his neck.

Next came the patented Princess Stephanie pout. A glower, a stomp of her foot, a puff of breath. "Fine. Next time, though, I want an important assignment. You should see my skills with nunchucks."

"True story. I trained her," Sorin said. "She's very good."

"Comforting," was Aden's only reply.

Stephanie flattened her hands on Aden's shoulders, rose on her tiptoes and kissed him on the cheek. "By the way, thanks for not killing my big bro."

Aden cast Sorin a sideways glance, the same *what's happening around me* glance he'd thrown Victoria a moment before. She liked that. Liked seeing them work as a unit. "I can't say it was the wisest decision I've ever made, but he *is* growing on me. Like a fungus."

Stephanie laughed, a tinkling sound. "Whatever. You like him. I can tell." With that, she turned to the boys and waved them over. "Come on, pesky humans. Let's get you home."

"Alive," Aden reminded her.

"Yeah, yeah," she replied, not turning back but throwing her hands in the air.

Shannon patted Aden on the shoulder before walking off, and Aden nodded at him. A silent communication. They would be talking soon.

"Pizza first," Victoria heard Seth say as the foursome pushed through the enthralled throng, "*then* home."

"And you'll have to convince Dan we were there all along," Ryder said. "Seth mentioned you guys have some kind of freaky voice."

"We do, so it's not a prob," Stephanie replied. "But I could also nunchuck his head and he'll—"

"Use your voice," Aden called.

A growl of frustration pierced the air. "You take the fun out of everything!"

Chuckling, Aden focused on Victoria. "Now that *that's* taken care of…" He reached out his hand, twined her fingers with his, and they left the party. Together.

SEVENTEEN

RILEY HAD BEEN ON plenty of stakeouts in his life, but this was by far his fave. Even though it was a last minute change of plans and rushed.

First, he and Mary Ann had caught a glimpse of Aden's parents as they drove a truck away from their house a few hours before. Or who they thought were Aden's parents. Driver had been male, early to mid-forties, with brown hair, and from what Riley could tell with his superior wolf-vision, gunmetal gray eyes.

The passenger had been female, possibly in her late thirties, with blond hair, and from what he could tell, brown eyes. Both possessed muddy green auras. From guilt, maybe. Or fear. Hard to tell when the color was so murky, even with his superior wolf-vision.

Perhaps Joe and Paula Stone were living with regret for what they'd done to their son. Perhaps they'd simply been panicked 'cause they couldn't pay their electric bill. Either was possible.

Riley and Mary Ann were waiting in another house, across the street from the small, slightly rundown one the Stones had left, hoping to catch another glimpse of the couple when they returned. Perhaps even listen in on a conversation or two when they did.

Riley would have searched the house while the couple was gone, but he'd spied cameras. The expensive kind with face-recognition software. Too expensive for a home as cheap as that one. And with that kind of cheese being spent on cameras, he'd bet good money there were motion detectors on every door and window. Not to mention special hinges and even silent alarms. So, if he didn't have to do a smash and grab, he wasn't going to do a smash and grab.

That would come later, if the couple failed to return.

Part of him hoped they didn't return for a while. Currently he had Mary Ann all to himself. Tucker the Flaming Engorged Rectum was missing and had been since the café. Where the demon spawn had gone, Riley didn't know and didn't care.

Right now, Riley was sitting at the living room window, peering through the crinkled blinds. Yes, he'd broken into the place. The locks had been crap, and so had the doors they'd been nailed to, so it had just been a matter of busting the already chipped glass pane, reaching inside and turning the knob.

When would people learn? Glass next to a door was like *begging* every thief in the neighborhood to come inside.

Mary Ann was sitting beside him. They weren't touching. Yet. But they would be. Soon. By warding her back at the motel, he'd taken care of the witch and fairy problem. The two races couldn't watch her with their magic and intrinsic abilities anymore, couldn't track her except through human means. A skill they most likely lacked, considering they'd never had reason to use it. Meaning, the danger level was now close to nil.

That meant one soul-rocking thing. There'd be no interruptions.

And *that* meant one more soul-rocking thing. Riley was through being Mr. Nice Wolf. He had experience. He knew how to charm a girl. And had. Often. He knew how to tease and taunt to heighten curiosity and awareness. Now, he would charm Mary Ann.

Since nearly feeding on him, she'd been distant, quiet. He had to do something to convince her she wouldn't hurt him. She wouldn't. He wouldn't let her.

Because Riley and Victoria shared such a deep mind

connection, allowing him to do more than simply read her aura, and because he was so in tune to everything concerning Mary Ann, he'd inadvertently culled Vic's thoughts about the girl possibly being related to the fae. Something he was ashamed to admit he hadn't considered. Fairies were drainers, too, and yet they could control their feedings. So, if there *was* a connection, there was hope for Mary Ann.

Not that she would search. Not yet. She was determined to save Aden. Riley was, too, but he wouldn't put Mary Ann's life on the back burner, even for his king. Therefore, tomorrow his digging into her history would begin.

Right now he had to ease her worries about hurting him. Otherwise, she'd continue to resist everything he suggested. For the mission and for their relationship.

He scanned their surroundings. The way the neighborhood was laid out, they had a clear view of both the street and Aden's (possible) parents' place. There were no cars, no one out and about.

"Victoria texted me," he said, starting casually. Cold wind blew through the crack in the bottom of the window, causing strands of her dark hair to dance in every direction, even in his face. "Her brother came home, challenged Aden, and Aden kicked his ass in front of everyone."

"Good for Aden."

"We need to tell him what you've found."

"What have I found?" The frown she tossed him said the rest for her: you gotta think before you speak. "I've got nothing concrete, so there's no reason to get his hopes up."

"Not true. He should know you think you found Julian." For all Riley knew, Victoria had already told him. "He should know you think you found his parents."

"And crush him when we learn I'm wrong?"

"So you're wrong now?"

"No. But I could be."

"And you could be right."

"Or not," she insisted.

"When did you become such a Debbie Downer?" Her aura was a dark blue, sadness practically radiating off her. Mixed with the blue, however, were specks of brown that were soon to darken to black. Not a color that represented death—not all the time. But with her, that brown represented hunger, her need to feed, to draw energy into herself.

Those specks had grown in the last few hours. Not

enough to concern him. Maybe because he also saw specks of red and pink. Red for anger—or passion—and pink for hope. He wanted to nurture both.

Her mouth fell open. "I'm not Debbie Downer." The red bloomed a little brighter.

"Honey, you're the textbook version of Doomsday. You expect the worst, always."

"I do no—" There at the end, she caught herself. "Fine. I do." She leaned forward and rested her elbows on the edge of the pane. "Better safe than sorry, though."

"Actually, no, it's not. But if we're going to cliché this conversation to death, here's one you need to memorize—better to have tried and failed than to never have tried at all."

"I *am* trying."

"You're coasting, and you need to lighten up." *Way to charm her, you idiot.* All he was doing was pissing her off. He could have apologized for taking the harsh road, but he didn't. What he'd said was true. However, he did flash her a quick smile when he nudged her shoulder with his. "Let me help you."

Instantly suspicious, she eyed him warily. "How?"

They'd switched roles, he realized. Once upon a time, she had charged full-speed ahead, and he had been the one to press on the brakes. Now he wondered what would she have done if the situation were reversed. "Tell me a secret. Something you've never told anyone else." Excellent. Something the old Mary Ann would have suggested—and enjoyed.

Her tongue glided over her lips. "We're kinda in the middle of breaking and entering and spying. Now isn't the time to share."

Oh, yeah. Their roles had totally switched. "Now's the perfect time. Hasn't anyone told you it's prudent to multitask?"

"I don't know…" A hint of the old Mary Ann.

"Come on. Live a little. Add one more chore to our ever-growing list." Not that talking to him was a chore. He hoped.

A pause, then, "Fine. You go first."

He had her and tried not to smile. "All right. Here goes. I've regretted not sleeping with you." Straight to the heart of the matter.

The red halo around her brightened so much, it was almost blinding. Passion, definitely. His body reacted, heating from head to toe.

"I don't think that's a secret," she said softly. "But… I've regretted that you didn't sleep with me, too."

He froze. Forget charming and convincing her. He

liked *this*. The raw honesty of her tone, the longing she cast his way. "Mary Ann," he said.

"I—I—" She had to know what he wanted. To kiss her, to hold her. To finally be with her.

She turned away from the window, watching him through wide eyes. In the haze of light, he could see flecks of green mixed with the brown. "We shouldn't," she said, but she was wavering, he could tell. "Not here."

"We should." He didn't want to regret anymore, didn't want to wait. As Aden could attest, no one was guaranteed a tomorrow.

Her fingers moved to the hem of her shirt, twisting the buttons. Did she realize what that action did to him? How it tantalized him? "What if the owner of this house comes home? What if Aden's parents come home?"

Still wavering, so close to the edge. *Fall, sweetheart. I'll catch you.* "Then we get dressed. Quickly."

"You have an answer for everything," she said dryly. "I might have become a Debbie Downer, but you've become a pain the butt. You know that, right?"

"I just realized we need to work on your perception, too, because it's kinda skewed."

A laugh escaped her. "Or it's finally on target."

"Hardly." He loved the sound of her laugh. Husky,

wine-rich. And that *he* had caused it, well, he felt like he was king of the world. "I'm a little slice of heaven and you know it."

"All right. I know it."

Smiling, Riley moved closer to her, making sure some part of them touched. Forearms, hips. Breath hitched in her throat, even as his own hissed through his teeth.

Before he could swoop in to claim a kiss, a car snaked the far corner of the road before speeding along, closing in on the house they were watching. Mary Ann noticed and stiffened. Riley did, too, zeroing in on the driver. Male, early-twenties. Not Joe Stone. The car bypassed the houses, and they both relaxed.

"I wonder where Tucker is," she said with a tremble.

"You want to talk about him *now?* Seriously?"

"Safer for us, don't you think?"

Not really. "Tucker's probably in the process of a human sacrifice."

"He's not that bad."

"You're right. He's worse."

She pushed at his shoulder. At this second contact, he sizzled. She must have, too, because she didn't withdraw her hand right away. In fact, she flattened her palms on him and spread her fingers, touching as much of his biceps as she could.

As her aura flared with all that luscious red, she licked her lips. "All right. We don't have to talk about Tucker." There at the end, her voice dipped, going low with need.

The heat returned, wrapping around him. "What do you want to talk about?" His own voice had lowered.

"Our secrets."

All the encouragement he needed. He gripped her by the waist, lifted and turned her, until she was poised over him, then he set her on his lap. "Straddle me."

She did, and he drew her closer. Not all the way but just enough. Her arms wound around his neck and back. "What about the cars—"

"I can still see out the window." Truth. He could. When he looked. At the moment, all he could see, all he cared about, was Mary Ann. "Now kiss me. I need you so much."

"I need you, too," she said, leaning down and meshing their lips together.

He kissed her deep and sure, his hands sliding to her back, under her shirt, gliding up the ridges of her spine, then down, then tracing the waistband of her pants.

"You'll tell me if…" she rasped.

If she fed. "I'll tell you."

"Promise?"

"Promise." This time he would. He didn't want her to doubt him, ever. "But let's try something, okay?"

"What?" she asked, hesitant again.

"If the urge to feed pops up, or if you feel yourself drawing from me, don't pull away from me."

"No, I—"

"Just listen." He cupped her jaw, gentle, so gentle. "If that happens, keep doing what you're doing, stay calm, and just try to stop yourself from feeding."

"Stay calm. As if that'll be possible with your life in jeopardy."

"I honestly think you can stop yourself, that it's just a matter of control, but we can't know for sure unless you try."

She shook her head. "That's the kind of thing I should practice on others. Not you."

"Just do what Riley tells you, and you might like the results."

A snort. "We're speaking in third person now? Because Mary Ann doesn't like it."

"Actually, we're getting back to our secrets." He returned his attention to their kiss, and soon she did, too. He didn't try anything else, even though they'd gone farther than this before, until she was breathing more heavily and moving against him as if she just couldn't sit still.

He removed his T-shirt, then removed hers and pulled her closer, until their chests were brushing together with every inhalation. He allowed his hands to roam, exploring her. She did the same, sensitizing his skin in the most primal way. Soon he was moaning with every brush of her fingertips.

The few times he heard the hum of a car engine, he would break the kiss long enough to peer out the window, discover the driver was no one important, then dive back in.

Twice, Mary Ann froze on him, every muscle she possessed tensing. Both times occurred sometime after the cars drove past, so he knew they had nothing to do with her reaction, and he wondered if she'd felt herself trying to feed but had stopped herself in time. She must have. Not once did he experience a single flicker of cold. And that's what happened when a drainer fed. The victim felt cold. A bone-deep cold not even a thick winter coat could warm.

"Riley," she said, and he knew what that meant. She wanted more.

He gazed around the living room. A couch. Old, torn in several spots. Stained. No way. He wasn't having sex with her on that couch. Not for the first time. But he wanted her so badly right now, he—

Saw movement. Across the street, in the bushes of another house. Leaves rattling, a glow of orange. The color of confidence and determination. Riley pulled from the kiss and narrowed his focal point. The orange glow was faint, as if concealed by a metaphysical scarf, but it was there all the same.

"Riley?"

"Hang on."

A girl stood from the center of those bushes. Blonde, familiar. *Witch*. She held a crossbow, the tip aimed directly at Mary Ann. Riley jolted to his feet, taking Mary Ann with him even while shoving her out of the way.

He was too late. The action had been anticipated.

The witch moved with him, fluidly shifting her aim. The arrow whizzed faster than a blink. Glass shattered, and that arrow slammed into Mary Ann's back.

She screamed, a high-pitched sound of pain and shock, her eyes flaring wide, her body jolting. She was so close to him, the tip sliced at *Riley's* chest. He jerked her to the floor just as another arrow slicked through the now-open window, this one sticking in the far wall.

"What…happened?" She was panting, her words

barely audible. Blood poured down her chest and back, soaking her with little crimson rivers. Her aura was blue once again, but fading, the other colors having vanished. *Her* energy was draining.

"The witches found us." He never should have discounted their ability to track like the humans. And he never should have kissed Mary Ann. Deep down, he had known the dangers, the risks, but he'd allowed his need of her to persuade him.

This was on him.

He couldn't shift and hunt the witch-bitches because he couldn't leave Mary Ann like this. And hell! She should have been protected from mortal injury. She should have started healing already.

He'd warded her for exactly this kind of thing weeks ago. A stabbing, gunshot, arrow, it didn't matter. She. Should. Heal. But the witch had seen her back, the ward, and had aimed accordingly, hitting her in the one spot guaranteed to prevent her from healing supernaturally: the center of the ward, disrupting the words and negating the inked spell completely.

Just then, Mary Ann was as vulnerable as any other human. Unless...

"Feed off me," he said, even as he calculated the best escape route. He'd already walked through the place and memorized the exits, but he didn't know if witches now surrounded the place. If they did, the moment he carried Mary Ann away, they'd start shooting again.

"No," she croaked.

"Yes. You have to. You need to." If she fed off him, she would be strengthened. He would be weakened, yes, but she could take the witches out in a way he could not. All at once, rather than one at a time. Besides, it was fitting. Her ability to drain was why the enemy had chosen to notch her up with holes. "Feed off me and kill them."

"No," she said again, the depths of her stubbornness more apparent than ever.

"If you don't, they'll kill *you*."

"No."

Done arguing, Riley stripped the rest of the way and shifted into his wolf form, his bones readjusting, fur sprouting from his pores. He was so used to doing this, it felt more like stretching after a nap than actually becoming something new.

He clamped his teeth on Mary Ann's arm, as gently as he could, which wasn't much, and forced her to climb onto his back.

Another arrow soared overhead, just missing her.

Hold on tight, he commanded, speaking into her mind as he bounded from the living room.

"O...kay," she said, her teeth chattering.

He was a stupid idiot fool. She needed what little warmth her clothes would offer, but he couldn't pull a shirt over her injury and he couldn't afford to carry the material in his mouth. Currently his teeth were the only weapon he had.

He really could have used Tucker just then. Words he'd never thought to entertain. But an illusion or two would have seriously come in handy.

Left with no other choice, Riley raced out the back door, bursting through the hollowed plywood without pause. He zigzagged off the porch, making himself a harder target to lock onto, and good thing. Arrows rained.

How many witches were out there? More than Jennifer and Marie, he knew that much.

"Hurt," Mary Ann said.

I know, sweetheart. He pushed the words into her head. *I'd take your pain into my own body if I could.*

An arrow homed in on him and lodged in his front left leg. He snarled at the pain, but didn't slow and didn't dare stumble. Mary Ann would have fallen, and he couldn't allow that. Gravel bit into his paws, making everything worse. A quick search of the area, and he saw eleven auras. All orange, and all faint. They must have bespelled themselves, hoping to hide from him. Well, their spell hadn't worked fully.

He narrowed his focus on the one farthest from the others and closed in. A blur of motion, never slowing, he raced past the witch and chomped her between his jaws, dragging her along. She struggled against him, but still he didn't slow. Kept moving, taking both females farther and farther away. Careful, so careful.

Drain her, he commanded Mary Ann. *Now!*

She must have obeyed, because the witch's struggles tapered off…stopped completely. She became a limp rag in his mouth, and he spit her out. Still he didn't slow.

Any better?

"A little."

He'd get her somewhere safe and doctor her himself. Then, the hunt would begin. No more letting the witches and the fae chase while he and Mary Ann ran. That had been his biggest mistake, and one he wouldn't make again.

The hunters were about to become the prey.

EIGHTEEN

TUCKER PERCHED ON THE highest limb of an oak and watched as the wolf absconded with Mary Ann. They left a trail of blood a blind man would spot. The wolf was unsteady and weaving, and Mary Ann limp as a noodle. She wouldn't last much longer.

The wolf read auras, but Tucker knew the siren's call of death. No question, Mary Ann was even then swimming out to greet the lyrical grim reaper, and nothing would stop her.

The witch's aim had been true. Her arrow had sliced through the ward preventing Mary Ann from receiving a mortal wound. The location alone was damaging, but the blood loss would be more so.

Wards worked—until they were closed. Or burned away. Or any number of other painful things. Some people opted to get a ward to protect their wards, so that something like this could never happen, but not many went that route. What if someone gave you a ward you didn't want? 'Cause yeah. Being held down and inked with all kinds of badness never happened.

Tucker would have snickered at his sarcasm, considering he'd told Mary Ann how ugly it was, but he was too afraid it'd sound like a sob. Only pansy-assed babies sobbed. He wasn't a pansy-assed baby.

He was a liar.

He hadn't been completely honest with Mary Ann. Oh, he'd run from Vlad after stabbing Aden all right—but he'd run *after* he'd "chatted" with the guy. Bastard had threatened him with a few wards of his own if he didn't man up and do as he was told.

Man up. Funny, coming from a guy who looked more monster than man while he hid in the shadows, but whatever.

Until yesterday, Tucker hadn't exactly followed the former king's orders. He'd helped Mary Ann rather than hurt her.

He liked her. More than he should, and more than was wise.

Why'd she have to let the wolf stick around?

Tucker would have continued to resist Vlad if she'd kicked the wolf to the curb.

Because, when he and Mary Ann were alone, he was fine. A halfway decent individual. Dirty-minded, maybe, but who wasn't? Then Riley had shown up, and *boom*. Vlad had made another move, and Tucker had lost the battle.

Poor Mary Ann. She was an unwanted casualty.

Tucker waited as the witches who'd just annihilated her congregated under his tree. Red Robed Bitches, that's what he called them. They were glaring up at him, pissed that they'd failed and blaming him. Even though he hadn't been the one to freaking fail.

"You said we'd have the pair cornered if we waited until they were inside the house," the blonde in charge said. Marie, he thought was her name. She was a pretty thing but vicious in her determination.

Having rifled through Mary Ann's things, he'd found the address she'd tried so hard to hide. Had known exactly where she would go, if not when. So, he'd cast an illusion when she and the wolf left the café and followed them. "That's when I thought you were competent," he replied. "Why didn't you give chase?"

"And risk a draining?"

"Again I'm struck by the words *thought you were competent*."

They spat expletives at him.

He shoved from the branch and fell…fell…and landed on his feet. In the center of the RRBs now, he spun, his arms splayed wide, his vibe all about daring them to try something with him.

He really wanted them to try something with him.

He deserved punishment, but then, so did they. Only difference was, he knew he deserved it. They'd be the first to tell you how righteous their cause, how they were on the holy path, blah, blah, blah.

They had lost Mary Ann's trail after Riley warded her, but they hadn't lost Tucker's. Apparently they'd magically locked onto him, too, but Riley had refused to ward him, so there you go. Because of Riley's refusal, they'd never really lost the girl. Tucker would not take the blame for that.

The fae had been trailing Mary Ann and Tucker, as well. They would have been here, extracting their pound of flesh like the witches, only the witches had…politely asked them to leave, sending the other race home to their mamas.

After that, Tucker had thrown the witches an illusion—one of Mary Ann and Riley talking, arguing, tossing out names and info Tucker had pulled out of his ass—hoping to send the little RRBs running in a thousand different directions. Of course, that's when Vlad had called him.

Tucker...my Tucker...

Just. Like. That.

Everything had changed.

Tucker...

He shuddered as that eerie, commanding voice continued to shove its way into his head, leading him around like a puppet on a string. Wasn't difficult to do, either. The darkest part of Tucker's nature—the part that enjoyed verbally ripping his little brother to pieces, kicking puppies, fist fighting his friends, cheating on his girlfriend, watching the girl pregnant with his baby lose the respect of her family—that part craved the vampire's guidance.

The other part of him was curled up in a little ball, weeping like a stupid kid, sad about all the pain he'd caused—all the destruction he would soon cause. But Tucker hated that side of himself, too, so really, there wasn't any part of himself that he liked.

Tucker, my Tucker, finish this.

The king's voice was stronger than before, louder, more...everything. Every day he healed a little more, and one day soon, he would be the man, the warrior, he'd once been.

Vlad had commanded Tucker to approach the witches, told him what image to show them, told him what to say and how to act. And he had. He'd done all of it. Assumed the image of someone they knew—who he was supposed to be, he still wasn't sure—and they'd believed him and done everything he'd wanted without question.

"—even listening?" Marie demanded.

"No."

"Argh! You were always frustrating, but now you're just a bastard."

"You can't blame your failure on me," he said. "I gift wrapped the pair and handed them to you like it was your birthday." Just saying those words caused guilt to claw at him.

Tucker...you know what to do. Kill the witches, find the wolf and the drainer, and finish them off.

Kill the witches? Fine, no problem. Consider it done. But... *You wanted the wolf and Mary—the drainer's deaths blamed on the witches.* He shoved the words out of his mind, into the air, and knew Vlad heard him. Wherever he was. *If the witches are dead, how can they be blamed?*

I'm sure you'll think of a way. Now, do what I told you.

No sense in fighting Vlad. He'd come out the loser. Tucker squared his shoulders, his gaze narrowing on the gaggle of females around him. He shook his arms, just barely, but enough. The blades he'd stashed under his shirt sleeves slid into his palms. He gripped the hilts.

"Why don't you gift wrap them again," Marie said primly. "And we'll go from there."

"No, I don't think I will."

Cleary she did not like to be thwarted. She stomped her foot, saying, "Why not?"

"You're not gonna be around to accept any more presents." Without another word, he struck.

RILEY LEFT MARY ANN behind a Dumpster, shifted to human, didn't care that he was naked, stole a bottle of vodka and a pass key to a motel room from the clerk at the desk, a bag from one of the guests and went back for Mary Ann. He carried her inside the empty room without being seen or dropping her. A shocker and a miracle, considering he was as twitchy as a junkie in need of a fix.

He settled his bundle on the bed as gently as he could, then ransacked the bag for something to wear.

"Don't move," he told her when she thrashed against the mattress.

"O…kay?" she asked.

"Yes, we're going to be okay," he lied.

Only thing he found that would come close to fitting was a pair of shorts that had the word *Princess* stamped across the ass in glittery pink. Now wasn't the time to care about fashion—or the lack thereof. Or the fact that the shorts were too snug and he might never be able to have children. He might need to do another endless dash, and he had to be prepared.

He peered down at his leg. The arrow had been pounded out of him when he'd accidentally run into a tree, but he could feel the wood shards embedded in the muscle, cutting at him, making him bleed harder rather than heal. He applied pressure to force the shards out, grimaced, but wasn't going to let the pain stop him. If he didn't staunch the flow, he wouldn't be able to care for Mary Ann.

So he doctored himself as fast as he could, using one of the T-shirts in the bag, and raced back to the bed, where he crouched in front of Mary Ann. Her skin was chalk white, the blue tracery of her veins evident. There were bruises under her eyes, and her lips were chapped. All cosmetic—until you looked at her chest. There was so much blood caking her skin, she looked like she was wearing a red sweater. Worse, the arrow still protruded from the front *and* the back.

"H-how b-bad?" she whispered.

She was on her side, her shoulders slumped, and her head lolling forward. She was fighting sleep, her teeth chattering. Never had he seen her this weak and helpless. And he never wanted to see her like this again.

What he did want to do was panic the hell out, but he wasn't going to let himself. Someone needed to stay calm, and bottom line, he was the only option.

"R–Riley?"

Brutal honesty, no more lies. "It's bad. Real bad."

"Kn–knew it. D–dying?"

"No!" he shouted, then more quietly added, "No. I won't let you." He pressed his fingers into her carotid and counted the beats that jumped up to meet him. One hundred and sixty-eight a minute. God. The speed at which her heart hammered was a testament to how much blood she had lost. If she reached one hundred and eighty thumps a minute, there'd be no saving her.

He had to act fast. "I've got to leave you here for a minute, okay? I have to get a few supplies so I can re-move the arrow."

That'd make her bleed even more, but he couldn't patch her up with it there.

"O...kay." Her eyelashes fluttered, as if she were try-ing to focus on him but couldn't quite manage it. He needed to go, now, now, *now,* but if he released her, she would fall on her face or on her back, and both options would do more damage to her already fragile body.

Moving like he was on a racetrack being timed, he propped pillows in front and behind her, holding her in that position all the while, and tucked the blanket around her legs to keep her warm. Then he washed the blood off himself and zipped out the door, stealing money from the front desk, then zooming to the convenience store across the street to gather up gauze, disinfectant and anything else he could find that he might need.

Yeah, his shorts got a few looks. When he had what he needed, he just sort of threw the money on the counter and left.

Mary Ann hadn't moved. Her eyes were closed, her entire body shaking violently. Not a good sign. He counted her pulse again. One hundred and seventy-three beats a minute.

He was trembling as he uncapped the half-gone vodka, held Mary Ann's mouth open and poured the contents inside. He worked her throat with his free hand, ensuring she swallowed as much as possible.

She didn't choke, didn't protest, hell, didn't notice anything was being done to her. Good for her, since he was about to hurt her worse than she'd ever been hurt, but a bad sign. A really bad sign.

"You will not die on me," he told her. "Understand?" He splashed a bit of the alcohol over the wound. Then, still trembling, he gripped the front end, breathed in and out, trying to stop his trembling, and snapped the wood in two, removing the tip.

He threw the piece on the floor, lifted Mary Ann into the light of the lamp, and studied what remained. The shaft had gone all the way through, so the wood was peeking out both sides of her. Okay. Good. The damage had already been done. The danger now was leaving shards inside her when he pushed the rest of the arrow out. Which he had to do quickly, smoothly.

Like that was possible when he looked like he had advanced Parkinson's. Riley claimed the bottle of vodka and downed the rest in three gulps. The liquid burned a path along his throat, scalded his stomach, then blistered through his veins. He'd had to do this kind of triage before. To himself, to his brothers and to his friends. Why was he breaking down now?

He pressed his fingers into Mary Ann's pulse. One hundred and seventy-five.

A string of curses left him, but at least the alcohol kept him from vomiting. He moved behind her. In the mirror across the way, he could see that her eyes were still closed, her expression still too smooth for what was happening. Another breath in, out. *You can do this. Don't hesitate. Just act.*

He raised his arm. Lowered his arm. *Come on!*

Raised. Lowered. He wanted to grab the end of the shaft and jerk, that would have been easier, or should have been, but the wood was slippery from her blood and he'd never be able to maintain his grip long enough. So, he had to punch one end to shoot the other end out the other side. The thought of punching her, however…

You would rather she die? You would rather puss out than do everything you can?

With a roar, Riley balled his fist and did it. He punched the broken end with all his might. He made contact with the wood, then Mary Ann's flesh, pushing the arrow the rest of the way through her body, and out the wound in her front. She barely twitched.

Okay. Done, the worst was done. Time for the easy stuff.

So why did he feel faint? The shaking only got worse as he cleaned and bandaged her, and when he finished, *he* was the one covered in blood. Again. And this was fresh. Meaning, she'd lost more than another spurt or two.

She needed a transfusion and fast. Only reason she was still alive was because she'd fed from a witch on the way here. That wouldn't save her much longer, though. She was wheezing. The death rattle, some called it.

Riley scrubbed a hand down his face. What should he do? Carrying her to a hospital would kill her, no question. She wouldn't survive the jostling. Being picked up by an ambulance might actually save her—if they got here at the speed of light.

What a nightmare. *Now* he panicked. He paced through the room, his gaze constantly straying to the phone. If he called 911, they would pick her up, but they would also hunt down her father. Dr. Gray would take her home, where any number of enemies could be waiting for her, ready to strike while she was too weak to defend herself.

'Course, you had to be alive to defend yourself, and that beat the hell out of dead.

He was decided, then.

Riley called 911, told them about the emergency—injured girl, blood loss, location—leaving out names, and then eased next to Mary Ann.

"Don't tell them your name," he said, hoping, somehow, that she heard him. "Whatever you do, don't tell them your name."

No response. Worse, she no longer had an aura. She was colorless.

She needed to feed again, or she wouldn't make it, no matter how quickly the first responders got here. There wasn't time to find her another witch, her preference, but there *was* a solution: she could feed off him.

Not allowing himself to think about his actions, or the consequences, Riley reached around her and flattened his hands on her chest, just over her now too-faint heartbeat. He'd never done anything like this, so he wasn't sure it'd work, but he was giving it a go anyway. Maybe, as stressed as her body was, she would simply feed automatically.

Closing his eyes, he imagined the essence of his wolf-self. Deep inside, embedded in the marrow of his bones. Saw the tiny sparks of golden light that swirled there, pushed at the sparks, pushed, pushed, forcing them out of his body, through his pores and willing them inside of Mary Ann.

Her entire body jolted, and she gasped. A moment later, she sagged against the mattress, her breathing, dare he think it, evening out. Determination renewed, he continued to push, until he was sweating, panting, his own pulse rate rising. Until his muscles were knotted painfully, perhaps permanently. Until his chest felt like ground-up hamburger meat with tacks mixed in. He was raw, stinging.

How much time had passed, he wondered as he, too, sagged into the mattress. He didn't have the strength to look around at the nightstand clock. Nor did he have the strength to switch into his wolf form, something he'd wanted to do before the emergency crew rushed inside the room.

Which they were currently doing.

The door had crashed open, but he hadn't heard it. Couldn't hear anything, he realized. Three human men were looming over the bed, two of them looking over Mary Ann, forcing her eyelids apart, shining bright lights into her corneas, attaching some kind of medical pads to her chest. The other human did the same to Riley. Was talking to him, maybe asking him questions, but Riley couldn't make out the words.

The world around him was hazing over, as if a morning fog had rolled in. Then he was being lifted, settled against something cold and semisoft. A gurney, maybe. He turned his head to ensure Mary Ann was being placed on a gurney, too, but the fog had thickened, and he saw only a stretch of endless white.

Something sharp in his arm, something warm in his vein. No, not warm, burning, whooshing through him. A moment later, his eyelids were too heavy to hold open. Darkness came. He fought it, needing to know

Mary Ann was okay, that they weren't being separated. Another sting, another burn. Still he fought.

The darkness intensified. Stronger and stronger, until Riley was completely consumed. Until he couldn't move, could barely breathe. Until he forgot why he'd been fighting in the first place.

IN A STOLEN CAR, Tucker followed behind the ambulance. Both Mary Ann and the wolf were inside. He'd watched the paramedics wheel them in. Both had been hooked to IVs already, the humans working frantically to save them. Which meant they'd still been alive. Surprising. He'd heard the grim expectation in their voices, and knew they thought they'd lose both kids before they reached the hospital.

Maybe they would, maybe they wouldn't. Riley and Mary Ann had held on this long. Why not longer?

Either way, the pair had to die. Just like the witches.

The witches. *Don't think about that,* he shouted to himself. He'd just relive the screams, the sobs, the pleas and then the fading groans. The footsteps as a few escaped him. The ensuing chase. Failure. Vlad's insistence that he let the escapees go and find the wolf and drainer instead. Apparently, offing the pair was more important than offing the witches, who would be desperate to avenge their fallen friends.

Something Tucker would be punished for later. Brutally.

All too soon he realized Riley and Mary Ann were headed to St. Mary's, the hospital where Mary Ann had been born. The hospital where Aden had been born. The hospital where Mary Ann's mother had died.

Upon arrival, Riley and Mary Ann were quickly wheeled inside. They'd made it, survived the trek. Tucker exited his vehicle and stood outside, the bitter wind blowing around him. No one noticed him. Not even the cameras monitoring the area could pick up his image.

"What do you want me to do?" he asked Vlad, knowing the vampire would hear.

A guy in scrubs, who had been in the process of passing him, stopped and frowned, looking around. As Tucker was currently casting an illusion, the human saw only the emergency parking lot, the people walking through it and the cars ambling in and out of it.

They're weak. Now is the perfect time to strike, Vlad replied.

Muttering under his breath, Scrubs moved on.

"You want me to..." Tucker gulped. He couldn't

say the words. Even after everything he'd done, he still couldn't say the words. Not Mary Ann, his human side screamed. Please not Mary Ann. Not again.

Kill them, yes. Both *of them. And don't disappoint me this time, Tucker.*

"I won't," he said, thinking, *one day I'll kill* you.

Oh, and did I forget to tell you what your punishment will be if you fail me this time? No? A cruel, cruel laugh. *Well, allow me to do so now. I will find your brother. I will drain your brother. After I play with him a bit.*

No. *No!* This was not happening. They weren't doing this.

Are we clear?

His kid brother, one of the only people he truly loved. In danger. Because of him. *No,* he thought again, teeth grinding, but he said, "Yes, we're clear," and got to work.

NINETEEN

"WAKE UP. ADEN, YOU have to wake up."

Aden latched onto the voice as if it were a lifeline. And it was. He'd been trapped in an ocean of nothing, no sound, no colors, no sensations, with no way out. He pulled himself up a mountain, found that the line dangled over a cliff, and let himself drop, ending up in a river of ice.

"Aden." His entire body shook. "Wake. *Up*."

His eyelids popped open. He saw that Victoria loomed over him, black hair falling over her shoulder and tickling his bare chest. Concern painted twin circles of pink on her cheeks, and a clammy sheen glazed her brow.

"What's wrong?" he croaked. He sat up, his entire body instantly throwing out I-hate-you vibes. His muscles were tangled around bone, and his skin stretched too tight, a rubber band ready to snap. His mouth was dry as a desert, and his stomach…his stomach was the worst offender. Distorted, grumbling, shrunken and probably in the process of eating itself.

"You worried me," she said, straightening. She stuffed one of her hands into her pocket and played with something that crinkled. A wrapper of some sort, he would guess. "I was about to start pouring blood down your throat."

Hmm…blood…

He licked his lips, trying to recall his last waking moments. He'd stepped into the ballroom, a party in full swing around him. His gaze had swept the attendees, and he'd somehow looked *through* a darkened glass wall and found Victoria. A new vampire ability, he supposed. How many more would he inherit?

They'd left the ballroom together and come up here to talk. He'd sat on the edge of the bed, and…he didn't remember anything else. He must have fallen asleep.

What a wuss.

He'd meant to tell her about the dancing woman and the vision he'd had. The one of little Victoria and her whipping. Of her *mother,* the cause of that whipping. Maybe his impromptu snooze fest was a blessing, though. The news would have distressed her, and right now she didn't appear capable of shouldering another burden. She appeared...fragile, easily breakable.

"What time is it?" He inhaled and—mistake! Every thought in his head derailed. His sinuses clung to that tantalizing whiff of her, shooting sparks of gotta-have-that through his entire body. Moisture finally flooded his mouth, destroying the desert as if it had never been. His gums ached, their favorite thing to do, it seemed.

"Are you all right?" she asked.

"Fine," he croaked. "I'm fine."

"As Riley says, I'll pretend I believe that. And to answer your question, it's dawn."

He shook his head to clear the cobwebs, but they proved thick and stubborn. "Still?"

"The *next* dawn."

Okay, then. That made more sense.

"You entered a healing sleep," she explained.

Healing sleep. He'd never heard the term before, but just as he'd known the names of his vampires, he knew the meaning. A comalike state of total sensory deprivation, where vampire and beast merged into a single being. Blood cell count rose to extraordinary levels, speeding the curative process.

Healing sleep or not, however, he felt like he'd fought a few hundred bruisers and lost. Unfortunate, since he had stuff to do. He couldn't snuggle up and go for round two of the mattress blackouts.

He threw his legs over the side of the bed. He would have stood, but Victoria placed a chilled hand on his shoulder and pressed. A puny move, but effective all the same. And necessary. With that one little movement of his, he'd set off a chain reaction of pain. And more pain.

"If I went into a healing sleep, why do I feel like crap?"

"Because the new tissue is untried. Don't worry, though. Once you get up and stretch out, you'll feel better."

No room for doubt with such a confident tone. "How often have *you* had to endure this?"

A shrug of her elegant shoulder. "I lost count a long time ago."

He didn't like that. At all. "Want to go into details?"

"Not particularly."

"I can have anyone you like punished." Another mistake on his part. He'd meant the words as a joke, something to make her laugh, but she didn't laugh, and he realized he'd told the truth. Anyone who hurt her, he wanted to hurt in turn.

Time to switch subjects before he started issuing demands and upsetting her.

Now would be the perfect opportunity to tell her what he'd seen. Her mom, Edina, trying to run away with her, her dad catching her, blaming her, whipping her. Would she be embarrassed? Probably. She shouldn't be, but yeah, it would still kill her that he knew.

After all, he would have been embarrassed if the situation were reversed. He never wanted this girl to see him weak, at his worst. Like now. He could barely stand that she was seeing him bruised and swollen. And he had to be bruised and swollen, despite that healing sleep. Aches and pains were not exactly liars.

But if *he* felt that way, she would, too. Vampires seemed to carry a thousand pounds more pride than their human counterparts. So. Okay. Yeah. Maybe this was one of those things he just needed to take to the grave. Knowing helped him understand her, and understanding caused him to toss a heap load of respect her way. No reason to ruin that by—what?—upsetting her.

Was that cowardly of him? His rationale to get him out of an uncomfortable situation? Maybe some would say so, but he honestly didn't think so. Sometimes full disclosure was cruel and silence kind.

He was running with that.

"Have you had any visions of my past?" he asked, counteracting his decision in a snap. He'd just opened the door for her to ask if *he* had. And if she asked, he couldn't lie.

"No. Let's talk about that later, though. Okay? Yes? You need to see something."

"See what?"

"This." She turned, some kind of black remote outstretched in her hand. After pressing a few buttons, the wood panel over her dresser parted, revealing a large television screen. Colors flickered together, then images formed. She scrolled through the channels quickly, stopping when she reached a news station. "Listen."

A somber-faced reporter stared out at him, an umbrella overhead, a light drizzle of rain falling. "—been dubbed the Red Robe Massacre of Tulsa," she was saying. "Ten women, all brutally slain. Police are working diligently to find clues as to who could have committed such a heinous crime."

"Tragic," he said, "but why did I need to know it?"

Victoria hit Mute and fell onto the mattress beside him. "Females wearing red robes. In Tulsa. Where Riley is. Where Mary Ann is. They're witches, Aden, and they must have been the ones chasing the pair. They were stabbed repeatedly, which means the fairies, vampires and wolves weren't responsible."

He jumped on the topic with the finesse of a freight train. "Are Riley and Mary Ann okay?"

Her hands wrung together, and when that wasn't enough, she twisted the fabric of her robe, leaving wrinkles in her wake. "I don't know. He hasn't contacted me in a while."

"Elijah?"

I don't know, the soul said.

Okay. So the soul hadn't seen anything bad. That beat the crap out of the alternative. "How can you be sure the creatures you named aren't responsible?"

"Fairies would not have caused bloodshed. Vampires would have, but they would have licked up every drop of that blood. And the wolves would have left claw marks, not knife slashes."

Hmm, blood...

The moment the thought registered, he sank into a dark pit of humiliation. People had died. Violently, painfully, and he craved a snack?

"Aden," Victoria prompted.

Right. He needed to comment. See Aden discuss murder as casually as the weather. "Who does that leave?"

Wait, wait, wait, Caleb suddenly said. *Go back. I was*

*just waking up and had to have misheard. Did she just say a
coven of witches was...murdered?*

Victoria was talking, too, but Aden heard only Caleb,
the soul's upset giving him volume. "Yes," he replied.
"I'm so sorry."

No. She's wrong, she has to be wrong.

"Caleb—"

No! Elijah. Tell him she's wrong. Tell him!

I'm sorry, too, Elijah said sadly.

No! A plaintive cry. A cry that must have opened a
dam of heartache, because Caleb began sobbing.

The soul had liked the witches from day one, and had
thought he was somehow connected to them, that he'd
known them in his other life. The one before Aden.

*You have to go back in time, Aden. You have to save them
from this.*

His reply was instant. "No. I can't."

You mean you won't.

"Too many things could go wrong. You know that."
It was the same answer he'd given Victoria, when she'd
asked. The same answer he would give anyone, *everyone,*
who asked. When you weighed the risks against the re-
wards, the risks always tipped the scale.

There was no reason good enough to tip the scale in
the other direction.

Please, Aden! Please.

"No. I'm sorry."

While Elijah and Julian attempted to comfort their friend, Aden met Victoria's curious gaze. "The news has…" *destroyed* "…disturbed Caleb."

"I'm sorry."

"Me, too." And he was, even though Aden had never liked the witches himself. How could he? They'd cast the death spell over Riley, Mary Ann and Victoria, and nearly ruined the life he'd built for himself. But he hated for one of his souls to suffer, and he would have spared the witches for that alone.

"The best thing we can do for him is figure out what happened and make sure it doesn't happen again," he said.

"I agree. You asked me who could be responsible. I don't think the goblins or zombies are smart enough, so that leaves…humans."

All the commotion woke Junior. The beast stretched inside his head, making little mewling noises. Aden tensed. Exactly what he needed. Another fight. Then he recalled what Elijah said, that Junior responded to emotion. If he remained calm, the beast wouldn't fight him.

Yeah, he could do that. Maybe.

"How could a few humans defeat a coven of witches?"

he asked. Good. Right track. "We've seen the power of
their spells firsthand. And humans, well, they're eudu-
cated when it comes to magic. Anyone who so much as
approached the witches would have been defenseless."

"I don't know."

"Maybe one of the races you named *wanted* humans to
be blamed and framed them."

"It's possible. But why do so? To send a message?"

"A we-know-what-you-are-and-we're-coming-after-
your-kind sort of thing?"

"Yes. No. Maybe. I don't know. Nothing like this has
ever happened before. We clean up our battles. All of us.
We rarely leave evidence for humans to find. That's how
we're trained from birth. That's how we survive."

"Times change."

"Yes," she said flatly. "They do."

What did that mean? He'd changed, and she no longer
liked him?

Junior belted out a hungry roar.

With a sigh, Aden fell back on the mattress, winced
and draped his arm over his forehead. "I'm not thinking straight. Let's talk about the murders after we eat,
okay?"

Her hesitant "Okay" gave him pause.

"Did you already eat?" For that matter, "Where did

you sleep last night?" He'd taken her room, and she had not been here. And he could have kicked his own butt for simply falling asleep on her, making her feel as if she didn't belong in her own digs. He knew how important having personal space could be, having been denied his own for most of his life.

Before, Victoria would have felt comfortable enough to snuggle up to him. After the way he'd treated her lately, she probably hadn't known if he would welcome her or reject her.

"I stayed in Riley's room," she said, her hand going back in her pocket to play with the wrapper or whatever it was.

A growl rose up in his throat before he even realized he was having an emotional reaction to those words. *Calm down.*

He recalled the first time he'd seen Victoria outside one of Elijah's visions. She'd been standing in a forest clearing just beyond the D and M ranch, Riley towering behind her, protecting her. Aden had wondered what they were to each other—and even when he'd learned they were just friends, thrums of jealousy had refused to leave him.

Closeness was closeness, no matter how you sliced it.

"You could have slept here," he told her.

"Well, did you, the king of heaven and earth, mention that a single time since coming here?"

No, she hadn't known. "I'm mentioning it now."

Crinkle, crinkle. She wasn't done. "That's great. Wonderful. Considering you've done nothing but push me away for days."

Annnnd there was the crux of the problem. "I'm sorry for that. I really am. But I'm improving. Right? I mean, you've changed, too." Great. Now he was throwing blame, something she didn't deserve.

"Meaning I'm more human?" *Crinkle, crinkle.*

What *was* that? "Meaning, nothing bad, I swear. But… yes, you have been more human. And again, that's not a bad thing."

"Yes, it is. You're saying I wasn't good enough as I was."

"No! That's not what I'm saying at all."

Still she wasn't done. "The fact that you're improving is great. Wonderful."

He was going to hate what came next, he just knew it.

"But I've decided to hold a grudge," she finished.

Yep. Hated. "Are you serious?"

"Am I known for my delightful sense of humor?"

When she gave in to the new human side of her, she really gave in. "Why are you holding a grudge?"

"Because I feel like it."

And how did you argue with that kind of logic? "Fine."

"Fine."

"I still need to eat."

Flames lit up the blue in her eyes. "Do you want me to fetch you a slave?"

No. Yes. "No." Only one name was etched into his menu of choice, and it was still hers. But he'd had Sorin's blood. And, hey, why wasn't he seeing the world through Sorin's eyes? He asked Victoria.

"The blood only works that way for a limited amount of time, and since you've spent an entire day dead to the world, your connection to Sorin, and his to you, has passed.

"Now," she added. "Why don't you want a slave?"

"I'll find someone to chomp on in a minute." He would force himself. "I need to clean up first."

Crinkle, crinkle.

"What's in your pocket?" he asked

Her checks flashed bright red. "Nothing. Now go. Clean up."

O-kay. He lumbered from the bed and hobbled to

the bathroom, certain he resembled an old man with a walker, and yes, he hated that Victoria was seeing him like this.

"Oh, and Aden? Thank you for not killing my brother," she said just before he shut the door.

"You're welcome."

He brushed his teeth, showered quickly, noticed Victoria had already stacked fresh clothes in the corner, and dressed in the plain gray T-shirt, jeans and his own boots. Everything was pressed and a perfect fit.

As Junior's roars came more frequently and Caleb's choking sobs finally faded, Aden studied himself in the mirror. It was still a jolt to see himself with blond hair. He'd been dying the mop for years. His eyes jolted him, too. Last time he'd seen them, they were gold. Now, they were a kaleidoscope of colors.

What stunned him most was his lack of bruises, swelling and punctures. He looked one hundred percent racer ready. His insides clearly had some catching up to do. Even after that steamy shower, he hurt. Considering he'd expected his lips to resemble something out of a horror flick and the fact that he'd lost a tooth—which, three cheers, had regrown during his healing sleep—he wasn't going to complain.

Could you please shut that beast up, Ad? Julian asked,

pulling him from his thoughts. *All that roaring on top of everything else is annoying, and I'm not sure how much longer I can deal.*

"If we want to quiet Junior—" at least for a little while "—we've got to eat."

Pick a blood-slave, like Victoria suggested. Please.

The term *blood-slave* was really starting to bother him. Yeah, that could have been his fate, and could still be his fate since he was jonesing so badly for the princess and only the princess.

His ears twitched. Footsteps in Victoria's room. Frowning, he threw open the bathroom door. Before he saw who had entered, he *smelled* who had entered. Riley's brothers. Maxwell and Nathan. They reeked of the outdoors and fear.

Nathan was pale from head to toe. Pale hair, pale blue eyes, pale skin. Maxwell was gold. Both were handsome—he guessed—but both were cursed by witches. (Who wasn't, nowadays?) Anyone the pair desired would see a mask of ugliness when looking at them. Anyone they did *not* desire would see their true faces, their beauty.

Aden, of course, saw their true faces.

Both were scowling and taut with their worry and trying to comfort a crying Victoria.

"What's going on?" he demanded, stalking over, ready to grind them both into powder if they'd hurt her.

He was just about ready to throw a punch, anyway, when she held out a goblet to him. "Here. Drink this."

He smelled the sweetness before he saw the blood. Junior went wild, his roars more of a yes, yes, *yessssss*. Or maybe *give me* was more accurate. Aden's mouth watered uncontrollably, his gums doing a little dance of anticipation. He knew without asking exactly whose vein the blood had been tapped from. Victoria's.

His arm was lifting, the cup at his mouth, his throat gulping back the contents a second later, and only when he'd consumed every drop did he even realize he'd moved.

After he'd drunk Sorin's blood, he'd considered himself strong. He'd been a fool. *This* was strength. A warm cascade that shimmered through him, lighting him up like a house at Christmas. His eyes closed as he savored.

The fog that had seemed to attach itself to his mind disappeared completely. His cells fizzed as if they were dancing with champagne. All the remaining aches and pangs from the fight with Sorin vanished. His muscles plumped up, and he might even have shot up an inch or two.

Junior purred his satisfaction, and like a baby who'd just gotten a bottle at bedtime, he slipped back to sleep.

Aden, though, well, he just wanted more.

No more for you, Julian said, conjuring the Soup Nazi.

How had the soul known what Aden was thinking? Had he said the words aloud? Was he staring at Victoria's neck? Wait. How could he be staring? His eyes were still closed.

He focused, realized he had dropped the cup and latched onto Victoria's arms. Was pulling her closer... closer...

Jolting out of his stupor, he released her. Backed away. Maxwell and Nathan were watching him with unease.

Later, he would see the world through Victoria's eyes. No healing sleep would stop it from happening. Would he also continue to want her blood, and only hers? If so, who cared?

Because—and here was the clincher—having her was worth the risk of addiction. He would endure *anything* to be with her, to have her blood. Everything that had ever bothered him and more.

Victoria shifted from one foot to the other. He was still staring at her, he realized. He lowered his gaze, and that's when he caught sight of her wrist. Though she wore a long-sleeved robe, the material had pulled back to reveal a wound stretching from one side to the other.

She'd cut herself, and recently, but she hadn't healed.

Why hadn't she healed? For that matter, her hand had been cold earlier. Her hand had never been cold before.

"Are you okay?" he asked her.

"No." She held her phone in front of his face. "Look what came in."

He read the screen. "Tulsa. St. Mary's. Dying. Hurry."

"That's from Riley," she said, chin trembling as she fought her tears.

That's not from Riley, Elijah said.

"How do you know?" Aden asked.

"Because he's been—"

"Sorry." He held up his hand. "Elijah knows something. Hang on."

She nodded, both worried and hopeful.

First, the soul continued, *deductive reasoning. If Riley was dying, he would not have typed so perfectly. And do you see any misspellings? No. Second, I just had a vision of Tucker typing those words.*

As the bottom of Aden's stomach fell out, he told the group what Elijah had said.

Then, he turned his attention inward again. "What else did you see? Show me. Please."

You won't like it.

"Do it anyway."

Silence. Such oppressive silence.

A sigh. *As you wish.*

A moment later, Aden's knees nearly buckled. In his mind he saw Riley strapped to a gurney, his skin the color of death and a gaping wound in one of his calves.

Mary Ann was also strapped to a gurney and being wheeled into an ambulance. An ambulance clearly marked *St. Mary's*. She wore a pair of jeans and a bra, and she, too, had a gaping wound. Only, hers was in her shoulder. Someone had obviously tried to clean her up, because she was streaked with dried blood, patches of blue-tinted skin between the crimson.

Paramedics were pumping her chest, but she wasn't responding.

"Tucker might have typed those words, but he wasn't lying," Aden croaked out. "They're hurt. Badly." If his friends died...

If they'd *already* died...

"What's wrong with Riley?" Maxwell demanded.

Aden explained what he'd seen.

The brothers cursed, dropping so many F-bombs

Aden soon lost count. Victoria pressed her knuckles into her mouth, but a sob still managed to escape.

"Could *Tucker* have killed the witches, then turned his sights on Riley and Mary Ann?" Nathan asked. "He's part demon, and he can cast illusions. So, if anyone could defeat a coven of witches, it's him."

Caleb dropped a few sobbing F-bombs of his own, each one directed at Tucker.

"Tucker wouldn't have been able to defeat Riley," Maxwell said.

Aden had to concentrate to hear past the sounds in his head. "Whatever happened, we have to get to St. Mary's." He didn't know a lot about the shifters, but what would happen if the paramedics discovered something different about Riley? "Can you teleport us, Victoria?"

To Tulsa? Yes, Caleb said, rousing himself from his anger and grief. *We'll go to Tulsa. We'll investigate. We'll savage Tucker if he did this.*

The thought of vengeance was like a shot of adrenaline, Aden supposed.

All the color drained from Victoria's cheeks. "N-no. I've been meaning to tell you…" Her gaze flicked to the shifters. "My, uh, brother…whatever he did to me must still be affecting my ability. I can't. But maybe, I don't know, you can."

"Me?" He'd never tried, had no idea how to begin and didn't want to waste time learning when he might not possess the ability anyway. "No, we'll drive."

There was a knock at the door, then hinges were squeaking as the beautiful Maddie entered. She wore the same expression she'd worn the day she'd told him about Sorin's visit.

"I don't know why I've been chosen to be the bearer of bad news *again*," she began, licking her lips in agitation, "but your human friends have returned, majesty."

"I don't have time to deal with them. Tell them to go home and I'll—"

You need to speak with them, Elijah cut in with an urgent tone. *Now.*

But the witches—

"Have to wait," Aden said, cutting Caleb off with the same sense of urgency in *his* voice. "I'm sorry." A muscle ticked below his eye as he motioned to Maddie to lead the way. "Take me to them."

Down the stairs, around several corners and into the foyer they went. There stood Seth, Ryder and Shannon. All of whom were covered in soot, smoke practically rising from their shoulders.

"What happened?" he demanded.

"The ranch," Seth began, then stopped to cough.

"B-burned down," Shannon finished. "Every b-bit of it. N-nothing left."

Aden stiffened. "Dan? Meg?"

"Alive, but injured, both of them," Ryder said. "And they're only alive because Sophia got them out."

Sophia, Dan's favorite dog. *Don't react. Not yet.* One reaction would lead to another, and he couldn't break down right now. He had to stay strong. But too much was going wrong all at once. Too many bad things piling up, weighing him down. *Crushing* him.

Looking so weary Aden wondered how he was even standing, Shannon massaged the back of his neck. Tears had dried on his cheeks, streaking through the soot. "S-Sophia didn't make it, though. Neither did Brian."

Brian, another boy who'd lived at the ranch. He'd never been a close friend, but still, Aden would not have wished such a death on him.

"Terry and RJ are moving out ahead of schedule. State's gonna break the rest of us up," Ryder said, and that's when the fatigue hit him. He hunched over, breath emerging heavily. "They're gonna send us to other homes. Maybe prison. Cops will think one of us set the fire."

"Did you?" Nathan asked.

Seth erupted, getting in his face. "No, we sure as hell didn't. That ranch was our *home*. Dan was the only person who ever cared about any of us. We would not have hurt him. Ever."

So, who did that leave? Tucker? But even a demon couldn't be in two places at once.

"My father," Victoria whispered, horrified. "He's begun to strike at you, I think. Which means he's getting stronger."

Yeah, Aden suddenly thought so, too. No longer were the boys safe. But if they ran, they'd look guilty of the crime. Plus, Vlad could clearly track them wherever they went.

There was only one place they'd be safe. Here.

Everyone was watching him, awaiting orders. Or answers. The burden of protecting them, all of them, was profound. He'd accepted the challenge, though, and won, so the burden *was* his to carry.

"Maddie," he said, turning to the girl. "Bring Sorin to me."

She nodded and was off, her black robe floating behind her.

As soon as Victoria's brother rounded the far corner, headed in his direction, Aden started throwing out more orders. "You're in charge, Sorin. Just don't get used to the position. I've gotta take off for a bit. Spread the word," he told Maddie. "Maxwell, Nathan, you're coming with me and Victoria to Tulsa. The humans are staying here. They aren't to be hurt."

"I'm g-going with you," Shannon said, the picture of stubbornness.

The vampires and shifters gasped at his daring. Seth and Ryder just looked confused by their reaction.

Wasn't worth arguing over. Besides, it might be nice to have a human by his side.

Wait. Had he really just referred to his friend as a human? He was even thinking like a vampire now. "He's coming with us," Aden amended. "And I changed my mind. So are Seth and Ryder." That way, he wouldn't have to worry about leaving them here. "Sorin, let everyone know the Draven/Victoria fight is on hold until I return. I want to watch it, and I can't do that if I'm gone. Anyone who says this is a ploy to save Victoria from a beating—"

"Will be punished," the warrior said. "I know how this works."

"Send a few of the shifters to Crossroads High. I want the building guarded day and night." Just in case Vlad tried to strike at him that way, too. "And I want someone protecting Mary Ann's dad at all times, too." No chances.

Sorin nodded, clearly happy with the turn of events. "It will be done."

Aden still wasn't sure he could trust the warrior, but he didn't know what else to do. Either Sorin was actually working for his father, here to spy on Aden, or would fight his father more fervently than anyone else and help Aden's cause.

Elijah hadn't protested, so Aden wouldn't worry—overly much.

"All right," he said, turning to his friends. "Let's go save Riley and Mary Ann."

If it isn't too late, Elijah said now.

"Unless you have something productive and *positive* to add," Aden told him, "don't speak again." Another cryptic warning would only grind him further into the dirt.

Elijah remained silent the entire drive to Tulsa.

TWEN+Y

ST. MARY'S. A SPRAWLING SET of buildings both long
and high, with orange sandstone and countless windows.
A large white cross stretched from the center of the tall-
est structure, which was situated in the center. Cars lit-
tered the parking lot, people coming and going in every
direction.

Aden sat in the passenger seat of the black SUV Maxwell had produced back at the mansion, studying the
entrances and exits, every face that passed him, all while
searching for any landmark that didn't quite fit the scene.
If Tucker were casting an illusion, he wanted to know.

Nothing seemed out of place. No one watched him.

He supposed, after the Red Robe Massacre, two injured teenagers weren't news. Unless the police suspected
they were somehow connected. Either way, Mary Ann
and Riley were going to be questioned. If they hadn't

been already. Guards were going to be stationed outside their doors.

Come on. Let's do what we came to do, Caleb said, impatient, *so that we can do what I need to do.* He wasn't crying about the witches anymore, but he was pissed. The cold kind of pissed where the need for vengeance seethed.

Aden preferred the tears. At least the soul hadn't tried to take over his body again.

"Not yet," he muttered, and everyone in the car leaned forward, expecting an order. "Souls," he explained.

A chorus of disappointed "ohs" filled the car. They were ready to act, too, but he wasn't going into this thing blind. They would have a plan and take every precaution.

You know, this place looks familiar, Julian said.

It should. Aden had been born here, and the souls had died here.

A wave of…*something* swept through him. Sadness, maybe. Fear. If Julian remembered how he'd died, who'd he'd been, he could leave. Forever. Aden had always thought that's what he wanted—time alone, the ability to concentrate—until he'd lost Eve.

Well, it doesn't look familiar to me, Caleb snapped. *But maybe that means I need a closer look. Hint. HINT.*

"What do you think you'll find inside, Caleb? The witch bodies?"

Yes. No. I don't know, okay. But it wouldn't hurt to check out the morgue, or, if the police suspect Riley and Mary Ann of being involved, getting a peek at their notes.

Morgue, Julian echoed, a hollow edge to his tone. *I don't want a closer look at it. I don't want to fight anyone in there. I'm creeped out. I want to leave.*

Yeah. The moment Aden stepped foot inside the morgue, crossing the living-people-reside-here/dead-people-belong-here threshold, every body in the room would reanimate and rise. Attack. He'd have to remove their heads to kill them—again—and just how would he explain *that?* No, thanks.

Elijah must not have had anything productive or positive to offer, because he didn't chime in.

Aden scrubbed a hand down his face, wishing he'd kept his own lips shut back at the mansion and not lashed out at the psychic. Elijah had only wanted to help him.

"With my abilities, I can't risk going in there," Aden admitted to the others. "Maxwell, Nathan, how good are you at tracking?"

"The best." Maxwell, the driver, twisted and eyed his brother, who sat directly behind him. "You bring the stuff?"

"Hell, yeah," Nathan said, lifting a nylon bag he'd stuffed under his seat. "Always."

They shared a semblance of a grin.

"We'll find them, no problem," Maxwell said to Aden. "And no one will suspect us of anything, even if we smack into a cop."

"Explain."

"Why don't I take it to the next level and show?" Nathan unzipped the bag, reached inside and tossed Maxwell a pair of sunglasses. As Maxwell pushed them over his nose, Nathan pulled out a few others things and then, right there in the car, he shimmied out of his clothes and morphed into his wolf form.

Seth, Shannon and Ryder dove over the backseat, into the trunk space, and pressed themselves against the window.

"How did—"

"T-that was—"

"No *way!*"

"You met the vampires," Aden said, "now meet the shape-shifters."

There was more floundering, and Aden could practically taste their fear and shock. Could definitely hear the increase of their heartbeats. Junior noticed, too, and offered up one of his patented roars.

"What else is out there?" Ryder asked, peering at the wolf as if he was toxic.

"Everything you can imagine."

His grin as grim as before, Maxwell exited the car and Nathan bounded into the driver's seat, then to the concrete outside. Maxwell loaded him down with a harness, service vest and leash.

Victoria, who sat behind Aden, giggled behind her hand. Half humor, half apprehension. "A Seeing Eye dog?"

Maxwell wiggled his brows over the rim of the shades. "No one asks a blind man what he's doing or why he's doing it."

"Brilliant," Aden said.

"We'll be back as soon as we can." With that, the pair was off, Nathan leading the way, trotting slowly, and Maxwell stepping tentatively behind him.

For a moment, as Aden watched them, he caught a glimpse of Edina the Dancing Mama winding through the cars. *Not now,* he thought, cutting off the moan trying to break free of his throat.

Maybe his unwillingness to deal with the woman shot this newest memory down before it could form, because he blinked and she was gone.

"That was close," he muttered. He wondered why she

kept appearing, if he saw her during times *Victoria* would think of her, when she would most want her mother's support.

What was close? Caleb asked. *Never mind, doesn't matter. I don't like waiting.*

It's been, like, two minutes, Julian replied. *Shut it for a bit, and we'll all get through this.*

Victoria climbed into the driver's seat, her shoulder brushing his. Even with their clothes between them, the sensation was electric. "How are you doing?"

"Good." Truth. The aches and pains had faded, as she'd promised. "You?"

"Good," she said, but she didn't sound convinced—or convincing.

"Still holding a grudge?"

She smiled sheepishly. "No."

"I'm glad." He reached out and traced a fingertip along her cheek.

Her eyes closed as she leaned into the touch. "Once the wolves find Riley and Mary Ann, you might have to risk going inside long enough to use your new vampire voice on the police, hospital staff, whoever happens to be around them."

That's right. He could do that now. He recalled telling Seth to leave the stronghold, watching the boy's eyes glaze over and receiving instant obedience. Recalled Victoria trying to use her voice and failing.

So he could, and she *couldn't?* "Why can't you use yours?"

Her gaze moved briefly to the boys in back, none of whom had left their perch against the window. "We'll discuss it later. Right now, you need to practice."

On the boys? No need to ask out loud. He knew. Who else?

He sighed and turned to them. "Bark like a dog." Simple, easy.

Seth flipped him off. Shannon and Ryder leaned toward each other and locked in a whispered conversation.

"Okay, *that* was productive," Aden said dryly.

"Want them to obey," Victoria instructed. "Then force that want into your voice." Propping one elbow on the console between them and resting her weight, she leaned into him and patted his chest, just over his heartbeat. "Push the words out from right here."

Her hand was still chilled, he noted. He latched onto her arm and turned her wrist up. The cuts still hadn't healed. Her ability to use Voice Voodoo was gone. She had been unable to teleport them. Something was going on with her, and he would find out what that something was the next time they were alone.

Now he closed his eyes and thought, *I want my friends to bark like dogs. I really want them to bark like dogs, it'll be funny as crap.* "Bark like a dog." His throat tingled, and his tongue felt thicker as the words tumbled out of his head—and his heart?

Immediately all three boys began barking.

Holy wow, Julian breathed.

Victoria smiled at Aden with a blend of triumph and sadness. "See?"

Captain, fire the shock at warp speed, because wow. He'd done it. He'd freaking done it. That quickly and that effortlessly. He looked back, and sure enough, all three boys sported glazed expressions. They were his to control. His to manipulate.

He cut those thoughts off at the root. He shouldn't want to control, and he shouldn't want to manipulate. And he absolutely did not want to listen to any more barking.

"Quiet," Aden commanded.

"Arf."

"Woof."

"Ruff. Ruff."

"Want it," Victoria reminded him.

Hands balled into fists, Aden closed his eyes, forced his mind on the necessary task. *I want them to stop barking,* he thought and then said the words. Once again his throat tingled, and his tongue thickened.

The barking instantly stopped, the boys glaring at him.

"How did you do that?" Seth spat.

"D-don't do that a-again, you ass," Shannon stuttered.

Leaping over the backseat, Ryder cranked his elbow backward, clearly intending to fly the rest of the way over and strike. Which he did. Aden caught the boy's hand just before contact, seeing and sensing his intent at the same time.

"Use your words like a big boy," he said. "I was just testing something out, making sure I'll be able to help Riley and Mary Ann."

Though Ryder was obviously shocked by Aden's speed, he jerked away and dropped his arm to his side. "Whatever, dude. You do that again, and I'm gonna... I'll...you don't want to know!"

Shannon climbed beside him and tried to put his arm around him, but Ryder threw him off, cheeks brightening. Shannon's cheeks brightened, too, and he turned away from his…boyfriend? Were they a couple? Or just getting there?

You know, I believe there's an entrance at the east side of the emergency building, Julian said, distracted, as if he'd been studying blueprints of the building during the entire exchange. *It's locked…maybe…and no one ever uses it. Maybe. Or rather, they didn't use to. Papers and photos were stored there. Records.* Pause. *I think.*

How's that supposed to help us? Caleb lashed out.

Aden, Julian said, ignoring him. *Check out that entrance, my man. Please. I want a peek at those papers. If they're there. Just, I don't know, stay out of the hospital, okay?*

"Why?"

"Why what?" Victoria asked.

He pointed to his head with an apologetic half smile, and she nodded in understanding. True understanding.

Maybe they'll remind me of who I was.

"No, I mean, why stay out? If we avoid the morgue—"

Don't want to risk it. Besides, I'm creeped out, remember?

"But not by the secret room, or whatever it is." A room that, if it really did exist, could very well be a lab for testing bodily fluids by now. His luck, he'd walk in, someone in a lab coat would be holding a vial of something black and smelly, and he'd have to beat feet, cries of "You ruined everything" ringing in his ears.

Right.

"You mentioned records. What kind?"

I...don't know. Just seems really important.

Important like stuff about the night the souls died? A long shot, but worth a peek. If there was a chance—and there was—he had to risk his neck to take it.

"Victoria, stay here with Shannon and Ryder. Seth, come with me. There's something I want to check out." The boy would make a good—and probably the only one who'd be eager—lookout.

"Sweet." Seth was standing outside the car and rubbing his hands together in less than point-six seconds.

"Wait. You're leaving me behind?" Sharp, bitter air blustered inside, causing Victoria to shiver.

To his knowledge, she'd never shivered before.

"I need you to guard the humans." Just in case Tucker was out there. And he probably was.

Even though Tucker was Vlad's ambassador, Vlad would not order anyone to slay his daughter. Beat her, yes, Aden thought with a tide of anger. Kill her? No.

"But I...I...oh, very well." She nodded reluctantly, shadows in her eyes. "I'll stay behind like a good little girl."

One day, he would find a way to wipe those shadows clean. She was meant for happiness. "Hey, are you okay?" he asked her. "Seriously." He cupped her cheeks and thrilled at her softness. "You can tell me."

"I'm fine. We'll all be fine."

"Yes, you will be." *Right, Elijah?*

Silence.

Aden sighed. He'd have to apologize to the psychic, but not here. Groveling might be involved, so private time was a definite necessity. He kissed Victoria, soft and lingering, uncaring about their audience. "I'll be back. Do you have your phone?"

She nodded.

"Text me when the wolves return. Or if you need anything. Or if you get scared. Or if you—"

"I will." She laughed now, and the sweet sound lessened the tension between them. "Go."

After another kiss—he couldn't stop himself, had to have it—he led Seth toward the east side of the building.

"What are we checking out?" Seth asked.

They reached a padlocked door, and dread overtook him. "I guess we'll find out together."

†WEN†Y-ONE

To a vampire or a shifter, a human guarding two other humans was kind of like having a toddler guard other toddlers. Useless. But Victoria had never been more certain of her status. She was absolutely, utterly human.

Earlier she'd cut her wrist to pour her blood into a cup so that Aden would finally eat without revealing her secret, or having to bite and addict her—or himself. There'd been no *je la nune* on the metal, yet the blade had sliced right through her flesh without any hindrance. The wound had yet to heal. And Chompers, well, he'd stopped roaring, even stopped mewling.

"You and Aden dating?" Ryder asked her, relaxing for the first time since he'd watched Nathan shift.

Leaning her temple against the driver's headrest, she peered back at him. "Yes." *I think.* Since waking up in her bed, he'd been kind, tender, sweet and affectionate.

More like his old self. She constantly battled the urge to throw herself into his arms and spill everything. Her fears, her frailties...her love. Fear of rejection formed a clamp around her mouth.

"You don't care that he's crazy?"

Maybe it was a good thing her beast was quiet. The question pushed all the wrong buttons, and she—or Chompers—might have dove over the seat and ripped out Ryder's tongue. "He's not crazy."

"He talks to himself. Or to the souls, as he calls them. I'm no doctor, but I'm pretty sure that's the textbook definition of crazy."

Twisting, she threw her glare at him. How like Draven he was. Clueless to the violence he stirred. "I drink blood." *Or I used to.* "And my closest friends turn into wolves. Are *we* crazy?"

The corner of his mouth kicked up. He should have appeared amused, but he just looked sad. "Probably."

"Sh-shut up," Shannon told him. "N-now."

"What?" Ryder thumped a fist into the roof. "This whole thing is fucked up, yet everyone is acting like it's normal."

"Then why are you here?" she demanded. "Why did you come with us?"

"I was bored." Flippant tone, challenging expression.

Shannon peered at him with growing horror. Why
the horror? She glanced at the clock on the dash, the
numbers glowing a soft red. Nathan and Maxwell had
been gone for twenty-three minutes, and Aden for nine-
teen. When would they return?

"'I—I was bored' says the b-boy who always t-talks
his way out of everything? No. I know y-you. Wh-what
did you d-do?" Shannon asked Ryder. "Why did y-you
want to leave Crossroads?"

"I did nothing." Ryder shifted uncomfortably in
his seat. "And I didn't want to leave. Aden asked us to
come."

Shannon wasn't giving up. "Wh-what the hell did
y-you do? J-just say it. S-say it b-because I already
kn-know. Didn't w-want to believe, but you were
g-gone last night, after w-we...just after. You reeked of
g-gasoline. I believed you when you s-said you'd been
working on th-the truck. B-believed you, but you...
you... S-say it!"

Cringing, seemingly in pain, Ryder rubbed the spot
just above his heart. The two boys glared at each other
for a long while. The pain must have been building,
must have pushed from him. A moan escaped him, followed by a spew of poisonous yelling.

"You want to hear the truth? Fine. I started the fire.

Okay? All right? There was a voice in my head, and he told me what to do. I tried to stop myself, but I couldn't. You know what else? He told me to kill you, to kill *all* of you, and I stood over your bed. I was going to do it, just like he told me, but I started shaking, and I couldn't. I couldn't do it, so I dragged you out instead."

Victoria listened, her own sense of horror growing.

"You…you…" Shannon let his head flop into his up-raised hands.

"The voice told me to go with Aden, wherever he went. He told me—" Ryder's entire body shook, as if he were having a seizure. His eyes rolled back in his head, until only the whites could be seen through the slits in his lashes.

"R-Ryder!" Darting into action, Shannon pushed his friend to his side, and shoved his own hand into the boy's mouth, trying to prevent him from swallowing his tongue. Then the shaking stopped as suddenly as it had begun.

The passenger door slid open, frosty air once again shoving inside the car to battle with what little warmth remained. No one had opened the door that Victoria could see, yet it had opened—and was now closing on its own. Victoria's horror morphed into alarm, the reason popping into place.

Tucker.

In a snap, he materialized in the seat. His clothes were ragged and bloodstained, his sandy hair plastered to his head and sporting matching streaks of crimson. His eyes held a corrosive sadness that would eat through the rest of him if he wasn't careful.

"Hello, Victoria," he said. "You got my text, I see."

She would not be cowed. She might be human, but Riley had trained her in self-defense. Weak as she was, she wasn't completely helpless. "Yes, I did." And having taken a page from the Aden Stone School of Ass Kicking, she'd stored daggers under the sleeves of her robe.

Motions fluid, Ryder sat up and pushed Shannon away from him. "Do not touch me with your filthy hands, human," he snapped, and despite his vehemence, his voice was formal, cultured, with a slight Romanian accent in the undertones.

A tremor slid down the length of her spine. She knew that voice. Both loved and hated that voice. But...but... *impossible,* she thought.

"A-are you o-kay?" Even though Ryder had just admitted to destroying Shannon's home, Shannon obviously cared about his welfare.

"I'm fine. Or rather, I will be." Ryder reached for

his boot, withdrew a dagger of his own—and stabbed Shannon in the heart.

He moved so quickly, Victoria only registered what had happened *after* Shannon screamed. After the blood was flowing. After Ryder twisted the blade deeper and deeper still.

Shannon gurgled, unable to form words. His eyes said it all. *What? Why? How could you?*

"No!" Victoria dove into the backseat, placing herself in front of Shannon while thrusting Ryder away from him. Using her back as his shield, uncaring if she was stabbed, she jerked the blade out and pressed her palms into the wound. Warm blood met her quaking hands.

Ryder gave a little laugh. She thought he might even have rubbed his hands together in a job well done. "Smells good, doesn't it, Tucker, my lad?"

"Yes," Tucker replied automatically.

There was nothing she could do. No way to help. Or to save. Tears burned Victoria's eyes, spilling onto her cheeks. "Shannon, I'm sorry. I'm so sorry. I should have…" Done something, anything.

Shannon was gasping now, desperately trying to lure oxygen inside his lungs. Blood seeped from the corners of his mouth. He was in pain, so much pain, and she hated that more than she hated the thought of his death.

"That," Ryder said to Tucker, "is how it's done. Had you done that to Aden, my daughter never would have been able to save him."

His daughter.

Not impossible, then. Vlad had possessed Ryder.

He'd done this. Vlad had done this. To Shannon. To Aden. To all of them. The man she'd once mourned the loss of had *done this*.

She couldn't teleport Shannon away. She couldn't carry him out of the car. Waiting for Aden would cause him needless suffering.

Aden. For a moment, she was thrown back to the night of *his* stabbing. He'd been in pain, too. He'd wanted so badly for it end. All of it, including his life. Anything for a little peace. At one point, he'd even begged her to let him go.

She hadn't, then. She could now.

"I'm so sorry." Hating herself more than ever before, she slashed into Shannon's jugular with her fangs. Fangs that were not as long or sharp as they'd once been, but there was nothing she could do about that now. His gurgling increased before it faded, but he didn't fight her, and as she gulped at the blood as quickly as she could, she tasted copper and what was surely despair. She didn't let herself dwell on that, not here, not now, and kept drinking, until there was nothing left. Until his head lolled to the side.

Until he was gone, his pain no more.

Distantly she heard the clomp and scratch of a wolf's paws. Nathan. Maxwell.

She straightened with a snap, panting, crying again, and scanned the area outside the car. Everything was blurry. Sniffling, chest heaving—how could she have done that to Shannon, even to set him free?—she wiped at her eyes with the back of her wrist.

There was Maxwell, still wearing his shades, and Nathan, still in his Seeing Eye dog uniform. They were bumping into cars as if they were *both* blind.

"They'll never find this car," Tucker said. "I've made sure of it."

"Your ability to cast illusions is the only reason you're still alive, boy," Ryder remarked. "I hope you know that."

They were having this conversation *now?* As if nothing had happened? Heartless monsters.

Victoria twisted to face the father who wasn't her father, not anymore, and the boy who had changed her life forever. *"How could you do this?"*

"So wonderful to see you again, my love." Ryder's smile was all winter ice and black dagger. "Even though you have betrayed me in ways I can never and *will never* forgive."

His intent to kill her shone so brightly in his eyes, she felt spotlighted. "You don't scare me. *Father.* Not anymore."

He tapped his chin with a fingertip. "Whatever can I do to change that?" A grin so heartless even his amusement was tainted. "I'm sure I'll think of something."

How did I ever look up to this man? "Shannon did nothing to deserve that kind of death."

Finally. An expected reaction. His amusement faded, his eyes narrowing to tiny slits and his lips peeling back from his teeth. The expression of a predator who'd spotted prey. "He aided Aden. Of course he deserved to d—"

Victoria dove for him, landed on top of him. Vlad might have possessed Ryder, but Ryder still had a human body. Which meant, Ryder was still vulnerable.

He had nowhere to go as she chewed on his jugular.

As a human, she wasn't so ineffective, after all.

TWENTY-TWO

ADEN HAD FILES STUFFED under his shirt, inside his pants and clutched under his arms. So did Seth. They'd busted into the small, dusty room Julian had led them to, and as promised, no one had been inside. No one had been inside for a really long time, he suspected. The lock had been rusted, the hinges on the door squeaking and practically falling off with the pressure he'd applied.

They'd hurried from one box to another, rifling through the papers—realizing *everything* related to the unexplainable. Unexplainable deaths, unexplainable injuries, unexplainable healings. They'd grabbed everything they could hold. Later, they'd come back for the rest. As for today, Mary Ann and Riley were priority one.

Now they were on their way back to the SUV, and he couldn't shake a sense of nervousness.

"Elijah," he muttered.

Seth cast him a strange glance but didn't say anything.

The apology couldn't wait for a little private time. "I'm sorry." The soul wasn't usually vindictive, but then, maybe Elijah *couldn't* talk. Maybe something was wrong. "I was frustrated." The words left him in a rush. "I didn't mean to take it out on you."

A pause. A familiar sigh. *I know.*

Finally. Blessedly. "Talk to me. Tell me what's going on with you."

I've just been thinking. What if all your problems stem from me? From my guidance? What if these bad things happen to you because I tell you they're going to happen? Like a self-fulfilling prophesy?

"Uh, that would be a 'hell, no.' I need you. Now more than ever."

What if none of this would have happened if I'd kept my mouth shut?

Aden didn't have to be a psychic to know where this was leading. "Don't do this to me, Elijah. Not now." Yeah, several times over the years, he'd asked the souls to keep their pie holes closed. A few times they'd tried. A few less, they'd succeeded. For the most part, they'd failed. Talking to each other and Aden was their only outlet, their only connection to a world they'd lost.

I have to. I'm going to.

This time, there was finality in Elijah's voice. He meant what he said. "No."

I'm sorry, Aden.

"No," he repeated.

We're going to try this. We're going to try silence.

"I'm serious. Don't do this to me."

I really am sorry, Aden. For the past. For...the future. So sorry. I just...I really think this is for the best. So this is it, my last words to you for a while.

"Define a while." The clouds had done a disappearing act. The sun was high, stroking his skin, making him itch and burn.

As long as it takes. Be careful, and know that I love you.

"Elijah."

Silence.

"Elijah!"

More silence.

Seth grabbed hold of his arm and jerked him to a stop. "What the crap is this?"

Elijah was momentarily forgotten as Aden's brain tried to make sense of what he was seeing. The once bustling parking lot was completely empty. Of people, of cars.

Except for Maxwell and Nathan, who were a few yards away and bumping into air.

No doubt about it, Tucker was here, casting an illusion. Aden dropped the papers he was holding and ran. Five steps in, and he, too, slammed into something solid, though there was nothing in front of him.

A human he couldn't see huffed out an angry, "Watch where you're going!"

Aden did his best to dodge the invisible person. And maybe he succeeded, but a few more steps, and he was slamming into something else. Most likely a car, since another protest wasn't forthcoming. He lost his breath the moment he hit the concrete. More papers made their way into the breeze, catching on indiscernible cars and staying put.

To be able to manipulate Aden's mind like this, without tampering with the humans around him, was *insane*.

Seth ran up behind him, fisting his shirt and yanking him to his feet. "You're the expert on all things whacked out. Tell me what's going on."

"Danger, everyone's in danger. Victoria!" he shouted, already running forward again. "Victoria!" If she'd just call out, he could find her.

He slammed into something else.

"Aden," Maxwell called. A good distance still separated them. "Can you see me?"

"Yes."

"I can see you but nothing else."

"Tucker's here. Be careful."

Maxwell nodded grimly. "We found Riley. He's alive. Guards at his door. Mary Ann was harder to find, we couldn't get her scent, but the guards at her door gave her away. What the hell happened out here? We smell blood, right—" he pointed to a spot about a yard away "—there."

Aden sniffed and realized he could smell the blood, too. Not Victoria's, but…Shannon's?

Like an engine had just been keyed, Junior roared to life, the scent whipping him into a frenzy.

"Calm down," Aden said, but that didn't help. "You ate just before we got here."

His response? Another *gimme* roar.

Though urgency rode him, Aden gingerly made his way through the lot, feeling his way, winding around cars he still couldn't see, until he reached the place where Maxwell had pointed. He reached out and felt—

The SUV. He knew it. The motor was still running, the metal warm.

He frisked the thing until he found the door handle.

Just as he was pulling, the lock caught and the car came back into view.

He was peering through the back window, with a clear view of Shannon. Shannon, at an odd angle. Shannon, blood all over him. Shannon, eyes open and staring out at nothing. Shannon, immobile. Shannon, throat ripped open. Shannon. Dead.

Look away, please look away. Caleb gagged. Aden could barely hear him over the roaring. *That can't be…that isn't…*

No. No, no, no, Julian babbled.

This was not an illusion. The smell of the blood couldn't be faked, he didn't think. And right now, Junior was more ravenous than ever, clawing and biting at his skull, desperate to escape, to have a go at all that crimson nectar.

Shock numbed Aden against the headache he should have experienced. But even numb, he wanted to vomit when he saw Victoria tearing into Ryder's neck. Blood, gore, other things, spraying, dripping, flinging in every direction as she shook her head, a ravenous shark.

Why would she…how could she…

To Aden's everlasting mortification, his mouth watered. Part of him, a part that had nothing to do with

Junior, wanted to slit the car in half just to get inside and go to town on that wound.

Ryder wasn't dead. His mouth was open, releasing a silent scream, and his struggles were weakening.

Body heat at Aden's side. A horrified gasp in his ear. Banging on the glass. "Stop! What the hell are you doing? Stop!" Seth hammered at the window, shaking the entire vehicle. When that failed to elicit results, he shoved Aden's immobile hand aside and jerked at the locked trunk.

The commotion jolted Victoria out of her craze. She stilled, head turning slowly, as if she feared what she'd find. Their eyes met. She was panting, blood dripping down her face. But...he didn't see a glaze of bloodlust, something that would explain why she'd gone after his friends. He saw sadness, remorse...fury. Frustration. Tears.

Her gaze darted to the passenger seat before turning to Aden, beseeching. He sniffed—and at last caught Tucker's dark scent.

Tucker hadn't appeared, but Aden knew he was inside that vehicle. Knew Victoria was in grave danger.

He swept around the vehicle and clawed at the metal as he'd imagined doing, ripping the door from its hinges.

Instantly the odor of blood intensified, but now it was mixed with the pungent scent of death.

He swooped in and gathered Victoria in his arms. She was trembling violently. As he straightened, she buried her face in the hollow of his neck, arms winding around him and holding tightly. She released a gut-wrenching sob.

"He...my father...possessed..."

Maxwell and Nathan bounded to his side. Maxwell tried to check Victoria for injuries, an impossible task since Aden refused to release her, and she refused to release him. Nathan snarled into the car, poison dripping from his canines.

"Call off your dog," Tucker's voice said, even though he was still nowhere to be seen.

"Eat him, and make sure there's nothing for anyone to find," Aden commanded, then had to catch Nathan by the nape to stop him from obeying as Tucker added, "You want to save your remaining friends, right? Because I'm the only person who can help you."

Victoria wiggled until she got her legs on the ground, but she still didn't release Aden's neck. "He's...he's... right. Don't hurt him. We need him."

Need him? When had *that* happened? And what the

hell had happened in there? "Tucker, don't you dare move."

A laugh, and Tucker appeared, no longer trying to shield himself. He sat in the passenger seat, as calm as you please. His blond hair was plastered to his scalp, and his face was splattered with blood. "Like you could stop me if I did."

Seth was shaking his head in time to his body's shaking.

"Victoria," Aden said, gentling his tone. "I'm going to move away from you now. Okay?"

Her sobs took on a frantic edge. "No! Please!"

"Just for a minute or two," he said, already easing away from her. He made sure she could balance on her own before lowering his arms. "I'm going to help Ryder. Okay?"

"Don't." She wiped at her tears with the back of a wobbly wrist. "Ryder killed Shannon. He started the fire at the ranch, and he would have killed me, but I...I... Vlad possessed him, worked through him."

"Vlad *possessed* him?" Maxwell echoed hollowly. "But...but...something like that is impossible."

"Actually, it's very possible." Thanks to Caleb, Aden had possessed other people himself. Many times. He'd simply stepped inside their bodies and taken over their minds. Was that what Vlad had done? Was Vlad inside Ryder's mind, even now? Would killing Ryder end them both? "As for now, I'm gonna help Ryder as best I can."

"You believe her? Just like that?" Seth banged a fist into the car, cracking the already abused glass. "You saw what she was doing. She had her teeth in his neck. *And. You. Believe. Her?*"

"Yeah, I do," Aden replied as he climbed inside the car. "Don't speak when you don't understand."

"Oh, I understand plenty," Seth said. "She's a murderer, and you don't care."

"She's not a murderer," he snarled from his post. There was one subject guaranteed to hurtle him into a fight. Victoria's honor. She wasn't a liar, and she was *broken* about this. He wouldn't have her hurt further.

Tucker didn't try to stop him as he whipped off his T-shirt and wound it around Ryder's gushing neck. He didn't let himself think about Shannon, who lay behind him, gone, unsavable. Or rather, he tried not to let himself.

Shannon, the first boy at the ranch to be nice to him.

Shannon, whose body might rise from the dead and attack him.

Shannon, whom he'd have to kill all over again.

Hurry, he told himself.

Poor Shannon, Julian said.

Another senseless death, Caleb cried.

The scent of blood was overpowering. Moisture pooled around his tongue, and his gums ached. Junior's roars laced with fury, and the banging against his skull became more pronounced.

"Keep an eye on Shannon," Aden said to no one in particular. "Tell me if he so much as twitches."

"Will do," Maxwell vowed.

"And don't worry," Tucker piped up. "No one but us can see what's going on here. I've made sure of it."

Good Samaritan Award, meet Tucker. Or not. "You'll pay for this," Aden told him. "All of it. I hope you know that."

"Oh, yeah," the boy said, sadder than Aden had ever heard him. "I know."

I could possess him right now, Caleb growled. *I could make him hurt himself.*

No. You heard him, and you heard Vic. Julian, a voice of reason. *We need his illusion.*

Aden lifted one of Ryder's limp arms and felt for a pulse. Weak, thready, but there. The ring Aden still wore, Vlad's ring, glinted in the sunlight. He'd had the thing refilled, so there was plenty of *je la nune* inside.

Best I can included cutting himself open and feeding the boy his blood. So that's exactly what Aden did. With the pad of his thumb, he slid the glittering jewel out of the way. The clear liquid swirling inside, so innocent-looking. He tilted his hand to the side, allowing a single drop to splash against his other.

The burn and sizzle were instantaneous, and he hissed between his teeth. But blood welled, and he let the ensuing stream fall over Ryder's neck, into his mouth.

"Shannon's twitching," Maxwell said.

Aden's heart gave a little leap. Maybe, despite everything, he'd *wanted* Shannon to rise. He wasn't ready to say goodbye.

If that were true, Aden had just committed his most dishonorable deed of the week. What he wanted shouldn't have mattered. Turning his friend into a zombie, that was low, even for him.

"Hold him down," he said.

The shifter jumped on top of the body the moment Shannon's eyelids popped apart. Dull green eyes locked on Aden, and blood-soaked hands reached out.

Seth reached in and batted Maxwell away in an attempt to prevent the shifter from hurting his friend. A friend who was now a zombie, a fresh corpse who would know only a hunger for living flesh. Whose saliva would poison Aden and make him crave a death of his own.

"He's alive and needs medical help. Let me take him inside the hospital," Seth said with a mix of panic and relief.

"He's not alive," Aden said, much as he wished otherwise. No, he shouldn't have done this to his friend. Either friend. He'd given Seth hope.

Tucker clapped, a round of applause meant to gain everyone's attention. It got their attention, all right, but it also upped the tension another thousand degrees. "You're all playing right into Vlad's hands. You're distracted and pulling in opposite directions."

"As if you care." Maxwell didn't budge from his perch atop the now-struggling Shannon.

"You have no idea what I feel! Vlad has threatened my brother. I'll do whatever it takes to save him. And yes, that includes murdering each of you if it proves necessary. I'm hoping you won't prove it necessary."

Whether the brother thing was the truth or a lie, Aden didn't know. He did know Vlad was capable of using anyone.

"Including," Tucker continued, "make a deal with you, when I know you'll kill me afterward. So here it is. Save my brother, protect him, and I'll help you save Mary Ann and Riley."

Yeah, they'd get right on that. Because everyone here was borderline certifiable. "And give you the chance to betray us? *Again?* No."

Tucker launched forward, in Aden's face a heart-beat later. "I hate what that bastard makes me do. I like Mary Ann. Do you think I enjoyed watching her suffer?"

From the corner of his eye, he could see that Maxwell had to stretch out his arm to hold Nathan back. Good thing he did. Otherwise the wolf's pearly whites would have been embedded in Tucker's cheeks.

Aden's wound hadn't yet closed when he shoved Tucker backward, the action ripping his skin farther. "Yes. I do."

"I want *Vlad* to suffer. Do you understand *that?* I hate him. I hate what he makes me do." Tucker's nostrils flared with the force of his breathing, but he remained in his seat. "I can't act against him until I make sure my brother's okay."

His concern seemed genuine, and much as Aden loathed admitting it, Tucker *was* the best way to get his friends out of St. Mary's. But. "You want my help with your bro, you help me with Mary Ann and Riley. First."

"First? No way. You'll get what you want from me and dispose of me. No, help me first, I help you second."

He studied Ryder's face, expecting some kind of change but seeing nothing. His blood would work, or it wouldn't, but there was nothing else he could do. He emerged from the car, Junior immediately calming down, and opened his arms to Victoria. She threw herself against him, her body still quaking.

"I'd rather kill you now," he said to Tucker, "and send your brother a Hope All's Well card." Cold of him, and he wouldn't let himself ponder whether he was bluffing or not. Not here, not now.

Tucker ground his molars together. "How can I trust you?"

"How can *I* trust *you?*"

More grinding. Then, "We have a deal. I'll help you now, you help me later."

No more argument than that? Huh. Was Aden playing right into some kind of plan? And Tucker had one, he would bet money on it. Hell, he was betting the lives of his people. "If I think, even for a second, that you're doing this for Vlad, I will…" What? There was no threat vile enough.

"I'm not. Not at this time," Tucker added. "He comes and goes, and right now he's gone."

"He possesses you like he did Ryder?"

"No. He…guides me."

Easy fix. "Resist him."

Tucker jerked at the collar of his shirt. "You don't understand. I *can't* resist."

"Free will, dude. You should try it." His gaze flipped back to Ryder. The flesh in his neck actually appeared to be weaving back together, and his features were contorted in a pain-filled grimace.

Pain was good.

Pain meant life.

"Maxwell, drive Ryder and Shannon back to the house," Aden said, issuing orders to get things rolling. Victoria had saved Aden; Aden would save his friends. Hopefully the consequences would not be as severe. Hopefully he could find a way to prevent Shannon from—*don't think it*—rotting. "Lock them in separate rooms, doctor Ryder up, and ignore everything he says, just in case Vlad tries to take him over. Have a vampire, Stephanie maybe, feed them both a little blood."

"Shannon's already dead, so okay, but Ryder won't

survive transport," the wolf said, and after restraining Shannon with the seat belt, knotting the length around his wrists and chest, he moved to the driver's seat.

"Will he?" Aden asked Elijah.

Silence, again such oppressive silence.

Very well. He'd move forward without the soul's aid.

"Why don't you go with them, Seth? You can help take care of both." What he didn't say: Seth was fully human, and Vlad could now possess humans. Aden didn't know how the former king was doing it—he himself had to touch a body to step into it—so he had to take every precaution.

Red suffused the boy's cheeks as he braced his legs apart in a classic attack position. "I'll go. But if either one dies…" His narrowed gaze lanced at Victoria.

He'd want revenge.

"It won't be Victoria's fault, and you won't touch her. Ever." He did, and they'd become enemies. Aden didn't want that.

There was no backing down on Seth's part.

A bowl full of cherries right there, but they'd have to deal with it later—if Seth made that necessary. "Victoria will stay with me." He didn't like the thought of her around Tucker, but he also didn't like the thought of her out of his sight. Look what had happened last time.

He reached into the waist of his jeans and tugged out the papers that hadn't flown the coop. He tossed them on a clean section of the floorboard. "Read everything. Call and tell me what you find."

Tucker emerged and moved to stand behind the car in the next slot over, using it as a shield. Seth took his place in the passenger seat.

"Can you make sure they aren't spotted on the drive home?" Aden asked Tucker.

"Yes."

"Will you?" Wouldn't be smart to leave things open to interpretation.

"Yes."

Aden had no choice but to believe him. "Then do it."

"How are you gonna get home?" Maxwell asked.

Good question. "I'll steal a car." And it wouldn't be the first time.

"All right, then. I'll see you when I see you." A few seconds later, the SUV was motoring away, leaving Aden, Victoria, Tucker and Nathan—in wolf form—to take care of business here.

"I still can't risking going inside the hospital," Aden told them. "As you can see, I'm still in the body-raising business."

"Nathan and I can go with Tucker," Victoria said. "We'll meet you out here."

He'd known she would step up. That didn't lessen his nervousness. She was strong, he told himself. She couldn't teleport, but she could move quickly. "If anything happens to her..." Everyone knew the words were for Tucker, and Tucker alone.

"I won't be at fault."

"I bet that's your excuse every time you hurt someone."

A muscle ticked below the demon's eye. "Your friend needed to be eliminated. I let her eliminate him. No excuses necessary. What's wrong with that?"

They weren't going to debate this now. Wasn't like they'd change their minds about each other. "Riley made the mistake of trusting you, and look where it got him. Believe me, I'll give you enough rope to hang yourself, but that's it."

"Meaning?"

"Meaning, she comes back to me in the condition she's in now, or I hunt you down and make it hurt when I finish you."

Tucker snorted, not the least intimidated. "Riley plans to make it hurt anyway. And guess what? I warned him. He didn't listen to me. This is his fault. So let's stop yakking and do this. I'll get your friends, and you'll get my brother. That's the deal."

Before Aden could respond, Victoria said, "I'll be fine," as she stepped between them. She offered Aden a small smile. "Besides, Nathan is with me. He won't let Tucker do anything."

Aden didn't point out that Nathan wouldn't be able to stop Tucker if the guy started throwing those illusions around.

He kissed her, hard and fast. "Do what you gotta do, but you come out of there."

Her pupils expanded, black consuming blue, and he knew she understood. If she had to rip out a few throats to get out safely, she would just have to rip out a few throats.

"We doing this or what?" Tucker snapped.

"We're doing this," Victoria said without looking away from Aden. Then she turned, and the threesome walked away from him, disappearing through the hospital doors.

Aden was left in the parking lot, on his own with his worries and regrets. They wouldn't help him steal a car, so he shoved them aside and cased the parking lot.

†WEN†Y-†HREE

DARKNESS.

Light.

Darkness.

Light.

The darkness offered solace, the light anguish. Therefore, it wasn't hard to pick which one Mary Ann preferred. Sweet, sweet darkness. But that stupid, *stupid* light
kept forcing its way into her mind.

Like now. *Bump, bump. Bump, bump.* Her poor, bat-
tered body was being jostled, each movement a new
lesson in agony. An advanced class of you-think-you-
know-what-it's-like-to-hurt-well-try-this she would
have been very happy to fail.

"You should carry her, Vic," a raspy male voice said
above her.

Familiar. Maybe…unwelcome? Or *too* welcome? Her heartbeat kicked up a notch in the speed department.

"Don't call me that. And why would I want to carry her?" Wait. *That* had sounded like her sorta friend and Aden's girlfriend, Victoria.

"Maxwell took off with my clothes, so I'm tripping on the toga I stole from little bro's bed," the male replied. Yes, he was familiar…somehow. She should know him, but couldn't quite place him. He just wasn't who she'd hoped he'd be, that much she puzzled out. "If I drop her, Riley will flip his lid."

Riley. Yes! That was the voice she craved but had yet to hear.

"You complain, yet I'm carrying the big guy." Hey, that had sounded like Tucker. "He needs to diet. Seriously."

"Just do your jobs," Victoria said with a weariness Mary Ann had never before heard from her. Usually, the princess was tireless. "We're almost outside. Tucker, are you sure no one can see us?"

Tucker grumbled under his breath. Something along the lines of *how many times can you ask me this already?* "Yes, I'm sure."

"What about the guards and nurses—"

"They can still see the bodies in their beds. In fact,

they're trying to revive them and failing right now. The kids are dying. So sad. Boo-hoo."

"Don't they feel—"

"No. First, my evil deeds increase my power. As you can guess, I'm pretty powerful. Second, the human brain accepts what it sees and fills in the rest. And if it doesn't, I do. So by the time the people here realize their suspects are dead and missing, it'll be too late. Now shut up. They *can* hear us."

"But—"

"Do you doubt Aden's skills this much? You do, don't you? FYI, he probably wants to cut off his ears and mail them somewhere else. Geez-us!"

Now Victoria was the one to grumble. "I thought you couldn't work with Mary Ann nearby."

"Things change."

"Yes," she said on a sigh, "they do."

Were they...rescuing her? Surely. But from where? Last thing Mary Ann remembered was kissing Riley, loving it, wanting more, thinking they were finally going to go all the way, wishing their surroundings were different, then a shooting pain through her shoulder, the flow of warm blood, Riley telling her to feed from him—wait, wait, wait, back up that train.

She had fed from Riley.

Was he okay? Was he nearby?

Reckless in her need to find out, she struggled for freedom.

Bands tightened around her. "Mary Ann. Stop, you have to stop." The familiar yet unfamiliar male again.

"Riley," she managed to squeeze out of her raw throat.

"He's safe. He's with us."

Good. Okay. Yes. She relaxed, the intensity of her relief forcing the light to go bye-bye, and just like that, the darkness returned.

LIGHT.

Mary Ann heard squealing tires. Then loud, pounding rock music. Then soft, quiet rock and a muttered argument. She was no longer being jostled but resting against something soft. Although, there was a small, hard object pushing into her side.

Her mind immediately went somewhere it shouldn't.

She pried her heavy eyelids apart. Someone must have smeared Vaseline over them because everything was hazy. Well, the joke was not funny, and she'd be lodging a complaint just as soon as she could pry open her mouth.

"—telling you, I'm good," Tucker was saying.

"Sorry, but you'll understand if I still take precautions," Aden replied.

Aden. Aden was here.

"Letting your girlfriend drive while you hold a knife to my throat is not a precaution. It's a death wish. Besides, you still need me, you know. Without me, you could be pulled over."

"And you still need *me*. Don't forget."

Silence followed, allowing her thoughts to align. Rescued. With Riley. Where was Riley? Her heart drummed in her chest, reminding her of something, but she didn't know what. She raised shaky hands to wipe at her eyes. Though nothing coated her fingers, her line of vision cleared slightly, and she was able to look around. She was in some sort of van, sprawled across the backseat.

Okay, so a seat belt was the thing poking her in the back, not some guy's... Well, that was a relief.

More relief: she spotted Riley propped up in the seat in front of hers. Even in sleep, he must have heard her moving around because he turned his head in her direction. His eyes were closed, his expression pinched.

Pinched was better than lifeless any day.

She reached up, her shaking getting worse by the second, and wound her fingers around his arm. He gave no reaction, but that was okay. Whatever had happened to them, they were going to survive.

A sigh escaped her, the darkness closing back in around her. This time, she was smiling as she drifted away.

MARY ANN AWOKE to a grumbling stomach.

Frowning, she blinked open her eyes, stretched the soreness from her body as best she could—which equated to not at all—and gingerly sat up. After a moment of dizziness, she was able to make out her new surroundings. The car had been replaced by a small, tidy room, and the backseat with an unfamiliar bed. Whoever had done the decorating really liked the color brown. Brown carpet, brown drapes, brown comforter.

"—have to feed," Victoria was saying.

"You do, too."

"Yes, well, I'm okay for now."

"How is that possible? I haven't seen you eat."

"Just because you haven't seen something doesn't mean it hasn't happened, right?"

"So you have? Eaten?"

Feed. Food. Eat. Mary Ann's stomach threw another growl into the mix, and both Aden and Victoria—who sat in a brown chair across from the bed, Victoria on

Aden's lap—leveled their gazes her way. Talk about embarrassing.

Unlike the other times she and Aden first encountered each other, Mary Ann was not filled with the urge to hug him and run. She just wanted to hug him. He was one of her best friends, she loved him like a brother, but their abilities—his to draw, strengthen, and hers to repulse, weaken—made them complete opposites. They were like two magnets forcibly pressed together, wrong ends up, and they just weren't meant to coexist. Until now.

She wondered what had changed but was too hungry to unravel the pieces.

"You're awake," Aden said, his relief palpable.

"Yeah." He looked different. A lot different. Gone was his dark hair, and in its place was a short crop of blond. His face was harder, harsher, his shoulders wider. If she wasn't mistaken, his legs were longer, too.

All that growth, in about two weeks time. Wow. But then, she probably looked different, too. She was tattooed, thinner, maybe even gaunt. "Where's Riley?"

"Right beside you." Victoria motioned to the other side of the bed with a tilt of her head.

Barely concealing her jolt of surprise, Mary Ann twisted on the mattress, the springs protesting. Sure enough. Riley was beside her. He was awake, propped up on pillows, and...in pain? His skin was pallid but for the dark circles under his eyes. The normally luminous glow of his green eyes had blunted.

She reached up to trace her fingertips along the edge of those circles, halfway hoping to brush them away, but he jerked his head to the side, preventing contact.

Astonishment? Yes, she experienced that. Then utter, absolute distress. He didn't even glance in her direction, just kept staring over at Aden and Victoria. He didn't offer an explanation, just kept his lips pressed together in a hard line.

What was wrong with him?

Had she done something, said something?

Or was he simply hurting too badly to be touched?

He was shirtless, his chest free of injuries, but his lower half was hidden under the covers. Maybe his legs were giving him fits, making the rest of him sensitive to any type of human contact. She wanted so badly to believe that was the answer, but deep down she suspected the worst.

He was done with her.

And if that was the case, well, she'd pushed for that, hadn't she?

"I thought I heard Tucker earlier," she croaked out, turning back to Aden and Victoria.

The vampire princess hadn't budged from his lap. Why would she? It was probably the most comfortable seat in the room. Although…her back was straight, her posture perfect, her hands folded neatly atop her thighs. Anyone else would have thrown in the towel and sprawled. Aden had, though he was running one of his hands up and down Victoria's spine.

They looked every inch the couple. In sync, *together* together. They might be having problems, as Riley had told her, but they were clearly working on them.

A pang of longing moved through her. Would she and Riley work things out? Did she want to?

No pondering necessary. Yes, she wanted to. Would she let herself be with him, though, placing him in even more danger than she already had?

Yes, she thought again. She would. After the kiss they'd shared, she would do *anything* to be with him. If he would have her. She'd run from him, yet he'd chased her. She'd tried to get rid of him, yet he'd stayed with her. And now…now she had no idea what was going through his guy brain.

Well, they would find a way around the draining

thing. He'd always been so confident about that, and it was time she believed him.

"Mary Ann? You listening? Tucker's gone," Aden said.

"Oh. Where'd he go?"

"We don't know." Victoria pursed her lips. "Riley was about to kill him, so his disappearing act was for the best."

"You should have let me do my job," Riley snapped at Aden. "Majesty."

Hearing the harsh rasp of his voice left her shivering. Or maybe shuddering. He hadn't lost his ability to speak—he just didn't want to speak to her. Ouch.

"Where's the other guy?" she asked. "The one at the hospital? The one who carried me?"

Victoria's brow furrowed, creating worry lines in her forehead. "You remember that?"

"Vaguely."

"Did you hear—never mind. That was Nathan, Riley's brother, but he didn't travel with us. His presence upset Tucker."

And they hadn't wanted to upset Tucker? Shocker. "Will someone please tell me what's going on?" Her stomach released another grumble, soliciting the return of her blush.

"Hungry?" Aden asked.

"I...yes." Wait. She hadn't been hungry for food, real food, for several weeks. Only energy. Magic. Power. Now, she would have killed for a hamburger.

Mmm, a hamburger...

All three sets of eyes regarded her strangely.

"That's...weird," Victoria finally said.

Her stomach protested the description with yet another growl. "That doesn't change the facts. I'm starved!"

"Well, then, let's feed you." The princess popped to her feet, her expression a little too eager. "I'll fetch you something."

"No." Aden shook his head. "Absolutely not. Tucker's out there. I don't want you—"

"I'll be fine. If not, well, I'll text you. As you've probably noticed, I'm getting good at using modern technology," she said and bent down to kiss his cheek. "Besides, you can't go. You have a lot to tell Mary Ann."

"You could tell her."

"Impossible. I've already forgotten half of what you wanted her to know."

"No way," he said. "You and Riley did that joining hands and exchanging of memories thing. You know more than all of us."

"True. Which means you've got some catching up to do, too."

She didn't wait for his reply, and shockingly, neither Aden nor Riley tried to stop her as they once would have done. The door shut with a soft snick behind her, sunlight pouring in for a moment, then vanishing like vapor.

"Stubborn," Aden muttered.

"Typical," Riley groused.

Chauvinists.

"What do you have to tell me?" Mary Ann asked, dread blending with her hunger and leaving a thick coat of acid on her sternum.

"Brace yourself." For the next half hour, Aden told her so many gruesome things, she wanted to scrub her ears with sandpaper.

A coven of witches, slaughtered. The D and M ranch, burned to the ground. Vlad the Impaler, possessing humans and forcing them to do despicable things. Tucker's little brother, potential kidnap and murder victim.

Shannon, stabbed to death. Currently a zombie.

Aden's voice wobbled a few times, as if he was fighting tears, but he battled them back and continued. When he finished, she kinda wished he hadn't.

"So much death," she whispered. Poor, sweet Shannon, who would die all over again if something wasn't done. Could anything be done, though? She wanted to sob for him, for what he'd lost. She wanted to bring him back *as he'd been*. Wanted to hug him. Wanted to punish Vlad in the most terrible way.

She wanted Riley to put his arm around her, to comfort her, to tell her everything was going to be okay.

Big shocker, she didn't get any of that. Even worse, the silence that followed her horrified whisper acted like a thick cloud of oppression. No one knew where to look or how to respond.

Hinges squeaked, and light once again flooded the room. Victoria stepped inside, shut the door and chased that light away. She held a paper bag, the scent of bread, meat and greasy fries wafting from it. Mary Ann's mouth watered, and she was ashamed of herself. After everything she'd just heard, she should have lost her appetite. For, like, ever.

But when Victoria handed her that oil-spotted bag, she was unable to help herself and dove in, devouring every crumb in record time. After swallowing the last nibble, she realized the hush hadn't lifted from the room. In fact, everyone was staring at her. Great. She probably had food in her teeth and mustard smeared on her chin.

She wiped at her face with the back of her wrist, her shame intensifying.

"Do you feel sick?" Victoria asked. She'd reclaimed her perch on Aden's lap. She wasn't quite as pale as before, and was that a ketchup stain on her robe?

"No?" Mary Ann replied, her amazement making the word more of a question than a statement. Her stomach actually felt grateful. Before, when she'd even *thought* about eating, she had battled nausea. "What does this mean?"

Pensive, Victoria tugged at her earlobe. "You were shot with a witch's arrow and lost a lot of blood."

She nodded.

"And you were given a transfusion at the hospital."

"Yes. At least, I think so."

The princess started chewing on her bottom lip again. A nervous habit? "Maybe the new blood, the human blood, has made you human again. At least for a little while. Or maybe it has something to do with Riley? He's always interfered with your ability to mute. Maybe he's now interfering with your ability to drain."

"So, at the moment, I can't, won't drain anyone?"

"If you keep the food down, and it seems like you will, magic and energy probably aren't on your menu selection."

"You won't have to run anymore," Aden said.

"Not if there's a way to stay this way," Mary Ann replied, trying not to leap off the bed and dance like a fool. There had to be.

"I don't know. We could ward you against the draining of energy, but if, say, your hunger for it returns, you would then die." Victoria studied Riley before returning her attention to Mary Ann. "I mean, we've warded drainers before. Not when they were without their ability, because, to my knowledge, that's never happened before, but always they starved to death."

If there was a worse way to die, she suddenly couldn't think of it. Did that stop her from plowing ahead? No. "I don't care. I want to try. I want a ward." If there was a chance, well, she'd take it. Anything to return to her dad.

Anything to be with Riley.

She'd rather die than hurt her boys, so, she had no qualms about risking her life. "Do we have the equipment?"

"Yes. Nathan noticed your new wards, and the scabs forming on one of them, and thought Riley might want to correct the damage, so he commandeered what was needed before he took off."

"We'll think this through before we do it," Aden said.

Mary Ann was shaking her head before he finished. "No. We'll do it. Here, now. Before we leave this place."

Aden, too, glanced at Riley, his expression more what's-going-on than help-me-make-her-see-reason. "What happened to our sweet Mary Ann who rarely argues?"

Riley shrugged, offering nothing else, and for some reason, that upset her as much as when he'd pulled away from her. "You told us what you learned this past week. Now it's our turn to tell you what we learned."

A pause. A shuddering breath. "All right." Aden braced himself for impact. "Go."

Another half hour ticked by as Riley explained Mary Ann's search for the identity of the souls, her success, her search for Aden's parents, and what they assumed was her success.

Aden listened, paling, stiffening. His eyes were changing colors so rapidly they were like a spinning kaleidoscope. Blue, gold, green, black. Violet. Such a glittering violet. The souls must be going crazy inside his head.

By the time Riley finished, the oppressive silence had made another appearance.

Aden propped his head on the back of the chair and stared up at the ceiling. "I don't know how to react to this. I need time. Like a year, maybe. Or two." He rubbed his temples, as if battling a persistent ache. "But you know what I hate most of all? That we've been running around reacting to everything, but not *causing* anything."

"I don't understand," Victoria said.

"Yeah," Mary Ann said. "What?"

"We've been letting Vlad pull our strings. He hides in the shadows, forcing people to hurt us, and we do nothing to stop him. We wait, we take it, we react, bumbling around without any planning, without delivering any retribution. He has no fear of us because we never strike first. Why haven't we struck first?"

"What do you have in mind?" Riley asked, hard tone laced with the kind of eagerness you might hear from a prisoner on death row who had nothing to lose.

"I'll talk to Tonya Smart myself. I'll visit…my parents, if that's who they are. I'll find out as much as I can about myself and the souls. Because in the end, I need to be at my best if I'm to have any hope of defeating Vlad. And I can't be at my best if I'm pulled in a thousand different directions."

He paused, eyeing everyone to make sure they were

listening. When no one offered a reply, he went on, "You two aren't ready to leave yet, you're both still pretty weak, and to be honest, so am I. So rest up. When the sun sets, we're rolling out and cutting some of those strings."

TWENTY-FOUR

MARY ANN COULDN'T REST. Shock and medication were wearing off, and emotions were slogging through her with the force of a battering ram. Aden and Victoria had left over an hour ago, staying in the room next door, but she couldn't even close her eyes. Riley was still beside her, quiet, motionless. So quiet her ears were ringing. So motionless he could have been dead.

Like Shannon was destined to be, all over again.

The only way to kill a zombie was to cut off its head. Thinking of her friend ending up that way, of never seeing or speaking to him again, she wept for endless minutes—hours? Wept until there was nothing left inside her. Until her eyes were swollen and burning, her nose clogged up. At some point, Riley gathered her in his arms, those strong, beloved arms, and held her tight.

When her body stopped shaking, she released a shuddering sigh. If only that were the end of her misery, but her mind still refused to quiet. Tucker would have to be dealt with, too. Even though she hadn't truly trusted him, even though she'd known what he was capable of, she hadn't expected *this*.

"You good?" Riley asked gruffly. His arms fell away from her.

She rolled to her side, peering over at him. He was on his back, staring up at the ceiling, reminding her of Aden as he'd searched his mind for answers. "I don't want to vomit out my guts, if that's what you're asking."

"Well, okay then."

"You'll ward me?"

"Yes, if that's what you still want. I'll fix the one that was damaged and give you a new one to prevent you from taking energy from others."

"Thank you." But why was he so willing? Because he no longer cared if she lived or died?

"No reason to wait, then, is there?" He threw his legs over the side of the bed, and she saw the wound scabbing over on his calf. Raw, red, angry. He must have been in serious pain.

She reached out and grabbed his arm, preventing him from standing. "How are *you* feeling?"

"Fine," he said, and shook off her hold.

As she watched, upset all over again, he dug through

the bag his brother had left behind. When he had everything he needed, he set up shop at her side.

"Roll over."

She obeyed. He didn't speak as he pulled at the hospital gown she still wore, the material draping down her shoulder. Fixing the ward on her back *stung,* the needle running over fresh scabs and healing flesh.

By the time he finished, she was a trembling, sweating mess.

"Where do you want the new one?"

There was a chance she would be human again. Normal. And that meant there was a chance she'd get to see her dad again. He'd flip when he saw the tattoos on her arms. No reason to add to those, thereby adding to his flip out.

"My leg," she said.

Her back was throbbing, so she didn't attempt to lie flat. She just propped herself up on a pillow and extended one leg.

Riley slid the gown over her knee, and for a moment, he didn't move. Just looked down at her, expression... heated?

"Riley?"

Her voice jolted him from whatever thoughts he'd been entertaining. Scowling, he got back to work. After the other one, this tattoo barely registered. But, wow, it was *big,* stretching from just under her knee to her ankle.

The gun's motor shut down, and Riley cleared everything away, then dabbed at her bleeding calf with a towel from the bathroom. "Victoria was wrong. You won't die if this doesn't work."

"What do you mean?"

"If you start to weaken, or can't eat regular food anymore, I can close the ward and you'll return to nor—yourself."

He'd stopped himself from saying "normal" self. But the gist was, she'd become a drainer again if he closed that ward. On one hand, she knew that meant he still cared about whether she lived or died. On the other, he'd just closed the door on a relationship, hadn't he?

"No matter what, I want it open," she said. "Working."

"Mary Ann—"

"No. So I need you to give me another ward."

His eyes narrowed, but he didn't protest. She knew him, though, and knew he was thinking he'd do whatever the heck he wanted. "For what?"

"You know for what. I want one like Aden's. One that prevents anyone from being able to close my wards ever again."

He was shaking his head before she finished.

"Admit it. The witches wouldn't have attempted to poke a hole in the ward preventing my death by physical injury if I'd had one." Witches could sense wards and exactly what they meant.

"Yes, but what will you do if you're captured? What will you do if a ward you don't want is added to your body?"

"So give me a ward that prevents me from getting any more wards."

"No one in their right mind *ever* allows themselves to acquire that ward. You'll leave yourself open to too many other spells."

"Riley."

"Mary Ann."

"I want the ward, Riley. The first one I mentioned."

"Too risky."

"Aden has it."

"And it's worth the risk with him. Too many people are drawn to him, want to use him, control him, hurt him."

"News flash. People want to hurt me, too." In fact, everyone Riley knew wanted to kill her. Even his brothers. Was she the only one who remembered the way they'd looked at her the night she'd slain those witches and fairies? With horror, disgust and fury. The only reason they'd gone to so much trouble to save her today was because Riley loved her. Or used to love her.

"With an unbreakable ward preventing death by physical injury, how do you think the witches will go about killing you next time?" he growled. "And they will try to kill you again. You'll be blamed for the Red Robed Massacre."

"But I—"

He didn't let her finish. "In case you can't figure it out, let me explain. They will lock you away, starve you and torture you without killing you, keeping you in that state until you die of simple old age."

Impossible. "That could be *decades* from now."

"Exactly."

She was letting him scare her, she realized. "Give me the ward." She'd already decided: she would rather die herself, painfully, torturously, than cause anyone else to die because she was hungry. He wasn't going to change her mind.

"I've already put the equipment up."

"Yes, and it's so hard to dig it back out."

"No."

"I don't want to be a danger to you anymore."

A muscle ticked in his jaw. "You're not."

"Oh, and what's changed?" she asked as casually as she was able. Finally she would know what was driving him to act this way.

He ran his tongue over his teeth, his eyes glittering with a familiar green fire. Not of desire, but of fury. Something he'd never truly flashed her way. "I can't shift anymore."

He couldn't—wait, wait, wait. *"What?"*

"I can't shift. I've tried. Multiple times since leaving the hospital. I just…can't."

"Because I…because I fed from you?"

"You didn't want to—you even resisted—but I pushed and pushed and force-fed you." The fury shattered, hopelessness taking its place. "Doesn't matter, though. The result was the same."

Doesn't matter? It mattered more than anything! He might have pushed, but *she* was the one to take. She'd taken his animal from him. His inner self. His *true* self. Gone. Forever. Because of her. No wonder he was acting like he hated her. He did.

"Riley, I'm so sorry. So so sorry. I didn't mean…I never would have…" There were no words to convey the depths of her remorse. Nothing that would make this okay.

Of everything she'd done, this was the worst. And those dried-up tear ducts? They suddenly remembered how to work, burning her eyes and tracking moisture down her cheeks.

"We knew it was a possibility," he said.

"Are you...human?"

A bitter laugh. "Pretty much."

Worse and worse. That had to be torture for him. He'd been a shifter all his life.

His very long life. A life that might now be cut short. Because. Of. Her. His friends were shifters. His family. And now, he was the very thing he hated more than anything: vulnerable.

Riley pushed to his feet and turned away from her. "I'm going to take a shower. Try to get some rest." He didn't wait for her reply but marched into the bathroom and shut the door.

Shut her out.

Now and forever, if she had to guess.

Mary Ann curled into herself and sobbed.

ADEN CURSED UNDER his breath. "Did you hear that?"

"The gutter your mouth just traveled through?" Victoria asked. "Yes. You basically shouted the profanities in my ear."

"Not that. What Riley just told Mary Ann."

"Oh. No. Did you?"

"Yeah." She lay against him, snuggled into his side, and he sifted his fingers through her hair, loving the softness of it. Their room was dark, but his gaze cut through that darkness as if he wore night-vision goggles.

"How?" she asked.

"Thin walls?"

"Then *I* would have heard. How?"

"Another vampire ability manifesting itself?"

"Now that makes sense."

He expected the souls to comment, to voice their thoughts. They didn't. Caleb was still in mourning about the witches, Elijah hadn't given up his vow of silence, and since hearing about Tonya Smart, Julian had been too busy trying to figure out who he'd been and what his last wish was.

Currently the only being giving him fits was Junior. Aden was hungry, again, and his beast wasn't gonna let him forget it. In fact, his roars were getting louder with every hour that passed.

All of Elijah's birth terminology had really hit the mark. Aden kinda felt like a brand-new dad whose kid had soiled his diaper and was demanding a change.

"Aden," Victoria prompted. "What did Riley say?"

Oh, yeah. He and Victoria were in the middle of a conversation. "Riley can't shift anymore."

She jolted upright and peered down at him, eyes wide with dismay. "What?"

"Don't kill the messenger." Aden tugged her back into his embrace, loving the way she curled herself around him. "He just told Mary Ann. Apparently she fed off him before they landed in the hospital."

"How…how did he sound?"

"Surprisingly fine."

"Oh, no. That's when he's the *most* upset." She banged her fist against Aden's chest. "I will kill her!"

She tried the sitting up thing again, but he tightened his hold, keeping her against him. "He's taking a shower, and I don't think she meant to damage him."

"I don't care. That's exactly why the races have always slain drainers when they are first identified. Accidents like that don't have to happen."

"Maybe he'll heal. Maybe—"

"Mary Ann stole his ability. There is no healing from that."

"Just like there's no turning a human into a vampire?" She'd once told him *that* was impossible, too.

"I…I…oh! I still want to put her in a sleeper hold. Forever! I know how. Riley taught me."

O-kay. Time to abandon that subject before she worked herself into a rage, and Chompers came out to play. Which would cause Junior to come out to play. Besides, Aden had a feeling he hadn't seen the last of Riley's wolf. Maybe that was just wishful thinking on his part, but honestly? He trusted his feelings.

He'd known he would meet Victoria before he'd ever laid eyes on her. Because of Elijah's visions, yeah, but as Aden was learning, the souls shared their abilities with him. And when they left, those abilities remained. Elijah wasn't the only psychic in this body. Aden was, too.

The reminder gave him pause. Could *Aden* peek into the future?

"Let me go, Aden. Now." The chill of her breath stroked his chest.

"Not yet. I want to talk to you about something."

"What?" she asked, reluctantly.

"I know you don't want me to feed off you, and I respect that." Even though he *still* wanted her blood more than anything. At this point, he doubted that was ever going to change. "Are you afraid I'll revert to the mindless being I was inside the cave?"

"No. If that were a possibility, it would have happened after you drank my blood from the goblet."

He believed the same. "Are you afraid I'll see the world through your eyes?"

"No. I mean, you haven't yet. You still could, of

course, but the thought doesn't bother me. You have before, and really, you already know everything there is to know about me."

"Then tell me what's going on in that head of yours. Please."

She traced a pattern on his chest, the tip of her finger tickling him, sensitizing him. "You won't like it."

"Tell me anyway."

Her lips pressed against the most sensitive spot, his heartbeat rushing up to meet her. "You know how you're becoming a vampire?"

"Yes," he said, and in that moment he knew where she was going with this. He knew, and he *didn't* like it. An insidious cold invaded his bloodstream.

"Well, I'm becoming…human. Completely human."

Bingo.

"My skin, it's like yours was. Easily cut. I can't teleport anymore. I can't use my persuasive voice. And I'm eating human food. I had a hamburger before I returned with Mary Ann's lunch. A hamburger! And I enjoyed it."

So many changes. Too many changes. "Do you still need blood?"

"Not me, not anymore, but Chompers does. His roar…at first it was stronger, because he was so hungry, but now it's weakening. He's so quiet, I'm almost afraid he's…he's…you know."

Yeah. Dying.

Aden pinched the bridge of his nose, trying to align his thoughts. He should have realized the truth himself. After all, this made perfect sense and explained so much. Her chilled skin, her reluctance to do the things she used to do. When he thought about all the chances she'd taken lately, all the chances he'd asked her to take, he wanted to knock a few holes in the wall.

Barring that, there was only one other thing he wanted to do.

"Okay. Here's our new plan. You're going to feed off me, and I'm going to feed off you. Another blood exchange, just like in the cave."

Her cheek rubbed against him as she shook her head. "We don't know how we'll react. How *they'll* react." The beasts.

"Exactly, and it's time we found out. We're being proactive now, remember? We're not simply reacting, we're causing."

A breath shuddered from her, gusting this time. "All right. You're right. I know you're right."

Good, because his mouth was already watering, desperate for a taste. And maybe he was pushing for this because he craved it so badly, not because he thought it would save them, but just then, he didn't care. "Ready?"

"Yes."

He rolled on top of her, and she softened against him, turning her head to the side to offer her hammering pulse. His gums started aching, throbbing really, and he ran his tongue over—fangs, he realized, shocked to his soul. For the first time, his teeth were as sharp as razors. Not as long as Victoria's, but noticeably longer than they'd been.

"You first," he rasped, wanting her as strong as possible for his bite.

A tremor moved through her, but then she was licking his neck, sucking, warming his blood, biting, drinking, and unlike before, her bite hurt, no chemical shooting through his vein, numbing him, but he didn't care about that either, he liked that she was taking what she needed from him; it was what he'd begged her for since the moment he'd met her. And when she finished, he was doing the same to her, licking, sucking, warming, biting, drinking.

She moaned, the sound echoing through the room. Her fingers scraped through his hair. "That feels good," she rasped.

Then he was the one moaning. So sweet, so delicious, filling him, flowing through him, strengthening him, quieting Junior, consuming them both. He was rubbing against Victoria before he registered that he was moving at all, but she didn't seem to mind, seemed to like it, meeting his every motion with one of her own.

But soon that wasn't enough for either of them. Aden pulled his teeth from her neck, surely the most difficult thing he'd ever done, but he didn't want to take too much, had to protect her, even from himself, and she groaned in disappointment. He couldn't move away from her.

"Aden," she said on a husky catch of breath.

"Yes."

"More."

"Biting?"

A soft, glowing smile. "More everything."

As if he needed further prompting. He kissed her until he was forced to come up for air, and then he kissed her again.

Sometime during that second kiss, their clothes disappeared and their hands began exploring. He hurt, but he'd never felt so good. He needed more as she'd said, but couldn't take much more. His thoughts were short-circuiting. This was everything he'd thought it would be, only better. So much better.

"Too fast?" he rasped. "Should I stop?"

"Too slow. Don't stop."

"C-condom," he said. He didn't have a condom. And he couldn't be with her without one. He wouldn't risk pregnancy. There were STDs out there, he knew that, too, and even though he knew she didn't have one, that vampires were immune to human diseases, he wasn't going to be stupid about that, either.

"I...brought one. After our conversation in the forest, I've been carrying one. All the time."

The crinkling wrapper at last made sense. If only he'd known at the time.

She wiggled out from under him to get it, and he mourned the loss of her. She was back a few seconds later, and they picked up where they'd left off.

Not once did the souls comment. Not once did Junior roar. Or maybe Aden was simply too consumed with what he was doing to notice them. There was only Victoria, only here and now. Their first time. His first time.

His...everything.

TWENTY-FIVE

Do you truly wish to challenge me, boy?

Vlad's words echoed in Tucker's mind, menacing, as sharp as a blade. The very blade he held in his hands as he paced the floor of his motel room. He'd rented this crap hole in the same dump where the others were—or rather, had been—staying, and on the same floor. Not that they'd known it. He'd wanted to be close to Mary Ann, to feel at peace again, but it hadn't worked. He could still feel Vlad pulling at him.

The bastard wanted his own daughter eliminated. Wanted all the players responsible for his downfall eliminated. And he was close to getting what he wanted. Those players were finally together and on the same board. Aden, the power. Riley, the security. Victoria, the eye candy. Fine, she was the intermediary. And Mary Ann, the brain.

Tucker should have offed them already.

At least Vlad had no idea Tucker had made a deal with them. A deal they had better honor.

After Aden had finished boning his vamp, the twosome had talked, all lovey-dovey and crap. Tucker was still shuddering. On the other hand, Mary Ann and Riley had sniped at each other, nearly drawing blood. He kinda preferred the cooing. Thankfully all that ended when the foursome had gathered together and left the comfort of the motel for the wide-open battleground of the outside world. They were still vulnerable to attack, and that's exactly what Vlad wanted him to do. Attack.

Are you listening to me, boy? I don't like being ignored. Bad things happen to those who irritate me.

Like Tucker didn't know that already. Look what Vlad had already forced him to do to Aden. What Vlad had forced Ryder to do to Shannon.

The pace of his steps increased, his boots digging into the carpet. How was he going to get out of this mess? *Without* casualties? If he killed Aden, Aden couldn't save his brother.

Tucker scraped a hand through his hair, the one holding the blade, the metal hilt leaving grooves in his scalp.

You're going to do what I told you to do. There's no fighting me.

There had to be a way.

I will kill your brother if you fail me. Have you forgotten?

"No, I haven't. But if you kill him, you'll have no way to control me," he snapped.

Vlad might be getting stronger, but his hold on Tucker was not. Every hour, it weakened a little more. Tucker figured he was building up an immunity. Not quick enough, though. Not nearly quick enough. Vlad could still force him to walk up to anyone, hurt them— physically or mentally—and Tucker could only grin and bear it.

But Vlad had to know his grip was loosening, and that's why he was threatening Tucker's little brother. An insurance policy in the form of his innocent, sweet little brother, a six-year-old kid whose only friends were invisible and whose own father treated him like dog crap on the bottom of his shoes. Ethan deserved happiness, but everyone was always dumping on him.

Tucker loved him, yet he had been the worst offender, and now he wanted, needed, to make amends. To save that kid once and for all.

There's always a way to control a puny human, Vlad said, laughing smugly. *I always find a way.*

Very, very true. But Tucker wasn't exactly human, was he? "I don't want to hurt anyone else." Didn't want to slay his...friends. Or frenemies, they'd probably say. They, however, would kill him in a heartbeat. With good reason. But they'd promised to help him save his brother, and Tucker had to believe they would try.

Would they succeed? Maybe. The way Aden had tamed those vampire beasts...maybe he could tame Vlad's and use it against him. Yeah, maybe. All Tucker knew for sure was that he couldn't defeat the former king on his own. He needed help. Aden was that help. So, kill him? No.

I don't care what you do or do not want. Do it. Do what I told you. Destroy them. Now.

Tucker's feet were moving toward the door before he could stop himself, the dagger at the ready once more. No. No, no, no. He ground his heels into the carpet, slowing his momentum. A few days ago, he would have been outside and doing as ordered immediately. He hadn't lied to Victoria. The more evil he committed, the stronger he became. Hadn't taken him long to figure that out.

A few days from now, and maybe Vlad would no longer be able to lead him around like this. But did he have a few days? Did his brother?

Probably not.

Tucker massaged the back of his neck. Right now, there was only one sure way to get what he wanted. He'd ignored the possibility before, but here, now, he couldn't. And didn't really want to anymore.

"Lead me to wherever they've gone," he said, his tone devoid of all emotion.

Vlad's glee practically slithered from the top of his head to the soles of his feet. *That's my good boy.*

TRY AGAIN, Julian said.

Aden knocked on Tonya Smart's door for the sixth time. She was home, no matter how much she might be wishing otherwise right now, and he wasn't leaving until she answered. Or called the police and they escorted him off the premises.

Riley and Mary Ann were a few miles away, checking out the Stones' place, making sure they were, in fact, his parents. Aden had declined to go, claiming it'd be easier and faster if they split up. In reality, he just wasn't ready to face the two people who'd betrayed and forgotten him.

Because what if they were good, decent people? What if they knew nothing about his abilities? What if those abilities had nothing to do with the reason they'd given him up? What if they simply hadn't wanted him?

Even the thought left him bleeding inside.

Victoria stood beside him, holding his hand. Now that he knew she was human, he wasn't letting her out of his sight for any reason. Someone had to protect her, and he wanted to be that someone. Now, always. Not just because her blood tasted heavenly, and he still craved it, would probably always crave it, but also because she trusted him, looked out for him, wanted the best for him and still loved him, after everything he'd done, everything he'd taken from her.

Again, Julian prompted. *Please.*

After the loss of Eve, the souls had stopped pushing Aden to learn who they were. They'd been as scared about parting as Aden was. But now that the information was within reach, Julian's fear had dissipated. He was all about the eagerness.

"Perhaps we should try again later." Victoria scanned the yard.

"We'd get the same results." Aden knocked again. "She's home. I can...smell her." He could even hear the rapid *thump, thump* of her heartbeat. And yeah, that was kind of freaking him out.

Junior, of course, liked the sound. Though it wasn't a

lullaby to him, as it would have been to any other new-born; it was a war drum. He heard, and he hungered, even though he'd been fed.

"If the woman is that determined to ignore us, we failed before we even arrived." Victoria's voice had dipped, becoming husky, like a pinup coming to spar-kling life.

His intensified senses were picking up details he'd never before noticed. "All—"

No! Julian shouted. *We're not leaving.*

"Not yet," Aden said.

A relieved sigh echoed. *Thank you.*

"I just want to speak with you, Ms. Smart," he called. "Please. You could save a life here."

The next few minutes ticked by with no results.

"This isn't working." Victoria did her chew-on-the-lip thing. "I wish I could...but I can't." She blinked up at him. "You, however, can."

"Can what?"

"Summon her. You can *make* her talk to you."

That's right. He could. He kept forgetting.

His head fell back, and he peered up at the sky. Dark velvet with pinpricks of starlight. Vast, never-ending. Like his ability. He could make anyone do anything he wanted. The same way doctor after doctor had forced

their wills on him, only with pills. The same way foster parent after foster parent had expected absolute, total
compliance for the "gift" of taking him in. Anything for
a check, he supposed.

To do that to others...to *keep* doing it... over and over
again, when he knew the awfulness of being on the opposite side of that stick.

It's a good plan, Julian said.

"I know." The more he did it, though, the easier it'd
be and the more he'd fall back on it, until he relied on
the ability for everything. "Just...let me think for a bit."

Victoria understood. "You don't like forcing people."

"Yeah." He pulled her to the porch swing, and they
sat down, the wood swaying and creaking underneath
them.

"I've never met anyone who resisted using The Voice
before. It's admirable."

Frustration gave way to pleasure, and he wanted to
cuddle her close. Of course, that led to another thought:
he wanted to be with her again.

Next thing he knew, that's all his mind could ponder. Sex. His first time, and he was so glad it had
been with her. Someone who understood him, who
knew what he'd gone through, what he was still going

through. Someone who didn't judge him and liked being with him.

"I will not talk to you about him," a woman's familiar voice suddenly said. "I can't."

Fabulous. This crap again.

And yet, there she was. From the corner of his eye, he watched Victoria's mother twirl in front of him, her black robe dancing at her ankles. For a moment, he wondered if she were a vision courtesy of Tucker, if she had been an illusion all along. If Vlad had told Demon Boy what Edina looked liked and Tucker had taken things from there, just to drive Aden insane.

But, no. The first time the flashes came, Tucker had been with Mary Ann. Not even the demon could be in two places at once, causing problems. At the hospital, Aden had wondered if Edina appeared at times Victoria would have been—was—thinking of her. Now, he discarded that idea, too. She'd made no mention of the woman, and she would have.

What suddenly seemed most likely was his ingestion of Victoria's blood. He'd drank from her—twice—and he still hadn't mind-merged with her. What if this was the way their blood connection would manifest from now on?

No one else appeared in the vision, and he didn't hear

the response to Edina's refusal to "talk about him," but she said, "No. *No!* I love him, and that's all you need to know. I'm running away with him, but I can't take you with us, darling. Your father might let me go, but he would never let you go. He's proven that, hasn't he?"

She was going to leave her kid behind? *Victoria* behind?

"Aden?" Victoria said.

"Need a minute."

"Oh. Okay."

She probably assumed he was listening to the souls, and he didn't correct her.

"I'll write you every day, my darling," Edina said. A ray of sunlight burst through the thick cloud cover and shone directly on her. Like the dust motes around her, she wavered. "I promise."

Pause.

"Be my brave little Vicki, and tell your father I'm in my room if he asks where I am."

Vicki. Victoria. Yeah. Aden's stomach rolled in tune with the motes as his understanding of his girlfriend deepened. No wonder she'd used her Voice Voodoo so much. Chaos had always surrounded her. Telling humans what to do had been her way of taking charge, of finally eliciting the results she wanted.

Aden? What's going on? Julian asked.

"Nothing."

In a snap, the vision changed. This time, the rest of the world faded away, black walls closing in around him. No time to react. Above him was a mirrored ceiling, below him a shiny onyx floor.

He lost his connection to his own body, found himself looking through someone else's eyes. Victoria's eyes. He knew this sensation very well.

Just in front of him, a man Aden could only assume was Vlad the Impaler sat on a gold embossed throne. Wow, the guy was impressive. Before, all Aden had seen of him were charred remains. Now, the vampire king was a hulking, towering figure of strength, even sitting down.

He had a thick crop of black hair and eyes so blue they were like sapphires burning in a ceaseless fire. Fine lines branched from the corners of those eyes, and rather than age him, they painted an expression of determination and cruelty. His lips were a thin slash, stained crimson and twisted ruthlessly. A scar ran from the arch of one dark brow all the way to a stubborn chin.

Girls would consider him handsome, Aden supposed, in a psycho-killer kind of way. Vlad had wide shoulders, his torso bared and roped with muscle. There was a ring on each of his fingers, making him a man assured of his own masculinity. He wore fawn-colored breeches that molded to his legs and boots that tied all the way up to his knees.

"You dare to challenge me?" Though Vlad spoke in a language Aden had never heard before, he had no trouble understanding because *Victoria* understood. "Well, I accept." He stood. Tall…taller…a giant of a man and solid muscle.

The vampire he spoke to was just as tall and just as muscled. "I did not doubt you would."

"You may choose the weapon."

Around them was a crowd of people, watching, tense, barely breathing. Except for one man. Sorin, Victoria's brother. He stood just below the dais where the throne rested, and he was shaking his head in resignation.

Victoria was a few feet away from him. Her gaze skidded over a mirror, and Aden saw that she was a little girl, perhaps two years older than she'd been in the vision of the whipping. Her mother stood on her other side, tears streaking her cheeks, her features tight with fear.

There'd been no hint of Victoria's emotions revealed in her reflection. She clutched her mother's hand, however, her knuckles leaching of color. She might have looked calm, but she was a mess of nerves inside and too afraid to let go.

"I choose swords," the man said.

"Excellent choice." Vlad glided down the stairs to the floor. "When? Where?"

"Now. Here."

A nod of satisfaction. "We are of one mind, then."

"Only in this."

Someone from the crowd threw a sword at Vlad and a sword at his opponent. Both caught the weapons with ease. A second later, the man lunged forward, throwing himself into the fight.

Vlad stood completely still. Until, just before the man reached him, he turned, a blur of motion, and slashed.

Blood and guts spilled all over the floor.

The man dropped to his knees, gasping, gurgling, his eyes wide. He clutched at his middle, not yet grasping the depths of his swift defeat. Without breaking a sweat or moving a step, Vlad struck a second time, and off went the man's head.

A collective gasp sounded from the crowd.

"Anyone else?" Vlad asked, buffing his nails on the waist of his pants. "It would be my pleasure to fight any of you."

Edina burst into sobs and rushed from the room,

leaving her little girl behind. A little girl who was shaking as her father turned the force of his displeasure on her.

"Why did you not stop her? 'Tis *her* lover in pieces on the floor. A man you would have called Father, I am sure. A man you *wanted* to call Father."

"No! I—I—"

"I will hear no excuses or false denials from you." He waved a hand through the air. "Go. Take the head and place it on a pike. The task is yours, and you will complete it or find yourself resting beside him."

Her trembling increased as she rushed to obey, wading through things no child should *ever* encounter.

Aden's first thought had nothing to do with Vlad, fighting Vlad or having no hope of winning against a man like that. His mind concentrated solely on Victoria. Knowing she had endured this undid him.

He wanted to run to the girl she'd been, whisk her away, protect her from such horrors. The man who'd just been gutted was the man Edina had attempted to run away with, leaving her daughter behind. The daughter who then had to clean up her mother's mess. Literally.

His poor Victoria. Once he would have placed good money on the fact that no one could have a childhood worse than his. Hers had been, though. In comparison, he'd been raised in heaven by doting angels.

The scene disappeared, there one minute, a cloud of vapor the next.

"Aden," Victoria whispered, shaking him into the present. "Someone's coming."

He rapid-fire blinked into focus as the front door of the house creaked open, Tonya peeking out. He hadn't summoned her, yet here she was. Checking to make sure he was gone most likely, but whatever. He'd take what he could get.

"What do you want?" she snapped when she spotted him. She didn't step out on the porch, but kept the screen between them. "Why won't you leave?"

Aden unfolded from the swing. "My friends visited you, asked you about your husband—"

"Yes, and I told the girl not to return."

"And so she hasn't. I'm here."

"Sorry, but I have nothing to say to you, either."

She made to close the door, and that's when Aden caved. Sick of waiting, sick of questions without answers and no longer willing to view his new gift as a curse, he said, "Leave the door open," putting all of his want into the words.

Victoria had loved her Voice Voodoo, but she'd

given it up. For him. Aden wouldn't make light of that anymore.

Tonya's eyes immediately glazed over, and she left the door alone.

Victoria stood beside him and twined their fingers, offering comfort.

"Your brother-in-law died, and he left no family behind. Do you have any photographs of him? Any personal effects?"

Silence.

"Tell her to tell you," Victoria instructed.

"Tell me what I wish to know," he added, wanting it, wanting it so badly.

"I—" Though Tonya's eyes were still glazed, she found the strength to deny him. "I can't tell you."

A frowning Victoria shook her head. "That's impossible. You have to tell him. He commanded you to. I don't know anything, but even *I* want to obey him."

"I...I can't."

Slowly Aden disengaged from Victoria and approached Tonya, doing his best not to spook her. Tonya remained in place. Though he was younger than she was, he was taller, a lot taller, and he had to look down...down...to meet that still-glazed stare. That's when he saw something besides a glassy sheen swimming in those gray depths. Something dark, like a shadow.

Julian saw it, too, and gasped in dismay. *What is that?*

"Don't know." Aden drew on every ounce of his need for answers. He let that need churn in his voice box, until his throat nearly steamed from the burn of it, before speaking again. "You will tell me what I want to know, Tonya Smart. Now."

The shadows coagulated, then broke apart and scattered, and Tonya relaxed a little. "Yes. I do have photographs and personal effects."

Answers, that easily. It was as powerful and addictive as he'd suspected. As powerful and addictive as a vampire's bite. That wasn't going to stop him. "Bring them to me. Give them to me."

"Bring. Give. Yes." She disappeared inside the house.

Half an hour ticked by, and Aden began to worry that he'd lost her, that she'd shaken out of his mental hold and taken off out the back door, never to return. But then, as suddenly as she'd left, she was back in the doorway, holding a box out to him.

It. Had. Worked.

He claimed the thing with a relieved, "Thank you."

Julian was dancing through his head. *I can't believe this! There could be a picture of me in there.*

Aden balanced the box with one hand, used the other to grab Victoria and headed back to the motel to study what was inside. Hopefully, Riley and Mary Ann were just as lucky.

Or not.

TWENTY-SIX

RILEY KICKED IN THE front door, wooden shards raining in every direction. No alarm sounded. That didn't mean one hadn't been tripped, but screw it. Last time he'd been in this neighborhood, playing it safe had almost killed him. *Had* killed his animal. So, no more playing it safe.

His hands balled into fists as he stomped into the house. He couldn't think about the past right now. He'd rage and destroy everything in sight. "We've got five minutes." After that, the authorities could arrive. "Let's make the most of it."

Mary Ann rushed in behind him. "So, just grab what I can?"

Joe and Paula Stone supposedly lived there. So, yeah, grabbing what they could was the plan. A plan they'd gone over several times already. He stalked down the hallway without bothering to reply. She knew the answer, she was just nervous. He wished he could comfort her, but just then, he was having trouble comforting himself.

There were only two doorways along this route. He entered the first. Master bedroom? Maybe. Small, sparse, with only a bed, a nightstand and a dresser. On the bed, the covers were in disarray, as if they'd been shoved away in a hurry. A cup on the nightstand was tipped to its side, the contents—water, from the looks of it—had dripped to the floor, where clothes were piled. The dresser's drawers were partly open. The only window was covered by thick black paint.

Clearly no one had been here for a while. Probably since the morning he and Mary Ann had nearly had sex in the house across the street, and both their lives had changed forever.

If so, well, Joe and Paula Stone had run. For good. And if they'd run, that meant they'd known Riley and Mary Ann were coming. But how could they have known? And *why* run? What had they feared?

"Riley," Mary Ann called.

He followed the sound of her voice and was soon standing beside her in the second bedroom. Toys lit-tered the floor, a fact that momentarily rendered him speechless. *"They have a kid?"*

"Either that, or they have a home day care."

"A day care that caters strictly to girls? No." There was nothing masculine in the room. No blue, no race cars, no action figures. Just pink, stuffed animals and dolls.

"Do you think…"

That Aden has a sister? "Maybe." Probably. And what a way to find out. He thought back to the couple, to the truck, but didn't recall seeing a car seat. That didn't mean the girl hadn't been with them. "Just…" What? He looked for a clock, couldn't find one. How were they on time? "Go to the kitchen, go through all the drawers. Grab any kind of bill you find. Anything with a name."

"Okay." She didn't run off, but stood there. "Riley, I—"

"I can't talk about it. Just go," he said and returned to the master bedroom before she could say anything else. Trying to force his mind to a Happy Place, he dug through the closet, every drawer in the nightstand, then searched under the mattress and bed. Nothing personal had been left behind.

Figured.

"Uh, Riley," Mary Ann called, her voice cracking.

His back was to her, but he could sense her fear. He jackknifed to a stand and turned toward her, only to freeze, his breath icing over in his lungs.

"Mary Ann. Walk to me. Slowly."

A strangling sound slipped from her. "Can't."

"You don't issue orders, little boy. I do," said the man standing behind her. The man pointing a gun at her head.

He was tall, blond and lean. He wore a flannel shirt, the sleeves rolled up halfway on his arms to reveal several tattoos. Wards. Against what, Riley couldn't tell. Yet. He needed a closer look. What he did know? Anger pulsed from the guy in dark, agitated waves. He'd shoot, and he wouldn't care about the dead bodies he left behind.

Riley cursed himself for not teaching Mary Ann how to react in this type of situation. "You hurt her," he said just as calmly, "and I'll kill you." That was not an empty boast.

Throughout his life, he'd done that and more. He'd never been one to strike without cause, but he'd never been one to sit back and take whatever was being served, either.

"That'll be a little hard for you to do if you're dead,

now won't it." A statement when it should have been a question. "But don't you worry. I'll make it fast."

The sad thing was, Riley had no argument. No real defense. Had he not lost his wolf, he would have heard the man enter the house. Failing that, he would have smelled him. Instead, he'd allowed his ex-girlfriend to be terrorized. He kinda deserved what he got.

Not Mary Ann, though, she didn't deserve any of this. Not…his ex. Only then did he realize he'd just thought of her in past tense, rather than present. Something he'd never done before, not with her.

The man pushed the gun into her scalp, which pushed her forward. She stumbled into the room.

"I'm so sorry," she whispered, tears pooling in her eyes. "He snuck up on me, and I—"

"Shut up, girl. I've heard enough from you."

When she was finally within reach, Riley latched onto her arm and jerked her behind him. She was trembling, her fingers clutching at his. There was no time to comfort her. To act as her shield, he had to release her completely. Her palms flattened on his back, then fisted in his T-shirt. Then she released him as he had done to her—and stepped beside him.

He stepped in front of her and glared over at the gun-wielding human, who'd watched the entire scene with a hard, seen-it-all-before expression. They were about the same height, which put the guy at about six foot three.

"Are you Joe Stone?"

There was a flash of surprise in the guy's eyes, but he ignored the question to ask one of his own. "Are you the kids who busted my neighbor's window and left blood everywhere?"

"Yeah," Riley answered. "So?"

"So?" Such blatant honesty left the guy reeling but only for a moment. "Who are you, and what are you doing in my house?"

Should he give the truth or a lie this time? Who *was* this person? He and Aden had the same hair color and the same square chin, but then, thousands of people did. Nothing else looked similar.

The man's face was rough, his nose slightly crooked, as if it had been broken a time or ten, and there were tiny scars crisscrossing on his cheeks. Aden had an angel's face, no suggestion of roughness.

"I asked you a question, boy."

"And I didn't answer it." *Don't poke at the bear.* Especially when his wolf couldn't eat that bear.

A new concept for Riley. On paper, he was older than this man. Used to be stronger—on paper and in a ring.

A lot stronger. And a lot meaner. Now what was he? Pathetic, that's what.

"We know your son," Mary Ann said with a calm, even tone. "Aden. Haden, I mean. Everyone calls him Aden."

No expression change from Stonehenge over there. Worse, his grip on the gun was steady, proving his strength. Anyone else would have already grown tired of its weight. "I have no idea what you're talking about."

"Oh, I thought…you should have…maybe we were… this isn't happening!" she cried. "What if we're in the wrong house?"

"We aren't," Riley said.

She spoke over him. "Sir, I'm sorry. Very sorry. We shouldn't have…"

A primitive part of Riley wanted to punish the man for crushing her fighting spirit. And maybe her recent brush with death was partly to blame, too, having dulled her brave streak and—hey. She'd just inched her way in front of him again. For the love of—she was trying to act as *his* shield.

So much for a crushed spirit.

He could have taken that as a sign she still maybe kinda sorta loved him. But all he could think was that she no longer viewed him as strong enough to take care of her. Why would she? He didn't.

Joe Possible cocked the gun, getting serious. "You got five seconds to start talking, boy, or your brains will paint my walls."

"Are you going to count out loud so I can spew all my secrets at the last possible moment?" There was no need to wait for Joe's reply. And he planned to treat the man like he was Joe from then on. Otherwise, Riley would flounder. "You know exactly who Aden is. He's your son." As he spoke, he shoved Mary Ann behind him. One step, two, he backed her up, trying to get her to the window. She could jump through and run, and he could deal with the situation without fear of casualties.

"I don't have a son."

"I don't believe you."

"Don't care. Why would you think I was this Joe?"

"News flash. Answering a question with another question doesn't make you smart or mysterious."

Those dark eyes narrowed farther, becoming tiny slits. "Watch the attitude, kid. I'm the one with the gun."

Another backward step. Almost there...

"I know what you're doing, so don't you dare move another inch." Joe advanced until the barrel of the gun was pressing into Riley's chest. "You're not leaving here. Not until I get some answers."

"Like yours is the first gun I've had pointed my way. You want me scared, do something original. You want answers, let the girl go."

"No," Mary Ann said, and he reached back to squeeze her arm, a silent command to shut the hell up. "I'm staying."

"Don't listen to her."

"Too late," Joe said. "I listened. She stays."

Oh, hell, no. They weren't playing that game. "You'll regret that decision." Riley put his hands up, palms out, as if he were submitting.

"Actually, I don't think I will."

Moving swiftly, Riley grabbed the gun and pushed down, hard. Joe fired off a shot, but the bullet slammed into the floor.

Riley didn't release him but held him like that and punched him once, twice, with his other hand. Then, while Joe was dazed, he used both hands to twist the gun, breaking Joe's trigger finger in the process. He could have fired off a shot himself, but he didn't. He just pulled the weapon from the now-loosened grip and aimed.

"Told you."

Cursing under his breath, grimacing, Joe held up his hands, palms out. Unlike Riley, he meant it. His broken finger lay at an odd angle, the rest of the appendage useless.

Riley kept the gun trained on him, certain he had other weapons stashed in other places. "Move, and it'll be the last thing you do. Mary Ann, call Aden."

"What? Why?"

"He needs to be here."

From the corner of his eye, he saw her withdraw her cell and scroll through her address book. A few seconds later, she was whispering into the receiver. All the while, he kept the bulk of his attention on Joe, on the lookout for a reaction. Besides a slight hitch of breath and a truckload of trembling, the guy gave no reaction.

"If you're not Joe Stone," he said, determined to uncover the truth before Aden got here, "who are you?"

A gulp. "All right. I'll play. Let's say I am this Joe Stone. What would you want with me?"

Okay. So. He was Joe, no doubt about it. Why else would he have asked that question? But why the subterfuge? "An apology for starters."

"For protecting my home?"

"For abandoning your son."

A twitch underneath his eye. From irritation? Or guilt?

"Mary Ann?" Riley said.

"Y-yes?"

"Come here."

She was at his side a second later. "Aden's on his way."

"That's good. Now hold the gun," he said, still not taking his eyes off Joe.

"What!"

Fear once again pulsed from her.

"Hold the gun, keep your finger on the trigger and squeeze if he moves."

"Okay. Sure. Yes. Okay." With trembling hands, she reached out and did as he instructed. The gun was heavy, and he doubted she would be able to hold it for long, so he moved quickly, stalking to Joe and patting him down, but always staying out of Mary Ann's line of fire. Riley found three blades, a syringe of something and a Taser. What he didn't find was ID.

Through it all, Joe stood completely still. Smart of him.

"Riley," Mary Ann said.

"You're doing good, sweetheart." He shoved Joe to the bed, away from the discarded blades, Mary Ann following with the barrel of the gun. "Sit down and stay down."

Joe sat, and Riley returned to Mary Ann's side. When he reclaimed the gun, she let out a relieved breath.

"Grab the blades and stand beside the door. Anyone besides Aden or Victoria walk into this room, stab them."

"No one else is here," Joe said. "And no one will be coming to my rescue."

Dude's default tone was emotionless, and he'd gone back to it. Riley arched a brow at him. "Paula, your wife, isn't going to come busting in to save you, then?"

Bronzed skin paled to a sickly gray. "No, she's not. And don't think to go looking for her. She's safe."

Oh, yes. This was Joe Stone.

Silence reigned, until an hour later, Aden arrived, Victoria behind him. Both wore wrinkled clothing, and both had total bed head. Victoria's cheeks were flushed, and there were two perfect punctures in her neck. Hell, there were even puncture marks in Aden's neck, though his were jagged, clearly torn, as if he'd fended off a human.

Victoria was getting sloppy. If only that were the least of Aden's worries. They weren't just feeding off each other now, which was dangerous, considering what they'd just been through, they were sleeping together. As Riley could attest, nothing productive happened when you mixed business with pleasure.

And if Aden's beast got free…if Victoria lost herself to blood lust…well, no one would survive. But both were steady on their feet, neither was trembling, and neither was salivating and staring at thumping pulses.

Good thing. Those vampire beasts reacted to aggression and testosterone, and there was a lot of that in the air right now, practically thickening into a fog.

Joe stiffened, suddenly on alert. And surprise, surprise, he wouldn't look in Aden's direction. He looked everywhere *but* at Aden.

"Rest of the house is clean," Victoria said. "And no one suspicious is watching from the other houses."

They'd been together a long time. She knew how Riley operated, and what information he desired without being told.

Aden looked Joe over, his expression remaining blank. "This is him?" But oh, he couldn't hide the anger in his tone. He was also intrigued.

"Yeah," Mary Ann said. "That's him."

Riley gave him a moment to gather his thoughts.

"I'm not who you think I am," Joe said, still unwilling to glance at Aden, who spent the next few seconds guiding Victoria beside Mary Ann and blocking both females from Joe's line of vision.

"Not a very good liar, Joey. I'd stop trying to sell that story. You already admitted to knowing Paula."

"Or I pretended to."

"Whatever." Riley lowered the gun, pointing the tip at the carpet. "Oh, and if you don't think I can aim and fire faster than you can grab one of my friends, test me. I dare you."

Joe's lips pressed into a thin line.

"Who do we think you are?" Aden asked, jumping back into the conversation.

"Your...father." He nearly choked on that.

"And you're not?"

Silence. Then, "Why are you looking for him?"

"That's something I'll discuss only with him."

Again, silence. Silence so tense Riley could have cut through it with a knife. He was shocked when Aden walked forward, slow and deliberate, and crouched in front of Joe.

Joe flinched but otherwise made no motion to dodge his attention.

"Tell me who you are," Aden said.

Mother of—Aden had just used Voice Voodoo, as Mary Ann called it, and he'd leaked enough power to force even a wolf to do what he wanted. Most times, wolves were immune.

And apparently, so was Joe. "No," he said, at last looking Aden in the eye. "So you're one of them." Emotion now, and a lot of it. Disappointment, incredulity, anger.

The muscles in Aden's back rippled under his T-shirt. "One of who?"

"The vampires. Who else?"

Those two words—*the vampires*—were a revelation. Joe knew what was out there. Joe knew about the otherworld.

"So you know they exist?" Aden choked out.

"At least you don't try to deny it," Joe said flatly. But his anger was draining, along with the rest of the emotions, and fear was taking over.

"Are you my father?"

"Why do you want to know?"

"This again." Another pause, this one longer. Then Aden gave Joe the answers he wanted. "I have three souls trapped inside my head. I can do things, weird things, like travel to past versions of my life, wake the dead, possess other people's bodies and predict the future."

"And?"

Aden laughed bitterly. "*And*, you say, as if all of that isn't enough. *And*. I want to know if anyone else in my family was—is—like me. I want to know why I'm like I am. I want to know why my own parents were unwilling to help me."

The slightest narrowing of his eyes, Joe's lashes the same chocolate color as Aden's. "And you think answers will help you understand?"

"They wouldn't hurt."

"Do you hope your parents will apologize? Tell you they were wrong? Welcome you back into their arms?" Now Joe was the one to laugh bitterly. "I can tell you right now, you're gonna be severely disappointed if so."

Riley didn't have to see his king's face to know he'd just been cut to the bone. Aden might never have admitted it, but he would have loved those things. Probably craved them in secret. A secret buried so deep he'd kept it from himself. But being rejected like that, no matter what lies he'd told himself about wanting nothing to do with his birth parents, he wouldn't be able to stop himself from caring now.

"Believe me," Aden said, reverting to his own emotionless state, "I want nothing to do with the people who left me to rot in mental institutions. The monsters who placed me in the care of doctors who hurt me and foster families who tried to beat the normal into me."

"That wasn't what was supposed to—" Joe pressed his

lips together, but he'd already said enough. Riley had already figured it out, and now Aden knew without a doubt.

"That wasn't supposed to be what happened to me?" Aden spat. "Was I supposed to die? Or did you think leaving me in the care of the state when I was so young was going to work out for me?"

Breath hissed through Joe's flaring nostrils. "That's right. Am I your father? Yes. Was there someone else like you? Yes. *My* father. I was dragged all over the world as a child because of the things he drew our way. And you call *me* a monster? You have no idea what a true monster is! I watched huge, ugly beasts kill my mother, my brother."

"And that excuses your behavior with me?"

Joe continued as if he hadn't spoken. "When I was old enough, I moved away from my dad and never looked back. He tried to contact me a few times before he died, killed by the same things that had killed the rest of my family, I'm sure, but I wanted nothing to do with him. I wasn't going to live that way anymore. I had my own family to take care of."

"You didn't take care of *me!*" Aden shouted. "Why did you risk having kids, if you knew you could pass on your father's abilities?"

"I didn't know. He was the only one. I thought... I hoped... It wasn't genetic, shouldn't have been genetic. He did it to himself. Messed with things he shouldn't have messed with."

"Like what?"

"Magic, science." Joe leaned down, getting in his face. "As for abandoning you, how could I not? You were just like him. About a week after you were born, they started showing up. Stray goblins at first, trying to crawl through your window, then the wolves, then the witches. Rogues, all of them, without true ties to their race, but I knew it was only a matter of time until you drew them in groups. Just a matter of time until we were running...until your mother was dead. Me, you."

"What about the girl?" Riley asked. Aden didn't know, not yet, but didn't betray his lack of knowledge by speaking.

"An accident."

"Is she—"

"I won't talk about her!"

"Well, I don't believe you about your reasons," Aden said. "I managed not to draw those monsters to me for over a decade."

"Because of the wards," Joe replied.

Aden balled his hand into a fist. "I got my first ward a few weeks ago."

"No. You got your first ward as an infant."

"Impossible."

"No. Hidden."

Nostrils flared. "Where?"

"Your scalp."

"The freckles," Victoria suddenly gasped out. "Remember?"

Aden rubbed at his head. "Then why did they stop working? For that matter, if you gave them to me, if they kept the monsters away, why not keep me with you?"

Joe closed his eyes, his spine sagging. He sighed. "Maybe the ink faded. Maybe the spell was somehow broken."

Aden and Mary Ann shared a look, and Riley figured they were remembering the first time they'd met, when an atomic bomb of power had been unleashed, summoning everything Joe had named and more.

"And as for why we didn't keep you with us," Joe said, "I wasn't willing to take the chance. I had to keep your mother safe."

"My mother." Absolute longing radiated from Aden. "Where is she?"

"That, I will never tell." Firm, final.

Riley refused to accept. "If you didn't want to be found, you should have changed your names."

Joe's gaze met his for about half a second. "I did. For a while. But Paula..." He shrugged. "She insisted."

Had she *wanted* Aden to find her?

Aden straightened as if a board had just been strapped to his back. "I've heard enough."

Actually, Riley thought he'd reached his limit. He might be veering close to a breakdown. Here was his dad—who still didn't want him. Who didn't want to help him, who didn't so much as throw him a bone.

"What about Joe?" he asked.

"Leave him. I'm done with him." With that, Aden walked out of the room, out of the house.

Riley motioned for the girls to follow him. When they were out of view, he tossed the gun on the floor. Rather than make a move for it, Joe stayed on the bed. "He's a good kid, and now he's leader of the very world you despise. And guess what? The monsters of your nightmares obey his every command. He could have protected you unlike any ward, and in a way no one else in the world could have, yet you just tossed him away like garbage. Again."

Blink, blink. "I...I don't understand."

"Well, understand this—he deserved better than you. A lot better."

Now Joe bolted to his feet. "You have no idea what I went through when—"

"Make all the excuses you want. It won't change the facts. You didn't protect your own son. You're greedy, selfish and an all-around bastard. Now give me your shirt."

The swift subject change threw the guy for a loop. "What?"

"You heard me. Give me your shirt. Don't make me say it again. You won't like the results."

Joe jerked the material over his head and tossed it at him. "There. Happy?"

Riley caught it. "Not even." There were thick scars all over Joe's chest—scars in the pattern of claw marks. There were also other wards, and Riley recognized the biggest. It was an alert. Whenever danger approached, his entire body would vibrate. No wonder he'd known to run when Riley neared. "Understand this, Joe Stone. If we want to talk to you again, there's no place you'll be able to hide now." He brought the shirt to his nose and sniffed. Though he could no longer shift and didn't know if he could track, his brothers could still do both. "We've got your scent."

With that, he, too, walked away.

TWENTY-SEVEN

THE REST OF THE DAY, the entire night, and most of the next morning, Aden spent locked inside another motel room with Victoria, Mary Ann and Riley. They pored through the photos and papers Tonya Smart had given them, taking only a few breaks to eat or stretch their legs.

Aden pounded back a pint of Victoria's blood, appeasing Junior, Victoria downed a pint of his and a Big Mac, Mary Ann three Big Macs, and Riley a chicken nugget Happy Meal.

When teased, he'd said, "What? I like chicken," then went back to scowling at everyone and generally acting as if he was on his period.

No one mentioned Riley's wolf. Maybe because they knew the top of his head would explode. And no one mentioned Joe. Not even the souls. Maybe because they knew the top of *Aden's* head would explode.

Joe. His father. He'd looked into those dark gray eyes, and he'd known. Part of him had even recognized the man. His father, he thought again. His. Father. The man who'd given him up. The man who hadn't loved him enough to keep him. The man who had thrown him to the wolves—literally. The man who had admitted the truth only upon threat of death.

If he'd shown any hint of remorse…but no, Joe Stone was ashamed of who and what Aden was, even denying him the opportunity to see his mother, his sister. And now Aden felt as if he were bleeding inside. Bleeding and unable to suture the wound. There was a steady *drip, drip* inside him. He had a sister; Riley had seen her toys. Joe apparently loved the little girl in a way he'd never loved Aden.

Drip, drip.

For years he'd dreamed about meeting his parents. About his dad coming to his rescue, telling him how much of a mistake letting him go had been, about how loved he was. Then, when none of that had happened, the want had sharpened into indifference, and eventually the indifference into dislike.

One look at Joe and the want had returned.

Yet no matter what Aden had said, Joe had regarded him as a liability. *I've made something of myself,* he'd wanted to say. *I'm king of the vampires now. More than that, I earned the title. It wasn't handed to me.* Would his father have regarded him with horror then? Probably.

That wouldn't stop him from wanting to be king. Or acting as king. Already he'd gotten texts from Sorin and Seth. Shannon sat in his cell and stared at the wall—until someone entered with blood for him. Then he attacked. Ryder was on the mend, yet inconsolable about what he'd done, and begged everyone who approached him to kill him.

Sorin wanted to grant his request; Seth wanted to eliminate Sorin.

Aden had commanded them both to leave the boy alone and let him heal. Oh, yeah. And to suck it. They were supposed to help him, not hinder him.

Hey, I think I know them, Julian said excitedly, cutting into Aden's thoughts.

Focus, he had to focus. He peered down at the photo in his hand and saw two men. Both were of average height. One had thinning dark hair and glasses, the other had a full head of dark hair and no glasses. They were standing side by side, though they weren't touching. Or smiling. The back of the photo read *Daniel and Robert.*

So. Here were the Smart brothers.

Do you think that's really me? Julian asked. *The one with the hair and without glasses, I mean. I would not have sported a comb-over.*

How do you know? Caleb asked. Or rather, grumbled. But at least he wasn't crying. *We don't know anything about our former selves.*

"I'm glad you recognize the guys, but do you remember anything about them?" Aden asked. "Or why there are spell books in this box?" Lots of spell books. And the papers? All about casting spells. Love spells, black magic spells. Spells to raise the dead. Spells to find the dead. Was that how Robert had done what he'd done?

If so, why didn't *Aden* need spells to do what he did? Joe had claimed even his grandfather had used magic.

Julian sighed. *No. I don't remember.*

Eve hadn't, either. Not at first.

Still. It was only a matter of time now.

"And the Boy King is back from la-la land," Riley muttered.

Boy King? Aden flipped him off, and Victoria batted his hand to the mattress. They were on one bed, and Riley and Mary Ann were on the other. Since leaving Joe's house, the pair hadn't spoken a single word to each other. They were stiff, unwilling to even glance at each other.

"Julian thinks he knows these guys. So, who's who?"

A yawning Mary Ann stood and clomped over to study the photo. "I saw pictures of Daniel on the internet. That's him, and that's Robert."

No way, Julian said.

Caleb snickered, and Aden was heartened by the sound. If Julian was Robert, as Mary Ann suspected, then Julian had indeed been the guy with thinning hair and glasses.

"He was known for communicating with the dead and helping the police find bodies. I printed out a few stories." She dug through a nylon bag Riley had fetched earlier and handed Aden a thick stack of papers. "Should have given these to you before. Sorry."

"No problem. We've all been pretty busy."

"I've been thinking," she said. "For you to absorb his soul into your mind, he would have had to die near the hospital. Which makes sense. His brother worked there, so Robert was probably visiting Daniel. What if he visited, raised one of the corpses in the morgue, and that corpse killed them both?"

"From what you told me before, only Daniel was

found dead in the hospital that night," Riley said. "And he'd been mauled to death."

"Right," Mary Ann agreed.

Well, well. Conversation.

Riley raised his arms as if she'd just made his point for him. "So where was Robert's body?"

"Never found." She shrugged. "He just disappeared."

"Well, he had to have died that night, too. And nearby, just as you said, or Aden wouldn't have absorbed him," Victoria said.

"What if Aden absorbed *Daniel?*" Riley asked.

Julian grabbed onto that rationale like a lifeline. *The one with the hair? I'm liking Riley's theory.*

"But Daniel had worked at the hospital for years," Mary Ann replied. "Why hadn't he raised the dead before then? Someone would have noticed."

Riley arched a brow, looking her up and down with a darkness Aden had never before seen from him. "Maybe he had latent abilities. It happens."

She popped her jaw. "Maybe. So?"

So, they all knew he was referring to her draining.

"Please don't make me referee," Aden told them. "Anyway, I think we can all agree Julian was one of the Smart brothers."

If by one of *you mean the handsome one, then yes, I agree,* Julian said.

Junior made a mewling sound in the back of Aden's mind. The ever-growing monster was hungry. Again. And he was getting harder and harder to appease, craving more and at shorter intervals.

"I'll read the stories," Aden said, "and see if anything jumps out at Julian."

"Going back in time helped Eve remember," Mary Ann reminded him. "Maybe you should let Julian take over and take you back and relive one of the stories through his eyes."

Time travel. Nearly everyone in this room had suggested he go back at some point, and he couldn't seem to make them understand the consequences. "Change something in the past, and you change something in the future—a something that could leave you snot-crying for what used to be."

"Look at us, Aden," Mary Ann said. "Can things get any worse than this?"

"Yes." Indubitably.

"Well, I don't see how."

Okay, how about this? "I could wake up and never have come to Crossroads. Never have met you."

Dark hope turned her eyes into fathomless pools. "Maybe that would be a good thing."

Victoria's chin trembled, as if she was fighting tears. "She's right. If you had not come to Crossroads, my father would not be after you."

"Think about it, Aden," Riley said.

What was this? Gang up on Aden hour? "There's another way to help Julian," he said. "And we're all going to be fine. Aren't we, Elijah?"

Silence.

Hated silence.

"Talk to me, please." He hunched forward, resting his face in his upraised hands. "At the very least, argue the pros and cons of what they're wanting." Not that Aden would ever consider going back. "Don't just leave me hanging."

A sigh, familiar, adored, necessary. *I'm not going to tell you what I've seen, Aden.*

Finally, a response, and Aden was as relieved as he was irritated. After all this time, *that's* what Elijah had to say? "So you've seen…what? What happens if I go back? What happens if I don't? The end of this entire mess?" He was used to hiding his conversations with the souls, yet here he was, talking as if the souls were in the room, too, and he wasn't embarrassed.

He knew why. He was going to lose them and was savoring every moment he had with them.

Another sigh. *Yes. I've seen the end.*

Stuttering heart, sweating palms, blood going cold in his veins. "What is it? What happens?"

Another dose of the silent treatment. Maybe they'd time-traveled back to five minutes ago, he thought bitterly. "Help me, Elijah. Please." *Otherwise I'll have to try and force a vision,* he thought.

My refusal is helping you. I've been getting things wrong, Aden. Leading you in the wrong direction, making things worse.

"Not every time."

Even once is too many.

Junior growled.

All kinds of sweetness suddenly filled Aden's nose. He lifted his head. Victoria had scooted closer to him, was tracing her fingertips up and down his arm. As they were, he had a direct view of her thrashing pulse, the scabbed-over punctures in her neck. His mouth was a waterfall, but he would *not* let himself go corncob on her vein.

"We'll revisit the time-travel thing later." Riley lumbered from his bed. "Right now, I want to see the wards on your head."

If by "later" he meant "never," then yeah, Aden was on board with that plan. Elijah hadn't told him anything useful. And until Aden attempted a vision on his own, well, there was no reason good enough to give himself a second chance to screw everything up.

The scent of Victoria's sweetness was replaced by the earthiness of Riley's as the shifter—ex-shifter—loomed over him. Hard fingers combed through his hair, tugging at the strands.

Riley said, "They've faded quite a bit and worked longer than they should have, but I know what they are. Joe wasn't lying. These stopped you from being mobbed by creatures."

"Until I met Mary Ann." Joe had expected Aden to be grateful about that. As if that were enough. *Why couldn't he have loved me?*

"The explosion of energy, or whatever it was," Mary Ann said, nodding her head. "That's what stopped the wards from working, guaranteed."

Riley let Aden go and plopped beside Victoria.

She rested her head on the wide berth of his shoulder. "The magic you guys created together must have overpowered the one Aden's dad, a mere human, created," she said.

"Don't call him that," he snapped. "His name is Joe." Seeing Victoria and Riley together always roused his jealousy. But just then, he experienced something more. Their ease with each other, their taking comfort from each other...disturbed him.

Her cheeks leached of color. "I'm sorry."

Great. Now he was taking his bad mood out on her. "No need to be sorry. I shouldn't have reacted like that." As he spoke, he watched as Riley rubbed her arm up and down. Again he was struck by their ease with each other.

That should be me. Instead, they relied on each other. Had for years. Decades. Another thought hit him, a subject that had been bothering him since it had first come up, a subject he'd buried as more important issues arose. A subject he couldn't dismiss at the moment.

When Victoria had wanted to rid herself of her virginity, so that her first time would not be with the guy her father had picked out for her, she would have gone to...

Riley.

Only Riley.

Aden jackknifed to his feet, his hands fisting, Junior's

growling more pronounced. And that's when Aden knew beyond a doubt. Junior wasn't just hungry. He truly was reacting to Aden's emotions.

"Aden, your eyes," Victoria gasped out. "They're violet, glowing."

"Get your hands off her," he said, shocked by his voice. Layered, one his own, one raspy with smoke. Both enraged. "Now."

Riley's eyes narrowed. At first, that was his only reaction. Then, he dropped his arm at his side and stood. "Yes, my king. Whatever you wish, my king. Anything else, *my king?*"

"Riley," Victoria said, her gaze never leaving Aden. "Leave the room. Please. Mary Ann, make him leave the room."

Riley just stood there. Mary Ann jumped into action, at least. She grabbed Riley's hand and tugged him out the door. He didn't resist, and a second later, there was an ominous *click*.

"You know," Victoria said, wringing her hands.

"I know." Harsh, menacing.

"I—"

"Don't want to hear it." Aden swiped up the box of papers and books, stalked to the bathroom, slammed the door behind him. On top of everything he was already dealing with, his girlfriend had slept with one of his friends. A long time ago, sure. But he'd always comforted himself with the fact that Riley and Victoria were friends, only friends. Now he couldn't do that.

He wanted to beat Riley's face into pulp. Instead, he closed the lid on the toilet, sat down, and dropped the box between his feet.

"See that one coming, Elijah?" he sneered.

No reply. Of course.

You can't blame Victoria for— Julian began.

"I don't want to hear from you, either. Let's just go over this crap and figure out who you were. Okay? All right?"

Silence.

Silence he was suddenly grateful for. At least he hadn't actually seen Victoria in bed with Riley, at least Edina had taken center stage in each of those visions. Visions. The perfect distraction. Maybe now was the time to try and force one.

Or not, he thought half an hour later as sweat poured down his chest. His turbulent emotions had interfered, preventing him from making any headway. Whatever. He'd try again later. As for now, he picked up one of the books and started reading.

Outside, cold air biting at her with teeth she couldn't see, Mary Ann whirled to face Riley. "What was *that* about?"

His expression was hard, completely blocking her out. "Nothing."

Nothing. Oh, really? "Do you hate me now? Is that why you won't talk to me or tell me the truth? Should I take off again?" The moment she realized what she'd said, she wanted to snatch the words back. What if his reply was an unwavering yes?

Wary, he scrubbed a hand down his face. "I don't hate you."

No mention of the other thing, she noted. "Do you resent me? Is that why you can barely look at me? Why you won't talk to me? Why you offer Victoria comfort but not me?"

One of his brows arched. "Do you *need* comfort?"

Something else of note: that wasn't an offer.

She'd hurt him. She'd destroyed his life. And there was nothing she could do to make it up to him. She knew that. But that didn't stop her from loving him. From wishing things were different.

"No," she lied. "I don't need comfort." She wanted to lean her head on his shoulder, that strong, strong shoulder, exactly as Victoria had done.

"You'll want to answer differently in a few seconds," a male voice said. A voice she recognized. Tucker's voice.

Riley spun, but the demon was nowhere to be seen.

Before fear had time to set in, a strong arm wound around her waist, and another around her neck. Cold steel pressed into her vein. "Riley," she gasped out.

He peered over her shoulder, his eyes narrowing. "Let her go."

"We've gotta talk," Tucker said. "All of us. Preferably alive, but I'm open to negotiation."

†WEN†Y-EIGH†

ANYTHING YET?

"No."

Well, look again.

"I've looked eight times already."

Look again.

"How many times can we have this conversation, Julian?"

Let's not find out. Let's look. Again.

Aden ground his teeth. He'd left the toilet a few seconds ago, and now crouched on the floor. His head fell back, resting on the cool porcelain of the tub, and he stared up at the ceiling. Frustration was eating at him, but he once again thumbed through the papers he'd brought with him.

His ears twitched, picking up…something, a rustle of clothing maybe, then nothing.

Not those. I don't like those. They give me the creeps.

Like the room at the hospital. That was something, at least. He read the spine of the book he held. *Dark Arts of the Ages.*

Show me the pictures again.

We've memorized them already, Caleb complained.

As promised, Elijah kept his figurative lips shut.

Aden heard another rustle of clothing beyond the bathroom door as he discarded the book and picked up the photos. What he saw as he shuffled through them: two little boys the same age, so alike they could have been twins. Yet, the older they got, the more dissimilar they became, Robert aging faster than Daniel. Also, the older they got, the unhappier their expressions became, until Robert—looking fortysomething—and Daniel—looking thirtysomething—were sullen and miserable.

And this was the man Tonya had loved so staunchly she hadn't gotten over his death seventeen years later? Seemed obsessive. Weirdly obsessive.

That one, that one, that one, Julian chanted.

Aden stilled. The picture he held was not of the brothers, but of Tonya herself. Younger, blonder, prettier, sitting under a shade tree, staring off into the distance as little pink flower petals floated around her. "What about it?"

I dismissed it every time because it's of a woman. Of her. But the more I see it, the more I think I was...there.

"Maybe you took the picture."

If I did, that has to mean I was Daniel. Right? She wouldn't have spent time with her brother-in-law.

Unless Robert loved her, too, Elijah said. *Wait. Ignore that. I didn't mean to say that out loud.*

Hearing his voice perked Aden right up.

I was not balding! Julian insisted.

I think that's something every baldy tells himself at some point, Caleb said.

"Okay, good. We're working as a team again. I like this. Let's keep this up."

Let's travel back in time, like Mary Ann suggested. To when the picture was taken, Julian said, practically rubbing hands together in glee. *I'll prove I had hair. Aden will open his eyes, and be in Daniel's body. With hair. Did I mention that part yet?*

Deep breath in, hold, hold. "Are you forgetting how many times we've woken up with new—worse—foster parents? Or in a mental institution we'd once been dismissed from? Or, the latest, with a new doctor in charge of our care—a doctor who wasn't human but a fairy in disguise who hoped to kill us?"

No. But—

"No buts. I told everyone else no, and now I'll tell you." Even if he wasn't exactly happy with his present, he didn't want to make it worse. "No, no, a thousand times no. And now that we've covered *that*. Who took this picture isn't important."

You don't know that.

"You died in December. This picture was clearly taken in the spring. And we both know you only need to remember the day you died to make this work."

A frustrated growl. *Well, I'm not remembering. We have to do something. Try something.*

"We'll visit Tonya again. I'll *make* her talk."

No. I don't want her hurt, Julian rushed out, only to pause. *I mean, I know you won't hurt her. I just...I don't know. I don't want her to suffer anymore.*

Intrigue sparked. Were Julian's past feelings coming to the surface? Had he loved the woman, as Elijah suspected? He—wait, wait, wait. Aden's attention snagged on a single word. "You said *anymore*. You don't want her to suffer *anymore*. Why was—is—she suffering?"

I...I...don't know.

Maybe you're thinking about this too hard, Caleb said. *Maybe if we relax for a little bit, the answers will just come to us.*

Aden doubted he'd be relaxing anytime soon.

Uh, Aden. Victoria's in trouble, Elijah burst out.

"What!" His head snapped up, his gaze automatically moving to the door. Unlike the mirror in the mansion, he couldn't see past the wood. He was on his feet a heartbeat later. "What's wrong with her?"

I know I'm breaking my promise to you, but Tucker's out there and he has a knife he's very determined to use. Mary Ann and Riley are there, too. I just thought you should know.

"Are they okay?" He never should have trusted that traitor.

As of right now, yes.

As of right now. Words that were like a noose around his neck. Exploding into action might cause *Tucker* to explode into action. Okay, okay. He had to think about this, plan how to strike. He might be upset with Victoria, but he didn't want her hurt. Didn't want any of them hurt.

Back and forth he paced. He tried to listen, but all he heard was that rustle of clothing. Why?

"Where's everyone located in the room? Do you know?"

Two seconds passed. Four. The rustling increased in volume, but that was it.

He and Riley are knife fighting, Elijah suddenly announced. *Both are cut up pretty badly. Blood is everywhere.*

A horrified gasp. *Victoria just tried to get in the middle. Now she's unconscious. Mary Ann is—*

Junior slammed against Aden's skull. Exploding into action, so not a problem anymore. Victoria was hurt. No one hurt Victoria. His mind was so focused on defending her, he didn't stop to open the door. He simply burst through it, shards spraying everywhere.

Took a moment for him to make sense of what he was seeing, hearing. Or not hearing.

First thing he noticed, the room was a wreck, the nightstand in shambles, the lamp shattered into hundreds of pieces, the phone embedded in the wall, but Aden hadn't heard anything more than that rustling through the paper-thin bathroom wall. Still didn't. Yet, the boys were going it at like animals in human form, throwing each other onto the beds, the floors, into the dresser.

Tucker's illusion could now control sound, he realized.

Second thing, Aden had fought Tucker before and knew the guy wasn't giving the confrontation his all. He was actually spreading his arms, allowing Riley to pound those meaty fists into his face. Well, until survival instinct kicked in and Tucker probably reacted without thought, bucking the shifter off him.

Third, the metallic scent of blood coated the air,

whipping Junior into more of a frenzy. The beast raced from one corner of his mind to the other, claws cutting deeply, making him grimace. Any minute now, and Aden's brain would be ripped into tatters. Surely.

Fourth, Mary Ann was dodging the combatants as she raced around the room, searching for a weapon.

Fifth, Victoria was in an unconscious heap at the door. Blood trickled from her nose.

No one hurts her. No one. Such a killing rage…blooming inside him…so strong he wasn't sure how he could contain it…had never experienced anything like it…not even when he'd fought Sorin…was going to detonate…

What's happening to us? Julian asked, barely audible as Junior roared and roared and roared.

Aden threw himself into the fray, batting Riley away with one hand and grabbing Tucker by the shirt with the other. His momentum gave him strength, and he was able to spin, slamming Tucker against the wall, then the floor, and pinning him in place.

Sensing his opportunity to strike, Junior burst from his skin, the roaring now directed at Tucker. Junior wasn't solid—yet—and caused no damage as he tried to bite. Tucker just lay there, taking the abuse. He looked as if he were smuggling golf balls under his eyelids, and a couple of his teeth were missing.

Riley must have gained his bearings because he was beside Aden a few seconds later. Junior had already decided Tucker belonged to him and wrenched around, snipping at Riley, teeth—solid now—slicing through his arm.

The shifter reared back, and Junior returned his attention to Tucker. Saliva dripped from sharpened fangs.

Tucker smiled. "Remember…promise…" he managed to get out. "Protect…brother."

Aden tried to rise, but it was too late. Junior had slipped from him completely, and attacked, feasting. Not once did Tucker struggle. And then, his head lulled to the side. His eyes were open, staring into nothing. Glassy, dull. His pulse stopped thumping—because he had no neck left.

Suddenly sound whooshed back. Aden heard a male scream—a bloodcurdling sound that echoed throughout the room, though no one in the room was screaming. He could hear Junior's snarls as he ate. Could hear Riley panting. Could hear Mary Ann fighting sobs. Could hear Victoria's shallow breaths.

He couldn't face any of them. Not yet. If Junior decided to turn on them…

"Riley, get the girls out of here." Aden wrapped his

arms around his beast, holding for all he was worth. "Now."

"Where and when should we meet you?"

"I'll call you and let you know. Now go." Before it was too late.

A pause. Footsteps. The squeak of door hinges. He stayed where he was until Junior had eaten everything. He could feel the beast's pleasure and satisfaction. Then the beast's discomfort from overindulgence.

"What did I just let happen?" he whispered, even as he petted Junior behind the ears.

Tucker wanted to die, Elijah said, sadness dripping from the words. *Vlad can't use his brother against him if he's dead.*

"I know. And Tucker needed to be stopped, but not this way." All Aden's threats aside, *not this way.*

These things happen, Caleb said. He didn't sound sorry or upset but vindicated.

Really? Julian sniped, *because I don't remember anything like this happening before.*

Aden continued to pet Junior, and the beast allowed it, not even trying to attack. Junior even fell asleep, his body misting before seeping back into Aden's pores.

He lay there for a long while, Tucker's blood pooling around him, soaking into his clothes, his hair. He'd known Junior was dangerous. But this…there'd been no controlling him, no reining him in.

That couldn't happen again.

You can ward yourself, as the other vampires do, Elijah said. *The ward will help keep Junior inside you. Help keep him calm, quiet.*

Uh, why are you so despondent? Julian asked. *Controlling that monster is a good thing.*

Yes, but the ward will quiet us, too.

What? Julian.

What! Caleb.

We will be aware, as Junior will be aware, but we will have no voice. Not any longer. No, don't protest, any of you. I knew we would reach this point. And I wanted to be sure Aden could exist without us. He can. You're strong enough, Aden. Smart enough.

So we'll just fade into the background? Caleb asked, incredulous. Upset.

That's not fair, Julian said.

Life never is.

So. Aden was supposed to choose between controlling his beast—who could emerge and kill everyone he loved—and destroying his dearest friends. No, life wasn't fair.

He sat up, saying grimly, "Right now, Junior's content

and maybe even battling a case of indigestion. Nothing needs to be decided right now."

What do you mean, nothing needs to be decided? There shouldn't be anything to decide, Caleb said.

Aden ignored him, couldn't yet deal with him. "Let's get cleaned up, find the others and pay Tonya another visit."

We don't have a car, Julian said, everything else forgotten at the mention of his...wife's?...name.

We don't need one, Elijah replied. *Not anymore.*

TWENTY-NINE

By THE TIME ADEN TEXTED to set the meeting place and time, Riley had already procured another room, was cleaned and bandaged, Victoria was awake, showered and changed, and she was pretty bruised up. Mary Ann was showered, changed and pissed. At herself, as well as everyone around her.

Tucker was dead, killed in the most violent, vile way, and no one seemed to care. She hadn't thought *she* would care. He'd caused so much pain and suffering—and would have caused more. But part of her mourned him. Mourned the boy she'd once known. The boy who had treated her with respect and kindness and made her feel pretty. The boy who would never know his kid.

How was she going to break this to Penny? She'd have to call, have to tell her. Just not now. Maybe after her own grief had settled.

Mary Ann didn't blame Aden for what had happened. If he hadn't killed the boy, Riley would have. There was simply no middle ground with these creatures. It was either kill or be killed.

What had happened to a good old-fashioned locked-away-for-the-rest-of-eternity punishment?

Adding to her sense of anger was Riley's treatment of her. Yes, he'd offered his beast, but she never would have taken it had she been coherent.

If Riley wanted to end things with her, he could end things with her. However, he was going to have to tell her straight out. No more giving her the silent treatment, then defending her "honor" with such fury, as if he still cared. No more keeping her at a distance, then looking at her as if she'd make a tasty snack.

If things were over, things were *over*. She needed to know—and cut all ties.

She loved him, she wanted him in her life, but she deserved to be treated right. That's why she'd broken up with Tucker, because he hadn't treated her right. She couldn't change her mind about that now, just because she craved Riley more than her next breath.

She wouldn't die without him. She knew that. She would miss him, yes, and would probably cry herself to sleep for weeks. But in the end, she would be okay. Right?

Next time she got Riley alone, they were going to hash this out.

They walked the few blocks to the meeting place, the parking lot of a deserted warehouse. Not much traffic this way, which was always a good thing. The sun was setting, shadows cast in every direction. Another good thing.

"I wonder if Aden is—" Victoria began, then stopped on a gasp.

Aden simply appeared. In a blink, he was hunched over and fighting for breath.

He could teleport. *He. Could. Teleport.* When the heck had that happened?

"That's…a little more…difficult than I…imagined," he panted.

"Aden!" Victoria rushed to him.

He straightened, and by the time she reached him, his arms were open to her. She threw herself at him, and he hugged her tight, burying his face in her neck. She winced a little, obviously hurting from her injuries.

"Are you okay?" he asked her. Having almost lost each other must have trumped whatever he'd been angry about.

"Yes. Just a little bump on the head when Tucker threw me into the wall. Are you?"

"I'm fine. I'm sorry I was so mad at you. I should have—"

"No. I'm sorry I didn't tell you before. I can't believe—"

"I was jealous, but if I'd just stopped—"

Lord above, they were talking over each other, making eavesdropping very difficult.

Victoria cupped his cheeks. "You have no reason to be jealous, I promise. It was a onetime thing, and it will never happen again. It wasn't even very good."

Mary Ann had no idea what they were blabbering about, but Riley must have because he mumbled something about "not his fault" and "better than good, as always."

Took a moment, but something clicked inside Mary Ann's head. *Onetime thing. Never happen again. Not very good. Better than good.*

Sex.

Glaring, she wheeled around. The wind blew, causing several strands of hair to Swan Lake over his eyes. He had his arms crossed over his chest, the pose casual and unconcerned.

"You told me the two of you had never been involved!" She threw the words at him as if they were weapons.

To his credit, he didn't pretend not to know what she was asking. "We slept together one time. That's not exactly an involvement."

Then what was? "Is there anyone you *haven't* slept with?"

There was no change in his blasé expression. He shrugged. "Just an unlucky few, but that just means I haven't met them yet."

"*Really?* You're using sarcasm now? *Really?*"

"What do you want me to say, Mary Ann?"

"When did it happen? Tell me that much."

"Before I met you."

And that made it okay? "What about before you dated *her sister?*"

A nod, as if he didn't hear—or didn't care—about her disgust. "Yes. Before then. I've never cheated on a girl-friend, and I never will, so this argument is pointless."

Pointless.

"Screw you," she said. Then, "Oh, wait. Fifty percent of the people in this circle already have!" Her math was off, but she didn't care. No wonder she'd always been so jealous when she watched him with Victoria. No wonder the pair was always at ease with each other. They'd seen each other naked! And once tasted, forbidden fruit was that much easier to taste a second time. And a third.

Mary Ann was proof of that. How many times had she made out with Riley when she shouldn't have?

"Look, it was awkward, all right?" Now he was the one throwing words like weapons. "Like she said, there's not going to be a repeat performance."

Again, as if that made everything okay. "Why don't I sleep with Aden, then, and we'll see how pointless—"

Riley leaned down, getting in her face, all hint of placating her gone. *"You will not sleep with Aden."* There was so much fury in the undercurrents of his rasping voice, she felt the brush of it all the way to the bone.

She could only blink in surprise. Now, here was a reaction she hadn't expected from him. It meant he still cared about what she did—and who she did it with. "Why? Because I'm still your girlfriend?"

A moment passed. The fury melted, and he straightened, gathered his wits. "I…I don't know. Neither one of us is the same person we were a few weeks ago."

Honesty. Well, *that* she had expected, and now she wanted more. "Just say it," she said, forcing the issue despite their rapt audience. *Please don't. Please don't say we're through. That we're over, done.*

A muscle ticked below his eye. A sign of his upset,

and something that had happened quite frequently lately. "I'm practically human. I can't protect you anymore."

If that was his only argument, he'd never get rid of her. "You did just fine back at the motel."

"And what about when a pack of wolves decide to make you their lunch?"

"So, if you could still shift, you would stay with me every second of every day?"

"No. Of course not."

"Lock me up?"

"No."

"Then how would you have protected me from that before, huh? I could become someone's breakfast, lunch or dinner, whether you shift or not. Stop making excuses and say what we both know you want to say." *Don't listen to me.*

He was breathing heavily, his nostrils flaring with the force of his inhalations. "We're…we…"

"Say it!" *No. Don't.*

A hard hand settled on her shoulder, and Mary Ann whipped around with a startled yelp. A frowning Aden stood beside her. Riley snarled at him, realized what he'd done to his king and cleared his expression.

"Let's head to Tonya's. I'll get Victoria there. Riley, you get Mary Ann there."

Warmth flooded Mary Ann's cheeks. Okay, so now she cared about her audience. "Why do you want to go back to Tonya's?"

"She has answers about Julian that I can't find in the papers and photos. So, meet us there in…" He glanced at a wristwatch he didn't have and had never worn. "Half an hour?"

Enough time to work through their current problem, he was saying.

Riley nodded. "Fine."

"Good." Aden and Victoria sauntered off, hand in hand.

Way to rub it in.

"Come on," Riley grumbled, taking off in the other direction. He rounded the far corner, Mary Ann close to his heels. Rather than picking up where they'd left off, he picked out a car to steal.

She didn't protest as he popped the door lock, removed a chunk of plastic around the ignition, then cut and twisted the exposed wires. She just acted as lookout and slid into the passenger side when the engine roared to life.

Soon they were winding down the roads a little too swiftly for her peace of mind, winding in and out of traffic. Which still wasn't heavy, but come on. Only took one vehicle to get in your way, and hello, wreck.

"Slow down."

"In a minute."

He'd never driven this erratically before. Not with her. "If I say what you wouldn't, will you slow down?"

His fingers curled around the wheel, his knuckles quickly losing color. "I don't need you to say it. I can."

She wouldn't react, she wouldn't react, she wouldn't freaking react. "Then do it." Good. There'd been no hint of turmoil in her voice.

"I can't," he said, contradicting himself. "I try, part of me wants to, but I can't."

There was no comfort to be had in his claim. "Can you ever forgive me for what I did? For what you asked me to do?"

He reached up, adjusted the rearview mirror. "That's not the issue, Mary Ann. If I hadn't done what I did, if you hadn't done what you did, you wouldn't be alive. And I'd rather you were alive and my animal dead than the other way around."

That, she could take comfort from—but it cost her. Suddenly she was bathed in shame, her skin tingling with it. "I wish I could give him back to you." But she'd absorbed him and must have chewed him up bite by tasty bite, because she couldn't sense him inside her. Not on any level.

"You can't," he said, confirming what she'd already known.

"If that's not the issue, then why are you so angry with me?"

"I told you. I can't protect you like this."

"Riley, I never liked you because of how well you protected me. I liked you because of how hot you look in your jeans!"

"Funny." The word was laced with sarcasm, but his lips were quirking at the corners, delighting her, uplifting her.

"But kind of true."

All too quickly, he sobered up. "My pack, the vampires, they all hate you, fear you and will be out for your blood."

"Even though I'm no longer draining?"

"Yes. A drainer has never been rehabilitated before. They won't believe you're no longer a danger to them."

And he didn't either, apparently. "A few weeks ago you would have said they'd never follow a human king, but look at them now."

He flicked her a glance, and the car at last slowed down. He was still breaking the sound barrier, but she took heart. "Do you *want* to be with me? Because I seem to remember you pushing me away again and again."

Now or never. She may as well lay it all on the line, since she was asking him to do the very same. "Yes. I want to be with you."

"And if you start draining again, will you run from me again?"

So not the response she'd craved. "I—" Crap. She had no answer for him. Would she? Wouldn't she? She didn't know, and then it didn't matter. Blue and red lights flashed behind them. A siren blared. "I think we're being pulled over."

Riley slowed the rest of the way, easing over to the side of the road.

Panic beat through her. "Does he know it's stolen? Is that why he stopped us?"

"No, or he'd have his gun out and aimed. Just stay calm, and say nothing."

A few horribly agonizing minutes later, the cop was standing beside their car, his elbow resting against the open window, and Mary Ann was battling a panic attack.

"Do you know how fast you were going, son?"

"Nope." And Riley didn't sound as if he cared.

"Thirty-five miles over the speed limit."

"You mean the sign wasn't just a suggestion?"

She wanted to curse. Why was he being so antagonistic?

Gaze narrowing, the cop focused on her, his lips turning down in a scowl. "License and registration. Now."

"Can't," Riley said easily. "This isn't my car."

She *really* wanted to curse. What was he doing? Did he *want* to be arrested?

"What are you saying, son?"

"That I don't know who it belongs to." Riley flashed a wicked grin. "I—" he air quoted the next word "—borrowed it."

Aaannd…that's when the cop pulled his gun.

Where were they? Victoria wondered for the thousandth time. The allotted half hour had come and gone, yet Riley and Mary Ann never made an appearance, never texted, and never answered *her* texts or calls.

"Maybe we should go look for them," she suggested to Aden. "Then, you can teleport us where we need to go."

She'd had to work for years to move even a yard, and even then, she'd always winded herself. Yet he had jetted them miles across the city, without having to stop and rest or check his surroundings to ensure he'd hit the right spot. She was baffled, impressed and, yes, jealous.

The jealousy made her feel guilty. He'd given up a lot to be with her. She could deal with the loss of her vampire abilities.

"They're probably arguing and lost track of time," Aden replied. "Come on. We don't need them for this."

"You're probably right." Riley had never had to work for a girl, so a resisting Mary Ann was good for him. Seeing them together, seeing the need Riley tossed her way when he thought no one was watching, Victoria had stopped blaming Mary Ann for what had happened to her friend. Clearly, they needed each other.

Aden gave her a quick kiss and dragged her up the porch steps. Hard and sharp, he knocked on the front door.

Several seconds ticked by. Victoria didn't see or hear anything, but Aden must have because he said, "You will open the door, Tonya, and welcome us inside." The polished cherrywood swung open, Tonya's eyes already glazed as she stepped aside.

Aden led Victoria into the living room. The furnishings were clean, yet clearly aged, the floral fabric on the couch faded in spots, the coffee table scuffed. In fact... Victoria studied the few magazines resting on top of that table. They were yellowed, a little brittle and dated seventeen years ago.

Grimacing as he made himself comfortable on the couch, Aden muttered, "Julian is going crazy. He recognizes the furnishings. He clearly spent more time inside than out."

"Well, there's a possibility the inside looks the exact same as it did before he died." She motioned to the magazines.

"Huh. Interesting."

Tonya sat across from them. "What do you want?" The words lashed, as if she were fighting the forced desire to welcome them. And those shadows…they were in her eyes and undulating madly.

"First, I want you to know that I will not hurt you," Aden said. "Do you understand?"

A frown. "Yes, but I don't believe you."

"That's all right. I'll prove it."

"What do you want?" she asked again, and wonder of wonders, she was less hostile.

"Answers. The truth about your husband and his brother. Tell me what I want to know, and I'll leave you alone."

"I don't like to talk about my darling Daniel and that rat Robert." Adoration mixed with revulsion. Her frown returned, and the shadows picked up speed. "I always call them by those names. And I feel that way, I do. I loved my husband and hated his brother, but…"

"But?" Victoria prompted.

"But I didn't always feel that way. I mean, I never

loved Robert, but I liked him. And I remember wanting to divorce Daniel." Her brow furrowed with confusion. "Or maybe I only dreamed that, because I love him so much. I will always love him."

Aden massaged his temple. Was Julian shouting? "Tell me about them."

"They…were…twins." Tonya acted as if she were having to push each word through a too-thin pipe. "Daniel worked at the hospital morgue…Robert was a good-for-nothing con artist. Yes. That's right." Flowing more easily now. "My Daniel was *not* jealous of his brother."

And yet, the words seemed so rehearsed, as if she were repeating something she'd been told over and over. Maybe she was. Those spell books…the shadows in her eyes…the faded black aura Riley had mentioned.

Perhaps Tonya's emotions and her unwavering loyalty were magic-driven.

Yes. That was it, Victoria realized with shock.

In unison, she and Aden sat up straighter. "I think I know what happened," they said.

THIRTY

MEMORIES FLOODED ADEN. None of them his own, all of them Julian's, and all of them devastating. His name was Robert Smart. Yes, he'd had thinning hair and had worn glasses. Daniel had been the good-looking one, the strong one, the smart one, but he'd never been the beloved one, and so he'd always been jealous of Robert's talent for the supernatural.

So Daniel had turned to spell books. Black magic, deeper and deeper into the occult, until finally delving into human sacrifice.

Robert's sacrifice.

Normal people would not have known to go that route, but Daniel hadn't been normal. His human parents had loved all things mystical, believing wholeheartedly in psychics, Ouija boards and enchantment of any kind.

Maybe that's why they had loved Robert so much

more. Maybe that's why Daniel had finally struck at him—fatally.

On the night of December twelfth, Daniel had called Robert and asked him to come to the hospital. Robert had gone because he'd wanted to talk some sense into his twin. But there had been no talking. Daniel had stabbed him over and over, trying to draw Robert's ability into his own body as Robert lay dying.

Only, Robert had been absorbed by Aden—his past buried, his mind reborn—before his twin could succeed.

Something else Robert had done to defeat his brother during those final minutes alive? Over the years he'd learned to control his ability to raise the dead, and he'd raised the corpses in the morgue. Several had disposed of Robert, eating him completely, and the rest had killed Daniel before help arrived.

Before all of that, however, Daniel had cast a spell over Tonya to gain her eternal devotion.

"Uh, Aden," Victoria said at the same time Julian said, *I loved her,* his tone sad, so sad and heavy with his memories, *but she never loved me back. She loved him, and she paid for it. Too late she realized Daniel's craziness and tried to leave him. That's when he cursed her to love him always. All*

I wanted, there at the end, was to set her free. And I could have done it, if my own brother hadn't betrayed me.

"Then we'll set her free now," Aden said. A wave of sadness moved through *him*. Doing this would set *Julian* free, as well. Smart-mouthed, fun-loving Julian, whom he adored. Whom he wanted to keep forever. Losing Eve had devastated him. Losing Julian would be even worse. Julian was like his brother, closer than blood.

"Aden?" Victoria tried again.

How, though? Julian asked. *I need to know what spell Danny used, and I don't know. I wasn't there. That's the real reason I went to the hospital. To see if I could trick him into telling me.*

"Aden, please."

What if you traveled back through her life? We could listen to the spell he cast.

"Aden!"

Wait, wait, wait, Elijah said before Aden could turn his attention to Victoria. *He travels back, he looks through Tonya's eyes, hears through her ears, and HE—WE—could become bespelled to love Daniel, too. I don't think any of us want that.*

And he, we, could not *become bespelled. It's worth the risk,* Julian replied with a huff and a puff.

They always thought the risks Aden took on their

behalves were worth it. For them, they were. For everyone else, no.

*He didn't go back for my witches, he's not going back for your
human,* Caleb said.

He told us he'd do anything to help us, Julian snapped.
*Correct me if I'm wrong, but time traveling falls into the category
of anything.*

"Guys, please. There's gotta be another way. How
many times do I have to say this—traveling through the
past is dangerous."

"Aden!" Cool fingers shook him.

Aden forced the room back into focus. "Victoria, I—"
The words died in his throat.

His father was sitting next to a too calm Tonya, a gun
resting on his thigh, the barrel pointed at Aden. Immediately Aden jumped to his feet, in front of Victoria,
acting as her shield. Junior belted out a snarl, responding
to the spike of aggression in Aden's veins.

The ward to control the beast suddenly seemed like a
brilliant idea, damn the consequences.

Aden did a little deep breathing, keeping his blood
pressure down and his head clear. Emotions were not
going to engulf him. Not this time.

"How'd you find me?" he asked.

"Do you really think I'd ward you and *not* make one of them a tracker?"

Joe had always known where he was, he realized. His father had simply chosen not to seek him, until now. *Don't react. That's what he wants.*

"Now, if I was going to hurt your girl, I would have hurt her already." Joe tapped at the trigger, light but threatening all the same. "Sit down."

Aden sat, angling his body so that he remained Victoria's shield. She trembled against him, her chilled breath shuddering over his neck.

"I'm sorry," she whispered.

"No reason to be."

"He snuck in, and…" Another shudder raked her.

He reached back and squeezed her knee.

"I'd be still if I were you," Joe said. "The slightest move makes me twitchy."

Warning received.

Tonya hadn't moved or spoken during the entire exchange. She wasn't dead, but she wasn't all there, either.

"I drugged her," Joe explained, having noticed Aden's attention on the woman. "One injection, and she's out but still functioning. Guy learns to use what weapons he can when he's always running for his life."

The first wave of danger had passed. Clearly conversation was up next on the chopping board. "You sound bitter. As old as you are, you should get over yourself already. Some people have had harder lives."

Junior kicked up a bit of a fuss, drowning out the arguing souls.

One sandy-colored brow arched. "Meaning *you?* You think you had a harder life than me, boy?"

Don't you dare react. "Meaning you're a baby. By the way, you should see what happened to the last guy who held a weapon on me. Oh, wait. You can't. He's dead."

Joe placed his free hand over his heart. "My son, the killer. I'm so proud."

First time Joe had ever willingly acknowledged their link. And to do it that way, full of piss and vinegar, well, that was a far more deadly weapon than the gun. "So you've never killed in self-defense, you—"

Reacting...

In and out he breathed.

Victoria linked their hands. Her trembling had intensified, though her expression was serene. Junior gave another roar. Much as Aden despised his...this man—no way he'd refer to the guy as his dad again—he didn't want Joe to become a Happy Meal for his beast.

"By the way, your conversations with yourself are more interesting now than they were when you were three." Joe's gaze shifted to Victoria. "Do you know what his first word was? Lijah. His second was Ebb. His third, Jew-els. His forth, Kayb. Yes, he had a slight pronunciation problem."

I was last? Caleb said. *Thanks for the love,* Hay-den.

Rather than getting caught up in a distracting conversation with the soul, Aden ignored him. There had been no affection to Joe's words. Just straight-up facts. No question, Joe was determined to flay him alive and leave him bleeding to death internally.

Murder with words. Smart. You couldn't be convicted for that.

Victoria tsked under her tongue. "You know, Joe— may I call you Joe?—Aden probably said the names of the souls first because they were better parents and friends to him than you had ever been or would ever be. Food for thought, don't you think?"

Joe popped his jaw, and Aden squeezed Victoria's knee, in warning this time, hoping to stop her from lashing out again. However sweetly she lashed out. *Do not poke at the armed bear.* Aden could, because well—fine, that wasn't such a good idea, either. Not while Victoria was so vulnerable.

"Enough of that. Let's get down to business, shall

we?" Joe said. "Why do you want to travel back through this woman's life?"

"I don't." But why not tell him the rest? Wasn't like Aden had been doing anything wrong. "However, she was bespelled, and I need to break that spell. To break it, I need to know what spell was used."

"You can't tell?" Asked with the same intonation Joe might have used speaking to a special needs kid.

At least he hadn't called Aden a liar. "You can?"

"Wait. You can time travel into people's pasts, you're apparently king of the vampires and wolves, and you can't hear the echo of the spell cast? Can't feel the vibe of its magic?"

Again with the special needs voice. "You can?" he repeated. "Wait. Don't tell me. You have a ward for that, too."

A shake of his blond head. "Practice." Then, "Why do you care about this woman anyway? She's nothing to you."

"I don't care."

Hey, now, Julian snapped.

Joe frowned. "Then why—"

"I don't," he went on, "but one of the souls inside my head does."

Okay, then. I can respect that.

"The souls. Of course. You always did love them best." Joe turned to Tonya. "Be a dear and fetch me a pen and paper, darlin'. All right?"

"Yes, of course," she said, slurring the words. "Pen and paper." She stood and stumbled off, unconcerned, unwitting and in a lot of danger.

Victoria made a play to follow her, but Joe shook the gun "no-no" as if he were shaking his head, and she remained in place. "Aren't you afraid she'll run?"

"No," was all the man said. "The drug opens her mind to suggestion. She'll do only what she's told."

Perhaps not the wisest thing to admit.

Victoria studied him for a moment. "You know, you're worse than my father, and I didn't think that was possible. He used to whip me with a cat-o'-nine-tails, you know. Just for fun."

"Yeah, and who's your father, honey?"

Aden squeezed her knee in another bid for silence. Much as Joe hated the creatures of the otherworld, he might try and punish Victoria for her origins or even the sins of others.

Joe offered him a small smile, content to let the mystery of her pass. "You picked a damaged girl with daddy issues. I guess we're more alike than I ever thought possible."

What was he saying? That Aden's mother was damaged? That she, too, had daddy issues? So badly he
wanted to ask. Despite everything, he was hungry for
information about his mother.

The few times he'd allowed himself to think about
her, he'd wondered what she looked like, if she'd been
as eager to give him away as Joe had been, or if she'd
wanted to keep him. Where was she now? What was she
doing?

Was she the woman Riley and Mary Ann had seen
with Joe that day in his truck?

"Don't ask," Joe said stiffly, sensing the direction of
his thoughts.

He opened his mouth to do just that, but Tonya returned with the commanded paper and pen and handed
them to Joe before reclaiming her seat beside him. Joe
balanced the notepad on his thigh and began writing, his
other hand never leaving the gun. When he finished he
tore off the paper and slapped it against the coffee table.

His gaze met Aden's, familiar and once again blank.
"Now you can't say I've never helped you."

Do NOT react.

He couldn't stop his heart from pounding in surprise
or Junior's consequent slamming against his skull. He

slanted his head to the side, motioning to the paper. "What's that?"

"Ms. Smart's ticket to free will."

Truth or lie? Either way, "Father of the Year award, meet Joe Stone. Or not."

Frowning, Joe leaned into the human. "Tonya, you're going to be a good girl, sit still and listen to Aden. You're going to do what he says, aren't you?"

"Yes. I will do what he says."

Those eyes lasered into Aden. "Spells are unbreakable unless the caster leaves himself a safe word, I guess is the best way to describe it. I can hear the spell this Daniel person cast inside my head, and he absolutely left himself a way out. Probably in case *he* stopped loving *her* and wanted to be rid of her. Or punish her. Or hurt her. There's always a reason, but those I can't interpret. Anyway, the words on the paper are her way out."

He would not thank the man. Too little, too late.

"Don't try to find me, Aden, and don't try to find your mother. I'm sure your friends told you about the toys they found in the house. Yes, you have a little sister. No, you cannot see her. She's not like you, and you'll only bring her pain and suffering."

Yeah, they'd told him about the girl, but hearing the words—*little sister*—and once again realizing he'd never get to see her, hold her, beat up the boys who hurt her feelings, well, Aden hadn't cried the two times he'd been stabbed, but he wanted to cry now.

"That's why I'm here," Joe went on, uncaring of the injuries he inflicted. "To tell you nothing good will ever come of your search for them."

Bang, bang. Junior, against his skull,

Easy. Easy now.

"You didn't kill me, and I didn't kill you," Joe said. "Let's leave it at that and parts ways. Forever."

"At least give him a picture of his mother, his sister," Victoria said, sympathetic to Aden in a way only she could be.

"No. Cutting all ties is best. Believe me." With that, Joe stood and strode from the living room. Though he did pause in the arched doorway for several heartbeats, as if he had something more to say, but in the end, he didn't. He left, the front door slamming shut behind him.

How could Joe do that to him? Let him go like that? Again. The most disturbing question of all, though— what would life have been like if Joe had actually loved him and kept him around? If Joe had trained him?

Junior nearly busted his eardrums with his next screech.

Calm, steady.

Tonya remained in her seat, unaffected.

Victoria threw her arms around him, settled herself in his lap and hugged him tight. "I'm so sorry. He doesn't deserve you."

Words she'd probably said to herself—or Riley had said to her—after her own father had broken her heart. Aden held her, letting her comfort him as only she was able, breathing her in, loving her scent, his mouth watering for a taste, not letting himself have a taste or think about tasting, not letting himself bite her but simply luxuriating in what she offered. Finally he calmed the rest of the way, and so did Junior.

Aden, please, Julian was saying.

Julian. His friend. Whom he *would* help, no matter the destruction to himself. He kissed Victoria on the temple, settled her on the couch, grabbed the paper, read it and stood. As he closed the distance between himself and Tonya, his hand fisted, crinkling the words. *This* was supposed to work?

He crouched in front of her. "Look at me, Tonya."

She obeyed without hesitation.

Will this work? Julian asked. *This has to work.*

Aden wasn't sure what his father had proposed, something so simple, so easy a freaking caveman could do it—too much TV?—would do anything more than embarrass him, but he said, "Tonya Smart, your heart is your own. Your soul is your own. Love may whither, love may die, but your truth will set you free."

She blinked down at him.

Why hasn't anything happened? Julian again.

"She's still drugged," Victoria said. "Maybe that's preventing her from showing a reaction."

"Fight your way from the drug's influence," Aden said, and just as before, she obeyed. Not because she'd been told to obey him, but because he'd used his vampire voice.

Her gaze cleared of that glassy sheen, revealing the shadows churning so violently behind them. A scream ripped from her, her entire body bowing, shaking her chair, then hunching over. She shook, she moaned, she writhed, her fingers gnarling.

Aden backed away from her, unsure how to help her.

Make it stop, Julian begged.

"I can't." All he could do was watch, horrified, as those shadows seeped through her pores, rising from her, enveloping her in a dark mist and screams, so many screams, echoing through the room.

Her screams? The ones she'd trapped inside herself,

every time the spell forced her to do something against her will?

Aden returned to Victoria—and the movement must have scared the shadows or something, because they shot up and out, disappearing through the ceiling. Leaving silence, such heavy silence.

Tonya sagged against her seat, slid to the floor and lay there panting. She was drenched with sweat, tears pouring down her cheeks, her skin flushed a deep red. "I...he...oh, dear Lord!" Sobs racked her entire body as she curled into herself.

Victoria slipped forward and reached out. Tonya caught the motion from the corner of her eye and reared backward.

"Don't touch me! Get out! Get out of my house! I hate you. I hate you all. I hate him. Hate, hate, hate." The sobs intensified, nearly choking her.

"Julian...Robert," Aden said. "Is there anything you want me to tell her?"

A pause. Then, *No. She wouldn't listen now, and besides, I don't know what I'd say. I don't love her as I once did, I just couldn't let her rot in the prison Daniel had built for her. She's free,* Julian said. *She's really free, and that's all that matters.*

With every word, his voice had become softer, quieter.

He was leaving, Aden realized, fighting a cry of his own. Just like that, without any other warning. *Don't go. I'm not ready.* He held the words inside himself. No reason to burden Julian with them. "How—how much time do you have left?"

Not long. A whisper now.

Victoria linked their fingers. "Aden?"

"Come on." He was shaking as he led her out of the house. He could have teleported them, but he was too emotionally messed up and wasn't sure where they'd land.

Cold air blustered around him, a storm clearly brewing. The sky was gray, the clouds bulky. The scenery fit his mood perfectly. He got them to a thick crop of trees before he dropped to his knees. "Julian?"

Still here. And I want you to know... I love you, Aden. Weaker still.

"I love you, too." So much.

Thank you for everything. You were a great host, and I will never forget you.

Once again he wanted to shout, *Don't go,* but he didn't. He'd just lost Joe—not that he wanted to be a part of Joe's life—but to lose Julian, too? Here and now, like this? His eyes were like twin coals just pulled from a fire.

"You were a great friend to me."

Julian, Elijah said, sad and happy all at once. Aden understood. He was sad for himself but happy for his friend. *We will never forget you, either.*

Dude, Caleb said. *I knew you were the one with the comb-over.*

Julian laughed. *I love you, guys. Even when you were being a pain in my ass.*

Caleb was the one to laugh this time. *You might want to rephrase that. You don't have an ass.*

"I'm going to miss you," Aden said softly. His chin trembled so violently, he barely got the words out.

Would it be gay if we attempted a four-way hug? Julian asked.

Yes, Caleb answered. *How about a mental slap on the back, instead?*

Another laugh, this one so weak Aden had to strain to hear it. *Yep, even when you're a pain.*

"Just…if you see her, tell Eve we said hi."

I will.

I bet she's a babe, Caleb said, his amusement gone. Like everyone else, he was fighting with his emotions.

Julian snorted. *I can't believe this is goodbye for us. Can't believe I'll never see you again. Never hear Caleb being per- verted, or Elijah bringing down the party or you Aden, the most honorable, loving person I've ever met, finding his way into the light. I'm no psychic, but great things are in store for you, my friend. I know it.*

The burning migrated to his cheeks, a wet tide, unstoppable. "We'll see each other again." Believing otherwise would kill him.

I love you so much, Julian said again, and then, just like that, he was gone. Aden felt the absence of him all the way to his bones.

Another goodbye he hadn't been prepared for.

He remained just as he was and let the tears flow. Victoria wound her arm around him and cried with him. He wasn't sure how much time had passed.

When they both quieted, she whispered, "Let's find Riley and Mary Ann and go home, Aden."

"Yes. Home."

THIRTY-ONE

"WHAT DID YOU DO to yourself?"

They were the first words Mary Ann had heard her father say in weeks—or what felt like an eternity—and she knew they were a precursor to all kinds of trouble.

She sat in the passenger seat of his sedan. He'd bailed her out of jail, or whatever. She wasn't really sure what had happened, only that she'd been cuffed, driven to the Tulsa P.D. headquarters downtown, stashed and questioned in a room for hours—not that she'd answered anything—and then uncuffed and ushered to her dad. Who hadn't spoken a word to her until now.

Since she hadn't given the cops his name and number, she could only assume Riley had. A reunion she'd wanted to both thank and slap him for.

The moment she'd seen her dad, she'd nearly run to him and thrown her arms around him. Anything to comfort him. As Penny had told her, he looked like hell. Bruises under his eyes, lines of tension branching from his mouth. His clothes, wrinkled and stained with coffee. But she hadn't let herself hug him, too afraid the strength of her riotous emotions would cause her new wards to fail and she'd start draining him, human though he was.

Rationally she knew that wouldn't happen, but fear… well, fear was illogical and all-consuming.

"Mary Ann! I'm talking to you. You take off without any warning, without calling, and I'm left worrying to death about you. Searching for you, begging the police for help, putting out flyers, and you're out there with that…that…" Fury crackled from him, so much fury his fingers nearly bent the steering wheel in half.

Guilt filled her, but she said, "We can't leave Riley there. We have to go back." She'd said it a thousand times before, but he'd ignored her each time. Riley could take care of himself, she knew that. Still. Leaving him behind felt wrong. Even though he'd purposely gotten them arrested.

She knew that now, too. What she didn't know was why. And there was a reason. With Riley, there was always a reason. The next time she saw him, she would find out. Because right now, all she could think was that he'd wanted to get out of a painful, we're-breaking-up talk. Except that wasn't his style.

"Please, Dad," she added. "Go back."

At least he didn't ignore her this time. "We *can* leave him, and we will leave him. I don't give a flying fig about your delinquent boyfriend. That boy is an outlaw who lives by no rules but his own, and who knows if he follows those even half the time. He stole a car, Mary Ann. While you were with him! And you should start praying those are wash-off tattoos on your arms."

The guilt intensified. "I…I'm sorry."

"Sorry? You're *sorry?* That's all you have to say to me?"

"Dad—"

"No. Be quiet. Are you doing drugs?"

What did he want? For her to be quiet or to answer? "No. I'm not doing drugs."

"Do you expect me to believe you?"

"Yes."

"Well, I don't. I don't know who you are anymore. So, guess what? We're going to find out together. Unquestionably."

"What? You're having me tested?"

Silence. Silence that cut her up and left her raw. He faced straight ahead.

Fine. She would ignore him, too. She turned her attention to the window, to the trees whizzing past. To the storm clouds hovering overhead. To the sign—for a town that wasn't on the way home.

Mary Ann flattened herself against her seat. Looked back at the sign, then at her father. Forget ignoring him. "Where are we going?"

"Clearly, I can't help you. So I'm taking you somewhere with people who can. No matter how long it takes."

Dread washed over her, leaving an icy glaze in its wake. "What are you talking about?"

"I'm talking about a psych evaluation. I'm talking about group therapy. I'm talking about medication, if that's required. I'm talking about figuring out the root of your problem, whatever it is, and getting my little girl back!"

"Dad—"

"No! I don't want to hear it. I wanted to hear from you for days, then weeks, and I got nothing but silence and worry. I couldn't eat, I couldn't sleep, couldn't work. I thought you'd been kidnapped. Thought you were being…raped and tortured. What do I find instead? You were out having fun. That isn't like you. Which means something's happened to you. Something you can't or won't talk to me about, so I'm going to *make* you talk to others."

The ice thickened, hardened. "Dad, don't do this. Please, don't do it."

"It's already done. It's the only way I could get you released without having to go to court or serve any time."

No. No, no, no. "I'm sorry I hurt you. I am." She couldn't tell him she'd done it for his own good! He wouldn't understand, and he wouldn't accept. More than that, she couldn't promise him that it wouldn't happen again. "But you have to trust me in this, okay? You have to—"

"Trust you? Oh, baby girl. You truly are delusional if you think that's happening. Trust is earned, and you did nothing but stomp on mine."

She had never seen her dad so angry, so hurt; she wouldn't be able to reach him through her usual means. "I'm not a little girl anymore. You can't just lock me away without my permission and think—"

"Legally, you're not an adult, and yes, I can do anything I want. You're about to fail the eleventh grade. Why? Because you're hanging out with the wrong crowd. So, I'll change your crowd by force."

"Dad—"

He wasn't done. "Ever since you became friends with that Haden Stone, you've been different. Harsher. You dumped your boyfriend to date a criminal."

If he only knew...Tucker, the boyfriend she'd dumped, had been more of a criminal than Riley ever had. And now Tucker was dead.

The thought kept hitting her at the oddest times, and tears would fill her eyes. Now was no different. "Riley is a good guy." Or had been, until she'd ruined his life. "You can't judge him because of this one instance."

"You keep telling me what I can't do, but you'll learn. Oh, baby girl, will you learn."

She gritted her teeth and tried to reach him from a yet another angle. "I'm not failing. I missed a couple weeks, and I can easily make them up."

"Yes, you can, but you'll make up the work in rehab."

"Rehab?" She almost laughed. Almost. "I told you. I'm not doing drugs."

"Like I said, we'll find out."

Rain suddenly burst from the sky and splattered all over the windshield. The wipers kicked on, and her dad slowed his speed just a bit.

"And when you learn that I'm clean?" she asked, hopeful. "You'll take me home?"

"No. You're staying there. It's not just a place for drug addicts. It's a place for kids who have gotten themselves into trouble, but can't find a way out. Not without help."

An institution. He was talking about locking her away in an institution. Shock slammed through her, joining the dread and creating a whole lot of horror. "Dad, you can't—"

"It's done, Mary Ann," he repeated. "It's done."

Acid nearly burned a hole in her stomach. Did burn a hole in her throat. "For how long?" she croaked out, thinking, *Riley will bust me out. Dating or not, he won't leave me in there.*

"As long as it takes."

RILEY WALKED the darkened, rain-drenched streets of downtown Tulsa, his hands in his pockets, his skin practically coated with ice, his hair plastered to his scalp, and breath misting in front of his face. A few cars drove past, but for the most part, no one was out and about.

The good, smart people of this town had already sought the warmth and dryness of the indoors. Mary Ann was probably warm and dry and headed home. Just as he'd wanted.

He'd given her back to her dad.

He'd disobeyed his king, his friend, and done what he'd thought best. He had never done that before. He'd always been a good little soldier, doing what he was told, his loyalty unwavering. And already he regretted his actions this day. Not because of the loyalty thing, but because he missed Mary Ann. Her smile, her sense of humor, her honesty, her kind heart.

He wanted her back.

But she'd fallen for a wolf, and he was no longer that wolf. She might think he was the same despite that fact, might think she still cared about him, but eventually she'd realize the truth: he was weak, vulnerable and soon to be an outcast among his kind.

Was he feeling sorry for himself? Hell, yeah. He didn't know who or what he was anymore. Only that he was no good. A failure. Worthless.

He couldn't protect Mary Ann, but he could make sure her dad did. And he would. He just had to take care of something first.

Riley turned a corner, the rain falling harder now. One thing Vlad had taught him was how to stay off human radar and how to keep his true identity hidden. After using his one phone call to leave a message for his brothers, telling them that they weren't to look for him, he'd busted his way free of lockup. An easy enough task.

Staying out would be a little more difficult, considering he planned to drink himself into a stupor. And why not? He wanted to forget everything that had happened, just for a little while. And if he was human, why not do what humans did?

Aden couldn't use him, and he couldn't protect Princess Victoria as he'd done for so many decades any more than he could protect Mary Ann. He was useless. So, mini-vacation, here he came.

He continued walking, searching for a liquor store, until he spotted something else. A dealer. He didn't mean to, but he stopped. The guy looked up and down and clearly judged him acceptable, since he didn't take off running.

Why not? This could work just as well. "What do you got?" he asked.

†HIR†Y-†WO

ADEN WATCHED THE FLAMES. Felt their heat. Heard their crackle. Tucker was dead; this wasn't an illusion.

He stood motionless. Disbelieving. Not an illusion, but this was a dream, a nightmare, surely. *Surely* the vampire mansion was not burning down before his eyes. Surely there was more than falling timber left.

He'd been gone only a few days. A while ago, Seth had texted him that things were okay. As okay as they could be, considering what had happened to Ryder and Shannon. But now...

"I don't...this can't be..." Victoria covered her mouth with her hand, her shock as deep as his.

The souls—the only two remaining souls—were shocked speechless.

Junior wasn't roaring. Maybe because Aden was numb. So numb.

He and Victoria had searched for Riley and Mary Ann, the rain battering at them, but they'd found no trace of the pair. They'd decided to come home and recruit a few wolves. Nathan and Maxwell hadn't picked up when he'd called.

Though his emotions had been raw, he'd somehow pulled himself together and teleported with Victoria, an ability that still amazed him. He just thought about where he wanted to be, and *boom,* he was there.

He'd expected to find Sorin, get a report about what had happened while he was gone, visit Ryder, make sure he was still on the mend, visit Shannon, gauge his condition for himself, visit Seth, maybe talk to Maxwell and find out if he'd learned anything new. The information he'd gathered in that secret room at the hospital might not have been important for Julian, but it could pertain to the other two souls. Then, Aden had planned to put the search party together. He'd felt no true urgency to do so, because he'd figured Riley and Mary Ann were still arguing. Or holed up somewhere making up.

He'd noticed the fire—how could he have missed it?—and at first, hadn't realized what was happening. He'd thought he'd simply imagined the wrong place. But, no. That was the vampire mansion in front of him, the ward in the ground the only thing untouched by the flames.

There was no one running from the crackling remains, no one screaming. No one was trying to stop the inferno from spreading.

How many had burned to death inside?

How many were hiding and safe?

He was king, and he should have been here. Should have protected them. He hadn't.

"I have no words," Victoria whispered. Then, she found them. "My sisters…my brother…my friends… they're all right. Tell me they're all right."

"They're…all right." He hoped. He prayed.

He doubted.

A whimper escaped her. "Who…who could have done this?"

Your father, he wanted to say but didn't. Vlad had burned down the D and M ranch, so why not his former home, too? The vampire was *that* vindictive and wouldn't hesitate to slaughter his own children to get what he wanted: revenge against Aden.

Victoria's knees must have given out, because she crumbled to the ground. The dry ground. Rain hadn't fallen here. Not yet. The sky was an expanse of black velvet, no twinkling stars in sight.

Fall, he thought. *Help us.*

A raindrop splashed against his nose. His chin. For several minutes, he felt a drop here, a drop there, then the heavens opened up and the storm descended with a fury. Soon, the fire sputtered to sparks, the sparks to smoke.

Maybe he could control the weather now, he thought with a bitter laugh.

How had things gotten this far? How had they come to this?

"What are we going to do?" Victoria asked shakily.

There were no viable answers to that question. Nothing he suggested would be good enough. Nothing he suggested would bring…everyone…back….

Light-headed, Aden eased beside her on the cold, now wet ground. There was a way. One he'd resisted. One he despised. Everyone always asked him to do it, and lately, he'd only said no.

He wasn't going to say no this time.

"I—I can fix this," he found himself saying.

No, Aden, Elijah said, pulling himself out of his stupor. *I know what you're thinking. Don't do it.*

Had the soul had a vision about this? "There's no other way." Flat, determined.

Victoria rubbed at her eyes with the back of her hand. "Aden?"

"Time travel," he said. He wasn't going to ask Elijah if, what, he'd seen. He wasn't going to try and force a vision himself. He didn't want to know, not now. He didn't want to talk himself out of this. "I'm going to time travel. I'll go back. I'll make sure this doesn't happen."

"Yes! Yes, that's perfect and...no." She vehemently shook her head. "Too much can go wrong. You told me that yourself."

And we don't know if the vampires were killed, Elijah said. *They could have run. They could have teleported like you. You might go back for nothing.*

Yes, some could have run. Yes, some could have teleported. But not all of them. Not the humans who had been inside. One death was too many. Going back wouldn't be for nothing.

The weight of this failure dragged him down so low he wasn't sure he'd ever see the light of day. Even if he managed to change things, he would not forget what had happened, and would know what to do—and what not to do. He never forgot.

They would forget, though. All of them. Victoria, Mary Ann, Riley. They would have no idea what had once transpired, the fate that once awaited them.

And if this worked, Vlad would not war with Aden—he would war with Dmitri, because Dmitri would become king. Victoria would be forced to marry the man. The thought caused Aden's hands to fist. He wasn't going to change his mind, though. *This* was being proactive.

Riley would keep his wolf.

Mary Ann would not become a drainer.

Aden would never meet Mary Ann. Would never summon the creatures of the otherworld here.

Ryder would live.

Hell, Tucker would live.

Shannon would not become a zombie.

The D and M ranch would not burn to the ground, and Brian would not die inside it.

Aden would not become a vampire. Junior would not be created.

Victoria would not become a human, would not lose her abilities.

Perhaps Eve and Julian would even return to him.

"I have to do this," he said. "I can't leave things like this." As Mary Ann had said, what could be worse than this?

Do you really want to find out? Elijah asked.

I should be on board for this, Caleb said. *I thought I would be. But something seems off. Wrong.*

"You're not usually the voice of reason. Don't start trying to be now."

"Aden, listen to me. Answer me." Victoria shook her head, wet hair slapping at his cheeks, then shook him. "Go back to when?"

"To the beginning."

Her eyes widened, the implications putting furious color in her cheeks. "Let's talk about this. Think it through. If you go back, will Eve return to you? Will Julian? What about you? Your beast? Will you still be a vampire?"

"Probably. Maybe. I don't know. Probably not. Definitely not. Maybe."

"Your wards—"

"Will never have been applied." He leaned over and pressed a soft kiss into her lips. "I love you. You know that, right?"

He should have done this a long time ago. Should have listened to everyone when they'd asked him to do it. Instead, he'd let fear and stubbornness rule him. And look where it had gotten him.

"Yes." Blue eyes studied him, sad, almost defeated. "I love you, too. But there has to be another way to—"

"There's not." If things worked out the way he hoped

they would, he and Victoria would never meet. Never get to know each other.

Never cause such a cataclysmic event.

He'd rather meet her and deal with this, but he wouldn't. And that was love.

Like his parents had given him up, he was going to give Victoria up. Unlike his parents, he wasn't doing it for himself but for her.

In the end, this was going to kill him. He could walk by her, and she would not know him, but he would know her.

"Aden, just give me a chance to—"

"This is the only way. I know that now." He kissed her again, a deeper kiss than he'd ever given her. A soul-shattering kiss. Their last kiss. He let her feel all of his longing, all of his dreams. All of his regrets. All of his prayers for the future.

And when he pulled back, he was trembling. She was crying. He tasted those tears in his mouth, a little salty, a lot heartbreaking.

He wiped those tears away with an unsteady hand, and then he did what was necessary. He closed his eyes and imagined the day he'd first met Mary Ann....

★ ★ ★ ★ ★

Glossary of Characters and Terms

Blood-slaves *Humans addicted to a vampire's bite.*

Bloody Mary *Queen of a vampire faction that's rival to Vlad's.*

Brian *Resident of the D and M, died when the ranch burned down.*

Brendal *Fairy princess, sister to Thomas.*

Caleb *A soul trapped inside Aden's head. Can possess other bodies.*

Chompers *Demon beast that lives inside Victoria.*

D and M Ranch *A halfway house for wayward teens.*

Dan Reeves *Owner of the D and M Ranch.*

Dmitri *Deceased betrothed of Victoria.*

Dr. Morris Gray *Mary Ann's father.*

Drainer *A human who feeds from and ultimately destroys those with supernatural abilities.*

Draven *Vampire female, challenged Victoria for the right to Aden.*

Edina *Victoria's mother.*

Elijah *A soul trapped inside Aden's head. Can predict the future.*

Eve *A soul formerly trapped inside Aden's head. A time traveler.*

Fairies *Protectors of mankind, enemies to vampires.*

Goblins *Small, flesh-hungry creatures.*

Haden Stone *Known as Aden. A human who attracts the supernatural and has three humans souls trapped in his head.*

Je la nune *A poisonous liquid that burns vampire skin.*

Jennifer *A witch.*

Julian *Soul trapped inside Aden's head. Can raise the dead.*

Lauren *Vampire princess, Victoria's sister.*

Maddie *Vampire female, sister to Draven.*

Marie *A witch.*

Mary Ann Gray *Human turned drainer. Repels the supernatural.*

Maxwell *Werewolf shape-shifter, Riley's cursed brother.*

Meg Reeves *Dan's wife.*

Nathan *Werewolf shape-shifter, Riley's cursed brother.*

Penny Parks *Mary Ann's best friend.*

Riley *Werewolf shape-shifter, guardian of Victoria.*

RJ *Former resident of the D and M.*

Ryder *Resident of the D and M.*

Seth *Resident of the D and M.*

Shannon Ross *Aden's roommate at the D and M.*

Sorin *Vampire prince, Victoria's older brother.*

Stephanie *Vampire princess, Victoria's sister.*

Teleport *To move one's body from one location to another in an instant.*

Terry *Former resident of the D and M.*

Thomas *Fairy prince, ghost.*

Tucker Harbor *Mary Ann's ex-boyfriend, part-demon illusionist.*

Vampires *Those who live off human blood and have a beast trapped inside them.*

Victoria *Vampire princess.*

Vlad the Impaler *Former king of Romanian vampire faction.*

Witches *Spell-weavers, magic producers.*

Q & A
with Gena Showalter

Q: Aden Stone has grown up with little understanding and a lot of pain and still has become a caring, compassionate person with a healthy sense of right and wrong. What was the inspiration behind this strong and complex hero?

A: I am surrounded by heroes. My father, husband, brothers. They are men who would take a bullet to protect their loved ones. (And, yes, even me.) I like to think Aden has their courage and their deep sense of loyalty. And I so admire them for those traits because, honestly, I curl into a ball and hide at the first sign of trouble.

Q: In Aden's first story, *Intertwined*, you included yourself in your dedication, "Because this one almost killed me," you said. Has writing the Intertwined Novels gotten easier as you've continued? How do you keep all the story threads straight?

A: Gotten easier? God, no! Each one has been more difficult than the last, and I swear *Twisted* grayed my hair. (I'd also swear that extra ten pounds I picked up is *Twisted's* fault, too, and has nothing to do with that bread pudding.) The characters are growing, evolving, and so are the happenings around them. As for keeping the threads straight, I'd love to tell you how organized I am, how I keep everything in a Word doc or a notebook. Yeah. I'd really love to tell you that. Instead, I have to admit that everything is jumbled inside my head, and I have to fit the pieces together after I've written my first draft.

Q: Which one of the Intertwined Novels characters do you relate to most, and why?

A: I'm probably a mix of Aden and the souls. All my life I've had people living inside my head—story characters— and they do talk to me. I talk to them, too, and it used to freak my family out. I'm a homebody who rarely leaves the house. My smart mouth sometimes gets me into trouble, and yet I'm a mediator who wants everyone around her to be happy (except when *I'm* the one who's angry, and then all bets are off). I love my family and friends more than anything, and—I'm just gonna say it—my mind sweeps through the gutter upon occasion.

Q: In the Intertwined Novels, vampires are living, breathing creatures who sleep in beds and can go out in daylight. How did you come up with the vampire mythology for this series?

A: One of my favorite things to do is play with mythology. Using certain already accepted aspects helps ground the world I hope to create in reality, and twisting those same aspects adds flavor. I knew I wanted my vamps to exist in differing stages. The younger vamps, who are the most humanlike (except for their raging need for blood), the middle-of-the-roaders, who begin to exhibit more vampirelike/supernatural abilities, and the elders, who are very much like the vampires of legend. That way, there is always a change to anticipate...or dread.

Q: Aden and Mary Ann have evolved from students working to get through high school into targets for all of paranormal-kind. What's your most memorable moment from high school, and how did it change you?

A: Once I walked in the cafeteria and a "friend" lifted my skirt—and held it up while I twisted and turned trying to cover my...assets. She thought it was hilarious. I was mortified. For several seconds that seemed like an eternity, everyone got a peek at my undies. While there was nothing I could do to change what had happened, I learned that being treated with respect is hugely important, there are boundaries friends should never cross, and that it's okay to end a toxic relationship.

Q: Riley's primary job is to guard Victoria, a duty that is both rewarding and frustrating. What are the best and worst jobs that you've ever had?

A: I've worked as an aircraft title searcher (interesting), a calendar sales girl (frustrating), a food service provider (stressful), a day-care worker (really stressful), and a nurse's assistant (really, *really* stressful). What I learned: I truly enjoy sleeping in, and I suck at customer service. My favorite job is, hands down, writing. I'm doing what I love: creating, weaving stories. And I get to sleep in. Of course, I work seven days a week and sometimes fifteen hours a day, but it's totally worth it!

Q: When did you first realize you wanted to be an author, and what was your journey to publication like?

A: I'd already dropped out of college three times and quit what seemed like a thousand jobs. Before I could allow myself to venture down the writing road, I had to prove I could actually finish a book. So, I wrote that first one in three months—and it sucked. But I'd done it, I'd written it from beginning to end, and as difficult as it was, I loved the process. I wrote another and another and kept sending them to publishers—and kept receiving rejections. Until that seventh book, about five years later. Finally, in 2004 I had a taker! Harlequin and I have been working together ever since.

Q: What advice do you have for anyone who aspires to be an author?

A: Read, read, read, and write, write, write. The more you read, the more you'll subconsciously understand story structure. The more you write, the more you'll understand your own process and how to maximize your strengths. Also, write from the heart, not what you think others would want you to write. You do, and you'll find your story magic. Oh, and never give up. Giving up is the only sure way to fail.

Thank you, Gena!

The *Twisted* Playlist

"Raise Your Glass" by Pink

"We R Who We R" by Ke$ha

"Only One" by Yellowcard

"All Over You" by The Spill Canvas

"Moth" by Audioslave

"If I Die Tomorrow" by Motley Crue

"That's What You Get" by Paramore

"Maybe" by Sick Puppies

"Secrets" by OneRepublic

"Basket Case" by Green Day

"Rebirthing" by Skillet

"I Gotta Feeling" by The Black Eyed Peas

"Homecoming" by Hey Monday

"Your Love is a Song" by Switchfoot

"Firework" by Katy Perry